1/05

D0368980

Busted Flush

Brad Smith

Busted Flush

A Novel

Henry Holt and Company, New York

Henry Holt and Company, LLC
Publishers since 1866
115 West 18th Street
New York, New York 10011

Library of Congress Cataloging-in-Publication Data

Smith, B. J. (Brad J.)
  Busted flush / Brad Smith.—1st ed.
      p.   cm.
ISBN-10 0-8050-7650-6
ISBN-13 978-0-8050-7650-9
    1. Historic buildings—Conservation and restoration—Fiction.   2. Lincoln, Abraham,
1809–1865—Collectibles—Fiction.   3. Inheritance and succession—Fiction.
4. Collectors and collecting—Fiction.   5. Gettysburg (Pa.)—Fiction.   6. Home
ownership—Fiction.   7. Divorced men—Fiction.   I. Title.

PR9199.3.S55148B87 2005
813'.54—dc22   2004054347

Henry Holt books are available for special promotions and premiums.
For details contact: Director, Special Markets.

First Edition 2005

Designed by Fritz Metsch

Printed in the United States of America

10 9 8 7 6 5 4 3 2 1

Busted Flush

ONE

Who's to say why a man will do the things he does? It's a mug's game to speculate on the reasons behind a man's actions, particularly when there's a very good chance that he himself doesn't know why he's doing whatever it is he's doing. A man doesn't go to a bar after work and drink a dozen bottles of beer because he's thirsty. He doesn't hit his thumb with a hammer because he wants to. He doesn't forget his wife's anniversary because it seems like a good idea. As often as not there are other forces at work and sometimes those forces are best left unknown. No one needs to know everything.

Fortunately, things are not always that complicated. In fact, there are times when matters are a hell of a lot simpler than they appear. Sometimes it's true—as Dooley Wilson so famously warbled—that a kiss is just a kiss.

It seemed as if everybody had a theory on why Dock Bass left town that fall. Of course, theories, as Dock's father used to say, were like assholes or elbows—everybody had one or two. And while any one of the theories surrounding Dock's sudden departure from Coopers Falls could have been right, the fact was that every one of them was wrong.

One popular and misguided conjecture was that Dock became unnerved after the incident at the Thursday night poker game at Ma

Harper's. They were playing jacks or better, and about an hour before the sun came up Willy Johnson shot Pooch McDougall—a rather unexpected development that woke up the neighborhood, put Pooch in the hospital, and brought the game to a screeching halt. Willy suspected Pooch of plucking a king of clubs from the slush, the addition boosting Pooch's hand from a pair of cowboys to three of a kind, a hand that would have won the pot had the gunshot not interrupted the proceedings. Actually, Willy more than suspected the deed; he himself had moments earlier discarded the king in question.

Nobody took the shooting too seriously. Somebody made a joke about whether Pooch should be taken to a veterinarian or a people doctor. Pooch had long been suspected of resorting to some sleight of hand when his luck was sour, although getting shot for his transgression did seem a tad harsh. But Willy only carried a little hammerless Iver Johnson .22, a relic that was at least as dangerous to the person holding it as to anyone out in front. Willy liked to brag that he carried the weapon in case a jealous husband came looking for him, but the truth was that the married women in Coopers Falls cut as wide a swath around Willy as did the single ones. In any event, the slug went into Pooch's shoulder and came to rest under the skin by his collarbone. The doctor who took it out closed up the wound with three stitches and refused to provide Pooch with so much as a Demerol, the denial of pharmaceutical relief actually pissing Pooch off more than getting shot.

By noon, the story around town was that Willy had gunned down Pooch in cold blood with a .357 magnum and that Pooch had been holding, of course, aces and eights at the time of his demise. That version held up pretty well until about nine that evening, when Pooch was spotted shooting pool at Soupy's Sports Bar.

Another theory had Dock pulling up stakes because of Terri walking out on him. This notion had a lot of support for a couple of reasons. The more romantic-minded of the couple's acquaintances garnered some perverse pleasure in the image of Dock leaving town with a broken heart, presumably with Patsy Cline or Hank Williams wailing away in the tape deck. But most people bought into the idea because Terri sold the hell out of the story. Her vanity wouldn't allow her to reveal the truth, which was that it was Dock who'd done the walking.

In fact, Dock had been waiting for Terri to leave for a couple of years, and he was quite sure that she would have earlier had he not—at her insistence—acquired his real estate license and gone to work for Phil McMurter. Dock was under the assumption that Terri was waiting around to see if he would become as successful as Phil, an eventuality that would make Terri quite happy and Dock quite miserable, as there was nothing about Phil he liked or envied, including his innate ability to make a lot of money.

The day after the shoot-'em-up at the poker game, Dock slept late, which was unusual for him, but then he hadn't arrived home until nearly six in the morning. He got out of bed at noon and was eating a ham sandwich in the kitchen when Terri walked in, dressed in her leather pants and a red silk blouse. She was flushed, he saw at once, which meant that he was about to be forced into a conversation about whatever it was that had her fired up.

"You're finally up."

"Yup."

She sat down across from him. "I went to see that house. On Loudon Road."

"Yeah?"

"Phil took me through it."

Dock knew that he should have asked why his wife went to look at a house with another realtor when he himself was in the business. He should have, but he didn't.

"It is absolutely gorgeous, Dock. It's even nicer than I imagined. I think we should put in an offer," she said then. "Phil thinks they're eager to sell."

"Why would I make an offer on a house I have no interest in?"

"Because I'm interested in it."

"Then you put in an offer."

"You know I don't have any money."

"Better make it a low offer."

She fell into a pout then. Terri could fill up a good-sized auditorium with her pout. Dock finished his sandwich and then carried his golf clubs out to the black Lexus parked in the drive. When he turned back toward the house, she was standing on the porch.

"Are we not going to talk about this?"

"I thought we just did."

"I'm not going to live in this little shit-hole forever," she said.

Dock looked at the house behind her. "Me, neither."

"And now you're going golfing?"

"I'm going out to the subdivision," he told her. "I have to show a house at one. I'm golfing later on with the guy who owns the stucco company. Business," he reminded her.

She stood with her lips pursed, arms crossed. After a moment she indicated the pickup truck beside the garage. "When you going to move that thing? It's a fucking eyesore."

Dock turned. The truck was a '91 Ford, faded red, with a 302 automatic and rally wheels; it had been his daily vehicle back when he was in the framing business. It had some rough on it, but it didn't qualify as an eyesore to him.

"One of these days," he told her and he got into the car and drove off.

The third popular theory on Dock's sudden departure was that he was embarrassed about getting fired by Phil McMurter. And while it was true that he was fired, there was no truth to the notion that he was in any way humiliated by the act. In fact, his dismissal was about as self-inflicted as a wound could be.

Coopers Falls was an unremarkable little town straddling the Cooper River in upstate New York, an hour's drive north of Albany. There were differing accounts as to how the town—and the river—got its name. One was that the area was first settled in the mid-1700s by a group of German immigrants who happened to be expert coopers. A conflicting view held that the esteemed American scribbler James Fenimore Cooper was the first to visit the area and to discover the rather unimpressive falls that eventually gave the town its name. This thesis seemed to suggest that the Mohawk Indians, who'd hunted and fished the countryside for generations, had done so without ever actually noticing the waterfall. That unlikelihood mattered little, as did the fact that the James Fenimore version was false. Apparently, the chamber of commerce had long ago decided that a famous author made for a better town-origin tale than did a bunch of mid-European barrel makers.

Oak Ridge Estates was the new subdivision on the west bank of the Cooper River. The old town was positioned on the east shore and it was showing its years, sagging here and there like a fading chorus girl. The downtown commercial interests had, predictably, moved to the strip malls outside of town. Many of the stores, three- and four-story brick buildings dating back a century or more, sat deserted, waiting for an unlikely resurrection. From time to time there would be enthusiastic talk of turning the core into an artists' community, but the plan was constantly stymied by the fact that there were no artists in the area to colonize.

Across the river, though, things were hopping. Several hundred acres of farmland had recently been rezoned from agricultural to residential, and this—along with the fact that young professionals working in Albany were willing to endure a daily one-hour commute for the combined benefits of fine country living and the opportunity to raise their children in a small-town atmosphere—had created a building boom.

The largest of the new subdivisions was Oak Ridge Estates. The first phase of the development was recently completed—150 houses of varying styles and shapes and price tags. The second phase, which would include an additional two hundred homes as well as a condominium complex, was now under construction, with some units nearing completion while others were waiting for start-up. The whole ball of wax was owned by Phil McMurter, who had quite presciently purchased most of the surrounding farmland before it had been rezoned. McMurter Real Estate, which employed Dock Bass, was the on-site realtor.

Dock arrived at the home he was to show a little before one. It had rained heavily the night before and the yard in front, not yet sodded, was a muddy pond. Dock made his way through the mire and used his master key to let himself into the house. The entranceway was a glassed-in foyer beneath a dormered roof; when Dock entered he found a puddle of water on the tiled floor. Looking up, he could see where the rain had come through the ceiling; the new paint was bubbled and the sodden drywall, bulging downward under the weight of the water, was about to come crashing down.

The prospective buyers—a young couple on the cusp of marriage—arrived, and Dock showed them in. He pointed out the leaky ceiling, and they asked what would have caused it.

"I'm not sure, but I'm guessing it wasn't Old World craftsmanship," Dock told them, quoting a phrase from the brochure. A moment later the woman suddenly remembered an urgent appointment and the couple, tossing their regrets over their shoulders, departed.

Dock found Phil McMurter over in phase two, standing in the living room of a partly constructed saltbox and talking to Stu Lewis, the building inspector, who was in the process of inspecting the insulation and vapor barrier.

"Hey, Dock," Lewis said when he walked in.

"Stu."

"Okay," Lewis said to Phil and he signed a paper on his clipboard. "This one's ready for drywall. Give me a call when the board's up."

Dock waited until Lewis was gone and then he said, "We got a roof leaking to beat the band in that unit I was showing over on Poplar."

"Shit."

"How can a roof leak in a new house?" Dock asked.

"I'd blame it on the rain."

"Or that peckerwood you got contracting for you."

Two young guys walked in then. They were in their early twenties and looked as if they'd been kicked out of Mötley Crüe for poor grooming. They immediately began to cut the plastic vapor barrier from the walls and then carry the new insulation outside. Dock looked out the window and watched as they carried the pink batts into the half-constructed house next door. Moments later they returned and repeated the act.

"What the fuck is going on?" Dock asked.

"I'm stretching my insulation dollar," Phil told him, and he smiled. "I'll have Murphy take care of the roof. I might have to stick my boot up his ass."

Dock, observing the ongoing insulation exchange, said nothing.

"I thought you were golfing with the stucco king," Phil said then.

Dock looked at his watch. "I am."

"Make sure he picks up the tab," Phil said. "The business I send his way."

On his way to the golf course Dock realized that Phil never mentioned showing Terri her dream house that morning. He wondered for a moment if his wife was fucking his boss. The possibility didn't bother him, but then the fact that it didn't began to bother him. It didn't seem the type of thing that a man would willingly let slide. If nothing else, it gave him a good excuse to give Phil McMurter a shit kicking, but he already had a half-dozen reasons to do that.

The stucco king was a pain-in-the-ass, ten-cent millionaire who wore Hawaiian shirts every day of his life and who insisted on picking up every check, in an effort to win friends or to lord his somewhat debatable wealth over others. He brought along two buddies, and they teamed up and played four-man Nassau for a hundred dollars a side. Dock wasn't interested in the golf or the networking or even being there for that matter, so of course he shot lights out and he and his partner—a fat flooring distributor who smoked a cigarette a hole and two on the par fives—won all of the cash.

They had a beer in the clubhouse afterward. When the stucco king started to complain about Phil McMurter's overdue accounts, Dock said he had to go.

Driving home, he decided on a whim to swing by the old place. He turned onto the river road south of town and wound his way north, following the meandering stream until he reached the cedar-lined lane leading to the house where he had grown up.

It had been a good place to grow up. As a boy, he'd enjoyed a

Huckleberry Finn existence, living on the shore of the shallow river, building rafts and catching turtles and fishing the deep holes his father had shown him. The family—there was just Dock and his parents— had lived in a two-story frame house on a rise above the river. Dock's father had a workshop alongside the house, where he kept his tools and also the table saws, lathes, planers, bandsaws, and countless other tools that he—and later Dock—used in the trade.

The house now belonged to strangers. Dock's father had sold it the previous year, and moved into a town house. The relocation may have contributed to his sudden death as Dock couldn't imagine his father in such surroundings, without his tools, his garden, his plank rowboat. Not to mention his purpose. It was, of course, all speculation on Dock's part and that's all it would ever be.

Now he turned onto the lane, crested the rise, and saw his child- hood home—the home where he'd learn to walk and to talk and to read and write, the home where he had begun to learn the difference between right and wrong (although lately that line had become a little blurred)—lying scattered on the ground, flat as the proverbial pancake. The bulldozer responsible for the flattening was still at it, pushing the debris that had so recently been a home into a large pile of sticks and bricks, broken windows and doors. Dock, nearly driving into a ditch, slammed on the brakes and just sat there for a time.

When he drove over to the wreckage, the dozer operator was lock- ing the cab. Dock recognized the man when he turned around.

"Charlie—what the fuck?"

"Hey, Dock." Charlie jumped to the ground. "Ain't this a corker?"

Dock stood with his arms out. "What happened?"

Charlie pointed his chin to the property to the east, where an ugly but supposedly palatial mansion had gone up a year previously. The house was a full three stories and the grounds covered four acres of land, complete with Greek fountains and ivy-covered stone walls and rock gardens. The owners were a computer programmer from Albany and his wife, a former flight attendant.

"It was blocking their view," Charlie said.

"What?"

"They couldn't see the sun set over the river from their balcony. So they bought it and hired us to tear it down."

"Sonofabitch."

"Ain't it?"

Dock walked around the house, kicked halfheartedly at what was left of his childhood, and then stood there.

"You know, Dock," Charlie said. "I always kinda wondered why you never bought the place from your old man."

Dock knelt down and extracted an ancient square nail from a collapsed doorjamb. The nail, despite its age, was in perfect condition. "I never knew he was selling. We didn't talk—I don't know—the last couple years. More like three or four, now that I think about it."

"Since you left the business?"

Dock nodded and put the nail in his shirt pocket.

"Funny thing," Charlie said then. "The owners came down when I got here earlier. Said that now they were thinking of buying some horses, putting a barn up right here on this spot."

"How they gonna see the sun set then?"

"I was wondering that myself," Charlie said. "Maybe they'll build the barn out of glass."

When Dock got home, Terri was sitting on the back deck, drinking wine and reading a copy of *The Wright Way*. Dock changed into jeans and then got a beer from the fridge.

"Hey," Terri called.

He stepped out on the deck, the beer in his hand.

"Phil called," she said. "He wants you to cover for him at the open house. He said he's going to be an hour late."

"Shit," Dock said and he opened the beer.

"And he said to wear a tie."

Dock sat down in a lawn chair and took a long drink of beer. Terri continued to flip through the magazine.

"Did you see the letter?"

"What letter?"

"On the kitchen table. From some law firm in Gettysburg, Pennsylvania. What've you got going on in Pennsylvania?"

"Nothing, far as I know. My dad and I went there once when I was a kid."

"What did you do there?"

"Nothing that would interest a law firm thirty years later. We looked at the battlefield and the museums and stuff."

She curled her lip. "I don't get what people find so fascinating about history."

"It doesn't change," Dock told her.

She held the open magazine out toward him. "Do you like that entranceway?"

"I thought she went to jail," Dock said.

"I was thinking it'd look great in the house over on Loudon."

"Didn't you say the house was perfect?"

"It is," she said.

"Then what do you need Sarah Jane Wright for?"

She pulled the magazine away. "I don't know why you're being this way. Why won't you at least look at the place? I guarantee you'll fall in love with it. It's got this great den with a wet bar. You could put in a plasma flat screen and hang out there with your old buddies from town."

"Not interested."

"Jesus, Dock. You're making real money for the first time in your life and look where you're living. I mean it, just look at this place."

"Maybe it'd look a little better if you cleaned it a couple times a year," he suggested. "What do you do all day anyway? Put on your leather pants and drive around with Phil McMurter?"

"Don't you dare accuse Phil and me of anything," she said. "He's a close friend and his wife is a dear, dear friend of mine."

"Irma? That snotty little blonde is nothing more than a mirror image of Phil. If an original thought ever entered her head, it would die of loneliness."

Terri sat staring at him for a moment. "What the fuck has gotten into you?"

He got to his feet and walked to the railing. Looking out over the back lawn, he slowly drank off the rest of the beer. He could hear her impatient breathing behind him and he could imagine the look on her face—the wounded set to her eyes, the bottom lip aquiver.

"I don't know," he said finally.

"You're just like your father, you know that? I see that in you more and more. You'll end up like him. Living in that shack along the river his whole life. Never owned anything but a shed full of tools. What kind of life is that?"

Dock took the square nail from his pocket, rolled it between his thumb and forefinger, felt the sharp edge. "My father was the smartest man I ever knew. And he was honest. You want to insult me, you're gonna have to come up with something better than that."

The open house was at one of Oak Ridge's showcase homes: a large two-story red brick with a stained-glass entranceway and a full porch accented by mock-Victorian gingerbread work. There were matching red oak trees in the front yard, on either side of the flagstone walkway, the trees transplanted from somewhere. Apparently, Phil McMurter had decided that a housing development called Oak Ridge should at least promise a few oak trees. Not that there was anything resembling a ridge within an hour's drive, but in Dock's estimation, when it came to Phil and promises, one out of two was probably way above average.

The real estate market was lively of late and a lot of people were there to see the house. Dock was on the premises from seven on, wearing a tie and a smile, as required. Phil showed at eight thirty. He wore khaki shorts and a golf shirt, sandals on his feet. Dock looked at him when he came in, and then he turned away and caught his own reflection in the foyer window and saw, to his dismay, a guy who looked like an actor in a real estate commercial. A guy with dark brown hair, cropped short, parted nicely on the left. Clean-shaven—in decent shape but carrying an extra ten pounds or so. He was not unpleasant to look at, but he was the type of guy whom Dock would normally do his goddamnedest to avoid. That sudden realization was more than a little disturbing.

A half hour later Dock found himself in conversation with a couple—both schoolteachers—who had just moved to the area from Georgia to teach at the high school and who were currently renting a house in the country while they looked for something to buy. They were, it seemed, quite impressed with Oak Ridge and the promised elegant living within.

"The taxes are somewhat higher than we anticipated," the man said.

"Did you ever hear anyone say their taxes were lower than they expected?" Dock asked, and as he said it he could hear the words but they didn't seem to be coming from him. He was watching across the room, where Phil McMurter was leaning against the curved staircase and talking to a young woman who wore a tight black skirt.

"We're from Georgia," said the woman, who hadn't a trace of an accent. "So we're not used to heating bills. Is a house like this expensive to heat?"

"Not if it's well insulated," Dock heard the voice say. "This is an R20 house."

Across the room, Phil was leaning into the young woman, whispering in her ear.

"And what does that mean?" the man asked.

"It has to do with the quantity of fiberglass insulation in the—" the voice said, and then Dock decided to put a stop to it. "Just a minute. Phil! You got a second?"

Phil said something to the woman and then followed his own dazzling smile across the room.

"Phil," Dock said. "This lovely young couple have some questions about this home. I believe they're very much in the market. Could you explain what R20 means in terms of insulation?"

Phil's eyes hooded over, but he held the smile. "Why, you know what it means, Dock. You having a senior moment?" He turned to the couple. "Your R factor is determined by the amount of insulation in the walls and attic. Here, you have six inches in the walls and twenty in the attic. That's a lot. It means that this house will be ridiculously inexpensive to heat."

"You understand what he's talking about, don't you?" Dock said then, and his voice was suddenly his own again. "It's that pink fiberglass stuff. You've seen it?"

"Well, no," the man said. "But I know what you mean."

"You've never seen it?" Dock asked.

"Well, we're schoolteachers; we're not in the construction business," the woman joked.

"Well, I can show it to you," Dock said. "Hold on."

His eyes locked on Phil's as he walked past him. When he reached the back wall of the dining room, he raised his heavy brogan and kicked a large hole in the drywall there. Then he reached his hand into the hole.

"By God," he said in mock wonderment. "There's no insulation in here at all."

He walked through to the living room and kicked a hole in the wall beside the beautiful bay window. "Nope, none here, either."

Finally, he went into the den and kicked a series of holes all along the side wall there. Then he walked back toward Phil McMurter and the two schoolteachers with the fast-disappearing interest in Oak Ridge Estates.

"I'll be goddamned, Phil," Dock said. "I don't believe there's any insulation at all in this house. Maybe you should have somebody check out the rest of the units."

"You're fired," was all Phil could think to say.

"No shit," Dock said.

Driving home, Dock stopped on the bridge over the Cooper River. There was a full moon just rising over the stream, casting a rippled and brilliant beam across the shallow expanse. He took off his coat and tie and threw them over the railing and then he popped the trunk and threw his golf clubs in the water, too. When he got home, Terri was sitting on the couch, watching a movie. He headed straight for his room.

"How'd it go?" she asked as he passed.

"I had a pretty good night."

He changed back into his jeans and packed a duffel bag with pants and shirts, underwear and socks. He tossed in a few CDs—Dylan and Eric Taylor and Neil Young and Coltrane. Lucinda Williams for good measure. He glanced at his books and decided on Hemingway, Steinbeck, and Richler, then added *Huckleberry Finn* to the collection. When he walked back out he saw the letter from Pennsylvania on the table and he put it in his pocket.

"Okay, you win, babe," he told her then.

She turned, her face every bit as bright as the moon outside. "Really?"

"Yup, I'm gonna move that old truck out of the driveway. See ya."

He got his fishing tackle from the garage and threw it in the back of the pickup. He headed north out of town and he never came back.

So it wasn't the shooting and it wasn't marital difficulties and it wasn't getting fired that caused Dock Bass to leave Coopers Falls that autumn. It was the insulation that did it. But, of course, in truth it wasn't even that.

It was the lack of insulation.

TWO

Amy Morris had given up on love at least as often as she'd given up on tobacco. She regarded both as evil, self-destructing habits, even as she was returning to them, offering her lungs to one, her heart to the other. Here she was—smitten again—and although she realized that she'd felt this way before, this time it really did seem different. The others had been trivial affairs, inconsequential flights of infatuation and whim, passing nods to fashion and fad. The Mustang, the Beemer, the Corvette—she looked back at them now with pangs of regret and remorse and even embarrassment. Especially the Corvette.

The new love in her life was a Porsche Cayenne Turbo. It was everything she wanted in a significant other. It had satellite navigation, even though she'd never been lost in her life. It had four-wheel drive that she would never use. It had a 4.5 liter, 340-horse V-8, six-speed automatic, an entertainment center with surround sound, eighteen-inch wheels, DVD player, computer, all sorts of other features she thrilled to own and never use. Success, maybe, was all about owning things one didn't need.

She picked up the Cayenne at eleven in the morning, chatted one last time with the fawning, jewelry-laden salesman, and then headed into Washington to the TransWorld studio. Sitting at a red light downtown, she succumbed to her old practice of admiring herself in the plate-glass fronts of the buildings. She couldn't help but conclude that she looked wonderful behind the wheel of the Porsche—at once hip and sophisticated, grace and elegance with a razor's edge. She had almost been talked into a Hummer, and she was glad now that she'd balked at the proposition. The Hummer was overkill—too big, too military, too ostentatious. And in the end, she decided that she couldn't be seen driving in a vehicle whose name was a synonym for a blow job. Not in this town anyway. Monica had spoiled it for everyone.

No, this was the one. And even though it was technically a truck, it was still a Porsche. Classic European engineering. At long last love, with a six-disc CD changer and lumbar support at her fingertips.

She parked in the underground lot and walked through reception and into the elevator. The lift stopped at the third floor and a man got on. He was wearing the bright blue blazer identifying him as one of the cast of the *News at Noon*.

"Hi," he said as he recognized her. He flashed brilliant teeth.

"Hello."

After a moment Amy decided he was either the weatherman or the sportscaster; she could not recall his name even though she'd seen him on air countless times. She sensed that he was nervous; he kept her in his peripheral vision and when she glanced at him his eyes snapped back to the elevator buttons, as if they were the object of his scrutiny.

"I really enjoy your work," he ventured finally. "I mean, really . . . you come across just so . . . I don't know. It's just *you*."

"Good—if it was someone else, I don't know what I'd do," Amy said. Confusion crowded his face so she added, "I like what you guys are doing at noon. Some terrific energy there."

"Well, hey," the man said and he actually blushed. "I'm just a weatherman."

"I started out doing the weather," Amy decided to tell him. "In St. Louis."

She watched in fascination as the falsehood elevated the man, actually made him stand taller, straighter. It might have made his teeth whiter, except that was impossible.

"It was a great jumping-off point," she said then, going with it. "I wouldn't trade the experience for the world."

When they stopped on the tenth floor, the man in the blue jacket thanked her and then strode away like the cock of the walk. Rain or shine, the Washington area was going to get one slam-bang weather report today.

When the elevator reached the top floor, she got off. Belinda, Sam Rockwood's private receptionist, offered her usual thin smile, a look stained with the resentment that Amy was one of the chosen few allowed to walk in on her boss unannounced.

The man himself was behind his desk, comfortably ensconced amid his collectibles and his newspapers and what *Time* magazine had referred to on the occasion of his seventieth birthday as "his restless contentment."

"Hey, kid," he said.

Amy tossed her purse on the couch as she said hello and walked over to help herself from a carafe of coffee on a table along the wall. He watched as she poured, taking in her disheveled appearance. She wore black jeans and a two-hundred-dollar T-shirt under a DKNY jacket; her hair was tied back in a ponytail with her shades propped on top.

"You're looking very casual today," he said.

She gestured toward his own appearance. His gray hair was as unruly as his reputation, and he wore a navy cardigan of indeterminate years, the elbows patched with brown leather. He nodded.

"But I have a feeling," he said, "that this soccer-mom look is a tad more calculated than it appears."

"Right—and you really *can't* afford a new sweater," she said. "By the way—I was just about to call you when I got your message to come down. I have a lead on the mysterious Cubby Stewart."

"Remind me who that is."

Amy carried her coffee to the couch and sat down. "He's apparently got a reputation as a go-between, one of these guys who are always popping up in trouble spots but never leave their fingerprints on anything. He was allegedly Howard's liaison in Haiti. He and the good congressman were seen together a lot in '94 and '95. On the island and off. I got a tip he's living large in Aruba these days."

"And what can he do for us?"

"Sam, there's still two hundred million dollars unaccounted for. If Congressman Howard is holding a chunk of that, and you know goddamn well that he is, then maybe this Stewart can provide us with some details."

"First of all, it's ex-Congressman Howard. You've already cost him his seat in the House. What more do you want?"

"I've got his seat but I want his ass. Man should be in jail."

Sam leaned back and crossed his legs. "How do you know Stewart's in Aruba?"

"I went for drinks last night with this guy, used to be on Howard's staff. Typical button-down ass kisser. He let it slip, rather intentionally. Claims to have visited Stewart's sumptuous digs, *with* the good congressman."

"Why would he tell you this?"

Amy, drinking from the cup, raised her eyebrows at him.

"Oh," Sam said. "I get it. Mr. Button-down was looking to get unbuttoned. Did he?"

"None of your damn business," Amy replied. "And *no.*"

Sam nodded his disinterest and uncrossed his legs, leaned forward. "Okay. If Stewart and Howard were in this together, then why would he spill to you? He's safe in Aruba, presumably with his share. He's not going to tell you anything."

"I won't know that until I try," Amy said. She put the coffee on the table beside the couch. "I want to fly down there, Sam. Why would you be reluctant to that? This could be good."

"You can go to Aruba," Sam said. He picked a cigar up from the desk, twirled it like a baton in his fingers. She'd spent enough time with him by now to recognize a stalling maneuver. He placed the cigar on the desk and smiled at her. "But first you're going to Chicago."

She felt her jaw tighten. "Really? What's in Chicago?"

"The World Series."

She instinctively reached for the cigarettes in her purse, then caught herself. She drew out a pack of gum instead, held it in her hand without opening it.

"The World Series," she said.

"Yes."

"The World fucking Series."

"I believe it's the baseball World Series. I wasn't aware there was one for fucking. You seem to have developed an affinity for that particular rogue adjective."

"So now I'm a sportscaster."

"You've done sports before," he reminded her. "The Olympics. You were quite enthused, as I recall."

"Only because I thought somebody was gonna blow something up. Which no one had the courtesy to do. What's going on, Sam?"

"Bob Brown went in for emergency surgery last night. Quintuple bypass."

"So somebody in sports flipped a coin and I lost."

"Oh, he's doing fine, so nice of you to ask," Sam said. "Bob's the grand old man in baseball. He's chewing tobacco and neat's-foot oil. What we lose with tradition, we have to make up with pizzazz. That's where you come in."

"Why don't you send Jimmy?"

"Jimmy's doing football now on Sundays. You know that. He can't exactly do that and the Series, too."

"Oh no, we wouldn't want to ask him to try and differentiate between an oblong ball and a round ball all in one week. His brain might explode."

"He's a valued member of the team," Sam said, his standard reply when addressing the topic of substandard members of the team.

She put the gum back in her purse. "Okay, let me get this straight. I spend the last two years breaking this story and in the process I bring down not just an oily congressman but also America's foremost right-wing lifestyle doyenne *and* a TV preacher so crooked he has to screw his shorts on in the morning and my reward is the World Series. Is that it?"

"I wouldn't characterize the Series as being your reward. You'll recall that I am paying you for these little assignments."

Amy got to her feet. "Is Simon behind this?"

"*I'm* behind this. I'm aware—as a select few are—that Simon is in love with you. Fortunately for everybody involved, he can be in love with you and do his job as a producer at the same time. Probably because he's resigned himself to the fact that you are incapable of love."

"I'm capable of love, goddamn it. I'm in love right now."

Sam laughed and he reached for a magazine. "If you're in love right now, it's with an inanimate object. A new pair of boots, maybe. Or an automobile. Have fun in the Windy City."

"Fuck you, Sam," she said and she started for the door.

"Oh," he called after her. "Could you get me an autographed ball?"

In the elevator she put her shades on and lit a cigarette. A middle-aged woman wearing a full-length mink got on at the tenth floor. She smiled until she saw the cigarette and then her face fell into a scowl that seemed to increase in intensity as they fell floor by floor. Amy knew the woman was caught between voicing her displeasure and merely allowing her expression to handle the job.

"I hope you realize," the woman said at last, "that smoking is frowned on by pretty much everyone in the medical community."

"I hope you realize that wearing fur is frowned upon by pretty much everybody except the Flintstones."

The woman stiffened as if she'd been jabbed in the back with a poker. She wore a double loop of pearls around a neck that was brown and wrinkled and in need of some simple cosmetic repair that would cost a lot less than the coat on the woman's back.

"I know who you are behind those glasses," the woman said then. "My husband is your boss."

"Sam Rockwood is my boss," Amy said. "Your husband is a fucking accountant."

★   ★   ★

She felt marginally better behind the wheel of the SUV, captured yet in the first blush. But just marginally. She fiddled with the CD player as she drove out of town. When she got on 95 she opened the truck up, ran the speedometer to 110 for the five miles to her exit. She put in Muddy Waters—what the hell, she was heading for Chicago— and with the CD blaring she never heard the cop's siren, and she didn't see the cruiser until he pulled up beside her on the off-ramp. The cop pointed to the shoulder, and she nodded. Pulling over, she reached into the console and found the vehicle's manual. She opened it randomly as she put the truck in park.

The cop was a young blond guy and he was bulked up in the chest and neck like a weight lifter. He approached the Cayenne with regulation caution. Amy powered the window down as he arrived.

"Oh my God—" she began excitedly.

"I'll have to see your license, ma'am. You're in a fair amount of trouble here."

Amy allowed a quaver in her voice. "I was so frightened."

"Ma'am?"

"I—I just picked this truck up an hour ago. I was trying to set the cruise control and it just kept accelerating."

The cop was doubtful. "Okay, I need to see your license."

Amy retrieved it from her purse. The cop recognized her after looking at the license. "Oh, I thought you looked familiar. I've seen you on TV."

Amy nodded absently as she began to leaf through the manual. "These things are like an NFL playbook," she said. "You need a degree from MIT these days to operate the dang cruise control. Look, I'm still shaking."

The cop was hesitant now. "You're saying the vehicle sped up on its own?"

"It was terrifying," Amy said.

"Then how did you slow down for the ramp?"

"I don't know. I just kept pressing buttons in a panic and finally something happened. As soon as it did, I headed for this ramp. This is not my exit."

The cop exhaled heavily and took a look around. "You're sure that's what happened? I was right behind you and I didn't get the feeling that you were in any kind of distress."

"Well, I was," Amy said. "But I guarantee you that I wasn't panicking as much as Porsche will, because—damn it—I'm going to do a story on this. This was a potentially life-threatening situation." She took a look at the officer, her face suddenly inspired. "Hey, would you be interested appearing on-screen as a witness? It would give my account credibility. I mean, you were right behind me."

"Uh, I would consider that. Yes, I would do it."

"That would be wonderful," Amy said. "Are you still required to ticket me? I absolutely understand if you do."

"Given the circumstances, I don't think that will be necessary."

"Are you sure? I wouldn't want you to get into trouble, you know, with your boss or anyone."

"I wouldn't worry about that, ma'am. Out on this highway, I am the boss."

Amy took his badge number and his home phone number on a slip of paper and then drove away on the exit she had claimed wasn't hers. If the cop was still watching, he would have seen the slip of paper float out the truck's window at the first intersection.

She arrived home in Old Town, parked the new truck in the drive, and then walked out to the street on the pretense of picking up the morning paper but in fact to see how the Cayenne looked against the backdrop of her Tudor-style town house.

It looked good. In fact, it looked magazine-cover good.

Inside, she opened the paper on the kitchen counter and then skimmed it absently as she drank a cup of tea and flipped through the TV channels with the remote. When MSNBC began a feature on the upcoming World Series, she turned the set off and phoned Peter.

His voice came on the line foggy and cracked and she wondered how late he'd been up the night before, and with whom.

"Hey," she said.

"Hi, baby," he said and she could imagine him reaching for a cigarette. The image was impulse enough for her to do the same.

"What're you doing?" she asked. "Besides just getting up."

"Just getting up."

"I'm coming out."

"Should I stay in bed?"

"Believe it or not, I need a little more romance than that," she said. "Make me some lunch."

Peter lived outside of Reston, in a stone mansion his great-great-grandfather had built after the Army of the Potomac had torched the original family farm in 1862. The fire had been the accidental result of a party celebrating a minor and rare—at the time—Union victory in a skirmish along a creek on the property. In fact, General George McClellan had afterward written an apology to the family for the tragedy; the note was framed and hung now in a rear hallway, its content and its author having been deemed too inconsequential to merit a spot in the sitting room, or even the parlor for that matter.

The great-great-grandfather in question had been a loafer and a drunk who had avoided service in the war, as well as anything resembling gainful employment afterward. His slothful ways had threatened the family fortune, built mainly in South Carolina on the backs of slaves and in fields of cotton. Peter's great-grandfather and grandfather had rallied, though, going into industry and then politics, respectively, thus saving the family's finances and social standing. Peter's father had continued along the political path, eventually serving in John Kennedy's cabinet.

In the face of three generations of overachievement, perhaps it was only natural that Peter should digress to the fourth for some ancestral inspiration. In any case, he was a loafer and a drunk.

Not that these two defining facets of his personality had always been obvious to Amy. She'd met him a year earlier, under circumstances that cast him in what proved, over time, to be his best light. Amy had been with TransWorld for just two years at the time and while it was apparent that she was being groomed as a high-profile correspondent, she was as yet without portfolio, so to speak. The big-name items, war and politics, were invariably handled by the veteran stars of the network—most notably John Walters and Eric Savannah—and they were protected in a rather zealous manner. Amy found herself covering everything from filibusters to hurricanes. But she was a team player and as such she took each assignment in stride, be it local or national. Like every other reporter on the planet, she was aware that a nickel-and-dime burglary at Watergate had changed the course of journalism history, and, like every other reporter, she was convinced she was due a Watergate of her own. A story on pig manure was not destined to become that, but it did introduce her to Peter.

A large national meat producer under the unlikely subsidiary name Superior Swine had acquired building permits to construct a number of intensive livestock operations—pig farms, to the layperson—along the valley of the Potomac. The mother corporation was well connected in Washington, and the permits were as clean as a hound's—or at least a hog's—tooth. Each blueprint was accompanied by a comprehensive nutrient management plan that detailed exactly how the millions of gallons of liquid pig manure created by the farms would be disposed of. The plans called for the sludge to be contained in large earthen lagoons, each holding several million gallons at full capacity, and then once a year injected into the soil of the surrounding farmland. In a perfect world, the pigs would then go to China for consumption, the corporation would grow as fat as the hogs by which they profited, and the liquid shit would not, it was hoped, find its way into the surrounding ditches, creeks, and streams and subsequently into the Potomac River.

All was fine until the local green types took note. Once news of the pending construction became known, it only required an afternoon's efforts on the Internet to turn up a plethora of horror stories—from North Carolina, from Holland, from Quebec—surrounding what one Montreal newspaper called "le paradis porcin." Lagoons overflowing into rivers and lakes, fish and fowl killed, aquatic life destroyed, water wells poisoned, farmlands injected with waste containing trace elements of antibiotics, steroids, and growth hormones. And if a subsistence farmer along the St. Lawrence River was unwilling to stand still for such unchecked environmental disregard, it was highly unlikely that the owners of multimillion-dollar homes in the eastern sector of Virginia would.

In the midst of the ensuing outcry, Amy took a camera crew to a lively town meeting in Herndon, where a panel assembled by Superior Swine was attempting to assuage the public's fears. Expert after expert approached the podium in the local high school auditorium, and proceeded to bat around like badminton birds words such as *containment* and *fail-safe* and the new catchall, *nutrient management*. Only when the microphone was turned over to the public, though, did the nutrient really hit the fan. Hell hath no fury like an entitled and outraged populous with access to the Web. Citizen after citizen bombarded the increasingly fidgety panel with tales of outright abomination regarding hog farms throughout the world. Peter was the last to speak. Dressed in khakis and plaid—every inch the gentleman farmer—he caustically tore wide strips off the folks from Superior Swine, the town council, and the building department that had issued the permits. Upon finishing, he reminded the audience of the danger of the lagoons leaking into the Potomac, upriver of the nation's capital, and then, following an appropriate and undoubtedly well-rehearsed pause, added that sending shit to Washington would be akin to sending coals to Newcastle. Amy decided at that moment that she would seek him out for further comment.

They remained in touch. Amy—who as a reporter could take no official stand on the issue—provided Peter and his group, Hogwatch Herndon, with data gathered clandestinely from the TransWorld research people. Eventually, they began to see each other. She was to learn, however, that the hog farm issue, like everything else in Peter's life, would hold his interest for only so long. Bored with the research, yet jealous of the successes of his more energetic Hogwatch cronies, he inevitably returned to his true loves: alcohol and recreational drugs. The wit and charm he had at first displayed soon fell away to reveal a cynical yet surprisingly dispassionate slacker.

But he could cook a little. When Amy arrived that afternoon, he had a very nice egg-white omelet waiting, with strawberries and yogurt on the side. They ate—or rather, Amy ate while Peter drank coffee and smoked French cigarettes—on the terrace outside the dining room. It was a southern exposure and warm in spite of the month. Peter wore shapeless cotton pants and a hemp pullover. His voice had improved slightly, from a scratch to a rasp, but his eyes were fairly bleeding.

"I got my new Cayenne," Amy said as she ate.

"Is it hot?"

"Don't do that," she said. "I'll take you for a ride after."

"I've been for car rides," Peter said. "What am I—a golden retriever?"

"I just spent eighty grand on a new vehicle. Humor me."

"I don't get that you care so much about cars."

"I don't get that you care so little about everything."

She watched as he poured more coffee for them both, his fingers on the carafe stained mahogany brown from nicotine. She finished her eggs and pushed the plate away, then turned her chair so the sun reflected more directly on her face.

"So what's up?" he asked presently. "I gotta admit, I was surprised you called. The last I saw you, I was getting the distinct impression that I was beginning to bore you."

"You probably were," she said. "Although the last I saw you, I was getting the distinct impression that you were about to boink Jessica Hardway."

"I probably was."

She took a drink from her cup. It was very good coffee. For all his indolent ways, Peter possessed a deft and natural hand in the kitchen. When it became apparent to Amy that their relationship was going nowhere, she had entertained for the briefest of moments the notion of hiring him as a housekeeper. Of course, he was too insufferably wealthy and intolerably irresponsible for that or any other job.

"You have a very discontented look for a girl who just picked up her latest dream vehicle."

"Yeah well, I was informed this morning that I'm chewing tobacco. Or neat's-foot oil. I can't remember which."

"You were probably confused by that. I know I am."

"The network's sending me to Chicago for the World Series. And after that—who knows? Maybe to Utah to cover that big Osmond reunion I keep hearing about."

"Chicago's a good town," Peter said. "I was locked up there once."

"That outlaw act doesn't work on me, Peter," Amy told him, and she yawned under the warmth of the sun. "If you were in jail, it was probably for possession of pot."

"It was kick-ass Moroccan hash, I'll have you know," he said as he lit another smoke. "So what's the matter, you not big on baseball? Isn't it the national pastime? You're unpatriotic, that's your problem."

"My problem," she said, "is that I've just found the guy who was opening portals for Cyrus Howard and Sarah Jane Wright in Haiti, and now I've been told I'm Chicago-bound. If I don't get to this guy quick, then somebody else will. I don't know what's going on at TransWorld, but it doesn't feel right. Not to sound overly possessive, but this is my story."

"Look at it as a vacation," Peter said, exhaling. "It's all on the network's dime. Don't forget, you're gonna be surrounded by all those ballplayers. I'm betting they're just as dumb as they are pretty. I gotta believe one of them could serve as a diversion for a high-maintenance gal like you."

"Sure, we can talk about huntin' and fishin' and such," she said. She set down her cup and looked out over the fields to the south. There was a stone fence a quarter mile away and past the fence she could see a flock of shaggy brown sheep, scattered across the field like dirty clouds against a green sky. "I could phone Fox today, you know," she said then and she looked at him. "If I wanted to. I could call Ted Turner, MSNBC, whomever. I've had overtures since I broke this thing, believe me. They like the idea of a high-profile black woman on the news. And I did say news, not fucking sports." She hesitated. "Jesus, it just occurred to me. Is Sam sending me to Chicago because of that?"

"First of all," Peter said, "you're not all that black anymore. You think the sisters in the hood relate to you? Shit, you could show up at that Osmond reunion and pass yourself off as a cuz."

"What're you talking about? I'm black."

"Your ancestors were black. And you used to be black—when it served you, back at the *Post*. But not anymore—not since you've become TV Barbie. You're in some weird racial limbo, babe. You're not black, and you're not white, either."

"Oh, yeah? Then what am I?"

Peter took a moment to consider the question. "You're a celebrity."

"You're a funny guy today."

"Really? I'm not trying to be. I need a drink." He got to his feet. "How about you?"

She shook her head and he went into the house. She took one of his cigarettes from the pack on the table. Leaning forward to reach for his lighter, she caught her reflection in the casement window. She looked at her nose, her lips, her eyes, the straight hair streaked with blond.

She lit the foul-smelling cigarette and turned away from the window. A few minutes later Peter came out, carrying a glass in one hand and a pitcher of Bloody Marys in the other. He sat down and poured from the pitcher.

"And who the hell you calling Barbie?" she asked. "Did you think I was going to let that slide?"

He dismissed the entire conversation with a flip of his hand. He was through with it, she knew, and she realized how rarely, other than during the early days after first meeting, they ever really talked about anything. She also knew that he didn't give a damn about her maintenance level.

"You sure you don't want a drink?" he asked.

"I'm sure."

"We could get drunk and fuck," he suggested brightly.

"My, but you make my heart go pitter-patter."

"There was a time when that was true."

"I'm not sure that's so." She got to her feet and came around to kiss him lightly on the cheek. She knew in that moment that she was finished with him. In truth, she'd known it for some time. "Thanks for lunch."

When she straightened, she caught her image in the glass again. "I think," she said, watching herself, "that I require someone with a little more ambition."

"Fuck ambition," Peter said, and he topped off his drink. "Look where it got you."

THREE

Like Robert E. Lee a century and a half before him, Dock Bass came upon the town of Gettysburg from the west, moving along the Chambersburg Road, through the lush farmland and hardwood forests of southeastern Pennsylvania. There the parallels pretty much stopped. Lee rode a gray horse; Dock drove a red truck. Lee had an entourage of about seventy-five thousand; Dock was traveling alone. Lee traveled through the heat and humidity of early July and he was furthermore burdened with the knowledge that he was fighting a war that, in all likelihood, he could not win. Dock drove in the cool of autumn and his load was light; he had shucked his past like a worn-out coat and he was surprisingly content with the uncertainty of his future. Lee had an appointment, although he didn't know it, with George Meade and the Army of the Potomac. Dock was there to see a lawyer named Tommy Trotter.

Dock held only ragged memories of his last visit to the town. He'd been eight years old, and his mother had gone to Rochester to stay with a sick aunt for the summer. Dock and his father had traveled to Gettysburg in the old station wagon. His father knew a little about the Civil War, as he knew a little about virtually everything. While there, he had bought a half-dozen books about the battle; the books were now Dock's, although they remained back in Coopers Falls. He had, however, revisited them from time to time—most recently at the time of the PBS series a few years back—and, as such, he was at least familiar with the bare bones of the three-day conflict. Of the town itself, though, thirty years removed from his last visit, he remembered only the unique town center. It was a traffic circle that acted as a terminal for the four main roads into town. It was a model of old-fashioned efficiency, accepting mergers and departures without requiring a traffic light.

At the northeast corner of the circle stood the venerable Gettysburg Hotel, established 1797. Across to the southeast was the house where Lincoln had stayed on the occasion of his famed address. A statue of the great man was planted on the sidewalk out front.

Tommy Trotter had an office on the second floor of an ancient stone building on Carlisle Street, maybe a minute's walk from the town center. The ground floor of the building housed a psychic, a dentist, and a taxidermist. Dock was directed by the dentist's receptionist to a flyer-strewn stairwell. The stairs were steep. The treads were of worn red oak and had apparently not seen fresh varnish since Lee's gray-coats were in town.

On the second floor there was a narrow hallway and at the end of the hallway was an office door featuring the attorney's name. Dock went through the door and found yet another receptionist, this one as skinny as Olive Oyl, with a hairdo to match, and rimless glasses that only accented the washed-out blue of her eyes. She sat at an aged wooden desk behind an older Apple computer. Behind her was another office. The door was slightly ajar, and Dock could see a portly man inside, sitting in a swivel chair behind a desk. The chair was turned around to face the window, and the man had his stubby legs propped on the sill. He was talking on a telephone.

The receptionist appeared to be rather surprised by Dock's arrival. "Can I help you?"

Dock produced the letter from his pocket. "I'm here to see Mr. Trotter."

"Do you have an appointment?"

"No. I just got into town. I have this letter—"

"You'll need an appointment."

"He can't see me today?"

"Mr. Trotter's not here," the receptionist said and when she saw Dock's eyes shift to the office door behind her she got to her feet and closed it. She sat down again and looked at Dock expectantly as she reached for an appointment book.

"Mr. Trotter's not here?" Dock asked.

"No, he's not."

"Who's the little fat guy on the phone?"

"He's . . . an associate of Mr. Trotter's. And that was uncalled for."

"Okay," Dock said. "But if I make an appointment with Mr. Trotter and I come back here and find out that the little fat guy on the phone is him, then you're gonna feel pretty goddamn dumb for lying to me."

The pale blue eyes misted over, and the woman's lip began to tremble.

"Jesus," Dock said. "Don't start that. I didn't mean anything. What's your name?"

"Olive."

"You're joking."

"Why would I joke about my name?"

"I guess you wouldn't."

Olive gathered herself. "When would it be convenient for you to see Mr. Trotter?"

"I got an opening right now," Dock said. "But apparently that's not gonna work."

From the inner office came the soft click of a door closing, followed by the sound of footsteps descending a back staircase. Olive turned her head at the noise and then looked back at Dock.

"I'm not always able to tell the absolute truth," she said. "It's my job."

"I had a job like that once," Dock said. "Let's make the appointment."

★   ★   ★

He got a room at the Motel 8 and then took a walk through the town. Certain things came back to him—the cemetery where Lincoln had delivered the famous speech, for instance, and the ridge beyond where the Union forces had turned away the Confederates in what was probably the best-known battle in American history. He walked through the cemetery and on to Culp's Hill and then back to the visitor's center, which was in truth a sizable museum. He looked at the maps and the muskets and the clothes and the saddles and the pistols and before long looking at all that dusty history made him thirsty, so he walked back to the town center and went into the old Gettysburg Hotel. There was a restaurant to the right and to the left, past the front desk, was a bar called McClellan's. Dock went in and sat at the bar and ordered a beer from a woman wearing a black skirt and a red velour top.

"Bottle or draft?"

"What's on tap?"

"We got Yuengling Lager. It's the oldest beer in the country."

"I'm not sure that's a selling point, but I'll give it a try."

The place was quiet. Other than Dock, the only customers were a man and a woman who sat at the far end of the bar, where they drank Manhattans and argued about the alleged insubordination of Ewell in the first day of the battle. Dock drank the lager and watched a preview of the upcoming World Series on the TV set above the bar. It was the White Sox against the Cubs, and the media had dubbed it the "El" series. The bartender leaned against the counter and watched too.

"Whatcha doing in town—you a tourist?" she asked during a commercial.

"Nope. I'm here to see a lawyer."

"Oh?"

"Somebody left me something."

"What'd they leave you?"

"I don't know. Whatever it was, I hope it was worth a long drive."

"Where you from?"

"These days I guess I'm not from anywhere. I spent the last couple weeks musky fishing in the St. Lawrence." Dock set the empty glass on the bar. "I'll have another."

The bartender went to the tap and drew another draft. "Who's the lawyer?"

"Tommy Trotter."

She laughed. "Good old Tommy Trots."

"What's that?"

"They call him Tommy Trots. There's a story behind it—something about a bad case of the runs and a pair of white pants. I wasn't there at the time, thank God."

The series preview came back on the set then, saving Dock from more on the history of Tommy Trotter's intestinal failures. The show ended just as Dock was finishing his second beer, which was actually pretty good. He got to his feet.

"So how was the fishing?" the bartender asked.

"Caught a twenty-eight pounder last Wednesday."

"That's a good one. You gonna get it mounted?"

"Nope," Dock said. "I let him go."

Dock was ushered into Tommy Trotter's office at precisely ten o'clock the following morning. Olive had greeted him like an old friend and even provided him with a cup of coffee. Apparently, having an appointment carried a lot of weight in the world of Tommy Trots.

With his dark hair and boyish face, the rotund attorney looked a little like a grown-up version of Beaver Cleaver. He wore a navy blue suit and a red silk tie, a Mason's ring on his right hand. As soon as Dock sat down, Trotter stood up and began to pace. He paced very quickly and the only thing quicker than his walk was his talk.

"I've been waiting to hear from you. Now, this is a complicated situation, so I'll go through it as thoroughly yet as expediently as possible. This is the story as I understand it and I will endeavor to make a long story short. Your grandfather, Ed Porter, left your grandmother when your mother was just a girl. He then moved to Binghamton, where he took up with a woman—you'll correct me if I'm in error—where he took up with a woman named Potter. Potter and Porter, an unusual combination. This Potter woman grew up on a farm not two miles out of Gettysburg. She became pregnant at a young age and was shipped off to New York State to live with her mother's sister until the baby was born, a common enough practice in those times. Well, as it turns out, she suffered a miscarriage and she never came back. However, she did at one point marry your grandfather. The marriage occurred in November of 1954. How does this affect you, you're asking? Well sir, eleven months ago old Ambrose Potter died. He was the brother of the woman your grandfather married. Her name was Winifred, did I mention that? Now old Ambrose was a lifelong bachelor—he may have been queer, there were rumors—but that has nothing to do with why we're here today, so why go into it? So Winifred is the sole living heir to the farm. Except for a slight technicality—Winifred is no longer living. When she died, however, she left everything to your grandfather. I suspect you can see where this is going. Your grandfather—who is also deceased, maybe you knew that, maybe you didn't—becomes the rightful owner of this farm. Your grandfather, possibly in an effort to reconcile with his long-estranged family—although that is pure speculation on my part and in truth none of my business—left everything he owned— although I'm sure he knew nothing of the farm—to your mother. Whom, we have discovered, is also deceased and has been so for twenty years. So, where does that leave us? Well—long story short— we have a bunch of dead people, we have a farm, and we have you."

Throughout the discourse Dock found himself following the lawyer, as he crisscrossed the room, like a spectator at a tennis match. When Trotter stopping talking, he also stopped walking; the little lawyer was, if nothing else, synchronized.

"I want to—" Dock began.

"I know exactly what you're going to say," Trotter interrupted, and he immediately resumed pacing. "Why has it taken nearly a year for you to hear about this? Well, let me tell you, it has been a game of hide-and-seek, and one of enormous scope. The principals in this thing were scattered to the four winds and—with the notable exception of yourself—for the most part deceased. When you add to the mix that I am a very busy attorney—I handle criminal cases, civil litigation, wills, real estate, and so on, I'll give you a card in fact—then I trust you can appreciate the task at hand. I might add at this point that I've been working on my own time in this matter. Ambrose Potter had a meager sum to his name when he died. I've run up a considerable expense in these endeavors and I've assumed all along that I would be compensated for my time when the farm is sold. I hope that that is agreeable to you. Back to the point, though—long story short—the reason for the delay is that there has been a lot of legwork on this case and just one set of legs to do it. I hope that answers your question."

"I didn't ask a question."

"What?"

"I didn't ask a question," Dock said again. "Sit down a minute. You need a rest."

"I can assure you, Mr. Bass, that I—"

"*Sit down.*"

Tommy Trotter sat.

"I want to see the farm," Dock said then.

"Why didn't you say so?"

Attorney Trotter drove a Lincoln. It was a big car and he was a small man, and whatever the psychology behind his choice of vehicle, it wasn't quite working as the Lincoln basically reduced the lawyer to the size of a gnat. He'd have been better off in a Mini Cooper.

They drove north on the Carlisle Road. In deference to his stubby legs, Trotter had the bench seat adjusted as far forward as possible—even then he could barely reach the gas pedal with his right foot. Dock, sitting beside him, had his knees pushed against the dash. Dock had suggested they take his pickup, but the lawyer had regarded the vehicle rather doubtfully. Trotter slid Kenny Rogers in the tape deck, cranked up the volume, and then proceeded to attempt to converse with Dock above the racket.

The farm was practically on the outskirts of Gettysburg, on Shealer Road, which ran east and west, on the north side of town. They drove past a handful of newer—thirty- or forty-year-old—bungalows and then a stretch of bush where there were no houses at all. There were new-growth pines along each side of the road and older hardwoods—oak and maple and white ash—farther back to the north.

The farmhouse was situated on the outer arc of a curve in the road. It was a fieldstone building, with a sagging porch and broken shutters. There was an addition, also of fieldstone, built onto the back of the house. It was square and the roofline extended at a right angle from the main house. To the right was a rock uprising, so close that the house appeared to be built hard against the rock. Beyond the house to the left was a small field that may have been an orchard at one time but was now a congested tangle of gnarled trees and weeds and fallen fencing. There was a small barn behind the house and behind the barn was another field, this one much larger, and it was planted in corn. The corn looked ready for harvest.

The stereo was still blaring as Trotter stopped the Lincoln in the gravel drive and turned the ignition off, killing the gambler and the engine in a single blow.

"I warned you it wasn't much," he said. "I don't want you to think I was gilding the lily back in the office. I was trying to convey—"

Dock got out of the Lincoln and walked down the drive, taking in the property and the outbuildings. Trotter followed, his legs pumping to match Dock's stride.

"I don't suppose old Ambrose put ten cents in the house in the last twenty years," he said, coming up. "Funny thing about old people, they get so concerned about money that they—"

"How many acres?" Dock asked.

"The farm? Twenty-five. Many of these local farms have been parceled—"

"Twenty-five? That's not a farm," Dock said and he headed for the house, Trotter on his heels.

"Like I said, old Ambrose never spent a dime on repairs or renovations. The prudent thing would be to knock the place down. I've talked to one of our local realtors, and he advised just such an action. Of course, I assume you'll just be selling it anyway, so it really doesn't matter which—"

"You got a key?" Dock asked. He was standing on the front porch.

Trotter sighed. "Yes, I have a key. You have a habit of interrupting people, did you know that?"

Dock put the key in the lock and opened the door. "And you got a habit of never shutting up," he said, smiling. "Together we're quite a pair."

The house inside was musty and smelled remotely of many things—tobacco and bleach and Vicks VapoRub were three that Dock could name. The interior looked exactly as the exterior would suggest: peeling wallpaper, worn carpet, kitchen cupboards with countless coats of paint. There was a staircase in the left rear corner. The upstairs was in fact a loft extending over roughly half the house; its railing ran along a hallway, behind which there appeared to be two bedrooms. Dock walked to the staircase and looked with interest at the posts that supported the loft. Then he walked along the wall, tapping the plaster with the back of his hand. At one point he stopped and tapped several times, his head cocked.

"Looking for treasure?" Trotter asked.

"I thought you were gonna put a sock in it, counselor," Dock said. He tapped once more before he moved on.

The kitchen was at the back of the house, and beyond that was the woodshed–turned–living quarters Dock had seen from the outside. It was a large open room featuring a potbellied woodstove as well as a lounge chair and a big-screen television connected to a receiver for a satellite system.

"Old Ambrose must've liked the tube," Dock said. When Trotter made no comment, Dock realized that the lawyer was in a sulk over his earlier remark.

There were no windows along the right-hand wall of the big room and Dock guessed that the building was indeed built against the flat rock. He walked over to tap his knuckles against the plaster there too. There was a back door off to the left, midway along the wall, and after a moment he headed for it.

"Let's have a look at the barn," he said to Trotter. "What's the matter, counselor, cat got your tongue?"

The barn was full of junk and the building itself qualified as the same. There were horse stalls that hadn't seen a live animal in generations, the frameworks rotted and fallen apart. A couple of steel stanchions, probably for milk cows, were still intact but rusted shut. There was the remains of a chicken coop in the mow and what could have once been a pigsty down below. Dock looked over everything, taking his time as he moved through the building. Twice he saw the muted attorney looking at his watch.

When he was done in the barn, Dock walked over to the orchard field and leaned on the rail fence there. He looked at the twisted and barren apple trees and then turned to Trotter.

"You're saying I own this place?"

"Oh, so now I can speak?"

"Yeah, I'd rather hear you babble than watch you pout," Dock told him.

"You're quite a funny fellow. Well, as the result of my yearlong quest, I'm quite confident in saying that you're the lone heir to this piece—"

"Okay, I'm gonna take that as a yes," Dock asked. "What do I owe you?"

"Well, as I said, I've spent a significant number of hours on this. Old Ambrose did have a meager sum, which is still resting in the bank in town and is now at your disposal. But I chased this matter across three states and two countries. Long story short—you'll end up owing me, after that which languishes in the bank in town, somewhere in the neighborhood of four to five thousand dollars. Now I have no way of knowing your financial position. If you would like to wait until you sell the place, I'm certain arrangements could be—"

"Tell you what," Dock said and he started for the Lincoln. "That sounds fair to me. But I'll warn you—I'm gonna deduct a hundred dollars from the total every time I hear you say 'long story short.'"

"I beg your pardon?"

"I figure we'll be even about sundown."

★   ★   ★

The Series was to begin on Saturday. Amy arrived in Chicago on the Tuesday before and spent three days conducting player interviews and preparing lame Windy City profiles to be aired during the pre-game show. The rest of the time she passed researching player stats, watching Series tapes from previous years, and searching out personal stories on various players whom she could potentially work into her coverage—the kind of uplifting, victory-over-adversity schmaltz that the network loved and that the real fan didn't give a shit about. She found that these types of stories were in short supply this year—just her luck—but she was optimistic by nature and held on to the hope that something of an inspirational—or better yet, scandalous—nature would pop up in the days to come. She'd give Sam Rockwood a Vin Scully for the new age, providing he accepted that she preferred base-ball broadcasting fame to be a fleeting thing.

By Thursday afternoon she was done with the prep work and, with time on her hands, she had little recourse but to pass the afternoon downtown shopping. She spent five thousand dollars in two hours and barely bought enough to burden her down as she walked along State Street in the late afternoon sun. Outside of buying vehicles or resi-dences, five grand a day was her shopping limit because that's roughly what she earned, each and every day of the year, and she was bound by some childhood sense of fiscal responsibility to adhere to that ceiling. Even with that restriction in place, she was aware that it was a terrific system, especially when browsing at Sak's.

After shopping, she was required to walk nearly a block before she found a Starbucks, and when she did she went inside to drink a latte and read *Newsweek*. Considering whether she should attempt sneaking a cigarette, she flipped through the magazine and was about to toss it aside when she came upon the scowling countenance of Sarah Jane Wright. The picture had been taken as Wright was being released from a prison in Connecticut a few days earlier. The scowl, it could be as-sumed, reflected Wright's feelings for her recent accommodations, al-though Amy, looking at the picture, could easily imagine it being directed toward her.

Former congressman Howard and the Reverend Stevie Save were

mentioned in the short piece that accompanied the picture, Howard relaxing on his Oklahoma ranch, untouched even yet, and the expansive TV preacher outside a courtroom somewhere, dancing through the appeals process and still smiling like the proverbial kid looking for a pony in a room full of shit.

It had all started with the good reverend. Stephen Austin Save was a congenial and somewhat dim-witted hustler from Dallas, a convicted felon, and an admitted alcoholic and cocaine addict who had somewhat incredibly converted these very failings into a wildly successful online ministry before moving to the world of cable television, where he eventually flaunted his warts-and-all persona to fifteen million viewers a week.

"If the good Lord can love a loser like me, just *think* what he will do for you!" he liked to exclaim at meetings.

"You see—it's all about redemption," he told Amy over lunch on his Long Island estate. "Your average citizen doesn't want to be told how to live his life by someone who appears to be untouched by perfidy. Your average citizen is a sinner."

Based, in effect, on there being no accusation too wretched for him to endorse, the reverend had hit upon an unlikely winning formula. Because it was impossible to hide the skeletons therein, he simply knocked down his closet walls and invited the world to have a look. It was a stroke of genius by a man who usually wouldn't be associated with the word. In his willingness to shine a spotlight on his sordid history, he convinced his flock that he was sincere in all things.

In truth, Amy didn't find Reverend Save to be all that interesting for that very reason. The country was indeed full of sinners. And she had no reaction to seeing, in his memento-filled den, the picture of him arm in arm with Sarah Jane Wright. Only when he casually revealed that the photograph had been taken ten years earlier in Haiti did she prick up her ears.

She made an inquiry regarding the matter to Sarah Jane Wright's office. She did not get a reply but she did, lo and behold, receive an invitation to Sarah's sixtieth birthday bash at the Waldorf in New York. There, engulfed in a tide of celebrities, she spent by her later estimation forty-five seconds in meaningless chatter with Sarah herself before being shuffled off to a separate room, where she soon found herself drinking warm champagne with Ann Coulter and Dennis Miller. She left knowing that something was amiss. She decided to take a closer look at the Fortune 500 phenomenon that was known to America as the Wright Way.

Sarah Jane Wright had in the past twenty-five years become conservative America's lifestyle maven of choice. She was a hard-line right-winger, a devout Christian who held rap music, on-screen nudity, and same-sex marriages in the same contempt that she did lumpy mashed potatoes. She'd started in Wisconsin, where she parlayed a five-minute weekly lifestyle segment on the noon news at a local affiliate into a syndicated television empire. Her sweet suggestion, "Do it the Wright Way," became her clarion call. It was now trademarked and used, in part, to market a line of books, CDs, furniture, towels, linen, jam, and even, improbably, rototillers.

Afterward, Amy likened her investigation of Wright's world to that of a child peeking into the big-top tent of a circus. And, like a real circus, each flap of the canvas revealed something different—some wonderful, some plain, some truly disgusting. When the revealing was done, she unearthed an elaborate scheme wherein Wright, Congressman Howard, Stevie Save, and a host of others collected several hundred million dollars for food and aid for starving Haitians after the 1994 insurrection. Some of the information was widely known; what wasn't was that barely a million dollars in assistance ever reached the island. Of course in the end, it wasn't the blatant embezzlement that brought Wright and Howard down. It was, as usual, the lying about it all.

Profile-wise, and given that the public rather expected the worst of politicians and TV evangelists, Howard and Save were considered small potatoes compared to Wright. After Amy broke the story in a weeklong series of reports in the *Post*, a stampede of media arrived and they didn't peek into the tent as much as trample it into the ground. The tabloids, as well, had a wonderful time of it all, in short order turning up Wright's ex-husband, who—perhaps bored with his

life back in Wisconsin or unhappy with the size of the annual al-
lowance he'd received for twenty years to remain mute—decided to
grab his God-given right to fifteen minutes. He was a dull sort who
didn't have a lot to say, but he did have stuff to show, including a tape
he'd made of his wife having sex with two of his hunting buddies back
in the seventies and a more recent audiotape upon which Sarah was
heard to say that "the fucking niggers" were ruining popular music.
Predictably, the Wright Way became a popular topic on late-night television, where it was soon dubbed the White Way and, of course, the
Three Way. In the end it was no way, as far as Wright's empire was
concerned.

Amy stayed away from the more sensationalistic elements of the
story, dug into the financial malfeasance instead, and ended up orches-
trating Howard's failed reelection bid and Wright's jailing. The investigation, which she continued after moving to TransWorld, made her a
star of sorts and won her a couple of awards. Howard, however, had yet
to be indicted on criminal charges, and the fact continued to eat at her.
She'd give back the awards to get him. She'd even give up the World
Series, but apparently that was not to be an option available to her.

She left the *Newsweek* on the table and walked back to the hotel.
She ate in her hotel room, a piece of salmon that had apparently been
cooked during last year's Series and some soggy steamed vegetables.
She ordered a half bottle of wine with the meal and she managed to
finish it off afterward, flipping through the movie channels for an hour
before finally turning off the set. She felt as if she'd been there for a
month already, and it would be two days before the Series even
started. She'd given up her bedtime prayers years before; she wondered if God would question her sincerity if she asked him for a sweep.

After all, he forgave Stevie Save.

Friday was sweltering hot. They spent the day at Wrigley, shooting
various World Series promos and teasers for the network. Amy was
decked out in a windbreaker bearing the TransWorld logo on the

breast, and a like-designed baseball cap, her shades perched stylishly above the bill. The final spot had her taking batting practice in the cage—equipped with a remote clip mike, she took turns swinging at baseballs and reciting from a cliché-ridden script. The director was new to Amy. He was young and brooding, and he was actually wearing a beret. His youth and his headgear Amy could forgive, but his broodiness was a bit much. The producer, Syd Greenblut, middle-aged and not even remotely a brooder, watched from inside the third-base line as Amy pretended to respond to a prompt from the nightly news anchor.

"Dan," she said, "I'm standing in the batting cage at Wrigley Field, where tomorrow tonight the Cubs and the White Sox will be squaring off in game one of the World Series. The rivalry usually generated in the Series is magnified a hundredfold as these two crosstown rivals duke it out for the right to be called the best in the world. There's been some trash talking from both sides and it looks as if the intensity is only going to increase in the next few days. Will the Cubs' pitching staff— with arguably the best bullpen in baseball—be able to shut down the vaunted White Sox defense? And how will this young, untested White Sox staff respond? Dan, I've been watching baseball since I was old enough to turn on the TV, and I can't remember being this excited about a World Series."

When she was done with the spiel, Amy took an awkward swing at a floating baseball and missed it by a foot and a half.

"Um," the director said, not happily. Of course, it was not a word that lent itself to glee.

"What?" Amy asked.

Syd walked over. "You said *defense*. It's *offense*. Will the Cub pitchers shut down the White Sox *offense*? Pitchers can't shut down a defense."

"Shit," she said.

"It's okay. We'll do it again."

"Um," the director said, again. Amy noticed now that the *ums* were directed at Syd.

"What?" Amy asked, again.

"Her sunglasses are blocking the TransWorld logo on the hat."

"Gee, maybe the home viewers will notice the giant TransWorld logo on my *jacket*."

"Lose the shades, Amy," Syd suggested.

"I paid two hundred dollars for these glasses," Amy told him.

"Money from your generous TransWorld salary?" Syd asked. "Oh, the irony."

Amy shot him a look. But she removed the shades, put them in her jacket pocket.

"Um," the director said. "The spot would work better if she actually hit the ball."

"Really?" Amy said. "I had no idea. Refresh my memory—when Jean-Luc Godard directed the classic Abbott and Costello routine 'Who's on First?'—or, as the French call it, 'C'est Qui Sur le Premier?'—did Costello hit the ball at the end?"

The director looked at Syd, who stood expressionless. "Try to hit the ball," Syd said.

"I'll hit it," she told him.

And she did. On the seventeenth take she topped a slow roller up the middle, and, flipping the bat like Reggie in his prime, she immediately walked away.

"Okay, that's it," Syd told everybody. "We gotta be back here, three tomorrow afternoon."

He caught up with Amy and walked with her off the field. She removed the TransWorld jacket and put on her sunglasses as she walked. When he arrived beside her, she handed the jacket to him without asking.

"The Godard shot was a bit much," he said.

"Was it?" she asked.

"Yeah, it was. You could be a little nicer to the guy. After all, you have something in common."

"What's that?"

"He doesn't want to be here either."

They headed for an exit to the street.

"Tomorrow, we just do the pregame, and that's it," Syd said then. "The color guys will take over. We can watch the game from the owner's box."

"You can watch the game from the owner's box," she said. "I'd rather watch a Three Stooges film fest."

"Who wouldn't?" Syd said. "I love those guys."

When she got back to the hotel, she had a bath and then drank a bottle of beer from the minibar while she read the issue of *Time* she'd picked up in the hotel lobby. She found she couldn't get interested in the pseudo-news, however, and after fifteen minutes she made her decision. She threw on jeans and a sweater and went down to the street and hailed a cab.

He was living on the South Side, in the walk-up where he'd been for thirty years now. She rang the buzzer a couple of times and got no response. She should have called, she realized, but then she had no idea that she would try to see him. She sat down on the steps out front and as soon as she did she saw him coming, moving down the street with that long, cool stride, dressed in tan cotton pants and a sports jacket, a T-shirt beneath. He was older, of course; she hadn't seen him in four years and his beard was scattershot with gray.

He spotted her, she was sure, from a distance—he was never one to miss much—but he didn't let on, in fact approached without really looking at her. He was carrying a couple of bags, one from the supermarket, the other from a liquor store. The staples, Amy thought.

He stopped short in front of her, executed a perfect double take. "I'll be damned. If it ain't Diane Sawyer."

Her hand went involuntarily to her hair. "That's a good one. You should send a tape to *Star Search*."

He went past her, up the steps. "You comin' in?"

"I was waiting to see if I'd be asked."

The apartment was as she remembered it. Small, one bedroom— the kitchen off the end of the dining room, the living room off the end of that. The place was in imminent danger of disappearing beneath his massive collection of books and records. She looked in vain for signs of a feminine presence, even of a temporary nature. She wondered how long it had been since he'd had a woman in his life.

She followed him into the kitchen and watched as he put the groceries away. Then he took the bottle from the paper bag. "You gonna have a drink?"

"No," she said, and then, "Yeah, what the hell."

They sat in the living room. He put on some Billie and then sat by the phonograph, his drink resting lightly on his knee. "I almost didn't recognize you," he said.

"You didn't recognize me? Come on, Dad."

"You're looking decidedly . . . Caucasian these days."

"Shit. Don't you start."

He shrugged and had a drink. "Why are you in town? You didn't arrive just to visit me."

"I'm covering the World Series."

"They've got you doing sports now? I suppose, the way things are, that that's considered a promotion."

"Not in my book, it isn't. I'm filling in, basically. Eating bacon every morning for fifty years finally caught up with Bob Brown. I'm being a good team player here, to leave no cliché unturned."

If he was amused, he sure as hell didn't let on. Sipped at his whiskey and nodded to the turntable.

"Did you see any of my stuff on Cyrus Howard?"

He gestured to the television in the corner. "Been broke for a couple of years. I guess I don't miss it or I'd get it fixed, wouldn't I? I do see you now and then, at the corner bar." He smiled. "Usually the sound is off."

"Supporting the old adage—children should be seen and not heard?"

He raised his eyebrows over the rim of his glass but said nothing. He seemed to be amused by her, and she was not happy with the notion.

"Would you like me to buy you a new TV?"

He placed the glass on his knee. "No."

She took a drink and almost gagged on the strong liquor. It had been a mistake to come.

"What the hell do you do all day, Dad?"

He nodded to the stereo. "This," he said, then lifted his glass. "And this. Been working for Councilman Granato—trying to get him reelected."

"You're working for the white candidate?"

"The black candidate's a crook."

"Free at last," Amy said.

This time he smiled slightly and looked for a moment at his bookshelves across the room. As she watched, his eyes narrowed, as if he noticed a title he didn't recognize. He took another drink.

"And what's next for you?" he asked then. "Now that you've removed the congressman from office and slapped Betty Crocker in leg irons?"

"I'm still following the money."

He rubbed his knuckles across his bearded cheek. "And TransWorld Communications thinks it might be buried at Wrigley Field?"

She would not let him get to her. "Well, we thought we'd try Chicago, then move on to Aruba. See where it goes from there."

"You couldn't have stayed at the *Post* and pursued this?"

"I could have. But why not move on to television? There's a significant difference in demographics."

"Ah, *demographics.*" He said the word delicately, touching upon each syllable, as if tasting a food for the first time. He smiled as Billie kicked into "I Can't Get Started with You."

"And what about you?" she asked. "You been back to Mississippi?"

"No. There's nothing for me in Mississippi. I guess that's one thing we have in common."

Amy took another drink. This time it was smoother. Probably not as smooth as it was on his tongue but smoother nonetheless.

"Why is it the only thing?" she asked and she was surprised that she did.

He shook his head without looking at her and she knew what he was thinking, that the two of them were too much alike to have a conversation like this. In fact, they had both spent their entire lives avoiding conversations like this.

So when he spoke, it surprised the hell out of her.

"You were the smartest girl I ever knew, Amelia," he said, still looking away. "And look at where they've got you. You ain't nothing but an ornament, girl."

The Sox took the first game by a score of 4–3. Not that Amy was there to watch, of course. She did her pregame duties, and then she took the limo back to the hotel. She got a massage and a facial from the hotel spa, and then she went back to her room, where she watched half of a Vin Diesel movie, most of *Mr. Smith Goes to Washington*, and five minutes of Meg Ryan pretending to know something about boxing. When she flipped to the ball game to check its progress, she caught the network in the act of running a blooper reel—a loop of her many failed attempts to hit the ball in the batting cage. She clicked the set off, adding abject humiliation to her list of grievances against Sam Rockwood.

She was back at Wrigley as Jefferson caught a fly ball in right center field for the final out. She did a quick on-field wrap-up, questioned the left fielder about the home run he'd hit ("In that situation, I was just looking for a pitch I could drive"), gushed enthusiastically about the game she hadn't seen, and then walked off, headed back for the hotel.

One down. Anywhere from three to six to go.

FOUR

Friday found Dock sitting on the front porch of the old farmhouse, eating a ham sandwich from the deli on Baltimore Street in town and drinking a Yuengling Lager. His truck was parked in the drive. He had the doors and the windows of the old house open in an effort to let the dust clear. In the meantime he was eating his sandwich and drinking his beer. And deciding.

While he was deciding, a black Lexus came down the road and pulled in the drive. The car was identical to the one Dock had driven back in Coopers Falls. It gave him a start; he feared for a moment that Terri had tracked him down. A thin man wearing a short-sleeve shirt with a tie got out, carrying a briefcase. He turned on a smile like he was turning on a light as he walked across the overgrown lawn.

"I'm gonna kick lawyer Trotter right in the nuts," Dock told him as he approached.

The man stopped. "What?"

"You heard me."

"Why would you do that?"

"For sending you here."

"You don't even know who I am."

"I guess I do. You're a real estate agent."

"Well," the man said hesitantly. "What if I was to tell you that it wasn't Mr. Trotter who sent me here?"

"Then I'd kick you in the nuts for lying."

The man considered this briefly. "Well, if it comes down to that, then I'd rather that Trotter took the kicking," the man said and he offered his hand. "Ron Orson. Penn State Realty."

Dock shook the hand reluctantly. "You already know who I am."

"Mr. Trotter tells me you're in the market for an agent."

"That what he said?"

"Yes," Orson said and he set the briefcase on the weathered planking of the porch and opened it. "I did an appraisal on the place at the time of Ambrose Potter's demise. As anyone can see, the house and the outbuildings are worthless. In fact, they're worth less than nothing because it's going to cost money to have them demolished and the debris disposed of. The property—twenty-five point five acres—is worth approximately eight hundred dollars an acre as farmland. That's on the high side as well, as the old orchard is not tillable at this time and the rock piece to the rear of the house will not be tillable ever. So you have the twenty-acre field in back, which is average to good farmland. Long story short—"

"Jesus, don't you start."

"Uh . . . what I was going to say was, you have a piece of farmland worth maybe twenty thousand dollars."

"Yeah?"

"However, that's less than you'd pay for a building lot in this part of the country. A lot is worth twenty-five to thirty thousand. I think you could put this piece on the market for thirty-five and see what happens."

"Do you think you could find a buyer at that price?"

"I'm sure I could."

"Any idea how old this house would be?"

Orson glanced at the building. "None. Sixty, seventy years."

"I'd say well over a hundred." Dock drank off his beer and got to his feet. "Come on inside."

Orson followed along. Inside the house Dock, using a rusty crow-bar he'd found in the barn, had pulled the lath and plaster from the wall of the living room to reveal the framing that supported the loft and the stairwell. The house was supported by six-inch-square white ash posts, the vertical beams held in place by a pair of diagonal sup-ports that formed a Y.

"You know what that's called?" Dock asked.

"Wood?"

"It's called post and beam. And this place is as square as the day it was built. I have a feeling the foundation's setting on bedrock. A man would have to be an idiot to tear this house down."

"Well," Orson said slowly. "We could advertise it as a handyman's special, I guess."

Dock looked at him. "I guess we could."

He walked over to the post beneath the staircase. He grabbed the support there and pulled on it. "See here. There's no nails in this. Everything is mortise and tenon, pegged together. It was an art."

"It's still a rundown house," Orson said.

Dock had a sudden urge to get the realtor out of the house. He led the way outside, where he stopped in the yard, made a point of looking over the failed orchard and the decrepit barn. He could feel Orson's impatience hanging in the air. Dock was aware that a man would put up with a lot for the sake of a commission, but it would be a pretty meager commission in this case. And that puzzled him.

"We could go a little higher on the price," Orson suggested then. "If that's what you're thinking. You can always come down."

Then Dock heard another voice. "Did he mention the proposal to develop this area?"

Dock turned to see a man standing at the back corner of the house. He was in his forties maybe, wearing a tweed cap and an expensive-looking twill jacket, corduroy pants, and hiking boots. He had a neatly trimmed beard.

Orson didn't try to hide the fact that he was pissed off. "What do you think you're doing?" he demanded.

"Eavesdropping," the man said. Then he looked at Dock. "There's been a proposal in the works for a couple years to rezone this area and turn it into residential housing. Did he mention that?"

"I don't recall that he did," Dock said.

"Who the fuck do you think you are?" Orson demanded of the man.

The man put two fingers in his mouth and gave a sharp whistle. A moment later a black Labrador retriever emerged from the cornfield and began a lopsided trot toward them. "Me?" the man asked. "I'm just a guy out walking his dog. No ulterior motives here."

He and the dog walked away then, heading across the road to a dirt lane running in the direction of town. Dock was watching Orson.

"Nobody knows how these things will go." Orson shrugged. "It's up to the whim of the town planners."

Dock nodded and in that moment his deciding was done. "Maybe so," he said, "but you knew there was the possibility. And you held that information back. I put this place on the market for thirty or forty thousand, and it'll sell in a day. To you, or one of your developer buddies, I'm guessing. I am just so sick of lying sons of bitches."

"Watch what you're calling me, boy."

"You'll let me call you a liar because you are a liar. And you won't be putting a sign up out front of this place. I'm sticking around."

The next morning he went down to the Gettysburg hardware store on York Street. His old tools were in the garage back in Coopers Falls, but he was pretty sure that by now Terri would have sold them at a yard sale or given them to Phil McMurter even though Phil wouldn't know a router from a slot screwdriver. Even if she hadn't, there was no way to get them without going back, and that was one move he'd already ruled out.

He bought a Skilsaw, reciprocating saw, level, apron, hammer, tape, chalkline, square, wrecking bars, cords, drills both corded and cordless, and an assortment of screwdrivers, pliers, and chisels. A big red toolbox. His bill came to six hundred and forty-two dollars.

"You're over five hundred dollars," the clerk told him. "You get a free T-shirt and a hat."

Dock put the T-shirt in a bag with his purchases and placed the cap on his head. "I'm gonna need to rent a dumpster," he said. "Somebody you could recommend?"

"There's a guy in Cashtown," the clerk said. "I'll give you the number."

Before leaving town, Dock went to the local branch of the Keystone Bank. He was able to check the balance on the joint account he held with Terri. It held forty-seven thousand and change, which meant that Terri hadn't figured out yet that he wasn't coming back. Dock arranged to open a new account, deposited twenty-three grand from the old, kissed the rest good-bye. There were term deposits, too, but he would worry about them later. He was told it would take a couple days for the transfer to come through.

Dock drove back out to the property and went to work gutting the house. He'd already carried whatever he considered salvageable of the furniture out to the barn and covered it with heavy plastic. Now he removed the doors and the baseboards and the door and window casings and carried them out as well. The trim was red oak; he labeled everything with masking tape and stacked it neatly in the barn. Then he went back to the house, put on gloves and a dust mask, and began the dirty task of removing the plaster and lath from the walls.

It took him two days to strip the main house down to the studding. The man from Cashtown delivered a large steel dumpster on the back of a flatbed loader; when it was overflowing he took it away and left another. The second dumpster was nearly full when Dock finished stripping the walls. The floors were covered with several generations of plywood, linoleum, and tile; he tore this up too, revealing the original pine underneath, and tossed it in the dumpster. Then he swept the house clean.

He had a cooler in the back of his truck with sandwiches and pop and beer on ice. When he'd finished sweeping, he removed the dust mask and opened a Coke and walked back into the house. All that remained were the stone walls and the post-and-beam framework. The roof rafters were sagging with a permanent bow and would have to be replaced. That meant tearing the entire roof off and starting anew. It would have to be done before the snow.

Dock walked through the kitchen and into the large back room, where there remained three walls to strip. He looked at his watch and then drank the soda and went back to work.

He tore out the lath and plaster from the left side and end walls first, leaving the windowless wall—the wall built against the rock overcropping—for the last. He worked until dark and then he packed up his tools and drove into town. He picked up a pizza and went back to his room at the Motel 8. He ate, had a shower, and watched the first game of the World Series. It was after midnight when Jefferson made a running catch for the final out of the game. The White Sox went up one game to zip.

He was back at the house by first light. He cleaned up from the day before and returned to the demolition. Early in the afternoon he was using a flat wrecking bar to pull the plaster from the back wall when he felt something brush against his leg. He looked down to see the Labrador retriever from a couple days earlier circling the room, sniffing frantically at everything in its path.

"Hey, pup," Dock called. He dropped to one knee and pulled the dust mask down. The dog came close, then veered skittishly away and out the open door. In a minute the animal was back, and this time he came nervously to Dock, who petted him for a moment before a man's voice called out.

"Casey! Where are you?"

Dock looked up and a moment later the dog's owner appeared in the doorway. He was dressed again in his hiking garb.

"Casey," the man said to the dog.

"He's okay," Dock said and he took the dog by the loose skin at the back of the neck and gave it a shake. "I don't think he's got any ulterior motives either."

"He might. Would you have anything dead for him to roll around in?"

When Dock stood, he extended his hand. "Thanks for the other day. I'm Dock Bass."

"Harris Jameson," the man said. "You buy this place?"

"Not exactly. But I own it."

"Old place has got a lot of potential," the man said.

Dock took a slow look at the house surrounding him. "I've been told the practical thing would be to knock it down."

"Is that what you're doing?"

"Nope," Dock said and he turned back to Harris. "I've decided to quit being practical, at least for the time being."

"Good for you," Harris said.

Dock nodded and then he pulled the mask up over his nose. Jamming the crook of the bar behind the lath strips, he pulled a large slab of plaster from the wall.

"You know this house is a hundred and sixty years old," he heard Harris say.

This time Dock removed the mask altogether. "How do you know that?"

"I checked it out. The records are down at the courthouse. Oh, I'm a professor at Gettysburg University."

"What kind of professor?"

"History. Mainly the Civil War. Lincoln, Lee, that bunch. I've done a lot of research in this area. Not that I'm exactly unique in that respect. Gettysburg is probably the most researched town in North America. But that doesn't make it any less interesting."

"So what do you know about this house?"

"Well, it was built in 1841 by a man named Thomas Burns and his wife, Eva. They had nine kids, which probably explains this back part. It looks to be an addition. Burns was a farmer. Back then everybody was a farmer or a merchant. The farm was two hundred acres at one time but then it got divided up over the years, a piece left to this son or that daughter. What's left now?"

"Twenty-five acres."

Harris nodded. "Nice piece of property. I walk through here quite often; we have a place about a mile yonder." He waggled his thumb over his shoulder. "So, you intend to renovate?"

"That's the plan."

"Mind if I take a look around?"

"Go ahead."

While Harris checked out the rest of the house, Dock went back to pulling down the plaster on the back wall. The Lab stayed with him, running back and forth, barking at the chunks of plaster as they fell, occasionally biting down on a piece of lath and dragging it across the floor. The studding behind the lath was at irregular spacings and loosely nailed; as a result sometimes a large slab of plaster would break loose suddenly, forcing Dock to move out of the way and allow it to fall. Such a piece—four or five feet wide—was coming down as Harris made his way back into the room. The plaster exploded into pieces when it hit the floor, raising a cloud of dust. Harris stepped back and waited for the air to clear.

"You plan to leave the post and beam exposed?" he asked.

"Yup."

"That's a nice look. What about the fieldstone where it's falling away?"

"Well, I'm no stonemason," Dock said. "I'll have to find somebody."

"We had a fellow from Chambersburg do our fireplace. A rough old cob—had a beard so long I was in constant fear he would mortar it into the hearth—but the work was good. I can give you his name"— Harris stopped short and looked past Dock, to the masonry wall behind the studding. "What's that?"

Dock turned. There was a doorway in the just-exposed portion of the stone wall, about six feet high and a couple of feet wide. The door had been filled in quite expertly, with fieldstone and mortar identical to the rest of the wall. At first glance it was evident only by the stone lintel above.

Dock walked over to the wall and brushed some dust away from the stone. "There's nothing behind here," he said. "Just rock."

"There's something behind there," Harris said. "You don't put a doorway in a stone wall by accident."

There were a couple of two-by-fours in front of the doorway. Dock took his hammer and knocked them loose, then tossed them aside to get a better look.

"An old root cellar would be my guess," Harris said. "I've seen it before. Could be a natural enclave in the rock. Makes for dry storage. Do you intend to open it up?"

"Yeah, I guess so."

"Who knows what you might find in there? Strawberry preserves, pickled beets. Maybe a jug or two of hard cider."

Dock went to his toolbox and picked up a cold chisel, then he looked at Harris. "Wanna help?"

"I'm afraid I can't. As a teacher, I'm not allowed to get my hands dirty. It's a union thing. Besides, I have to walk into town to buy the *New York Times.* My wife is from Westchester and she needs her paper. Casey!"

In a moment the dog trotted in from the main part of the house. Harris and the animal went out the back door. Outside, Harris turned back. "Maybe I'll stop on the way back through."

Whoever had sealed the doorway shut had known what they were doing. It took Dock the better part of an hour to remove the first stone. He started with the chisel and then switched to a hammer drill with a masonry bit, boring a series of holes along the mortar joints and then driving the mortar out with the hammer and chisel. Once the first stone was gone, the rest came easily.

By the time Harris came back along the lane, it was late afternoon and Dock was sitting outside the house in an aged ladderback chair he'd found in the barn, drinking a bottle of Yuengling from the cooler at his feet. He saw Harris from a distance, the Lab alternately at his heels or running along ahead, tongue lolling, nose to the ground. It was warm in the afternoon sun; Dock was down to his shirtsleeves.

"You're not going to tell me you found that bottle of beer in the root cellar," Harris said, approaching.

"I found this bottle of beer in that cooler. Grab one if you want."

Harris helped himself.

"Where's your newspaper?" Dock asked.

"I dawdled away half the day and by the time I got to the drug-store they were sold out. Mrs. Jameson will not be impressed."

"I wouldn't worry about that, Professor."

"No?"

"No, sir," Dock said, and he took a drink. "It wasn't a root cellar."

"What was it?"

Dock reached behind him and picked up an ancient sign made from a slab of cedar planking, about two feet square. Burned into the wood were the words:

WILLY BURNS
Photographer
Tinker
Inventionist

"Well, well," Harris said. "What else did you find?"

"I guess you could call it a workshop. Willy Burns's workshop."

"Anything interesting?"

"Have a look," Dock said and he got to his feet. "There's a good chance you won't be talking about newspapers by the time you get home."

It was nearly dark when they left. Dock offered to drive Harris and the dog home, but Harris declined.

"It's only a ten-minute walk," he said, and he set out. Dock drove into town, parked at the motel, and, after a shower and a change of clothes, walked into town to find something to eat.

The Blackbird Café was on Chambersburg Street, a block from the town center. The place was busy; Dock found a spot at the bar and waited to get the bartender's attention. He was a young guy, college kid, Dock guessed, and he was kept hopping, supplying the waitresses and the drinkers at the bar. Finally, he approached Dock and just as he did Dock felt a large shoulder ram into his side. He turned to see a huge bearded man, wearing a filthy buckskin jacket and a slouch hat. The man's beard and the hair beneath the hat were both long and unruly; he smelled like a cocker spaniel that had just come in from a rainstorm. He gave Dock a look of dismissal and spoke to the kid behind the bar.

"Whose ears I gotta box to get a beer around here?"

The kid was cool for his years. He ignored the giant and looked at Dock.

"A draft and a menu, please," Dock said.

Dock kept an eye on the big man as he waited for the kid to return.

"What the fuck you gawkin' at?" the man demanded.

Dock smiled. "I was thinking that maybe Darwin was on to something."

The bartender arrived at that moment. "Gimme a beer, you little prick," the big man demanded.

Dock took his own beer and the menu and found an empty table in the corner and sat. When the waitress came, he ordered a hamburger and another beer. The place mat featured a map of the town and a mélange of obscure trivial facts about the Battle of Gettysburg. At the bar, a half-dozen college kids were arguing about the week's NFL matchups, a subject that, Dock had noticed, had pretty much supplanted political debate in the gin mills of the nation.

The waitress brought his meal, and hard on its heels arrived an unwelcome side dish—the lawyer Tommy Trotter. Trotter wore another ensemble from his junior Brooks Brothers collection, although he had loosened his tie, presumably in deference to the hour. With him was a pale-skinned wisp of a man who could have been anywhere from fifty to sixty-five. He was thin to the point of emaciation and he had lank blond hair and unusually red lips. He wore what appeared to be a tracksuit of sky blue velour. His chin was cocked and uplifted; his nose seemed to have encountered something disagreeable.

"Mr. Bass," Tommy Trotter said. "I thought that was you."

Dock nodded and then took a bite of the burger.

"This is Thaddeus St. John," Trotter said. "Perhaps you've heard of him."

"Nope."

Thaddeus St. John smiled as if skeptical of the denial, but he nevertheless offered his hand delicately to Dock. He had stooped shoulders and small yellow teeth, like a rodent. Dock reluctantly put the burger down and took the soft, cold fingers in his own hand. St. John pulled his hand back quickly.

"Thaddeus is probably the foremost authority on the Civil War in the state," Trotter said and he turned to St. John. "Mr. Bass is the fellow I was telling you about; he's taken over the old Potter place, on Shealer Road. He intends, it appears, to renovate the place. Given the years of neglect accorded the house and the potential structural problems therein, it's quite an enormous undertaking. Not a practical move, if you ask me."

"I can't imagine anybody ever does," Dock said.

"Renovate?"

"Ask you."

St. John smiled his chipmunk's smile but said nothing. Trotter pursed his lips; Dock thought for a moment the lawyer might stamp his heel like a petulant schoolgirl.

"Well," he said instead, "if you have any questions of a historical nature, Thaddeus is the man to ask."

"I can't think of a single one, right at this moment," Dock said. "Unless he has some insight on the history of the hamburger."

Trotter stiffened; it seemed he'd expected Dock to be impressed by the little man in the velour suit. "Then there's the matter of your bill," Trotter said.

"The bill for my dinner?" Dock asked. "I've barely started to eat."

"The bill for my legal services."

"Oh, my," the man named Thaddeus said. He had a soft southern accent. "I never talk business after six o'clock. And I daresay never in a public house. I'll take my leave and afford the two of you some discretion." He smiled again at Dock and then moved away, toward the door. Before leaving, he stopped at the bar and spoke briefly to the behemoth in buckskin. The man turned and looked over at Dock as Thaddeus exited through the front door.

Dock turned to Trotter. "I'm having my bank account transferred. Should be done by tomorrow, they said."

"Well, we should really get it looked after," Trotter said. "Seems to me a person would be inclined to pay what he owes before sinking money into renovations. I would not enjoy taking action against you."

"You don't look to me like a man who enjoys much of anything, counselor," Dock said.

As he spoke, the bearded man from the bar approached. Dock noticed now that under his jacket he wore a T-shirt that promised "The South Will Rise Again." His swagger was slightly undermined by the bits of food clinging to his beard.

"This is Stonewall Martin," Trotter said as he arrived.

"Another colorful character?" Dock asked. "I really lucked out, coming in here."

"Word is you're renovating out on Shealer Road," the big man said. "I buy and sell antiques. You find anything—you call me." He made the request an order.

"Why would I call a hobo with french fries in his beard?" Dock asked.

"Oh, this guy's a sweetheart," the man said, turning to Trotter.

"You're right—I really should apologize," Dock said. "I don't know what I was thinking. Coming in here alone. Sitting in the corner. Minding my own fucking business." He paused. "How about you and I come to an agreement, counselor? You'll get your money, and then in return you'll stop sending these clowns my way. I'm talking about that weasel realtor who showed up at the house and the duck in the velvet suit who just left. Stonehead here too, for that matter."

"His name is Stonewall."

"Is it really? I bet his parents agonized over that one."

Dock saw the veins bulge in the big bearded man's neck, and he checked himself. Insulting a guy who outweighed him by 150 pounds was probably not the smartest move he could make. But the man simply reached across and gathered a handful of Dock's fries in his dirty fingers and, stuffing them into his mouth, turned and went back to the bar.

Dock would rather have been punched.

Trotter thrust a finger at him. "You, sir, have a very rude manner," the lawyer said. "Is that the norm where you come from? Do people just blurt out whatever pops into their heads?"

"Most people wouldn't say shit if they had a mouthful," Dock said. "Maybe that's what's wrong with the world. I figure I'll try it the other way around for a while. Say what's on my mind."

"Well, I for one don't care for it," Trotter said. "Therefore, once our business is concluded, I'll thank you to find another firm to handle your legal needs. I like to think that I'm rather selective in the company I keep."

"You've certainly proven that here tonight."

"You just can't resist, can you?"

Dock pushed his Stonewall-tainted plate away and got to his feet. "What can I say, Tommy? You're simply irresistible."

Dock walked back to his room and watched the fifth game of the Series. By the time Sullivan grounded out to Sanchez to put the Sox up two games to none, he was sound asleep in a chair. He had to wait until the next morning's sports update to hear the outcome. He ate breakfast in the motel coffee shop and then he went to the hardware store and bought fifty feet of fourteen-two wire and a half-dozen electrical pigtails. He was to meet Harris at eight; when he arrived at the house at a quarter to, the professor was already waiting, standing by the back door with a large steel coffee cup in hand. The Lab was in the orchard, feverishly on the scent of something or other. Dock unlocked the back door and then he took the wire and the pigtails and hooked up a string of lights for the back room. Then he and Harris set about documenting the contents of Wiily Burns's workshop.

The room was about twelve foot square and had apparently been built into a natural undercropping of the rock. It had a low ceiling and a plank floor. Virtually every square inch of space was taken up by workbenches and shelving and tables, all occupied by tools and textbooks and notebooks and drawings. There was an Ebenezer Gordon plate-glass camera on a shelf, above which sat dozens of photograph-plate negatives. There were engravers and molds, sealed jars filled with unidentifiable liquids, gizmos of unknown use and origin. And vises and clamps and lanterns and lamps. Scientific journals from the mid-1800s, scraps of yellowed newspaper with notations scrawled in the margin.

It took them half the day to document the room's contents. By noon the list was nearly complete, at least with respect to the larger items. Things like penny nails and string and tacks were listed under miscellaneous. A partial inventory read like this:

1 Ebenezer Gordon camera
first-edition *Notes on the State of Virginia*
223 plate-glass negatives
1 posing table
1 Jenny Lind photographer's head stand
2 developers
1 .58-caliber Enfield musket
1 foot-pedal wood lathe
8 full notebooks
quantity of bullet molds, several pounds of lead
1 small barrel of gunpowder
1 Bacon American Navy .38-caliber revolver
I Grisley saddle
1 phonograph, manufactured by Secretan, Paris
copy *Small Arms Report of 1856*
1 set *Thomas Scientific Journals,* pub. 1858
copy *Aesop's Fables*
3 kites
box of musket and pistol parts
1 apple peeler (broken)
1 brace and bit (various extra bits)
several handsaws
1 set of axle spanners
7 bone-handled knives in varying states of repair/construction
14 oil lanterns
9 candle molds
quantity of steel hinges

1 walking stick

drawings of mechanical ideas, concepts, on coarse brown paper

3 wooden mallets with box of square pegs

When they had finished, the two men sat down, Dock on a rough bench that had been tucked beneath the worktable and Harris on a low shelf that supported the photography equipment. Harris held one of the plates to the lightbulb overhead. He'd been wearing the same smile all day.

"What do you know about those?" Dock asked him. "I assume they're negatives."

"Collodion plates," Harris said.

"And what does that mean exactly?"

"Well, they're plates made with . . . collodion . . . and . . . it's a complicated process."

"You don't know what you're talking about, do you?"

"No, but you might have the common courtesy to pretend along with me." Harris held another plate to the light. "This is of the town," he said. "You can see the corner of the Gettysburg Hotel. Taken sometime, I don't know, mid to late 1800s. I couldn't say for sure, but I know somebody who could."

"A lot are of the town," Dock said. "I looked at maybe twenty or thirty yesterday. You can see the seminary and you can see the college. None of the students are pierced or tattooed, so I'd say they're not real recent."

Harris put the plate down. "People have been combing the countryside around here for a hundred and forty years. It's been generations since anybody's discovered anything bigger than a minié ball. Lord, man, you're not here a week and you hit the bloody jackpot. Life is strange."

"I don't know that I'd call this a jackpot."

"It's a significant find, I daresay. The room is obviously uncontaminated from the date it was sealed off. Whatever that date turns out to be. We should be able to pin it down when we get around to examining all of this. These plate-glass negatives should tell us something. The newspaper they're wrapped in—this one, for instance, is the *Gettysburg Sentinel*, from April 1861. You've got yourself a mini-museum here, Dock."

"Well, I'm no curator. What am I gonna do with it all?"

"Your first order of business would be to invest in a couple of sturdy padlocks to secure this place. The next thing, if you want my two cents', I think you should get Klaus Gabor involved. Have you heard of him?"

"Any kin to Zsa Zsa?"

"With Klaus, nothing would surprise me. He's a fellow professor at the university. He's a Lincoln scholar and he probably knows more about the history of the town of Gettysburg than anybody alive. Show him these glass plates and he'll not only tell you the year they were taken but probably what style petticoats the women were wearing that season. He's also a bit of a technical nut when it comes to collodion-plate photography, daguerreotypes, things like that."

"What's his name again?"

"Klaus Gabor. You may have seen him on public TV. Eccentric type—delights in mangling the mother tongue."

"Do you think he'd have a look at this?"

Harris smiled. "It'll be like asking a five-year-old to tour a chocolate factory."

Whether by divine intervention, or just a superior bullpen, the Series was over in five. About the time the first bottle of champagne was popped in the Sox clubhouse, Amy Morris was on a plane for Washington, her mood at least as buoyant as the Dom-soaked players she'd left behind. She arrived at Dulles at three in the morning; there was a driver waiting for her and she walked into her house at a quarter to four. She wasn't tired, she found, so she stayed up, flipping through the satellite channels in an effort to find out what was happening in the world. The stations she consulted now were, of course, the same that she'd watched all week in Chicago. But it was different nonetheless. She was back in the loop.

She finally went to bed as the sun was showing over the river. By eleven she was up and showered and behind the wheel of the Cayenne, headed into the city. When she walked into Sam Rockwood's office, she tossed the autographed baseball at his head. The old man was still pretty quick; he caught it with his left hand and then took a moment to scan the signatures.

"Don't worry—they're all there," she told him. "Take it out to McLean and file it away with the rest of your junk."

He ignored her, stood, and walked across the room to place the ball on a shelf already cluttered with sports-related mementos: footballs and pucks and photos of himself with various stars, present and past, everyone from Tiger Woods to Secretariat.

When he moved back to the desk, Amy noticed that he walked gingerly, as if pained with the effort. He was a big man who suffered chronic back problems; when his weight went up, it seemed the problems worsened. His wife, Marie, was constantly lecturing him on his eating habits. Sam Rockwood wasn't an easy man to lecture.

"You did a nice job out there, kid," he said as he sat. "I'm always amazed at your ability to personalize something that I know for a fact you don't care a fig about."

"Can you say that again? I'd like to get it on tape, play it back to you come contract time."

"I'm well aware of your impoverished condition, Amelia. I suspect the retail sector of the state of Illinois took a huge leap forward having had you as a resident for a week."

"You've got your nerve, Sam. What was it you scored at Sotheby's last month? George Washington's jockstrap? What'd that run you—a couple mil?"

"It was his riding crop, and I got it for twenty-two thousand. A bargain."

"I'll take your word on that. Sears handles all my riding-crop needs."

Sam got up and walked across the room to adjust the blinds. "So what can I do for you this morning? You know, a normal person might think about sleeping in after being on a plane half the night."

"I'm a company mule, Sam. I'm here to work. I'm thinking you might want my ass on a plane to Aruba today."

"You're thinking that you'll do my thinking for me," Sam said. "And that's not going to happen anytime soon. Before you rush off to the airport—what does the ex-congressman have to say about this Stewart? What does Sarah Jane Wright say about the guy? Now that's she's paid her debt to society, as CNN so cleverly phrased it, she just might want to get something off her chest."

"I haven't talked to either of them, not about this. I thought I'd get his story first."

"You get their story first. Then, if he tells you something different, you've caught them in a lie. Don't give them the opportunity to tailor their stories to his. I shouldn't have to tell you this, Amy."

She turned away from his tone. "Well, you know . . . I've been out in the boonies, interviewing balls and bats."

"All right," Sam said. "You've got your nose out of joint because you had to cover a sporting event. I get it, Amy. And don't give me your 'I'm gonna go to Fox or NBC' look because we both know that they'll take one look at your pretty face and put you on a morning show, where you'll spend the next twenty years interviewing fad diet authors and introducing insipid pop acts to the world."

Amy sat down on the couch and fell silent.

"By the way, I consider sulking worse than complaining," he informed her.

"Sarah Jane Wright is *not* going to talk to me."

"Don't be so sure. She's just out of jail. A woman with her ego will have one thing in mind and that's to get her old life back. Remember, her name is her livelihood. She has to restore her reputation. And if she has to make nice with the devil that's Amy Morris to facilitate that, you never know."

"She threatened to beat me up, you know."

"She's twice your age. You can take her."

She stood. "But I am going to Aruba."

"Of course you are, but do your homework first," he told her. "And hey—we're having a dinner party Saturday night. The usual bunch. I want you to come. I seem to recall you telling me that you were in love. Bring him along."

"That wouldn't work."

"Why not? Where is he?"

"In the underground parking."

"So I was right again. Well, bring someone or come alone, doesn't matter. But call Marie and let her know, okay?"

Amy shrugged. "Okay. What's the occasion?"

"Didn't you hear? I just acquired a baseball signed by the world champions."

FIVE

Stonewall Martin was behind the wheel of the five-ton cube van with the logo Stonewall Enterprises on the side. The inside of the cab was in its usual filthy state—a forensic team could probably determine most of what had gone into the big man's stomach over the previous month just by examining the debris inside the truck. Pizza boxes, McDonald's wrappers, soda cans, burrito wraps, as well as various bits of food that had not actually made it to Stonewall's mouth and clung now to the upholstery, the carpet, the steering wheel. If he was ever trapped in a blizzard, he could probably survive at least a few days on the scraps.

But then, Stonewall's body required a lot of fuel. He stood six-five and weighed, he said, 270 pounds. In reality, he was 310, but he didn't count the additional forty pounds as he was always on the verge of dropping the extra weight. The fact that he'd held on to this intention for at least five years indicated to him that he meant to do it. A man of lesser will would have given in by now and admitted to his true weight. Such was Stonewall's capacity for logic.

He'd received a call from Thaddeus St. John that morning, advising him of an elderly couple in downtown Carlisle who were looking for a consignment house. The couple were moving to a senior housing complex in Harrisburg, and as a result of the downsize they needed to sell off most of the contents of their home, where they had lived, according to Thaddeus, for nearly sixty years.

Stonewall drank coffee and ate a package of sticky buns as he drove Highway 30 north to Carlisle. He was decidedly unenthusiastic about the trip. The contents of a house like the one in question were usually worth less than the gas he would burn checking them out. Thaddeus was constantly sending Stonewall all over the state on these unprofitable jaunts. Anything high-end—and there were many monied estates in the area—Thaddeus would handle himself. At least Carlisle was close, just thirty miles north of Gettysburg.

He parked on the side street, a few blocks from the town center. Getting out of the van, he removed his dirty buckskin and pulled on a tweed sports jacket, which was unfortunately sized to fit him when he got back down to 270.

The house was a small and sorry-looking clapboard, with a tiny front stoop. The couple were waiting for him. They were gray and skinny, the both of them; they came out together and greeted Stonewall like he was a man of great importance. The old lady had even baked cookies.

The house's contents were typical—Sears appliances and stuffed chairs and couches, veneered tables and ugly ceramic lamps. There were pictures everywhere, presumably of the sorry couple and their sorry family. Snaps of bucktoothed kids and grandkids crowded the mantle; those of graduations and weddings and family vacations crowded the walls. Decades of middle-class mediocrity, the type of thing Stonewall came across time after time. The type of thing that pissed him off only because it reminded him that he'd never had anything close to it in his own life. He left the two fogeys in the kitchen and moved through the two-story structure at a clip, munching on the cookies, which were pretty good, and dismissing the rest of the goods at a glance. There were a couple of maple dressers upstairs that might fetch two hundred each, and a cast-iron bed frame worth a hundred. The odd bentwood or pressback chair, hidden under countless coats of paint.

He went back downstairs to the kitchen, where the couple were standing formally under a cloak of anticipation. He was about to tell them that their wonderful collection was not right for Stonewall Enterprises when he spotted an enclosed back porch. He opened the door and had a look. There was a washer and dryer of recent vintage in the center of the room and what appeared to be an old dining room table against the wall, covered with an oilcloth. Stonewall took notice of the legs.

"What's that?" he asked.

"Oh, that's just our old kitchen table," the man said. "I use it for a fix-it bench."

Stonewall stepped over and removed the oilcloth. A sheet of quarter-inch plywood had been tacked onto the original top. He pulled the corner of the plywood up, saw the inlays and marquetry underneath. He quickly stepped away and then feigned interest in the laundry appliances.

"How old are these units?" he asked.

"Four years," the lady said. "They're Maytags."

Stonewall looked them over, stroking his matted beard. "Maytags," he said thoughtfully. "I have to make a call."

He got his cell phone out of the truck and dialed the shop on York Street. Thaddeus St. John's dulcet tone replied.

"I'm in Carlisle," Stonewall said.

"What do you have, my boy?"

"I'm not sure, but these old fucks have got a table—I think it might be a Seymour."

"Oh, my."

"How will I know?"

"Look for the initials *J.S.* on the underside of one of the corners."

"What's it worth? The condition is good, I'm guessing original finish."

"A Seymour card table sold in '98 for half a million dollars. Do they have any idea?"

"The old coot's been mixing fucking paint on it."

"What else do they have?"

"A bunch of junk."

"Well, if it's a Seymour, we certainly don't want it in an auction. It will draw dealers like flies to a manure pile. You know what to do."

Stonewall entered the house through the back door and was able to check out the underside of the table before the fogeys knew he was back. The inscription was there. He walked back into the kitchen and helped himself to more cookies.

"So you were set on an auction?" he asked.

"Well, that's what we were thinking," the man said. "Isn't that the best?"

Stonewall, his mouth full, shook his head doubtfully. "Problem with an auction—you're really at the whim of the public. Sometimes the weather's bad and nobody shows up; sometimes people show but they're just not buying."

"What do you suggest?" the woman asked.

Stonewall made a show of calculating, turning around as he did, taking in his surroundings. "You put the whole lot up for auction—I would say you'd take in somewhere between three and five thousand dollars. Of course, you lose ten percent of that to the auctioneer. Is that what you were thinking?"

The man looked at his wife. "We had no idea. We have to be rid of it, though. We've left this too long. We're leaving in the morning and the house has been sold."

Stonewall performed another pantomime of calculation. "Tell you what, seeing as I have the truck here . . . I'll give you four thousand dollars for everything and take it away today."

The couple went into the front room to discuss the offer. Stonewall finished the last of the cookies and then helped himself to a Coke from the fridge. The man came back into the kitchen.

"Could you leave our bed?" he asked. "We have to stay here to-night."

"Absolutely," Stonewall said. "I am not in the habit of taking advantage of people."

★   ★   ★

That afternoon they packed the glass plates in two cardboard boxes and loaded them in the back of Dock's pickup and then drove to the university. The day was cold and overcast; as a precaution against rain they covered the boxes with a heavy canvas tarp Dock had salvaged from the barn.

They found Klaus Gabor at Weidensall Hall, in what his students referred to as Klaus's Lair—the artifact-filled classroom/laboratory where the professor held forth. Klaus was seventy-two years old, and although he'd left Budapest in 1955, he'd never quite conquered the English alphabet. His *t*'s were no longer *z*'s, except when he became excited, but his *w*'s would remain *v*'s forever. He was very tall, and he had a bald pate with a thick fringe of gray hair at the sides and back. This day he wore Kmart jeans and a heavy cable-knit cardigan, rubber duck boots on his feet, and irony on his sleeve.

"Here you are," he said as Dock and Harris walked in, carrying the two boxes. "Vut is this big mystery, Harrison James—you have found some old Beatles recordings?"

Harris introduced the two men as he set a box carefully on the counter, then opened it and pulled out a glass plate. Klaus's eyes narrowed as he took it. He held it to the light for a moment and then carried it over to a simple overhead projector and placed it on top. The image—a street scene from the village—appeared on the projector's screen.

"Vere you find this, Harrison James?"

"Old farmhouse on Shealer Road. Dock found it; he's renovating."

"Is in very good shape, this plate," Klaus said.

"It was in a room that was sealed off. Dry, practically airtight. And dark, which I assume is the reason the plates are good."

"Yah, the light destroys them."

"I was telling Dock a little about the collodion process," Harris said.

"You, Harrison James?" Klaus asked, his eyebrows arched. "And I suppose next you vill split an atom vith your pocketknife?"

Harris looked at Dock. "See what I mean?"

Klaus picked up the plate. "Vut you have here is photographic plates from vet collodion process. This is very new about the time of the

Civil War—this is process used by Gardner and Brady and others—they take hundreds of thousands of these during that war. You take ordinary glass plate and you coat it with collodion—vich is liquid made from nitric and sulphuric acid strained through cotton—then plate is dipped in silver nitrate. Ven plate is partly dry is placed in camera and the picture exposed. A print can be made from the plate. I could make you print from this plate, in fact."

Harris gestured to the plate on the screen. "So what do you think?"

Klaus looked at the image again and shrugged. "Is Gettysburg, of course. Looking to Emmitsburg Road."

"Any idea of the year?"

"Is hard to say. Sometime before second July, 1863."

Harris stepped forward. "How do you know that?"

Klaus pointed to the image. "See here—this is corner of Pierce barn. This is barn that burn down on second day of fighting. Harrison James, this you know. About photography you know nothing, but this you know."

"You're right," Harris said after he'd looked closely.

Klaus was looking at the two boxes. "You have more of these plates, Doctor? Vut are you doctor of?"

"Doctor of nothing. My name's Dock."

"You have more of these plates?"

"Two hundred and twenty-two more."

"Ah." Dock could see the excitement in the old man's eyes. "And I can see them?"

"That's why we brought them," Harris said. "We didn't know if we should be handling them."

Klaus took the plate from the overhead. "Is okay, is not nitroglycerin. Who is photographer of these plates, do ve know this?"

Dock went into one of the boxes and pulled out the cedar slab.

"Inventionist?" Klaus read. "He is bad speller, your Villy Burns. Like me. Also—he is left-handed, like me."

"How do you know that?" Harris asked.

"See here," Klaus said and he held up the plate. "You can see the man's thumbprint—this is from vere he holds the plate ven he pours the collodion. Your Villy Burns holds the plate vith his right hand; this means he pours vith his left. See, I am Sherlock Holmes. You vill leave these plates?"

"We were hoping you'd check them out," Dock said. "Maybe do some sort of indexing?"

"Yah, I do that," Klaus said. He was clearly trying to hide his enthusiasm behind a nonchalant attitude. "Maybe ve find picture of Pickett pooping his pants, third July."

When Dock got back to the house he used concrete screws to fasten a sheet of plywood over the entrance to Willy Burns's workshop and then put the room out of his mind for the time being. He still needed to replace the roof before the weather got bad and to do that, he first had to remove the old roof. He passed the weekend doing this; first tearing off the asphalt shingles, then the cedar shakes beneath, before pulling down the planking and the bowed and twisted rafters themselves. The dumpster was gone now; he made a burn pile in the orchard for the rafters and the sheeting and the cedar and stacked the old asphalt by the barn. He would haul it to a landfill at some point; for the here and now, he was more concerned with beating the snow.

By Monday morning he was left with a stone farmhouse that was completely without a roof. He went to the lumberyard, which was called the Lumber Yard, in town and priced a set of roof trusses. The cost was within reason, but he was told it would take at least a month to have them manufactured. So he decided to frame the roof the old-fashioned way, which, given the age of the place, seemed appropriate enough. He stood at the counter and figured out what he needed for rafters, ridge boards, and rafter ties and then arranged for everything to be delivered that afternoon. On his way out of town he stopped at the bank and discovered that his money had arrived. He withdrew a few hundred for spending money and then had the clerk supply him with a check for Trotter.

Olive was there, sitting behind the wooden desk and reading *Vogue* magazine and drinking tea. The door to Trotter's office was open; there was no sign of the tiny attorney.

"Hello," Olive said brightly when she saw him.

"Hello, Olive."

"I heard that you were sticking around."

"I bet you did," Dock said. "Do you have my bill?"

She turned to the computer. "I will have—just give me a minute. You know, I was glad to hear that you were restoring the house."

"You'll be lonesome on that side of the fence."

She found what she was looking for, and then the printer on the stand beside her kicked into action. "Don't be too hard on Thomas," she said. "He's actually a very good man. He just wants so badly to be a . . . big cog in the wheel. The sad thing is—he's a better man than all these people he envies. I keep hoping that someday he'll realize that."

Dock looked at the bill and decided that it was fair. He wrote the check leaning over Olive's desk and as he did he had a sudden thought. "Is Trotter married?" he asked.

"Yes," she said at once. "His wife has no idea who he is."

As he handed her the check, Trotter himself walked into the office. Dock watched Olive as she looked at him, her eyes shining.

"Hello, counselor," Dock said.

"Well?" The voice was cool.

"We're settled."

"Well," Trotter said then. "Good luck to you then."

Dock smiled at Olive. "Did he tell you we're breaking up?"

"Ah yes, more of that crude wit," Trotter said. "Speaking of which, you shouldn't have insulted Stonewall Martin the other night."

"I don't remember that I did."

"You called him Stonehead."

"Like it's the first time that's happened."

"He's not a man to trifle with," Trotter warned. "He's quite a character. He's a Civil War authority in his own right—"

"I'm looking forward to meeting someone who isn't," Dock said.

It seemed that Trotter was getting used to being interrupted; he pressed on without complaint. "He's also a reenactor of note. He's what they call hard-core. When he goes to a reenactment, he's as authentic as it gets, right down to the buttons on his shirt, the boots, the socks. Even his underwear is made of . . . oh, burlap or something."

"Gee," Dock said. "If I'd known he was wearing homemade shorts, I'd have been nicer to the man."

"You like to mock," Trotter said. "You're a stranger here; you should keep that in mind. The town of Gettysburg is all about history. As such, there are people in this town who are worth knowing. Thaddeus St. John is one of them. Stonewall is another. He's a genuine character, a force of nature."

"Oh, I know the type," Dock said. "Strong like bull—smart like tractor."

He drove out to the house and spent the rest of the morning laying out the top plates for the rafters. The lumber arrived shortly before one o'clock. He put the ridgepole on the main house up first, temporarily securing it with two-by-fours at each end. Then he cut his first rafter. It was tough to get a measurement on his own, and he had to adjust the cut several times. He could see that his carpentry skills were more than a little rusty, and that distressed him. It had been five years since he'd worked in the trade, but he'd always taken more pride in his ability as a carpenter than, say, his skill as a real estate agent. Of course, he took more pride in his ability to spit than to sell real estate. He eventually had a suitable pattern rafter, though, and he cut the rest, using two-by-eights on a six-twelve pitch.

He was spiking the first pair into place when a fifteen-year-old Volvo with the front grill smashed in pulled into the driveway, with Klaus behind the wheel and Harris in the passenger seat. They both climbed out the passenger side; Dock had to assume that the driver's door wouldn't open due to the damaged front fender.

"So you are carpentry doctor," Klaus called up. "Now I see."

Dock drove home the last two nails to secure the rafter and then he climbed down the ladder leaning against the end of the house. Although it was nearly fifty degrees out, Klaus was wearing a down-filled parka and leather gloves. Harris, dressed again in his hiking duds, stood leaning against the crunched Volvo. He looked like a cat that had just swallowed a dozen canaries.

"What's up?" Dock asked.

"Do you know Lincoln's Gettysburg Address?" Harris asked.

"You asking if I can recite it, or do I know of it?"

"Of it."

"Yeah, Harris. I think maybe I heard something about it in school."

"Well, Lincoln gave that speech in Gettysburg."

"Ah," Dock said. "What do you teach—kindergarten?"

"Would you happen to know how many pictures exist of Lincoln at Gettysburg?" Harris asked then.

"No, but my guess would be none."

"You'd be very close," Harris said. "The answer is one. And the image is so bad that there's some argument about whether or not it actually is Lincoln."

Dock looked past Harris, to where Klaus was doing his damnedest not to smile. He looked like a schoolkid acting up in the back row during class pictures. Dock turned back to Harris.

"You're kidding me," he said. "We've got a picture of Lincoln at Gettysburg?"

"I said nothing of the kind," Harris said. He looked over at Klaus, and now he smiled. "We've got seven pictures of Lincoln at Gettysburg."

Klaus stepped forward and with a flourish drew a manilla envelope from his parka. He took a number of black-and-white prints from inside and handed them to Dock. The photos were of several men seated at a dais or table, in the midst of a throng of people. Two were near-perfect images, three were fair but blurred slightly, and two were rather fuzzy.

But there was no question that the bearded man in the left center of each picture was the old Emancipator himself. Dock took a second then a third pass through the prints.

"Holy cow," he said finally.

"Yah," Klaus said. "This is a holy cow."

"You're sure it's Gettysburg?" Dock asked.

"No question," Harris said. "See the guy in the frock coat? That's Edward Everett; he was actually the keynote speaker that day. One newspaper referred to him as a gasbag—he went on for an hour and a half. It's a wonder anybody was still there to hear Abe talk. One would assume the taverns were closed. Klaus can identify the rest of the dais for you—mostly a bunch of local politicians and other assorted scally-wags. But it's Lincoln, no question."

"Yah, is Lincoln, nineteen November, 1863," Klaus said and he reached into the envelope again. "And you have other interesting plates, Doctor. Your Villy Burns, he vas here in July 1863. Here is plate of Meade's headquarters, after bombarding that make him scoot. Dead horses all around, fences knocked down. Picture vud have been made very soon after third July."

"There's some incredible stuff," Harris said. "Look here, that's Winfield Scott Hancock, on his horse, probably taken soon after the battle. Appears to be Culp's Hill. And about ten feet behind him—would you know who that fair-haired boy is?"

Dock looked at the print. "Nope."

"George Armstrong Custer."

"Before the Indians shoot him full of arrows," Klaus said. "Nin-compoop."

Dock looked up. "I'll be damned," he said.

"These are unusual because they appear to be candid shots," Harris said. "It was normal back then for people to pose for a picture. In fact, it was preferable because of the slow shutter speed. But a good number of these look as if Burns just set up and shot. You can see a lot of blurred figures in these prints. By the way, Klaus is making you a complete set."

Klaus had fixed Harris with a beseeching glare.

"Yes," Harris said. "Klaus was hoping to have a look at the room it-self, Dock."

"Sure," Dock said.

The three men walked into the roofless house. Dock used a cordless drill to remove the screws holding the plywood over the room's opening. He plugged in the string of lights overhead and then stepped aside.

"My, oh my," he heard Klaus say.

Dock leaned against the workbench and watched as Klaus moved slowly, almost with reverence, about the room, touching the textbooks and notebooks gingerly, turning the pages as if they were made of dust.

"Thomas Jefferson, first edition," he said quietly, as if speaking to himself. "Adams, Vashington . . . Ben Franklin, old kite flier."

After a moment Dock looked over at Harris, and when he did Harris indicated the outer room and then walked out through the doorway and into the yard. Dock followed.

"You just made that old Hungarian very happy," Harris said.

"Glad to do it," Dock said.

"One thing I should mention," Harris said then. "You're going to have to start thinking about safeguarding what you've got here. Civil War memorabilia has become a huge cottage industry, and when the word gets out these plates will be a hot item. And like everything else—if it represents big money, then it attracts all kinds. Dealers, collectors, auction houses. Some of these individuals might not be of the highest moral fiber. There's a man in town here, goes by the name Stonewall Martin—"

"We've met."

"Don't tell me he's been here already."

"Nah, I met him in a restaurant. I think he was sent my way by a fancy-pants named Thaddeus St. Something."

"That's quite likely. Thaddeus St. *John* is the man when it comes to Civil War collectibles. He's kind of the private sector's Klaus Gabor, always popping up on PBS or the History Channel. He presents himself as this old-school Southern gent and he's got this elaborate way of speaking. Dresses like he's off to a costume party every day. He's actually a very good writer, surprisingly; he's had a number of articles published in Civil War magazines, *Harper's*, a couple of things in the *New*

Yorker even. He's got a shop on York Street, very high-end stuff, big money. I have a feeling he's as phony as his accent, but he's built himself quite a reputation."

"So what's with him and this Stonewall?"

"They're a real Mutt-and-Jeff team. Thaddeus is this genteel dandy, and Stonewall likes to present himself as a living antique, a nineteenth-century frontiersman, even to the point, rumor has it, of not bathing regularly. I've been told he usually smells like a damn goat. Did you notice that?"

"I really don't know what a goat smells like."

"The two of them turn up some nice items. Mainly from estate auctions. There have been rumors about their methods, but to be fair that could come from other dealers envious of their success. It's true, though, that these types like to prey on the elderly and the uninformed. What did Stonewall have to say?"

Dock shrugged. "He offered his services, but I got a feeling he was just speculating. I haven't told anybody anything."

"Well, neither have I. And Klaus won't either. But if I were you, I would think about moving the big items somewhere secure. The university is a good spot, but then I'm biased on that account. There's the college down the road at Carlisle, there are schools all over Pennsylvania that would just salivate at this. I'm sure the Smithsonian would send a U-haul tomorrow. The thing is, you should come up with some sort of a plan. You're a sitting duck out here."

"Okay," Dock said.

"And another thing," Harris said then. "I don't know how much money you're worth."

"Well, my marriage just ended, so about half what I was worth a month ago."

"That's about to change," Harris said. "You just won the lottery. Forget about everything else in the room for a moment. Those seven plates of Lincoln alone will fetch enough for you to retire on. Start tallying up the rest of it, and—well, put it this way, I think you can hire someone to put your new roof on."

"Then I'll end up sitting on my ass."

"You say that like it's a bad thing."

They went back inside. Klaus was standing at the workbench and he had the old phonograph in front of him. The old man was bent at the waist, his neck twisting back and forth like a curious goose as he looked at the device from every angle. He glanced up when they came in.

"Harrison James!" he said. "You forget to tell me about zis!"

Harris shrugged off his offense. "I assume it's an Edison copycat."

"Your Mr. Edison vas in short trousers ven zis vas made. Zis is vut you call phonautograph. Made by a Frenchman. See, Harrison James— you Americans did not invent the whole vide vorld."

Harris turned to Dock. "Keep in mind that this fellow is from Hungary. Their main cultural contribution to the planet is goulash."

"Hah," Klaus said. "You are a real Jake Leno."

Klaus's attention remained on the machine. "This is built by Frenchman Edoard-Leon Scott, probably in 1860s. But not to play sound. To study sound, in laboratory. Your Mr. Edison, this I give you, is first to play back sound. Is his fault ve have rock and roll."

"This isn't exactly a laboratory," Dock said.

Klaus took a look around. "It is, though. Is Gettysburg laboratory, 1800 and something. Your Villy Burns, he's renaissance man, no?"

"I was looking through those notebooks," Dock said. "I found a drawing of a glider, powered like a bicycle."

"Yah, maybe he vas going to beat up on the Wright brothers, is that vut you think?"

"Maybe he was. I wonder what happened to him."

"Ve find out," Klaus said, nodding eagerly. "Ve find out. This pho-nautograph, can I study vith it? Back at the university? This is very rare machine."

Dock shrugged. "Sure."

"What about the plates?" Harris asked. "At some point, you'll have to go public with them. These aren't exactly nude shots of Pamela An-derson here. This is the sixteenth president of the United States—at Gettysburg. It's a very significant discovery."

Dock looked around at the contents of the room. "Give me a day or two."

"You should think about getting a telephone out here, too," Harris said. "They're becoming all the rage, you know."

Dock looked at him doubtfully. Klaus smiled. "Hah, this doctor does not care for your modern machines, Harrison James."

"Modern machines," Harris said. "Alexander Graham Bell invented the telephone in 1875."

"Yah, is my point," Klaus said. "He is Johnny-Came-Lately."

SIX

She didn't take a date to the dinner party. The only feasible candidate was Peter—his family background held an acceptable mix of history, politics, and money, and as such he would be considered an appropriate escort. But she also knew that, along with his name and standing, he would bring his propensity for mixing pharmaceuticals and liquor with sarcastic commentary, and at some point in the evening he'd end up either lying on the floor, biting people's ankles, or sitting very straight in a chair, insulting everyone in the room. Either eventuality would put a damper on the evening for Amy and in all likelihood would culminate in Sam Rockwood punching Peter's lights out.

So she went alone. Upon arriving, she discovered that Marie Rockwood had invited Russell Smythe to the soiree, in yet another effort to throw him and Amy together. Smythe was the fortunate son of a wealthy Newport family, and a sailor of note whose main claim to fame was losing the America's Cup ten years ago. Marie had met him at a fund-raiser several months earlier and apparently was so determined to play cupid that she had yet to notice that Smythe was fundamentally a buffoon, a fact that had not escaped Sam's judgmental eye. Amy, for her part, had no interest in the man but had, in the couple of times she'd been in his presence, at least been courteous to the supercilious salt. The same could not be said of Sam.

Sam and Marie Rockwood owned fifty pristine and pastoral acres on the outskirts of McLean. The house was redbrick, an antebellum mansion that had somehow passed through the Civil War, reconstruction, and the Great Depression without being blown up, knocked down, built onto, or turned into apartments. Marlene Dietrich was alleged to have slept many a night there, back in the 1930s, in the arms of a senator whose name Amy could never recall. A shallow, pebbly brook meandered through the green fields, cutting the property in half. Peruvian saddle horses grazed the fields on one side; hay for the animals' winter forage grew on the other. Sam's Chesapeake Bay retrievers roamed wherever they pleased.

Amy arrived at eight and Marie let her in. Amy wore a black Halston blouse and a brightly colored full-length wool skirt she'd bought in Argentina the previous year.

"I think it cost me about eight bucks American," Amy said when Marie complimented her on the skirt.

"If you don't count the airfare," Marie said.

"Sam picked up the flight."

Tom and Louise Marchand rounded out the group of six. They were to have been eight until a stomach bug had knocked Senator and Bliss McDonnell out of the equation.

"Stomach bug, my ass," Sam Rockwood said after his third martini but then, under Marie's baleful eye, declined to elaborate.

Tom was an editor at the *Post*, and Louise was a self-described socialite, the type of woman Amy usually avoided but whom in fact she liked a lot, especially after Louise had saved her one night from a potentially embarrassing situation in an elevator with a movie director fired up on testosterone and Vicodin.

They were all sitting in the sunroom, and they drank martinis with the exception of Russell, who, as a sailor of some note, was apparently required to drink rum. He played the part to the hilt and was in fact wearing a cable-knit sweater, while the other men were in shirt and tie. Amy would not have been surprised if he had shown up sporting a patch over one eye and a parrot on his shoulder. What he did bring along was his usual supply of jokes.

"There was a young man from Texas," he was saying now, posing against the French doors leading to the rock garden, "who received a full scholarship to Harvard. On his first day there, he approached a senior, a typical Ivy League type, walking across the square. The young Texan asked, 'I was wondering if y'all could tell me where the library's at?' The Harvard man looked him up and down and replied, 'My good man, I realize that you are out of your element here and that you haven't had the social and educational privileges of many, but I must inform you that here at Harvard we do not end a sentence with a preposition.' The Texan considered this for a moment, and then he nodded and said, 'I was wondering if y'all could tell me where the library's at . . . asshole.'"

The group responded with polite guffaws.

"You couldn't have made it a Yale man?" Tom asked.

"Then I'd have Sam on my back," Russell said. "I *am* drinking his liquor. Let's just say I have the utmost respect for higher education, wherever its origin, and leave it at that. But I have another one—"

"Let's eat," Sam said and he got to his feet and led the procession into the dining room. Russell slumped along behind.

"So Amy," Louise asked when they were seated and waiting for their soup, "where did you go to school?"

"Mississippi. At Jackson."

"Really?" Tom said. "Are you from Mississippi?"

Amy nodded. "I would be the hick in Russell's story."

"Beats being the asshole," Louise said.

Sam came out of the kitchen then, carrying a cauldron of steaming clam chowder, which without the slightest coaxing he admitted to cooking himself. Nettie, a black woman of indeterminate age who served as the Rockwood's maid but who had long ago taken on the persona of an eccentric aunt, glided into the room in Sam's wake, carrying large ceramic bowls that she helped to fill.

"Hey, old lady," Amy said to her.

"Hey yourself, child. Looks like you became a blonde."

"The sun did it," Amy told her. Nettie swatted away the fib like she was shooing a fly.

"I don't detect much of a Mississippi accent," Tom said.

"Oh, Amy shed the South a long time ago, Tom," Sam said as he passed the bowls around. "Ole Miss was not about to hold this one. She's always known that she was bound for bigger things."

"Don't we all feel that way, Sam?" Marie asked.

"Don't bother, Marie," Amy said. "He hired me because I'm ambitious, and he disparages me for the same reason. The only thing the man's got going for him is that he makes a passable soup."

"I'll have you know that this soup is a damn sight better than passable," Sam said and he sat to eat.

"I do all the cuttin' and dicin' anyway," Nettie said. "All he does is stir."

"That's a goddamn lie," Sam said. "It's the seasoning, people. It's the seasoning."

"Hang on, folks," Amy said. "We're about to be hit by a metaphor."

"Nettie, sit and eat with us," Marie said.

"No, thanks, I'll eat in the kitchen. I'm watchin' the hockey game. I be cuttin' and dicin' them, they don't get some defense on that team."

A couple of hours later the six of them had moved on to the den, if a room large enough to host a game of touch football could qualify as such. Nettie rolled in a cart that was covered with desserts and coffee and tea, cigars and liqueurs. They settled in a corner of the room featuring a stone fireplace, which Sam laid with kindling and birch logs and then lit. The chairs and chesterfield were leather, and the tables and sideboards of quarter-cut oak and bird's-eye maple. Some of the pieces, Amy knew, dated back to before the Revolutionary War. Also scattered about the room were prizes from Sam Rockwood's lifetime of collecting. American history was his passion; displayed about the monstrous den were flags and saddles and guns and documents and books and swords and maps. There were Frederick Remington busts perched on teak pedestals, Paul Kane oils on the wall, treaties and writs and proclamations both famous and obscure. There was a Winchester rifle that Buffalo Bill Cody had used to hurry the near extermination of the bison, and the flintlock pistol carried by Meriwether Lewis on his cross-continental jaunt.

Russell, perhaps inspired by the plainsman and the cartographer, set out upon an exploration of his own, circling the room while examining the artifacts on display, a brandy snifter instead of a firearm in his hand. The others, less adventurously, lounged near the fire.

Sometime during the evening Russell had assumed a standoffish pose toward Amy; throughout dinner, he had quite deliberately ignored her, even to the point of not answering when she'd asked him a direct question. She was quite sure that this hard-to-get act was his latest assault on her affections—everything else pretty much having failed—and that his detached demeanor was a last desperate attempt to garner her attention. Whatever his reasoning, his boorish behavior had succeeded only in pissing off Louise.

"You're not having a cigar, Sam?" Tom asked.

"I'm down to two a day," Sam replied. "I shot my wad before lunch."

"Doctor's orders?"

"Mine," Marie said. "I outrank the doctors in this house."

"What about you, Amy?" Tom asked. "I see more women partaking all the time."

"Yes, and it's pretty damn disheartening," Amy said. "Maybe we're as dumb as men after all."

Sam was pouring cognac and he looked over to Tom. "That about it for the cigar talk, Tom?"

"I'm good."

Russell was making his way back to the group. He stopped to look at a cutlass mounted above a glass case on a drop-leaf table. He ran his fingers over the gilded hilt of the sword, then looked down into the case. "Sam," he said, "knowing you, this is probably a stupid question. But is this an original copy of the Declaration of Independence?"

"It goddamn well better be," Sam said.

"Very impressive," Russell said. "There are, what, a dozen of these in existence. What do you pay for something like this?"

"Don't be crude," Marie told him. "Honestly, why do you care so much about money?"

"Um, because I don't have any?" Russell suggested.

"Oh," Louise said. "The same reason you care so much about intelligence."

Amy was drinking tea and she nearly spit into her cup.

"What do you mean you don't have any money?" Sam asked.

"My family's got plenty," Russell said. "But not me. In fact, there's been a suggestion put forth recently that I go to work."

"Those bastards," Louise said.

"Do I have a bull's-eye painted on me somewhere?" Russell asked her. "I was just inquiring about Sam's knickknacks."

"Knickknacks," Sam repeated darkly.

"Speaking of *collectibles*, Sam," Tom said. "I'm sure you've heard about the fellow in Gettysburg who found the pictures of Lincoln."

"I have."

"Do you think they're legitimate? I'm told there are a lot of snakes in the collectible game these days."

"Oh, I suspect they're genuine," Sam said. "The University of Gettysburg thinks so, too. Klaus Gabor has seen them. That old Hungarian knows more about Lincoln than Carl Sandburg and Ken Burns and Doris Kearns Goodwin put together."

Russell, finally sitting, poured himself a glass of cognac. "I saw an interesting piece about it on *Entertainment Tonight*. Apparently Tom Hanks has expressed interest in the collection."

Louise laughed out loud.

"My question is," Russell continued, shooting her a look, "why is this such a big deal? Surely there are plenty of pictures of Honest Abe."

"Actually, there aren't that many," Sam said. He'd had enough to drink that he was in a mood to lecture. "Your problem, Russell, is that you live in a world of sound bites and photo ops. You have to realize that a large part of the population back then had no idea what Lincoln even looked like. Newspapers couldn't run photographs yet; political campaigns were mainly confined to debates that took place in one or two large cities. Obviously, there was no video or audio. Just think: Lincoln delivered some of the great speeches in the history of the Republic—the Gettysburg Address and the second inaugural address, for instance—and nobody today has any idea what he sounded like. Was he a great orator? Did he speak as well as he wrote? Was he nervous, was he impassioned? Nobody knows."

"Where was Larry King when we needed him?" Russell asked.

"Be quiet, you dunderhead," Sam told him. "You asked why people would care about this. Pictures of this country's greatest president giving what is arguably this country's greatest speech? I would say they have some significance."

"And considerable worth," Tom added.

"In a society where Princess Diana's champagne glass fetches six figures," Louise said.

"JFK's golf clubs sold for seven hundred and fifty thousand," Tom said.

"Bill Clinton's cigar—" Russell began.

"All right, all right," Marie said. "We get it." She was now looking at Russell like a woman who'd paid a lot of money for a carpet only to realize she hated it when she got it home.

"The question is—what *are* the plates worth?" Louise asked.

"By his feigned disinterest, I'd say that Sam has already given that question some serious thought," Tom said.

Sam shrugged. "Who knows what'll happen? I'm sure the plates will come up for sale at some point, but it might be years. Some university could end up with them. Or the Smithsonian."

"Or perhaps some wealthy collector?" Louise suggested.

Sam looked at her. "Of course I'd be interested. All you have to do is look around this room to know that."

Amy stood and crossed the room to have a look at the Declaration.

"What do you think, Amy?" Marie asked. "Have we all gone collector crazy?"

"Why does it matter who owns this stuff?" Amy shrugged. "Sorry, Sam. But it just seems to me to be vanity. I mean, this is a first-class piece of prose—if we can ignore the fact that the man who wrote that all men are created equal was a slave owner. But it is what it is. It doesn't change just because it happens to be in your hands. A photocopy would read the same. This is nothing but materialism."

"This from a woman who will quite happily spend three hundred dollars for a pair of jeans," Sam said.

"But they're brand-new jeans," Amy said and she gestured around the room. "All this stuff is used."

"Aha," Louise said.

"I would think that Lincoln would be a president you'd be particularly interested in," Russell said. He was suddenly quite earnest; Amy suspected that he was smarting a little from being called a dunderhead.

"Oh, becuz he done freed all us niggas?" Amy asked. "Listen, Russell—it might surprise you but black people aren't that interested in the Civil War."

"Why not?"

"Because it didn't actually accomplish anything," Amy said. "You think the Emancipation Proclamation changed anything? Tell you what, Russell, wander over to Blockbuster some day and, instead of renting *Braveheart* for the fortieth time, pick up *Roots*. Then tell me what you think the Civil War accomplished."

"Just the same, I would think you'd be a little less callous about this," Russell said.

"I'm from Mississippi, remember?" she told him. "You want to know why I don't care about the Civil War? Because I know what was still happening a hundred years later. Tell me what you know about Medgar Evers, Russell. Tell me what you know about Emmett Till. You want to go for the hat trick? Share your thoughts on Hattie Carroll."

Russell raised his palms in surrender. "Hey, I'm just saying that Lincoln was the man who put an end to slavery. I would think that that might mean something to you."

Amy took down the cutlass from its mounting above the document. She pulled the sword from its scabbard and then dramatically lowered the tip toward Russell. "Well, now, that's funny, because I would think that you white folks would be more sensitive to the subject of slavery," she told him. "After all, you invented the game. My people just filled out the rosters."

"At the risk of being obvious," Louise said, "touché."

Attorney Trotter was lounging in the outer office, reading the *Philadelphia Gazette* and drinking a cup of coffee. Several feet away, Olive was working on some accounts on the computer. It was a lazy afternoon and the atmosphere in the room was more relaxed, domesticated even, than professional. Trotter had spent the morning in court, defending a Cashtown youth who had stolen a car from his mother and hit a pedestrian in downtown Gettysburg while joyriding. The youth had no license, no insurance, and, to attorney Trotter's eyes at least, no brains. The pedestrian had survived, fortunately, and Trotter had managed to convince the judge to hand the kid a year's probation under the condition that he pay for all damages. What might be done about his lack of gray matter was out of the court's—and now Trotter's—hands.

The tranquil scene in the office was soon interrupted by the large and noisy arrival of Stonewall Martin, who came through the door in a rush of bad energy, sweat, and tobacco smoke.

"What're you doing sitting out here, Trots—they fumigatin' your office again?" he demanded.

Trotter got to his feet and he smiled as he attempted to match the hearty tone. "Hello, Stonewall." He considered for a moment giving the big man a playful punch on the shoulder, then thought better of it.

"Hey, Stick," Stonewall said to Olive. "How 'bout a cup of coffee for the Stonewall?"

"Don't call me that," Olive said.

"Come on, Trots," Stonewall said and he started for the inner office. "We need a little privacy."

He headed into the office. Trotter made to follow, stopping by Olive's desk for a moment. "Could you bring a coffee?" he asked apologetically. "Yes, I'll talk to him."

Stonewall was in Trotter's chair, his black boots up on the desk when Trotter joined him. A moment later Olive came in with a cup of coffee that she placed beside the boots. She closed the door when she left.

"Thanks, Stick!" Stonewall called after her.

"She really doesn't like to be called that," Trotter said. He was deciding where to sit down. He usually sat in his own chair.

"You poking her or what?" Stonewall asked. "You like those skinny girls, don't you? Your wife's a fucking pool cue, man. How's it go—the closer the bone, the sweeter the meat? Not for me, though, I'm a meat-and-potatoes man. I gotta have tits and ass."

"Could you just call her Olive? Do me this one favor."

"Why should I do you a favor? The way that you and that piss-ant Orson fucked up that situation out on Shealer Road."

"He didn't want to sell, Stonewall. That's the man's prerogative. Since when are you interested in real estate anyway?"

"I don't give a shit about the fucking land. You didn't hear the latest?"

"What's the latest?"

"Thaddeus called me this morning. Little fucker's really got his panties in a twist over this one. That cocksucker Bass found some collodion plates of Lincoln at Gettysburg in the house. At least, that's what he's claiming."

"What kind of plates?"

"Photography plates, you moron. Pictures—you get it? Pictures of fucking Lincoln at Gettysburg."

"Oh—when did this happen?"

"I don't know when he found them, but that asshole Gabor from the college made the announcement yesterday. Hungarian bastard was almost pissing himself on public TV."

"Listen, there was nothing we could do. Orson made an offer and Bass turned it down."

"Then you *up* the offer," Stonewall said. "You pay whatever's necessary to get the place. If you develop the land, you're gonna get it back a hundred times anyway, right? If you'd done that, then I'd have the salvage rights, as usual, and right now our girl Thaddeus would be telling the world that *we've* discovered some snaps of Lincoln. You got any idea what they're worth?"

"I don't know. A lot."

"Take whatever number you got floating around that giant, empty head of yours, and add a couple of zeroes," Stonewall said. "Fucking Orson—that Jew bastard. I should cut his nuts off and feed them to my pit bull."

"I don't think there was anything we could have done," Trotter said. He was smarting from the remark about his head. He'd always been sensitive about the size of his head; that Stonewall had questioned its contents merely added insult to insecurity. "He's a different sort of fellow, this Bass. I found him rather pugnacious. And so did Orson."

"You guys would find Shirley Temple pugnacious."

"Fine," Trotter said. "Whatever you think—what's done is done. Did Thaddeus get my e-mail about the sword for sale in Reading?"

"Thanks for reminding me," Stonewall said. "He made me drive over to look at it. It's a genuine Confederate cavalry cutlass . . . made in 1977 in fucking Taiwan or someplace. Maybe I'll buy it and use it to castrate Orson."

"I didn't know."

Stonewall shook his head. "You didn't know. That's your excuse for everything. You should put it on your business card. I didn't know. Might cover you if somebody decides to sue your ass for misrepresentation. Hey, I didn't know."

"All right, Stonewall. I get it. We messed up. But we didn't do it on purpose—did anybody know about the pictures beforehand? We're all on the losing end with this thing. So take it easy."

"Right," Stonewall said and he took a drink of coffee then made a face and looked suspiciously into the cup. He set it aside. "You know, maybe you shouldn't have busted your hump finding this clown in the first place."

"I was doing my job. I could get disbarred otherwise."

Stonewall looked around the office. "Yeah, you wouldn't want to lose all this."

"Next time, I'll let you pick out a beneficiary of your choice," Trotter said. "Then you won't have anyone to blame but yourself."

"Fuck you, Trots. The last guy I ever blame is myself."

Dock slept at the house that night, in his sleeping bag in the back room beside the door to Willy Burns's shop. The next morning he picked up a newspaper and, after perusing the classifieds, he drove out to a campground on the Taneytown Road and bought a twenty-seven-foot Airstream trailer from a couple who were moving to a condominium in New Mexico.

He stopped at the Motel 8 on the way through town and carried his clothes and other belongings down to the trailer and then checked out. By noon he had the trailer at the farm, and he had water and hydro hooked up within the hour. The trailer had two bedrooms and a living area and a kitchen with a propane oven and range. It came equipped with pots and pans and various other household items, both essential and non, and was actually a big improvement over his cramped motel room.

He went back to framing the roof that afternoon. An Indian summer had set in and the day grew warm and then humid. Dock worked in his shirtsleeves. He finished the main house by midafternoon and then he laid out the top plates of the back room and cut the rafters for the roof there, this time at a ten-twelve pitch.

It cooled off as darkness approached. By five o'clock, when he climbed down the ladder for the last time that day, it was nippy enough that he ducked into the trailer for his jacket. When he came back out, a van was pulling in the drive. The logo on the side advised that the vehicle was from PHWX, a television station in Philadelphia. The same logo adorned the breast of the windbreaker of the man who emerged from the passenger side.

"Ted Harkness, *Nightly News*," the man said by way of introduction. "I'm looking for the man who found the Lincoln pictures. Dock Bass."

Dock looked at the man, who was offering his hand, and in that instant he imagined a thousand men just like this, rolling out of a factory on a conveyer belt somewhere, with their timbred, empty voices and their bland good looks. When he shook the hand, it was as soft as a child's.

"We've been driving around all afternoon," Harkness said. "The press release from the university just said the Gettysburg area." He turned toward the van. "This is it!"

The driver's door opened and a man got out. He wore a dirty ball cap over a ponytail and a Flyers' fleece; he walked around the back of the van and a moment later he approached carrying a large camera on his shoulder.

"Do you mind doing a short interview?" Harkness asked. "It's too late for the six o'clock, but we can still shoot for eleven."

"You should probably talk to the university," Dock said. "They've been taking care of things."

"We already did a phone hookup with them, some loopy professor, said he was too busy to appear on camera," Harkness said. "But you're the one who found the pictures. Right? You did find the pictures?"

"They weren't pictures. They were collodion plates."

"Pictures, plates, whatever. You're the man I want."

The other man was adjusting something on the camera. "It'll take a minute to set up," Harkness said. Then he looked at the house. "So this is it. Tell me—where exactly did you find the pictures, er . . . plates?"

"In a box," Dock said, which was technically the truth.

"Up in the attic or something like that?"

"Something like that."

"Have you found anything else interesting?"

"It depends what interests you. To some people a spider is interesting."

Harkness gave Dock a long look, then he turned to the cameraman. "We ready?"

"I did turn up a few," Dock said then.

Harkness turned back quickly. "A few what?"

"Spiders."

"Are you playing games with me here?" Harkness asked. "Have we even got the right guy?"

At that moment Dock decided that they did not. "Aw, I owe you an apology," he said. "My name's Willy Burns. I'm just a carpenter. Dock Bass hired me to put a roof on this place."

"For fuck's sakes," Harkness said. "Where's Bass?"

"Musky fishing, some place in the Thousand Islands. I'd give you the number if I had it. I don't know that they even got phones up there."

"Pack it up," Harkness said to the cameraman. "This guy's a fucking carpenter."

"Hey, Jesus was a carpenter," Dock said.

Harkness turned back to Dock. "You're a fucking asshole, you know that?"

A minute later, Harkness and the cameraman-driver were packed and gone. Dock watched as the van spun gravel and then fishtailed down the side road. He knew that the next bunch wouldn't be so easy to fool.

He packed away his tools, and then he went into the trailer. He opened a can of spaghetti and set it to simmer while he had a shower. He drank a beer with the pasta and when he was done eating he rinsed the dishes in the sink.

After a while he went into the house and walked back to the workshop. He sat on the stool and looked absently about the room, at the tools and the musket and the man-powered lathe. Turning toward the doorway, he noticed a screwdriver or chisel, wedged into a gap in the fieldstone above the lintel. He carried over the bench from beneath the worktable and climbed up to retrieve it. It was a slot screwdriver, with a cracked wooden handle and a heavy patina of corrosion on the blade.

Carrying the bench back across the room, he tipped it slightly and felt something inside shift. Setting it down, he noticed for the first time two small hinges, mortised skillfully beneath the overhang of the bench top. Taking a closer look, he saw that the top was actually a shallow box, fastened shut with penny nails. He used the screwdriver to pry the lid open. Inside was a cedar box with a brass clasp and inside the box were dozens of pages of handwritten notes on yellowed, brittle paper.

Dock carried the box into the trailer and then carefully removed the pages. There must have been two hundred or more, and as he began to read he realized at once that he was holding Willy Burns's diary. The pages were like rice paper; the edges broke when he handled them, and the writing itself was nearly transparent in places. The script was very small and cramped, obviously written with a quill. Each entry was dated. The earliest was from 1854.

> *Me and Elisha cumb back from Lancaster last night, where we was heping Uncle Thomas with the threshing. The wheat harves was a goodly one. Cousin James alowed it would run twenty bushells to the acre. He will sell it at markit cumb Saturday along with two fat shoats he has rased. It was after sundown when we got home and Josh Burrel was here. He is still determind that I should sell him Bess my mare. I am parshal to the animal and besides I hav no desire to deel with Josh as he is the kind to travel dolar down and dolar a week. I do not trust him as far as I could toss a gran piano.*

Dock sifted carefully through the pages until he came to the last. It was marked December 14, 1863. The writer's hand was more mature now, the quill, if not the spelling, more sure of itself.

> *This war is a right crimenal thing with nether side alltogether right and nether side alltogether wrong. I reckon now that I cain't keep away from it any longer. It was fine to sit back and treat it all like it didn't cuncern me but Mr. Lincoln has showed me that it cuncerns everybody. The people, as he said. And if fighting is the only way to stop people from fighting, then I guess I have to do my part. And when it's over then I hope nevver have to fight any body agin.*

Having read the entry, Dock was immediately sorry for having jumped ahead. He felt as if he'd cheated somehow. He put the pages together and started at the beginning. He would read the diary as it had been written.

The next day was again sunny and warm. By noon he had the rafter system finished over the back room, and he was tying that roof to the main house, framing in the valleys with the last of the two-by-eights.

The telephone installer had arrived at shortly past ten. It took him five minutes to reconnect Ambrose Potter's old wall-mount phone, which hung on a nail on the bare studding inside the back door. The installer wrote the new number on the two-by-four with a felt pen.

"You're the guy found the Lincoln pictures?" he asked before he left.

"Yup."

"I got a feeling that phone's gonna get a workout."

The diary was on Dock's mind as he finished the rafters and then nailed together the fascias for the overhangs. He'd read until midnight and, with the spelling and the faded handwriting, had barely made a dent in the stack of pages. When he stopped work at noon, he put on a clean shirt and drove into town, to the visitor's center he'd stopped at a few days earlier. The place was moderately busy. Dock got the attention of an overly pleasant, balding man in a sports jacket who offered to give him a guided tour of the battlefield for eighty bucks. When Dock declined, the man grew decidedly less pleasant. When Dock told him what he was looking for, the man dismissed him outright.

"Try the Historical Society."

"Where's that?"

"At the seminary," the man said and he walked away, fixing his sights on a likely pair of tourists wearing matching yellow outfits and expressions that fairly begged for guidance.

Before leaving, Dock went into the gift shop and bought a half-dozen books—two on Lincoln and the rest on the battle itself. The seminary was off Hay Street in the west end of the town. It was easy to find—the cupola was visible for miles around. Dock parked on the street and climbed the steps. Inside he was greeted by a woman wearing a blue blazer with an American flag on the lapel. She had high cheekbones and a firm jaw, and she was probably in her sixties.

"Something I can help you with?" the woman asked.

"I'm looking for some information about someone who lived here in the 1860s," Dock said. "Might be a wild-goose chase."

"Maybe not," the woman said. "Gettysburg has undergone a fair amount of scrutiny the past hundred and fifty years or so. There was quite a shindig here back in 1863."

Dock smiled.

"The fact is, we actually know who a good number of its residents were from that era. Census reports, newspapers from the era, that sort of thing. Do you have a name?"

"Willy Burns. Son of Thomas and Eva."

The woman looked at her watch. "I'm just going to lunch. I can do a search when I get back. If you'd like to stop by later?"

"Sure."

"I'm Betty Walker. I'll see you this afternoon."

When Dock got back to the farm, he hammered together some makeshift scaffolding from two-by-fours and rough planks from the barn, crisscrossing the braces as his father had taught him. Of course, everything he did had the old man's stamp on it, at least when it came to carpentry. In trade school, he'd been taught slightly different framing methods. After getting his papers, though, he found himself gradually returning to his father's way of doing things. Sometimes, but not always, it was a matter of efficiency. The rest he would have to ascribe to something else. Possibly his stubborn nature but maybe something as simple as loyalty.

Once on the scaffolding, he chalked a line along the new rafters to keep the sheeting square; then he began to nail the plywood onto the roof. The work was slow at first; he was constantly climbing up and down, cutting and carrying the sheets. After the first row was completed, he spiked two-by-two cleats onto the roof to walk on as he ascended.

A little after three o'clock a white cube van pulled in the driveway and stopped behind Dock's pickup. The passenger door opened and after a moment Thaddeus St. John climbed gingerly to the ground, like a bather stepping tentatively into a cold stream.

"Hello!"

Dock looked down and wondered what the visit would cost him, in terms of time. He was nearly at the peak, nailing a two-foot strip of plywood that would finish that side of the roof.

Stonewall Martin got out of the van now and the two men approached the house together. Thaddeus wore a bush jacket of heavy canvas twill; the coat featured numerous pockets and slots, apparently designed to hold knives and ammo, binoculars and compasses, and any other items a person might require on safari. The pockets appeared to be empty; presumably, the little man's mission today was not one of blood sport. He wore green pants, of a shade one might see in Sherwood Forest, tucked into expensive hiking boots, above which a precise band of striped wool sock was evident. The ensemble was topped off by a Aussie-looking bush hat, the right brim of which was pinned fast to the crown. The entire outfit appeared to be just-out-of-the-box creased and clean; Dock would not have been surprised to see a Minnie Pearl–ish price tag dangling from the hat.

Stonewall was sporting the same rough-spun attire he'd worn in the bar a few nights earlier. Dock regarded the pair for a moment—to look any more ridiculous at least one of them would have to have an arrow through the head—then he went back to work.

"I hear you've fallen upon a fortuitous find," Thaddeus called up, his tongue tripping just slightly over the alliteration.

Dock had a mouthful of nails and he hammered them home, one by one, before he spoke. He did not look down. "Where'd you hear that?"

"Why—practically everywhere. My manicurist could speak of nothing else this morning," Thaddeus replied. "I'm told there are collodion plates."

"Yup."

"Can we see them by chance?"

"Nope."

"Dear me," Thaddeus said. "And why not?"

"They're at the university," Dock said. He finished his nailing and then took a seat and looked down at the two, Stonewall grungy and rank, Thaddeus the would-be Nimrod cool and coiffed, undoubtedly sprinkled with whatever perfume he considered complementary to his costume. Dock was relieved he wasn't close enough to smell either one of them. "You can get the pictures off the Internet if you're interested. The university has a Web site."

"You'll have to indulge me my elitism, but I'm really not interested in looking at images on the Internet, especially when everybody else in the great wide world can do the same," Thaddeus said. "Besides, as an authority, I really would have to personally inspect these plates before I could even think of authenticating them." He smiled up at Dock.

Dock smiled back. "Who asked you?"

Stonewall was walking toward the back door, which, Dock remembered, was open. "What else you find in there?" he demanded.

"A lot of lath and plaster," Dock replied, and he started to inch his way down the steep roof. He was glad that he'd screwed the plywood covering over the workshop door before going into town at noon.

"Yeah, I bet you did," Stonewall said.

He was looking into the house when Dock reached the ground. Thaddeus was hanging back near the orchard, and he appeared to be posing along the rail fence, perhaps imagining his image against the rustic backdrop. He was absently fingering the brim of his hat, like a man waiting for something to happen.

"You don't mind if I take a look around?" Stonewall asked and he made to step into the house.

"I'd rather you didn't," Dock told him.

Stonewall stopped, and his face grew almost as dark as his beard. "Why the fuck not?"

"Now, Mr. Martin," Thaddeus said in reproach, and then he looked at Dock. "You have to understand that young Stonewall here is a man born of the wrong century. I consider him a throwback to the old frontier, a time when men were men. However, I will admit that occasionally the primitive gains the upper hand on the courteous. Allow me to apologize on his behalf."

"You don't have to apologize," Dock said. "Not your fault he doesn't know his ass from a hole in the ground."

At that Thaddeus shot Stonewall a quick look. Stonewall glared at Dock but held back, a dog who recognized the length of his chain.

"I must say," Thaddeus hurried on, "that I am curious as to where exactly you discovered the plates. I've actually been in this house many times. I knew old Ambrose quite well. He was a wonderful old fellow—perhaps not the most fastidious of housekeepers, but there are worse vices in life. I bought a few furniture pieces off him over the years, as well as a Colt Navy revolver with which he used to scare the crows out of his corn patch. My point is, I never saw any collodion plates. And there was never a mention of them, in spite of Ambrose's constant attempts to sell to me virtually every other item he possessed. So it begs the question: where'd you find them, Mr. Bass?"

Stonewall was inching toward the door again as Thaddeus held forth.

"Why don't you tell frontier boy to stand still?" Dock asked and when Stonewall stopped, he added, "Who said I found the plates here anyway?"

"The rumor abounds, Mr. Bass," Thaddeus said. "Are you saying it is false?"

"I can't for the life of me recall where I found them," Dock said. "The fact is, they're at the university now. Next you're gonna ask what I'm gonna do with them. Well, I don't know, but I do know I'm not gonna sell them to you."

"I'm afraid you're in error there," Thaddeus said. "I'm not here on a mission of trade but rather as an authority of the period in question. I'd hoped to offer my services with regards to authenticating whatever you've found. My only compensation would be the pleasure I'd receive in examining the items."

"Klaus Gabor is handling all my authenticating needs," Dock said.

"Ah yes, the illustrious Mr. Gabor," Thaddeus said, and he showed his squirrel's teeth again. "He seems to have attached himself to Mr. Lincoln and the history of our Republic. I suppose we are to assume that nothing of note ever occurred in Hungary."

"I wouldn't know about that," Dock said.

"Well, we all strive for our little niche in life," Thaddeus said, then turned to Stonewall. "Come, Mr. Martin—let us leave Mr. Bass to his carpentry."

With that, Thaddeus turned on his heel and walked to the van, where, scrambling and clawing like a toddler climbing onto a kitchen chair, he managed to deliver himself back into the passenger seat, knocking his hat off in the process, an act that required him to climb back down to retrieve it from the dirt. It was an undignified exit, especially for so theatrical a character, and by his expression he was clearly dismayed by it.

Stonewall headed for the van now. He passed by close enough that Dock could smell him; today there was a hint of burned cannabis to go along with the wet spaniel scent. "If you were as smart as you act, you'd at least listen to an offer," he said.

"Nope."

"Why the hell not?"

"I don't know," Dock said. "There's something about you I don't like."

"I've had about enough of your smart mouth," Stonewall said. "You're not gonna like it when I knock you on your fucking ass."

Dock smiled. "And you're not gonna like it when I get up."

SEVEN

The blond woman was waiting on the street in front of the apartment building when attorney Trotter pulled up in the Lincoln. She was wearing sunglasses and shivering under a thin cotton jacket. She had a takeout coffee in one hand and a cigarette in the other. Trotter was late. He prided himself on punctuality and he'd been hoping that the woman wouldn't be waiting; then he could claim he'd been there on time. He parked across the street and hurried over to her, nearly getting squashed by a stake truck as he did.

"I have to apologize," he said. "I was delayed in court. You are Ms. Anderson, I assume."

She nodded.

"It was inexcusable," Trotter said. "A simple matter—should have taken no more than twenty minutes. But the attorney for the other side chose to be obstreperous. Demanded that all documents be read in full, decided that he would re-cross-examine two witnesses, made mountains out of the slightest of molehills. And then, just as it appeared—"

"Can we, like, go in?"

The woman removed her sunglasses to reveal bloodshot eyes. Trotter went through his pockets for the key, reflecting as he did on the demise of civil conversation in the world.

It was a studio apartment on the third floor. It appeared that nothing had been moved since Trotter had been there two weeks earlier. There was a television on a steamer trunk in the corner, a fold-out couch across the room. A sideboard with the mirror missing. Fridge, stove, odd chairs and tables. A ceramic lamp with a flamenco dancer on the base.

Trotter stood inside the door and watched as the woman took a quick inventory of the room. He had no idea what she expected to find—probably nothing more than was there. She'd told him on the phone that she'd been away for several years.

"Have you been here before?" he asked.

"No. Mama moved here, I don't know, maybe three, four years ago. I just haven't been back. I mean, I been in touch," she added quickly, "by the phone and whatever. I was always in touch. But I've been busy, I've got a career, and it's been hard to get back. But I have been in contact all along. More than the rest of 'em."

"You have siblings, Ms. Anderson?"

"You can call me Leona. It's my name. Yeah, I got siblings coming out of my ears. None that made it to the funeral, I noticed."

"I wondered, is all. Yours was the only name in the will."

"What's that tell you?"

"Indeed. Have you been to the bank?"

"Yeah, that's all taken care of. Just the apartment, and then that's it. I met a guy last night said he'd buy whatever furniture there is. Don't look like I'm gonna retire on the proceeds, does it?"

"Well, it's just something you have to do," Trotter said. He was about to elaborate, but for some reason he didn't have the desire. He wondered if he was coming down with something.

The woman picked up a blanket from the couch, held it in her hands for a moment. It seemed to Trotter that it might hold some significance for her, but then she tossed it aside and looked at him.

"So we're done?"

"Yes. You can leave the key with the landlord on the first floor. That is, whenever. The rent is actually paid until the first. Will you be staying in Gettysburg?"

"Fuck Gettysburg. I been trying to get away from here my whole life. This is the end of it for me."

Betty Walker was waiting for Dock when he arrived back at the seminary at half past four. She had a loose-leaf binder in her hand.

"Willy Burns was a photographer," she said as he approached the counter.

"Yes," Dock said. "He was."

"This place has been buzzing for two days about the pictures of Lincoln," Betty said. "Is he the one that took them?"

"I think so."

"Then you would be the Mr. Bass I've been hearing about?"

"Yes, ma'am."

"You didn't want to bother the quaint old lady with all these details?"

"Well," Dock said and he smiled.

A man walked by then and said good night to Betty. Looking around, Dock realized that the place was closing for the day. When he turned back, Betty was still working her feigned indignation.

"What would Spencer Tracy do?" Dock asked.

"He'd probably offer to buy me a gin and tonic."

They went to the bar at the Gettysburg Hotel and sat at a table by the fireplace in the front room. The place was half full—men and women in office attire, a couple of students sharing a pitcher of beer, a tourist fiddling with a digital camera. Betty opened the folder as they waited for their drinks.

"Willy Burns was a photographer," she said again. "And a tinker, and an inventionist."

"Where'd you hear that word?"

She produced a photocopy. "From an ad he ran in the newspaper in 1862. We have some of the old *Adams County Sentinels* on microfilm. Not all, but some. But there's your Willy Burns."

Dock looked at the copy. The ad read:

WILLY BURNS
Photographer Tinker Inventionist
Fixer of Clocks, Watches, Muskets, Pistols
& all other items
15 Shealer Road (past Peart's Apiary)

"I found a cedar plank with this burned on it," Dock said. "Or most of it. His shingle, I guess."

"You'll see that ham was twelve cents a pound that year," Betty said. "And eggs were three cents a dozen."

"A man could breakfast for a month on a buck."

The waitress arrived with the gin, and a beer for Dock, who paid.

"His name came up several times," Betty said then. "He was quite prominent around fall fair time. Always winning a ribbon for something or other. There's one here—hold on while I find it—where he invented some sort of sluice system for watering your vegetable garden. Powered by a windmill. Here it is, from 1860."

Dock looked at the article. The text, presumably transferred from yellow newsprint to microfilm to photocopy, was blurred but legible. "No pictures of him?"

"Newspapers didn't run pictures back then. They didn't have the technology." She took a gulp of the drink. "But I heard that you found over two hundred collodion plates—were there no pictures of Willy Burns?"

Dock shrugged. "We don't know what he looked like. There are a lot of people on the plates."

"Not just famous presidents?"

"Not just famous presidents. A lot of citizens—maybe your ancestors, who knows?"

"No," she said and she finished her drink and, to Dock's amazement, signaled the waiter. "My people were still in New Hampshire at the time. We didn't get here until the 1870s."

"So you're a newcomer," Dock said.

"We're still unpacking."

Dock indicated the clippings. "Does it give Willy's age in 1860?"

"He was seventeen."

"A pioneer whiz kid."

A fresh gin arrived and Betty took a drink. "Everybody's yakking about the Lincoln pictures. Are you being hounded yet?"

"It's just starting."

"Well, you'd better get used to it. People are crazy when it comes to this stuff. And money, apparently, is no object."

"I've had my share of suitors already."

"I'm sure. Anybody you'd trust?"

Dock stole a phrase from Willy's diary. "Not as far as I could toss a grand piano."

"Right. You'll never know who to trust until you know who not to trust."

"Who said that?" Dock asked.

"Probably some great shyster of yore." She drank off the second gin. Dock had yet to make a dent in his beer.

"You have time for another?" he asked.

Betty looked at her watch. "Sure. The old boy's out deer hunting. He won't be back until dark."

Dock ordered another round, and they went through the rest of the folder on Willy Burns. There was a news item that told of Willy's trip to a scientific exposition in Philadelphia in 1860 and another on a sojourn he made to New York early in 1861, to study wind power. There was also a piece noting that he'd photographed a Shakespearean troupe—starring the "mesmerizing Petunia Carp"—that had passed through town. Betty downed her third, and then her fourth, gin and tonic and then she began to gather the papers.

"These are all photocopies," she said. "You can have them. I'll keep looking, see what else I can turn up. I have to go."

"Yeah, you might have a deer to skin out."

She laughed as she stood up. "He hasn't brought a deer home in ten years. And he's a good hunter and a crack shot, so there you go. I think he just likes being out in the woods."

Dock took the folder from her. "I appreciate this." He looked at the clippings. "A kid like that, you wonder whatever happened to him."

"Oh," she said. "Don't you know?"

It was pitch-dark as Dock drove back to the farmhouse. As he was walking in the back door, the telephone began to ring. He had come to consider the house as a remnant of the nineteenth century, and as such the phone—like the lawyers and the realtors and the Stonewalls and maybe Dock himself—had no business being there.

But he answered it anyway.

"Yah, carpentry doctor."

"Hello, Klaus."

"Vut are you building today?"

"I'm done for the day. It's dark out—don't you have a window?"

"Then come here, to university, I need to show you something."

The old Hungarian hung up before Dock could reply. He got in the truck and drove back into town, wondering how Klaus had managed to get his phone number so quickly.

Harris was there when he arrived at Klaus's Lair. The phonautograph was perched on a counter in the center of the room, beside a computer and a tape recorder and some other equipment Dock didn't recognize. Klaus was actually wearing a lab coat and he was hovering over the machine, looking every inch the mad scientist. Harris, in cords and a bulky sweater, was leaning against the windows running the length of the room. He looked at Dock, his eyebrows arched.

"What's up?" Dock asked.

"He wouldn't say," Harris said and he mimicked the older man. "Ve vait for Dock."

"Here I am," Dock said.

"You listen," Klaus ordered, and he started the tape machine. Dock saw now that he'd added what appeared to be a crude stylus to the cylinder of the phonautograph. Now a scratchy, irritating sound filled the room. Seconds later a man's voice was heard.

"Somebody reciting the Gettysburg Address," Dock said after a moment.

"Better than your Mr. Edison and his little lamb," Klaus said.

"The first words ever recorded and played back were from Edison," Harris explained. "He recited 'Mary Had a Little Lamb.'"

They listened. Sometimes the sound would almost disappear into the background noise and then return. The entire speech was recited and at the end a cacophony of static and unidentifiable noise burped from the machine. Klaus stood to one side with his arms crossed as the recording played; he looked like a man who'd just taught his grandson how to ride a bicycle.

"How'd you get it to work?" Dock asked when the recording finished.

"I tinker vith it. See—this paper on drum is called kymograph—it is scratched vith bristle from a pig. So I steal some from the Frenchman Scott, steal some from your Mr. Edison—vut, they are going to sue me?"

"Nowadays you just never know," Harris said.

"Vut I do, I first make digital image of recording," Klaus went on. "Then I linearize it. That is 'make flat' to you, Harrison James. Then I use computer program to scan this image and make vave form. Is simple thing."

"Right, any four-year-old could do it," Harris said. "So whose voice is on the cylinder?"

"Villy Burns?" Klaus suggested, then he shrugged. "Is just a guess. But vere ve find this cylinder? Villy Burns's shop."

"So," Harris said, thinking. "Willy Burns—or Villy, as he's apparently known in Budapest—hears about Thomas Edison's invention, does a little research, probably sends away to France for this gizmo, and builds his own recording machine."

"Hold on," Dock said then. "When did Edison first record sound?"

"You mean, when did he first play it back?" Harris asked.

"Yeah."

"1876," Klaus said.

"Then it's not Willy Burns," Dock told them.

"Why not?"

"Because he died in 1864," Dock said. "At Cold Harbor."

"How do you know that?"

"I had a conversation today with a feisty old girl from the Gettysburg Historical Society. Name of Betty Walker—she's got Katharine Hepburn's profile and W. C. Fields's liver. She did some digging on Willy Burns for me."

"Hah," Klaus said. "Now the history teacher gets a lesson. Harrison James, you have eggs on your face."

"I do?" Harris said.

"So is not Villy Burns on recording," Klaus said. "Who is it?"

"Could be anybody," Harris said. "The thing could've been made in 1950 for all we know."

"No, is too crude, this machine. This thing is around time of your Mr. Edison."

"Or before," Dock suggested.

"What do you mean—before?" Harris asked.

"I got thinking after I heard that Willy died in '64," Dock said. "Is there anything in that room that you can date later than 1863? You guys are the experts. Think about it—the guns are black powder, the books are all older editions, even the newspapers the plates were wrapped in are dated '63 and older. Name one thing that isn't."

Harris looked at Klaus.

"Is smart, this doctor," Klaus said.

"And didn't you say, Klaus, that this machine was made in the 1850s?" Dock asked.

"Yah, is available but to *study* sound. For laboratory."

"But Willy could've bought one?"

"Yah, sure."

"And he was obviously the type of kid who might have," Dock said.

Harris crossed the room and sat down behind Klaus's large, paper-strewn desk. He laced his hands behind his head and propped his boots on the desk.

"The boots," Klaus protested.

Harris ignored him. "Let's just weigh anchor here for a moment.

Because you guys are about a heartbeat away from saying that Willy Burns beat Edison to the wire by more than a decade when it came to playing back sound. Okay, let's pretend that it happened—gee, don't you think that maybe the papers would have picked up on a little story like that? Are we suggesting that Edison had a better press agent than the kid?"

"The boots," Klaus told Harris again. Then he looked at Dock. "But is good point."

"I don't know," Dock said. He walked over to the machine and looked at it, thinking. "What if he wasn't finished with it? What if he got it to record, but he hadn't figured how to play it back? Look what you had to do to get it to play, Klaus."

Dock turned to Harris, who had managed to remove his feet from the desk. Harris stroked his beard for a moment and then he looked at the Hungarian. "Play it again, Klaus."

They listened to the recording once more. Dock leaned close to the tape recorder this time. The voice on the recording was thin and the tone flat as the prairie. When it was done, Dock straightened up.

"There's a lot of background noise," he said.

"Static," Harris said. "This was before Dolby."

"Something else," Dock said. "Especially at the end."

"Yah, I hear it too," Klaus said. "Is not static."

"Well, whatever it is," Harris said, looking at Dock, "you're pretty much convinced yourself that it's Willy Burns on the recording."

"I'm not saying that," Dock said. "But Betty Walker found a bunch of newspaper clippings on the kid. He was always winning ribbons at the fair or inventing something. Now, think about his parents. A kid like that would be the apple of their eye. After he got killed in battle, all that his parents had left of him was in that room. Which they sealed off."

Klaus nodded. "Is little shrine, that room."

"That's right," Dock said. "And you don't mess with things in a shrine. I think there's a chance that everything in that room was there when Willy Burns left in 1863."

"Everything?" Harris asked.

"Everything," Dock said.

★   ★   ★

Amy passed the next few days trying to elicit some sort of statement from the camps of Cyrus Howard and/or Sarah Jane Wright with
regard to their involvement with Cubby Stewart. She soon came to realize that the only thing more bitter than a congressman voted out of
office for complicity in a scam to syphon off charitable donations destined for a Third World country was a lifestyle guru banished to prison
for the same crime. Cy and Sarah Jane weren't talking.

At least not to her. Wright, looking svelte and none the worse for
wear for her time in stir, was rather busy, popping up here and there in
various right-leaning newspapers and on certain political forums,
where she delivered rehearsed and virtually verbatim attacks on the
liberal establishment, which had conspired to bring her down. Citing
ongoing legal battles (there were none), she was unable to directly
comment on the "new" evidence that would eventually prove her innocent on all charges, except to suggest that she was a dupe of "certain
individuals."

Ex-congressman Howard, presumably on the advice of counsel,
was not talking to anybody about anything, a prudent enough move
considering that he was, although unelected, still at this point in time
unindicted.

Amy did talk to the Reverend Stevie Save, again in the trophy
room where she'd first spotted the incriminating picture of Sarah Jane
Wright. The good reverend was quite obviously not on his game,
though, possibly due to some pharmaceutical interference. He admitted at first to knowing Cubby Stewart, then later confused him with
Jimmy Stewart, whose acquaintance he also claimed. When he started
to ramble about the allegorical nuances of *Harvey,* Amy knew it was
time to go.

At this point, she was convinced that Sam was wrong. She needed
to get Stewart's side of the story first. Anything damning he might have
to say would presumably force the others into responding.

So she had Marla, at TransWorld, book her flight for Aruba. She
would leave Saturday morning. Thursday afternoon she was at home,

wearing her sweats and drinking tea and rereading her notes on the entire Haitian debacle when Peter called and invited her to the house for dinner. Being yanked from the reality of the impoverished Carribean, she was even more suspicious than usual of Peter, whose social conscience had no more grounding than a butterfly in a tornado.

"How many people will be there?" she asked.

"Me," he said. "And you. Let's see—that's two."

"I can't, Peter. I'm leaving Saturday, and I have tons to do."

"First you ask who's gonna be there and then you turn me down when you hear it's just me. What's your problem?"

"Peter, you're looking for a fuck buddy."

"Okay—something wrong with that?"

"Only if you're looking in the wrong place," she told him. "And guess what?"

She hung up on him then and as soon as she did the phone rang again. It was Sam Rockwood. From her call display she knew he was at home.

"Sam," she said.

"Jesus, I detest those display phones," he said.

"Hey, I answered, didn't I?"

"I need to see you, Amy. Can you come out to the house?"

"Um, I guess. Is it about Aruba?"

"You could say that."

She changed into khaki pants and a cotton sweater and then got into the Cayenne and drove out to McLean. Marie was walking out the door when she arrived—heading for a charity art auction in the city, she explained—and she gave Amy a quick hug but then a short, imponderable look that Amy found rather perplexing. Nettie was in the kitchen, sitting at the breakfast counter, smoking a cigarette as she leafed through O magazine.

"Hey, old lady," Amy said. "Got another one of those?"

Nettie reached into a drawer and produced the pack, tossed it over. Amy lit up and sat down on the stool opposite.

"What you doin' here?" Nettie asked.

"Command performance," Amy said and she gestured in the general direction of the inner house. "Since when do you read *O*?"

"Belongs to Marie. I'm just checking it out, y'understand."

"What do you think of the fabulous Oprah?"

"Shit. That girl further from the hood than you."

She found Sam in the den, behind the desk that had once belonged to either Jefferson or Madison, Amy could never remember which. He was in a heavy swivel chair, reclining in thoughtful repose, a glass of liquor in his right hand. He smiled when he saw her, but his expression held the same inscrutable quality as Marie's.

"Hey, kid. Grab yourself a drink and pull up a chair."

"I'm all right," Amy said, to both offers.

There was an unusual item on the desk. It looked like an antiquated version of the famous RCA Victor phonograph, minus the cute little doggie with the black eye. There was a dent in the horn about the size of a silver dollar. In a room chock-full of disparate-looking items, it would normally not draw Amy's attention, but, by its positioning on the desk and the predatory gleam in Sam's eye, she was at least aware of the thing, whatever the hell it was.

"What's going on?" she asked. "I've been up to my ears in research on Aruba. First settled by the Caiquetios, by the way."

"Do you know what this is?" Sam asked and he indicated the object on the desk.

"Barney Rubble's record player?"

Sam had a thin-lipped smile that he used when he was not amused and he produced it briefly now. He leaned forward, placed his glass to the side, and put his hand on the thing. "This is a Leon Scott phonautograph."

"Yes," Amy said. "That was going to be my second guess."

"Edouard-Leon Scott was a scientist from Martinville, France," Sam said then. "And he invented this in the 1850s. It was used to record sound and sold all over the world, primarily for scientific use. I bought this one in London thirty years ago. There's maybe a half dozen of these in the country. Maybe."

Amy moved to sit down. Apparently, she would be there for a while. "You realize I'm not really the collecting kind of woman—unless we're talking shoes or purses—"

"We're not."

"Didn't think so. So what do we have here? You bought this gadget thirty years ago, and you have a sudden need to share it with me. Is it possible that there's more to this story?"

Sam got to his feet and walked to the sideboard, where he poured more bourbon for himself. He held the bottle toward Amy, but she refused again. "The phonautograph is a sort of prototype to what Edison used when he invented the phonograph. Before Edison, you could record sound on the cylinder, but you couldn't play it back."

He crossed back to the desk and sat down.

"Okay," Amy said. "I *have* heard of this Edison fellow."

Sam laid an affectionate hand on the phonautograph, as if it were a favored family cat. "You see this dent? Legend has it that George the Fifth bounced a golf ball off this thing when he was still in kneesocks and short pants. Back in the old country."

"And you believed that?"

"No, but I bought it anyway." He looked at her across the desk. "They found one of these in Gettysburg last week. With the cylinder intact."

"Let me guess—the same guy who found the Lincoln pictures?"

"Same guy. And they've already rigged it up for playback. There's a voice on the cylinder, somebody reading the Gettysburg Address. Now they are suggesting—there's a couple professors from the university down there and this man Bass—that this Gettysburg photographer beat Edison to the punch. Which would be very significant and would lead to some controversial rewriting of American scientific history."

"You sure this guy's not running a scam?" Amy asked. "Come on, Sam. All of a sudden he turns up a barnful of Civil War memorabilia a hundred and fifty years after the fact? Nobody stumbled on any of this in all that time?"

"This room, as I understand it, was built into a stone wall, the doorway mortared in. Nobody even knew it was there."

"Which is exactly the kind of story I would invent if I was a scam artist. Anyway, how do they know this thing wasn't recorded twenty years after Edison? How would you ever prove otherwise?"

"They're maintaining that the phonautograph was in the room and the room was sealed off in 1864," Sam said. "And what's more—Klaus Gabor is one of the guys saying it. I've met him on a couple of occasions; the guy's won a Pulitzer and a Guggenheim and he still walks around looking like a refugee from a Budapest slum. Point is, he's not interested in money. And he sure as hell wouldn't trade his reputation on some fly-by-night scheme that would eventually be exposed."

Amy smiled as she stood up. "Well, either way, I guess I know what you want for Christmas this year, Sam. However, if this Gettysburg dude scooped Edison, I have a feeling this little record player is going to be way out of my price range. I do have my eye on a Richard Nixon shaving mug I think you'll like."

"You're right, I want it. It's one of a kind and there's nothing more valuable than that. I have an original copy of the Declaration of Independence, but there are eleven other copies out there. If this thing is legit, it's on its own."

"You know, Sam, I'm actually jealous that you can get so excited about these things. However, I have things to do. What exactly did you want to see me about?"

"I just told you."

"You did? I must have missed it."

"I want that goddamn phonautograph," Sam said. "Gettysburg is going to be swarming with all kinds of media and collectors and dealers. Eventually, they're going to decide if it's genuine. I want that machine before that happens, before the price goes through the roof on it. I'll pay now, not knowing, and take my chances."

Amy was staring at him now. "Tell me again how this concerns me," she said deliberately.

"Why, you're going to Gettysburg."

"The fuck I am. I'm going to Aruba."

Sam dismissed the island in question with the back of his hand. "You can go to Aruba next week. First, you have to do this. We have to preempt these people. The more attention this gets, the more difficult the situation becomes."

Amy looked at the ugly antique on the desk and she could feel her blood rising. "I'm going to go down there and do what?"

"You'll cover this as a news story," Sam said. "And you'll get close to this guy." He paused. "All right, I don't know what you'll do exactly. You're going to have to go down there and scope out the situation."

"For Christ's sakes, Sam," she said then. "Man finds old record player in barn—isn't this the kind of story the local news does just before the goat that ate the lady's hat? Don't do this to me, Sam. Shit, I just got back from a fucking sporting event. You're gonna pull this on me?"

"You'll go to Aruba next week. Stewart's not going anywhere."

"But somebody will get to him first," she said. "I found him. So will they."

"We'd know if somebody else had him. Do this for me first, kid."

Amy indicated the contents of the room they occupied. "Are you telling me you don't have somebody that buys all this junk for you? Send them."

"Ignoring for the moment your irreverence for what is arguably the best private collection of Americana in the country—yes, I have people who act as agents for me. And I've made inquiries through them about the Gettysburg situation. But the guy who found this stuff isn't biting. I get the impression he's not your run-of-the-mill, money-grabbing citizen. Just my luck."

"So why send me?"

"Because, my dear, of the intangibles you'll bring to the situation. You're smart and you're sexy and you're appealing and you have great instincts. You can connect with people, even when you don't have the slightest interest in them or their lives."

"I guess I'm supposed to be flattered by that."

"I'm not trying to flatter you," Sam said. "You're in my employ, I don't have to. Which brings me to the other reason I'm sending you."

"What's that?"

"You want to go to Aruba. When this is done, you'll go."

"Ah, the carrot and the stick," Amy said.

"If you will."

She was smiling at him but her mind was racing. Quitting on the spot was out of the question, she realized. She could only move on from a position of power, one that a freshly unemployed TV journalist would not possess.

"They used that carrot-and-stick routine on donkeys," she said then. "And donkeys like to kick and bite. You sure you want to treat me like a donkey, Sam?"

"The problem with metaphors is they grow old so fast," he said. "It's only a two-hour drive. Jump in that fancy new Porsche Turbo and visit historic Pennsylvania."

"How do you know I bought a Porsche? I never told you that."

"I know everything about you," Sam said.

"No," she said at once. "You think so, but you don't." She hesitated, looked again—this time with transparent disdain—at the gizmo on the desk. "Jesus Christ. What's this guy's name?"

"Bass. I assume it's pronounced like the fish, not the fiddle," Sam said. "Dock Bass."

"Sounds like a hillbilly action figure," she said unhappily. "How exactly am I supposed to handle this? I don't ever recall Dan Rather showing up at the space center with a pocketful of cash, trying to buy a used shuttle. There are credibility concerns here, Sam."

"Just get close to the situation. Find out what this guy's story is. If it looks as if he'll sell, I'll have somebody there in a heartbeat. I know people in the area. You can keep your distance, do a fascinating little historical piece for the six o'clock and hit the road. But don't think you're going to be the only dog in the hunt. This thing is already attracting a lot of attention, on the Lincoln pictures alone. Throw in the Edison controversy and it'll be Katie-bar-the-door."

"Oh yeah, it's very exciting," she said and she turned away. "It's the one I've been waiting for, Sam."

She was in a decidedly foul mood when she left and the new Cayenne took the brunt of her sulk. She was in the left lane and running along at a hundred and twenty when she reached her exit for Old Town. She crossed the four lanes without looking back and hit the ramp—among much horn blowing and fist shaking—at about a hundred. She put the Cayenne up on two wheels and then righted it just in time for the merge onto Delaware. The design engineers from Porsche would have been impressed.

Back at home she sat in her living room—recently described as "spacious, stylish yet functional" by *At Home* magazine—and felt sorry for herself for a full hour. When the hour was up, she logged on to her computer, went straight to Google, and typed in the word *Gettysburg*.

EIGHT

For a man who had, just a month earlier, driven off into the sunset with the sole purpose of uncomplicating his life, Dock Bass had somehow succeeded in accomplishing just the opposite. While the irony of that fact was not lost upon him, what he couldn't decide was what the hell to do about it. The only solution available seemed to be to mount up and ride off again. But that wasn't something he was considering at this point.

Pick your spots, his father used to say.

Any chance he had of fading back into the simple life evaporated when he agreed to allow Klaus Gabor, Lincoln scholar–slash–mad Hungarian professor, to release to the world the news of the discovery of the Burns phonautograph, as it was now called, and to suggest—and Klaus stressed in the press release that it was merely conjecture at this point—that Willy Burns might have trumped old Tom Edison's ace.

The busy little town of Gettysburg became busier.

Across the country, the news was greeted with doubt, excitement, disdain, and humor. Museums and universities demanded to examine the recording machine; Edison scholars proclaimed their outrage; news outlets were hot for salient details on the actual discovery; collectors and antique dealers phoned, e-mailed, and arrived in person in hopes of acquiring the recording machine, the collodion plates, or anything else that might have been discovered. David Letterman pronounced the recording as the second oldest known to man—the first being an early disk of the Rolling Stones.

Dock, in the midst of all this hoopla, was having difficulty getting any substantial work done on the house. And winter was getting close. Hardly an hour went by that a car or truck or van didn't pull in the drive. And even though he advised any and all comers that the university was handling questions and requests, he invariably was forced to stop whatever he was doing to talk about the findings.

On the Friday after Klaus's announcement he met Harris at the Gettysburg Hotel for dinner. He'd spent the day finishing up the sheeting on the roof. Finally. He would start shingling the next day, weather permitting. The forecast was for rain.

"Better than snow," he told Harris as they waited for their meals to arrive.

"Did I mention to you that you could hire this stuff out?" Harris asked.

"A couple times."

"So—you don't believe me when I tell you that you're about to become rich?"

"Sure, I believe you. I had a guy at the house today, offered me a hundred grand for the Lincoln plates."

"Oh yeah?" Harris asked. "Who was he?"

"Claimed to be a collector from Boston. I might have believed him if he hadn't been wearing a Hooters T-shirt and driving a beat-up Chevy pickup with Pennsylvania plates that I've seen around town about twenty times. I wouldn't be surprised he's working for old Stonehead."

"Old Stonehead is at the bar."

"I saw him."

The waitress showed up then with their meals. Harris had salmon in dill sauce, and Dock a T-bone steak. Harris was working on a half carafe of white wine. Dock ordered another beer.

"So what did you tell this enterprising chap?" Harris asked.

"I told him Bill Gates was by this morning, offered me a million a plate."

"What'd he say to that?"

"Asked me who Bill Gates was."

"Obviously a man of the world."

Dock cut a piece of beef and then glanced toward the bar as he lifted his fork to his mouth. Stonewall Martin was turned on his barstool, watching him. He was again wearing his buckskin coat with the "The South Will Rise Again" T-shirt underneath. Dock wondered if his intention was to wear the shirt until the event actually came to pass.

"By the way," Harris said, "I'm to invite you to dinner tomorrow night. Mrs. Harris is keen to meet you—I lied through my teeth, told her you were an interesting fellow. Be a few people from the university there along with an eccentric raconteur or two. And Klaus, of course."

"Do I have to dress up? I threw my tie in the river."

"You're okay the way you are," Harris told him. "Speaking of Klaus, I was talking to him today—or I should say I was listening to him today. And he told me something interesting. You know he put the recording on the Internet, so anybody who wants to can actually hear it. Well, for every request he's getting from scoundrels looking to score and TV stations looking to boost their ratings and museums looking for a freebie, he's getting e-mails and letters from grade schools and high schools. Apparently, this whole thing has spurred a renewed interest in Lincoln, and subsequently the Gettysburg Address, which leads to the Emancipation Proclamation and on down the line. So on one side you've got a whole bunch of people trying to make hay out of this, and on the other side a new generation of kids who are actually interested in it. It's the MTV thing—if it's in a book, it's boring, but if it's down-loadable audio, it's cool."

Dock took a drink of beer. "I bet the old rail-splitter would like that. The part about the kids, I mean, not these other peckerwoods. I'm glad to hear it myself—I gotta admit every now and then I find myself regretting that I ever tore that wall down."

"Fate, my son. It's what led you to Gettysburg."

"A screwy wife and a fucked-up life landed me in Gettysburg."

"No, you would've gotten that letter either way. And you'd have shown up here."

"Maybe not," Dock said. "If I'd been content where I was, maybe I'd have just told Trotter to sell the place and send me the money."

"There you are," Harris said. "That's where fate took a hand."

"So I can blame fate every time I fuck up? That's good to know." Dock took another drink of beer and then wiped his mouth with his napkin. "What about you, Harris? How'd you end up in these parts?"

"I grew up less than a hundred miles from here. On a dairy farm in Bedford County. First time I came to Gettysburg I was eight years old."

"And you decided right away that teaching history would be more fun than shoveling Holstein shit?"

"Guernsey," Harris corrected him. "But that's pretty close to the truth. Problem was, I was the only son out of five kids. My father was of the opinion that I should take over the family farm. On top of that, he's the kind of guy who doesn't regard teaching as a real job. If you don't end up at the end of the day with a sore back and dirty hands, then it's not work."

"Is he still pissed?"

"Not really. My sister married a German she met at school and they're running the farm. My sister's a lovely girl but I'm sure she became much more attractive once Gunther saw the acreage out in Bedford County. Do you know what farmland's worth in Europe these days?"

"So you and the old man are all right?"

"I never really got back in his good books until a couple of years ago when I introduced him to Wilfred Brimley."

"Pardon?"

"There was a film crew in the area shooting a miniseries on the battle. They hired me as consultant. Klaus too—you should've seen these TV types trying to deal with him. Network nincompoops, he called them. But Wilfred Brimley played Meade and I introduced him to my dad. My dad loves Wilfred Brimley."

Dock smiled. "Maybe I should've introduced Wilfred to my old man. I didn't know it was an option."

Harris looked up from his fish. "I don't know what that means but then I never got that throwing your tie in the river thing, either."

"Long, boring story, Harris. And I haven't had enough beer to tell it."

"Okay," Harris said after a moment. He took a drink of wine. "Klaus has sure kicked open a hornet's nest with this thing about Edison. I wasn't aware that Thomas Alva's supporters were such a possessive bunch. It's not as if the phonograph was his only claim to fame. There was the lightbulb—which has really caught on—and about a thousand other things."

"Edison's got one thing going for him," Dock said.

"What's that?"

"He's dead. If he was still alive, people would love to knock him off his pedestal. That's the way we are. As soon as he died, he became a legend. And we don't fuck with legends, not in this country. Or any other, far as I know."

"Speaking of legends," Harris said. "Stonewall approacheth."

Dock turned to see the bearded man headed their way. When he got close, though, he merely stared Dock down and then went out the side door. Dock went back to his steak.

"A little intimidation tactic?" Harris asked.

"Shit, I can hardly eat," Dock said and he took another mouthful. "Trotter was telling me that Stonewall is a famous reenactor. Said he was hard-core, whatever that means."

"That sounds like the kind of pablum Stonewall would feed Trotter. First of all—a reenactor would run a bayonet through you if you called him that. He prefers *historical interpreter*. Secondly, the genuine hard-cores are an obsessive lot—they starve themselves down to about a hundred and thirty pounds, to get that authentic look. These guys are as tough as leather—they march, bivouac, eat period rations, sleep on the hard ground. They'd laugh Stonewall Martin out of the state of Pennsylvania. The only thing Stonewall could reenact is half a Laurel and Hardy routine."

They finished their meals in silence. There was a country-and-western band setting up in the corner, and the singer, a buxom woman with a Loretta Lynn hairdo, was doing a sound check by singing an impressive a capella version of "Your Cheating Heart."

"You've never said what your plans are," Harris said then. "You intend to stick around?"

"I'm gonna restore the old house," Dock told him. "After that, I don't know. Gettysburg might be a quiet, normal little town, but to tell you the truth—nothing's been normal or quiet since I arrived."

"Nothing's been normal or quiet *because* you arrived," Harris reminded him. "Knocking down walls, rewriting history. You're a bloody rabble-rouser, Bass."

"That's good to know, too. This country was founded by rabble-rousers."

When Dock got back to the farmhouse, there was a station wagon parked in the driveway. The driver was a farmer from the Harrisburg area—a stooped man of perhaps seventy, wearing overalls and a dirty John Deere cap. He had with him a squirrel gun, which he was quite certain was of an age and pedigree that it might have been involved in the Battle of Gettysburg. He wondered if Dock might be able to sell it for him. Dock advised him to find a reputable dealer and to ask him about the weapon. As the man drove off into the darkness, Dock watched his taillights disappear, reflecting on the fact that he was suddenly an expert on things he knew nothing about.

The night was growing cold. Inside the trailer he turned up the propane heater and opened a beer and then retrieved the box of papers from its hiding place above the bunk. He was now in the year of 1860, and Willy Burns was seventeen years old.

I am alive at a time when grater things are posible than at any other. Mankind is saleing in uncharted waters and the doors that sciense will open in the next generation are without paralel. The times will reqwire men that are eqwal to the chalenges. I am

*keen to read the papers ever chance I get. From Pitsburgh and
Philadelphia and Baltimore, altho I do not get the drift that the
men in Washington today can hold a candle to Adams and Jefferson and Burr. I helped old Willis split some rales today and when
I got home Maddy Poynton was here and looking for me. I tole
her again that I ain't innerested in no girl and particlary not her,
as she is ugly as a mud fence. In the stead of crying, she give me a
smile and went off. I expect she'll be back soon enuf.*

In between the pages Dock found a scrap of paper with a short
verse.

*A man's life is a vessel,
To be filled as mutch from within
As from without.*

It was after midnight when Dock put the papers away and went to
bed. Sometime just before dawn he dreamed that he was riding across
a large pasture field on a stolen bay mare. A woman—the horse's owner, it seemed—apprehended him as he stopped to open a gate leading
into another field. The woman was not overly concerned with the theft,
and before he discovered the reason for her nonchalance, he woke up.
Lying awake in the narrow bed of the trailer, he realized that the
woman in the dream was the country singer from the hotel in town.

The next morning he ate a bowl of oatmeal, then stood looking out
the trailer window to the old house as he waited for coffee to brew.
There were dark clouds stacking up like cordwood above the tree line
to the west. After his coffee he put his work clothes on and went outside and began to nail the eaves-starter on the roof. After maybe ten
minutes, the skies opened up and soon it was raining so hard that he
had to give up and head back inside. He spent the rest of the day inside
the house, nailing in rafter ties as he dodged the raindrops where they
leaked in between the cracks of the plywood sheeting overhead.

Throughout the course of the day he was interrupted five times,
twice by reporters and three times by dealers pretending to be

tourists. He directed them all to the university. The phone rang constantly, but he never answered. He had an unlisted number that he'd changed twice already, though it didn't seem to matter. Finally, he unplugged the phone in mid-ring.

At noon he ate his lunch in Willy Burns's workshop. It was the only dry spot in the house. He could have eaten in the trailer, but he liked to sit in the shop. He suspected that the comfort came as much from what wasn't in the room as what was. He read more of the diary as he ate. In 1860 Willy Burns wrote of the Philadelphia trip that Betty Walker had mentioned.

> *I think that it must be the gratest city on the continent. The streets are as strate as a musket shot, lined with sugar mapels and oaks and ash, and lit up at night by lamps fueled by wale oil! Market Street is a whir and a bustle—butchers and candle-makers and coblers and tailors and farmers hawking fat shoats and geese and sheep. At the Exposition my windmill sistem was accepted with much ardor and innerest. It fairly makes me dizzy to think that the men in this grate city should pay heed to a farmboy from an unherd of vilage like Gettysburg. I must work hard to earn their futture respect.*

He showered at five and then fumbled through his clothes to find a shirt that would qualify in passing as clean. The Jameson home was only a mile away, but he had to drive into town and pick up a bottle of wine first. Harris lived on Charmed Circle Drive ("I bought the bloody house, I didn't name the street," Harris had protested when giving Dock directions), a short cul-de-sac off Harrisburg Road, home to a half-dozen nearly new upscale residences of disparate size and design. Dock parked the pickup along the drive, between a Ford SUV and a GM SUV.

The house was sand-colored stucco, two-story, with three shuttered dormers across the front and some struggling ivy on the southern wall. The dog, Casey, was lying on the front lawn as Dock approached, its four paws in the air, tongue lolling lazily to the side. Dock stopped to rub the animal's belly; when he continued on, the dog got up and followed.

It was a warm evening, one of those nights that threatened to be the last of its kind for the year. The guests were gathered on the patio and the lawn out back. There were probably two dozen people there. Klaus, wearing what appeared to be a pith helmet, was in the yard, talking with a woman in a green dress.

"Yah, here is the doctor!" he shouted when he saw Dock, then continued his conversation with the woman.

Dock was introduced all around by Harris and promptly forgot most of the names, a transgression he admitted to Harris's wife when she brought him a beer.

"Did you remember mine?" she asked.

"Yeah, it's Lynn."

"Then to hell with the rest of them."

She was tall and very fit in the manner of a tennis player or golfer. She had short blond hair and freckles on her face and her arms. She wore tan cotton pants and a navy V-neck displaying yet another splash of freckles on her chest.

The rest of the guests were scattered across the patio, sitting and standing, drinking and eating hors d'oeuvres. The dress code went from jeans to shorts to one woman who wore what appeared to be an evening gown of crinkly black material. She kept explaining that she'd been to a "function" in town and had come directly to the party.

Lynn was drinking red wine. "Come," she said to Dock, indicating a bench alongside the house. "I want to talk to you before this bunch carries you off."

They sat on the bench, with Casey still in Dock's wake, remembering—as dogs will—the earlier belly rub. Lynn told him to go, though, and he went, casting her wounded backward looks as he did.

"Well, Mr. Bass," she said as they sat. "You're a notorious guy in these parts. Did you have any notion what you were getting into when you rolled into town?"

"I swear, I had no idea."

"I'll bet you didn't. Harris says you came from the Albany area."

"Yup."

"Yup," she mimicked. "And what did you do in the Albany area?"

Dock took a drink of beer. "I sold real estate."

"Really? I thought you were a carpenter."

"I was. That was before I sold real estate."

"You don't look like a guy who would sell real estate."

"What do I look like?"

"I don't know," she said and she turned slightly, the better to see him. "You look like the type of guy who would hate people who sold real estate."

"I did."

"So you hated yourself?"

"Don't tell me—you teach psychology at the school," Dock said.

"Naw," Lynn replied. "I used to be in sales; these days I'm a freelance writer—finance, business, that sort of thing. We're not all teachers here."

"I thought you were."

"That's just one of those college town myths. You can't hang around with teachers all the time—for one thing, half of them are as boring as death. Take Lucy, for instance, wearing twelve yards of evening gown over there. If she tells me once more about her function in town, I'll stick her head in the birdbath."

Harris approached them then, carrying a scotch on the rocks. Lynn stood and kissed him lightly on the cheek. "And then there's my husband," she said. "Who, lucky for both of us, is not as boring as death."

"Incomprehensible compliments are always welcome," Harris said. "Dock, I want you to meet Dan Ryder. He's got something interesting for you."

"Go," Lynn said. "I have to check on the prime rib."

Dan Ryder was standing by the fence separating the patio from the pool, drinking a beer, and talking to no one. He wore a goatee and wire-rimmed glasses, a sports coat, and black jeans. Harris introduced him as an ex-hippie.

"I'm forty-two years old," Dan protested. "I was too young to be a hippie."

"In spirit," Harris explained to Dock, "in spirit, he was a hippie. *Is* a hippie, in fact."

"In spirit, you are a shit disturber," Dan told Harris. He looked at Dock. "Do you know who J'Makir Slim is?"

"I know who Slim Pickens is," Dock said.

"J'Makir Slim is a rapper," Dan said, and as he spoke he produced a CD from his jacket. "J'Makir Slim and the Word. One of my students burned this off the Net today. It's a new rap song—and it's based on the Gettysburg Address."

Dock looked at Harris. "That was quick."

"Come," Harris told them and he led the way inside.

They followed him through the French doors and down a staircase off the kitchen. The bottom of the staircase opened directly into a rec room, which was equipped with an elaborate stereo and video system. Harris took the CD and slid it into a player. A second later a hip-hop rant—a seething indictment of the enduring racism in the land—filled the room. Phrases from the Gettysburg Address made up the chorus. Dock sat on the edge of a couch and listened.

"*Shall not perish, shall not perish,*" Harris sang along, badly. Harris rapped like a white dairy farmer from Bedford County.

"I'll be go to hell," Dock said.

"We're uniting the country," Harris said and he began to dance. He danced like he sang.

"Doesn't sound to me like this guy Slim is feeling all that conciliatory," Dock said.

"Either way, this thing has taken on a strange persona," Dan said.

"This is nothing," Harris said. "Wait until you hear my new composition—'The Emancipation Proclamation Waltz.'"

"With that voice?" Dock asked.

"You cast aspersions on my musical talents?" Harris demanded.

"I'm surprised you could operate the CD player," Dock said.

It remained warm enough that they could eat outside, buffet style, the guests seated on lawn chairs, benches, the patio steps. There was considerable interest in Dock and his recent exploits, but after a while the conversation predictably moved on to other things, to his relief.

After dinner, Harris lit a fire in a potbellied firepit, and Dan Ryder produced a guitar from somewhere and played a few songs, singing along. Harris, by unanimous consent, remained silent. At one point Dock found himself, beer in hand, standing along the fence when he was approached by the woman in the voluminous black dress.

"Here you are—our local celebrity," she said, and for once she did not apologize for her attire. She'd had enough wine that she may have forgotten what she was wearing.

"You must be starved for celebrities, ma'am," Dock told her.

The woman tilted her head then and looked at him closely, as if seeking some great truth, on this patio, under the strains of "Heart of Gold."

"It's ironic, isn't it?" she said after what seemed to be a very long time.

"I guess it is," Dock said, hoping to avoid hearing whatever it was that was ironic.

"No," she plowed forward. "It's ironic—look around, all these educated people, and yet somehow you are the one who makes this great historical find. It's so . . . unlikely."

"Just the way it goes, I guess," Dock said. "One time when I was a kid I found a quarter, and I wasn't even through first grade yet."

He left her there with that, puzzled and overdressed and holding an empty wine glass. Dan, by accident or design, began to sing Dylan's "From a Buick Six."

At midnight there was just Klaus and Dock left with Harris and Lynn—the four of them sitting close to the fire as the night had finally grown cool. Harris brought out a bottle of cognac and four plastic glasses.

"Time to break out the good liquor," he said. "Now that the riffraff has departed."

"Hear that, Klaus?" Dock said. "At least we're not riffraff."

"Yah—but if ve have leave early, then ve vud be riffraff like the rest. Better to stick around, vait for the good liquor."

"Amen to that," Lynn said.

Harris poured and then added a log to the fire. "Did Klaus tell you about his TV appearance today, Dock?"

"I tell him now," Klaus said. "Earlier, he is too famous to talk to me."

Harris sat down. "They shot a piece for the Discovery Channel, at the university. They brought in a brace of hotshot Edison scholars from the Smithsonian, squared them off against our own Klaus Gabor. They brought their own Scott phonautograph, which looked very similar to yours. Professor Gabor was quite, well, professorial. Wore a tie, in fact."

"Yah—so I vear a tie. You find that funny, Harrison James?"

"It was a clip-on."

Lynn put her arm around Klaus's shoulders. "That is a *little* funny."

"Anyway," Harris said, "these two chaps were quite meticulously checking out the phonautograph, and you could see it in their eyes— they were just dying to prove Willy Burns a fraud."

"Well, they won't," Dock said.

He made the statement with such emphasis that nobody spoke for a moment.

"You're pretty sure about that, aren't you?" Lynn said at last.

Dock shrugged. "I seem to be. Yeah."

"Why is that?"

Dock took a sip of brandy, looked into the fire. He thought about the diary.

"I don't know," he said. "I guess I just got faith in the kid."

Thaddeus St. John lived in a stone cottage on a half acre of land backing on a creek in the woods beyond Seminary Ridge. The cottage was built in 1946, by a returning GI who was looking for a place to fish for brook trout and to hide from his memories of a gruesome day at Omaha Beach two years earlier. In 1949, with the fishing bad and his recall as vivid as ever, the soldier packed up his old kit bag and lit out for Alaska, never to be heard from again.

The place sat empty until Thaddeus bought it for back taxes in the 1980s. Over the years he'd demolished, renovated, refurbished, and built on until the finished product now resembled a quaint little place in the Irish countryside—a place where John Wayne might have taken Maureen O'Hara for a good old-fashioned ravishing. At one point Thaddeus had actually considered a thatch roof for the house but had had second thoughts when he learned that the coverings were usually infested with all legions of insects, snakes, and rodents both large and small. Instead, he added a rock garden reaching down to the bank of the creek, where the trout—stocked by the state—had made a triumphant return. Not that Thaddeus was an angler; his idea of spending time outdoors was to sit on his back porch with a glass of Dubonnet and the latest copy of *Vanity Fair.*

In the midst of the renovations—during which time he himself never actually lifted a hammer—Thaddeus also took the time to reinvent the history of the place. It was now generally accepted that the GI had merely fixed up the place and that the house had actually been constructed in the 1850s and had been heavily damaged by the Union artillery preceding Pickett's charge. Thaddeus had somehow managed to convince the Historical Society that this was true and had even held forth on public television on the fascinating history of his home, mentioning that it was rumored to be where James Longstreet had billeted back in July 1863. A few of the local farmers—old-timers—should have known that the stories were nonsense, but if they did, they made no effort to set the record straight. They regarded Thaddeus as an odd little man and his propensity for telling tales was hardly the strangest thing about him.

Of course, Thaddeus was a master of reinvention. He'd been born Thomas Stevens in Pittsburgh, and he'd suffered a difficult, allergy-ridden childhood. In his younger years, he'd imagined himself a tragic figure, an American Oliver Twist. He'd never actually read the book but had watched, with his mother, an early film version on television.

At age sixteen, deciding that his lavender sensibilities would never survive in a blue-collar town, Tommy left home and headed south. Louisiana seemed a likely refuge, and he spent most of the next fifteen years there. At one point he took a part-time job in an auction house in

Baton Rouge, and it was in the midst of all that clanky Cajun history that he began to realize that the merchandising of the past could be a pretty lucrative game. He educated himself in the marketing of collectibles and even made an abortive attempt at becoming an auctioneer—a career move that died when it became apparent that his voice was too soft to be heard outside a range of about twenty feet. Of such restrictions are great men thwarted.

Upon deciding that his field of expertise would be the perpetually popular Civil War, he headed back north. The two most obvious destinations were Virginia and Pennsylvania and he chose the latter out of some vague sense of home state loyalty. He arrived with a lilting southern accent that owed more to Vivien Leigh than to heritage or birthplace, and a phony history degree from LSU. And, of course, a brand-new name, one suited to his elegant and freshly refined background.

Thaddeus St. John now sat disconsolate in the cottage where Longstreet never slept, looking across the rock garden to the gray stream where the government-sponsored trout occasionally splashed. The day was as gray as the stream. Thaddeus sat wrapped in a kimono, drinking apple cider laced quite liberally with spiced amber rum. The cup was nearly empty when he heard the car pull up, the door slam. A moment later Carl walked in. He looked at Thaddeus as he removed his coat.

"Aren't you a morose thing?"

"Where have you been?" Thaddeus asked.

"Town."

"Town," Thaddeus repeated. "Been chasing college boys, have we?"

"I don't chase." Carl went to the fridge and poured himself a glass of wine. "What's your problem, dear heart?"

"As if you care."

Carl walked over and plopped himself on the couch like a teenager, which he practically was. "You gonna spill or am I gonna have a nap?"

Thaddeus pushed his bottom lip out farther. "Klaus Gabor is my problem," he said. "This should be my discovery. He's a fucking school-teacher. Fucking Euro-trash fucking schoolteacher. He has no business being involved in this."

There was a glass bowl of cashews on the end table. Carl reached over and grabbed a handful. "You talking about the Lincoln pictures?"

"No, I'm talking about the *Titanic*."

Carl smiled and popped a nut in his mouth.

"Of course that's what I'm talking about. And not just the pictures. Did you know that Gabor is going to be on the Discovery Channel, talking about his precious fucking phonautograph?"

"Actually, I didn't."

"It's not right. This is my bailiwick. Why doesn't that Hungarian gypsy freak stick to his books? Memorabilia is my game. I have worked hard to get where I am. I am the authority on these matters and I am being ignored. I am being ignored!" Thaddeus watched as Carl went for more cashews. "Am I boring you?"

"A little. You've been rehearsing this, haven't you?"

"Get out of my house!"

Carl wiped his hands on his jeans. "Come on, dear heart."

"Don't call me that."

"It's a term of endearment."

"Not when your voice drips with sarcasm when you say it."

Carl got to his feet. "Now, now. I'll make you another toddy."

Thaddeus snatched the cup away, held it to the side like a little child denying a playmate a toy. "I don't want another toddy."

Carl put his hand on the older man's neck. "Then what do you want?"

Thaddeus looked out over the landscape once more. It was just beginning to rain, tiny drops peppering the surface of the creek.

"Sympathy," he decided.

"I can do sympathy."

"I would also like Klaus Gabor's head on a platter," Thaddeus said, giggling as he handed over the cup. "But for now, sympathy will have to do."

NINE

Amy Morris came into Gettysburg from the south, moving up the Taneytown Road from Maryland as had General Meade and the Army of the Potomac a century and a half earlier. It was a brisk November day in contrast to the hot July of Meade's trip. But unlike the war-weary Union troops, Amy suffered not from the weather, nor from random musketry or cannon fire either. She put the Cayenne on cruise, set the climate control to sixty-eight degrees, and slipped Aretha in the CD player. She eschewed the hardtack and beans that had fueled Meade's army, drank Evian water, and munched on rice cakes instead. Her most serious tactical setback of the day came on the outskirts of Baltimore, where she was forced to pump her own gas. The mission went off without a hitch.

Seeking a certain anonymity, she'd booked a room at the Holiday Inn on Baltimore Street, a few short blocks from the town center. It was after dark when she arrived. She gathered her bags from the back of the Porsche and walked to the front desk to check in. The clerk, a young woman with cropped hair and black-rimmed glasses, recognized her at once.

"You must be here about the Lincoln pictures," she said.

"I must be."

"The PBS crew is also staying here. Should I put you near them?"

"Better not. Mixing public and network can be volatile."

The woman gave her a look. "You're joking."

"I'm joking," Amy said and it was close to the truth. She smiled at the young woman. "I really like your hair."

In her room she turned on the TV and unpacked, then ordered a club sandwich from room service. She logged on and checked her e-mail while she waited for the sandwich. She had seventy-two messages; most were cc's from various TransWorld producers and coordinators and as such didn't require a reply. The last message was from Sam Rockwood, wishing her a safe and successful trip to Pennsylvania.

"Christ," she said, hitting the delete key. "And he thinks I'm transparent." After she ate, she put on a jacket and took a walk through the town, looked without interest at all the battle-related merchandise in the store windows, and then walked up to a kiosk in the town center where she bought the local papers. Back in her room, she went through them, scanning without reading, discarding sections one by one until an item caught her eye in the "recommended viewing" page of the *Harrisburg Times*.

At nine o'clock she turned on the television. Minutes later she was watching a wild-eyed Hungarian defend in broken English the authenticity of the item she'd come to find. The phonautograph—to her untutored eye a dead ringer for the one in Sam Rockwood's possession—was on a table in front of the man. Across the table two men—both bearded, both wearing tweed—were playing devil's advocate to the Hungarian, whose name, she saw flashed on the screen, was Klaus Gabor, a history professor from the University of Gettysburg. She'd known that, though, as soon as she'd laid eyes on him.

"No one is arguing the fact that this is a Leon Scott phonautograph and that it was available in the 1850s," the first advocate was saying.

"Yah," the professor said.

"And no one is challenging your claim that the cylinder contains what appears to be an early recording," said the second advocate.

"Yah."

"But to suggest that there's anything more than that here is just not practical," the second man said. "Theoretically, the recording could have been made last Tuesday."

"Maybe it vas Tuesday," the professor said. "But not last Tuesday. Some Tuesday, 1863."

"How can you defend that?" the second man asked.

"This machine is locked away in little room since then. Hey, maybe a ghost sneak in and make the recording."

The first advocate sighed. "Your problem is—there is not a single shred of evidence that proves that this recording predates Thomas Edison. And even if there was, there is nothing to suggest that this man Burns ever played back the sound."

"Aha," Klaus said. "So you say Villy Burns does not record sound before your Mr. Edison."

"That's our position," the second man said.

"Yah. But then you say if he *does*, he does not play it back before your Mr. Edison."

"You're really taking this thing out of context," the second man said.

"Vut if I tell you that I think Villy Burns ties his shoes before your Mr. Edison?"

"What?"

"Just checking."

Amy, sitting cross-legged on the floor in her hotel room, smiled.

The next day she set out to find him. She was on her own for the time being. If a crew was needed, she would be provided with one from the affiliate in Philadelphia. In the morning she walked to the town center again and bought the papers and some fruit. Around mid-morning she called the university from her room. The receptionist told her that Klaus Gabor was tied up for that day and many to come and that no, she would not put her through. Amy called back two minutes later and got the same receptionist.

"University," the woman said.

"Yes," Amy said, affecting a midwestern accent. "This is Claudia calling from the dealership. We have Professor Gabor's car in for repairs, and we've run into complications. It looks as if the fuel injection system is gone. It's gonna run about two thousand dollars to replace."

"Oh," the woman said, clearly alarmed. "Well—I'd better let you talk to the professor."

"Yah," Klaus Gabor answered a half minute later.

"Professor Gabor, it's Amy Morris from TransWorld."

"Yah."

"TransWorld," Amy said again. "We're a news network."

"I know who you are. I am vaiting."

"I wanted to speak with you about the phonautograph. Do you have a free moment?"

"My moments are all free. Vut I don't have is spare moment."

"What about lunch? I can meet you at the university."

"I am going out for lunch. To meet with more nincompoops. Are you nincompoop?"

"I have my good days and bad in that regard."

"Hah. Me, too."

"Listen, maybe I can meet you beforehand—what time is your lunch?"

"Twelve thirty, but I have no time. Maybe next veek. Good-bye."

Amy hung up the phone after he did and then sat there for a moment, looking out her window. She could see the monument in the distance, in the cemetery where Lincoln made his speech. The day was overcast and the leafless trees surrounding the cemetery stood stark naked against the southern sky, an ethereal photograph in black and white.

At noon she got directions from the front desk and drove to the university. The school was a sprawling complex of buildings, randomly situated beneath aged oaks and maples, perimetered by Washington Street on the east and Lincoln Avenue to the north. Amy drove slowly around the campus a couple of times, looking for a sign that would identify one building or another as that which housed the history department. The buildings, however, were identified only as halls—McKnight Hall, Hanson Hall, Rice Hall—with nothing to indicate just what lofty ideals were disseminated within. Students were walking to and from the various buildings, singly and in groups. Finally she stopped, powered her window down, and waved to catch the attention of a pair of students—a guy in a jean jacket and a girl wearing a windbreaker.

"I'm looking for the history department," she said.

"It's the big red brick building," the guy replied.

All the buildings were big and constructed of red brick. Amy smiled. "Just my luck—I'm here on open mike night."

"It's Weidensall Hall," the girl told her then, and she pointed to the building.

"Do you know a professor named Klaus Gabor?" Amy asked then.

"Yeah," the girl said. "He's my prof."

"I have to drop a package in his car," Amy said. "Do you know what he drives?"

The girl pointed out a dented Volvo in the lot behind Weidensall Hall. Amy drove over and in full view of a dozen students let the air out of the left-front tire of the car. She got back into the Cayenne and parked a short distance away. While she waited, she read the owner's manual from the glove box. The Porsche had an impressive array of options she didn't know about. She was immersed in the fuel-data-center information when she looked up to see Klaus Gabor hurrying across the parking lot. He wore an open trench coat that had seen a number of years, and he had a pair of reading glasses perched on his balding head. He was moving like a man who was late.

She glanced at the dash and saw that it was twelve thirty-one. She watched as he got close to the Volvo and then pulled up short; the look on his face was as deflated as the tire. She dropped the Cayenne into gear and idled over beside him.

"Professor Gabor?" she asked.

He answered absently, still regarding the tire. "Yah?"

"I'm Amy Morris," she said. "We spoke on the phone."

"Yah." He turned now and gave her a look.

"I drove out hoping to get a look at the phonautograph—hey, is this your car?"

"Yah."

"Don't you have an appointment at twelve thirty?"

"Yah."

"I can give you a ride."

There was a long pause as Klaus regarded her narrowly. "Yah."

With the professor giving directions, they headed downtown. Klaus sat upright in the passenger seat, his knees pressed together, and as they drove he kept lowering his glasses and looking at the Porsche's interior like he was seeing the inner workings of a spaceship.

"Quite a gas guzzler," he said as they sat idling at a light.

"It is," she agreed. "The company pays."

"Is the planet that pays," Klaus said.

"I know," she said. "I'm a little conflicted about that."

"Yah—but just a little."

She smiled. "I give you a lift and you presume to lecture me about my mode of transportation? Would you be more comfortable on a bicycle built for two?"

"On that I vud freeze my ass," he said.

Amy made a show of admiring the surroundings as she drove. "This is such a beautiful little town. Do you live here?"

"Chambersburg," he said brusquely and he pointed. "Down the pike. Vut questions you have, Amy Morris?"

"Well, I'm just like everybody else. Did this Burns character get the jump on Thomas Alva Edison or not? I'm quite familiar with the Leon Scott phonautograph—I first became intrigued by it when I was in college—and I know its capabilities. So I know that on a purely technical level, this is absolutely a viable suggestion. But the question is quite obvious—how do you prove the time frame?"

"The phonautograph is found in sealed room."

"By this man Dock Bass."

"Yes, the doctor."

"That's my point—just how credible is this Bass character? I'm told that the memorabilia game is rife with fraud these days. Were there any reliable witnesses around when this guy stumbled on this stuff?"

"None. But I have seen this room. No one can duplicate vhat is there. Obscure textbooks, tools, lanterns, molds—things that can only be seen in this time."

"Anything in the room that you didn't recognize?"

He gave her a look. "No. Vy you ask that?"

"Because, if everything there is recognizable to an expert like yourself, then the contents of the room *could* be duplicated."

"Ah," Klaus said. "Is good point. You are sharp cookie in your guzzler. So you say—maybe the doctor Bass collects these things—books and tools and guns and drawings—and then he finds phonautograph with this recording. Or maybe—aha—maybe he puts recording on phonautograph himself. He puts this all in room and then says to the vorld—come here! See vut I have found."

Amy smiled with reserved triumph. "I'm not saying it happened, Professor. I'm playing devil's advocate here. I'm just saying it could have happened. It's conceivable."

"Yes, I think is conceivable. Is very good theory. Tell you vut, Amy Morris, I help you promote this theory if you tell me one thing."

"Sure."

"When the doctor Bass is collecting these things, vere does he find pictures of Lincoln at Gettysburg? Maybe on eBay or Home Shopping Network?"

Amy looked over. "Shit. I forgot about the goddamn pictures."

"Yah, you forget about goddamn pictures. Turn left here. You have ten seconds—you have other theory you vant to try on the silly old Hungarian?"

"I'm pretty much tapped out, theorywise." When she looked over, she was relieved to see that the old man was smiling. "But I would like to see the room where all these marvelous things were found. Could you set that up for me?"

"No."

She waited for an elaboration that did not come. "Okay," she said slowly. "Could you give me directions to this place then?"

"No," he said again. "You find it, though. Everyone else finds it, so vill you. But I don't tell you how. You vill bother the doctor, like all the rest." He pointed. "The yellow building, vith the shutters."

"What does Bass plan to do with all this stuff?" she asked then. "He's got to know he's sitting on a fortune here."

"He knows this, yah," Klaus said. "But he is different sort of man maybe than you think, this doctor. He is practical man. Busy man. Busy in his head and busy vith his hands. I don't think he is the kind of man who sits around counting his pocketbook."

She pulled over to the curb. "Another thing—I wasn't aware that Bass was a doctor," she said. She put the gearshift in park and quickly shut the engine off, hoping that the act might keep him a moment longer. "What is he, a medical doctor?"

"Doctor of carpentry," Klaus said. "My little joke. Hey, maybe ve are all doctors. The carpenter, the teacher, the inventor. Even you, Amy Morris. Vut are you doctor of?"

She smiled and shook her head. "Nothing. I told you—I'm just like everybody else. Looking for the story."

"But you are not like the others," Klaus said. "You are only one to somehow get me in your guzzler."

"That was just blind luck," she said, smiling. "Serendipity."

"Ha," Klaus said and he opened the door. "I think maybe you are doctor after all. Doctor of bullshit."

Thaddeus St. John had a shop on York Street, which was the old York Pike, a couple of blocks from the town center. He'd rented the building when he arrived in Gettysburg twenty-two years earlier and had, at first, dealt only in battlefield finds and Civil War–related merchandise. He gradually expanded into period furniture and other household items—lamps, crockery, books—and after five years he bought the building. As his fame as a historian grew—his phony diploma from LSU was framed and hanging rather unobtrusively in the corner—so did his business. Presumably, people who were willing to drop hundreds or even thousands of dollars on a pressback rocking chair or a Kentucky long rifle preferred to do business with a man who could be found periodically on public television, holding forth on anything from Ewell's caution to Chamberlain's courage.

Thaddeus was at the shop most days from ten o'clock in the morning until five in the afternoon. The days when he wasn't there—when he was off on a speaking tour or chasing some object across the eastern seaboard—Stonewall Martin would fill in.

Ninety-five percent of Thaddeus's business came from other dealers and bona fide collectors. The remaining 5 percent was generated from tourists—the mom and pop types who wandered into the store with a couple of mouthy, bored kids in tow, at first oohing and ahhing over the displays of muskets, swords, uniforms, and so on before expressing shock over the price tags on everything. Then buying a couple of the cheap Gettysburg T-shirts that Thaddeus imported from Taiwan and sold for a patriotic 150 percent markup.

Thaddeus was not a big fan of tourists. From a historical standpoint, they were usually uninformed or worse, misinformed, and they often arrived eating or drinking something, the residue of which as often as not ended up dripped or smeared or fingerprinted across Thaddeus's merchandise.

The blond woman in the sunglasses who walked into the store this afternoon was not of that particular species, he knew right away, and so he was obliged to reserve judgment on her. She was maybe thirty or thirty-five, attractive but not destined, to Thaddeus's clinical eye, to remain so. She wore jeans and a leather jacket with a navy sweater underneath. An impressive pair of breasts, from what he could see, not that he had ever been particularly intrigued by the female body.

Thaddeus couldn't say how he knew she wasn't a tourist, but he most definitely knew. It was November, for one thing, and the tourist business was slow. Besides, the woman didn't look like a history buff, even of the amateur stripe; in fact, she looked like a woman who'd done her share of partying, probably as recently as last night. Her dyed blond hair hung limply to her shoulders, and her eyes, when she removed the shades, were narrow and rimmed with red. What makeup she wore he was sure was left over from the night before.

And he was guessing she was broke. She had a Piggly Wiggly bag jammed in her jacket pocket, and in that bag, Thaddeus knew from experience, was an item she was hoping would be of interest to him. She wasn't a buyer, this woman. She was here to peddle.

But, typically, she was taking her time, going through the motions.

She said hello when she came in and then took a slow walk around the store, stopping to admire this sword or that flag, glancing at the stemware, then moving along as if she were at a shopping mall and not in the presence of history.

Thaddeus had been looking at himself in the mirror when she arrived. He was wearing a vintage frock coat, which he'd picked up in New York City a month earlier, over black Calvin Klein jeans, with black cowboy boots. He was going for a period look, a fire-and-brimstone prairie preacher, but it was not working. He'd been thinking that he required a hat of some description to carry it off when the woman walked in. He retreated behind the counter, where he went back to his morning paper and his green tea. He watched her patiently, knowing that she was waiting for some sort of opportunity to arise when she could broach the reason for her visit and then, in the likely event of that not happening, just getting to it.

When she stopped for an inordinate amount of time in front of the glass display of handguns, Thaddeus knew what she'd come to sell. Everything else in the room had received only token attention. She gave the pistols and revolvers, though, a thorough going over. And then, finally, she walked over to him, smiling wearily as she approached.

"Are you the owner?"

"I am."

"Good." Her voice was a little ragged, well on its way to acquiring one of those whiskey-soaked cigarette tones that most guys, he'd been told, found sexy.

"What do you have for me, my dear?" he asked then.

She reacted slightly to his knowing manner but then pulled the bag from her jacket and opened it up to produce a small revolver, which Thaddeus immediately took from her, reflecting as he did that his was the only store in town where a stranger could walk in off the street and pull a gun from her pocket and not create panic. Of course, the gun in evidence was unimposing on its own; barely six inches in overall length, it looked like a toy.

"Wherever did you find this, dear?"

"It's been in my family forever," she said. "My mother had it. She died last week, and I found it with her stuff. Do you know anything about it?"

"Of course," Thaddeus said, and he reached under the counter for his copy of *Flayderman's*. "It's an Allen and Wheelock sidehammer twenty-two. Probably made somewhere around 1860, I can tell you in a moment, dear. It was quite a popular carry gun during the conflict between the states."

"The what?"

"The Civil War."

"Oh. So what's a carry gun?"

"A gentleman's sidearm, they'd say," Thaddeus told her. "A man-about-town would carry a weapon such as this for protection, in the event he was set upon by thugs or ne'er-do-wells on an evening out."

"I've met a few of those boys myself," the woman said, and she laughed hoarsely.

"Yes, I'm sure," Thaddeus said. As he spoke, he was leafing through the book with his long delicate fingers. When he stopped, he broke open the cylinder on the gun and checked out the serial number there, then looked back at the book. "Here we are—1858. This is an early model."

"Some guy told me it was just a Saturday night special."

"Where did you encounter this expert?"

She looked for a moment as if she was going to take offense to the question, but then she let it go. "A friend," she said, shrugging.

"It is most definitely not a Saturday night special," Thaddeus said. With the cylinder still open, he held the barrel to the light and had a look inside. Then he gave the cylinder a spin and gently closed it. "These were quality revolvers. You wouldn't have the original grips, by chance?"

"What are grips?"

"The handles, the wood here."

"They're not original?"

Thaddeus ran his polished thumbnail across one grip. "These appear to be pine or some other softwood. The originals would be walnut or possibly rosewood. From where do you hail, my dear?"

"I hail from right here, Gettysburg."

At that Thaddeus perked up. "Indeed? Are there any other . . . items?"

"That's it."

"You sure now? Oftentimes people have bric-a-brac stowed away in the basement or the attic which they assume to be junk. Where did you grow up?"

"Shealer Road. But the house is gone; they tore it down years ago. It was a fucking shack anyway." She laughed again, pointlessly.

"Shealer Road," Thaddeus said.

"Hey, did you hear about the dude that found the pictures of Lincoln?"

"I hadn't heard."

"Well, that was old man Potter's place. He was our neighbor."

"Indeed."

"He was a good old guy. Well, he tried to grab my tits once when he was drunk, but it was just the one time and he gave me ten bucks the next day and said he was sorry. I remember he was good to my mother—I didn't have a father growing up, and we didn't have much money. I think he helped out." She laughed the husky laugh. "Who knows? Maybe he grabbed her tits, too."

"Perhaps he did," Thaddeus said thoughtfully. "What happened to your father?"

"He split when we were kids. He was a fucking piss tank anyway; he never married my mother. I don't even know for sure he was my dad and I don't give a fuck. I've done all right without him."

"May I ask your vocation?"

"What?"

"What do you do, my dear?"

"I'm, like, a hostess. In a club. Or I was anyway. Right now I'm between jobs. That's why I'm selling the gun. Plus, I don't like guns anyway. So—are you interested?"

Thaddeus regarded the revolver in his hand and then laid it softly on the counter. "It's not in the best of shape—very little original finish, in fact—and unfortunately it's missing the grips, so it's not an original piece anyway. It's worth about a hundred dollars."

"Shit—that's it?"

"If I could locate a set of grips, it'd be worth more to me."

She reached out to pick up the gun, and he noticed that her hand shook slightly. He guessed that she hadn't been out of bed more than an hour.

"What's your name?" he asked her then.

"Leona."

"Do you enjoy a libation, Leona?"

She laughed her ragged laugh again and didn't bother to answer.

"I'll give you two hundred dollars for the gun," he said after a moment. "Hoping I'll get lucky and locate some original grips. And to sweeten the deal I'll buy you a chardonnay at the hotel bar across the way. I'm anxious to hear more about your family. I'm regarded as a bit of a history buff in these parts—you might have information which could be of interest to me."

She pushed the gun toward him. "Make it a double Jack and you got yourself a deal."

Amy regrouped back at the hotel, eating take-out pizza in her room while figuring out her next move. Embedded as she was in the atmosphere of the town and the history that lurked at every turn, she felt as if she herself were conducting a military campaign. Her first skirmish, against the eccentric professor, had been entertaining as hell but inconclusive. She did learn one thing from the evasive Hungarian: if she approached this guy Bass in the guise of some on-air TV personality, she was likely to get routed and pretty damn quickly.

So she ditched the TransWorld warm-up jacket, put on jeans and a sweater, pulled her hair into a ponytail, and tucked it beneath her *No Fear* cap with the stitching gone in the bill. She looked at herself in the mirror above the bed and then went into the bathroom and removed her makeup. Looking again, she wavered and then put on eyeliner and a little blush. Even low-rent had its limits.

When she got to the parking lot, she realized at once that the Cayenne was way too much vehicle for the mission. She considered and dismissed the notion of a cab; it would seem too calculated, too urban. She lit a cigarette and leaned against the Porsche as she pondered her dilemma. While she was smoking and pondering, a black Sunfire drove into the lot and parked a couple of spaces over. The car was dirty and there was a diagonal crack across the windshield. After a moment the desk clerk from the previous night got out.

"Hi there," she said. She was wearing low-cut gray pants and a hooded sweatshirt with *Cornell* across the front—obviously not her working duds.

"Hi." Amy dropped her smoke to the ground, stepped on it.

"Nice wheels," the clerk said.

"Thanks. Going to work?"

"No, I'm off. Just here to pick up my check." She smiled. "Which I'm gonna cash and take to the city and spend."

"I can relate to a plan like that," Amy told her. "What city?"

"Baltimore."

"Baltimore," Amy said. "That's quite a drive, isn't it?"

The Sunfire was a stick, and the last time she'd driven a stick had been during her college days when she owned a Volkswagen bug. The car idled roughly, and she stalled it a few times starting out, but then got the hang of it quickly enough. The steering was quirky as well; she had to keep a firm hand on the wheel or risk veering sharply to the left. She had a feeling that the desk clerk—on the road to the factory outlet malls in Baltimore with an extra hundred in her purse—was having no such problems with the Porsche.

Klaus had been right about one thing: she had no trouble finding information on the old Potter place. She got directions from three people downtown—each one in contradiction to the others—as well as an offer from a man in a long gray beard and Confederate army jacket to guide her there for a hundred dollars. Using a compilation of the information gathered, she found the farm in less than ten minutes. After all, it was only two miles out of town or, she reasoned, about fifty bucks a mile from old graybeard.

What she found was an ancient fieldstone house, with the stone crumbling in one corner and the front porch falling off. The house did have a new roof, however, the fresh plywood of which she'd seen from a quarter mile down the road.

She stalled the Sunfire again pulling into the drive and she left it that way, coasting to a stop behind a faded red pickup truck that itself was parked behind a large silver house trailer. When she got out, she could hear nailing from the far side of the house and she walked around toward the sound. There she found a man, wearing a carpenter's apron, standing on the scaffolding and nailing shingles onto the new plywood eave. The man was probably thirty-five or forty years old; his dark brown hair was in need of cutting and it appeared as if he hadn't shaved in some time. He did not look down at her but she was quite certain that he knew she was there.

"Hi," she called up. "I hope I'm not bothering you."

He actually smiled at that. He had several roofing nails in his mouth, and he smiled around the nails—to himself, though, not to her—and he continued to drive the nails into the shingles, a bundle of which was secured on the roof above where he was working.

"I, um . . . I'm sure you've had a lot of visitors lately," she said then. "I mean, it's pretty exciting—the pictures, especially. I'm just visiting from the Washington area, and I had to come and see. Abraham Lincoln is my . . . I don't know . . . my patron saint, you could say. And as far as I'm concerned, the Gettysburg Address is the greatest speech in the history of our country. Are you Dock Bass?"

The man who was obviously Dock Bass took the nails from his mouth and looked down. "Pretty much everything's at the university."

"I understand that," Amy said. "But this house is not at the university. I mean, this is the place. I had to see it."

"Good," the man said. "Mission accomplished." He went back to his nailing.

Amy rolled her eyes and had a look around, took in the dilapidated barn, the overgrown orchard, the cornfield beyond. "Where did you find everything?"

"Inside."

"Could I have a look?"

"Nope."

He went back to his shingling. It took her several moments to realize that the conversation, as least as far as he was concerned, was over.

"Excuse me," she said. She was speaking to his boots and his back.

"Yeah?"

"I'm still standing here."

A second later he began to climb down from the scaffold. She thought for a moment that he was going to physically remove her from the property, but then she noticed that there were no more loose shingles on the roof and he was, presumably, coming down for more.

On the ground he removed his apron and hung it on the ladder. He walked over to her, stopped a couple of feet away. He had dark brown eyes and a scar on the bridge of his nose. There were flecks of gray in his fledgling beard.

"So what are you—a collector or a dealer?" he asked.

"Neither," she said. In that moment, though, she decided she wouldn't lie to him. Not overtly, anyway. That the guy didn't suffer fools gladly might as well have been tattooed on his muscular forearm. One little fib and he might nail *her* to the roof.

"Then what are you?"

"I'm here on vacation. I work for a company called TransWorld Communications, out of Washington. Big media conglomerate— Internet, TV, radio, all that stuff."

"Yeah?" He tilted his head slightly, as if to see her better beneath the brim of her cap.

"Yeah," she said. "You've probably heard of us. Do you . . . um, watch much TV?"

"Hardly ever," he said, and he turned away. "*The Honeymooners* still on?"

She smiled. "You know, I think it got canceled."

She watched as he walked to a skid of shingles at the rear of the house. He hoisted a bundle onto his shoulder and then went back over and climbed up the scaffold. Upon reaching the eave, he flopped the bundle onto the roof, above where he was working, and then tacked a couple of nails in the plywood to prevent it from sliding off. Then he climbed down and repeated the act.

"Can I help?" she asked.

"I doubt it."

She watched as he carried six bundles up to the roof. When he was finished, he was perspiring heavily, in spite of the coolness of the day. He walked toward her again. For the first time in memory she was having trouble thinking of anything to say; she chose to lay the blame for that on his taciturn manner. When he got close, he kept walking, past her and toward the trailer. At the door he stopped, hesitated, then looked back.

"You want something to drink?"

"Yes," she said immediately.

He went into the trailer and came out a moment later with two cans of ginger ale. He handed one to her and then sat down on the open tailgate of the pickup and popped the top on his own can. As he drank, he looked at the roof of the house, as if making some decision or calculation.

"So you're restoring the old place," Amy said.

"I'm trying," he said pointedly.

"Yes. I'm assuming you're attracting a little more attention than you're comfortable with."

"A little more attention than I'm comfortable with," he said, still looking at the roof. "Yeah, that about sums it up."

"Well," she said, and she smiled. "It's pretty remarkable, what you've found. I was watching TV in my room last night and I saw something about some type of recording machine that you discovered."

"A phonautograph."

"Is that what it was? And it has an early recording on it that can actually be played?"

"Yup."

"It was Edison who first recorded sound, right? Was it Edison or Einstein—I always get those two mixed up."

"It was Edison," Dock said and he drank the last of his soda. "Maybe."

"Maybe," Amy repeated. "That's the interesting part. Now this phonaut-whatever has a recording of the Gettysburg Address on it? At least that's what they said on TV. Whose voice is it?"

"Hard to say," Dock said. "Could be Willy Burns."

"Right. The guy who allegedly recorded it. Of course, if you can prove the recording was made before Edison, it doesn't really matter whose voice it is, does it? I mean, it's the recording itself that's important."

"I guess so," Dock said. "But myself, I'd like to know."

"Why?"

He shrugged. "Because I'd like to know if it's Willy."

He said the name as if he was speaking of an old drinking buddy. She waited for him to go on, but instead he got down from the tailgate and walked over to the house. The man wasn't much on elaboration.

"So what're you going to do?" she asked, following him.

"Finish shingling this roof," he said.

"What are you going to do with the recording?"

"Haven't decided," he said. He stopped. "You know, lady, for somebody who came here all excited about the pictures, you haven't asked me a damn thing about them."

"Asking you questions is not a real fruitful experience anyway, Mr. Bass," she said, keeping her voice light. "Besides, I mentioned to you that I'm a Lincoln buff and that I think that the Address is just a beautiful, beautiful speech. It's his greatest achievement. This might sound a little too apple pie for you, but I quite often recite it to myself. You know, when I need a little inspiration?"

He was reaching for his carpenter's apron, and he stopped. There was something about the way he stopped, and the subsequent look on his face, that made her pause. He straightened up, smiling that same noninclusive smile. "You do that?" he asked.

"Why, yes."

"You recite the Gettysburg Address? Out loud?"

"Absolutely."

"I kinda like that," he said. "What do you say we recite it together?"

"Oh, I don't think so," Amy said but as soon as she said it she knew that she was in trouble.

"Come on, it'll be fun," he said. "Four score and seven years ago our fathers brought forth on this continent a new nation, conceived in liberty, and dedicated to the proposition that all men are created equal." He stopped. "Hey, you're not reciting—come on, join in."

"I'd rather not. I'm a little . . . shy."

"You don't seem all that shy. Come on now—just the two of us here," he said, and he began reciting again. "Now we are engaged in a great civil war, testing whether that nation, or any other nation so conceived and so dedicated, can long endure—"

He bent down again to retrieve his apron, put it on as he talked.

"We are met on a great battlefield of that war. We have come to dedicate a portion of that field, as a final resting place for those who here gave their lives that that nation might live. It is altogether fitting and proper that we should do this—"

He turned and went back up the scaffold, continuing the recitation.

"But, in a larger sense, we cannot dedicate, we cannot consecrate, we cannot hallow this ground. The brave men, living and dead, who struggled here, have consecrated it, far and above our poor power to add or detract—"

Amy stood and watched, wishing he would shut up and knowing as well as she'd ever known anything that he wouldn't. She had expected the man to be obstinate; it appeared now that he was unbalanced to boot.

"The world will little note, nor long remember what we say here, but it can never forget what they did here. It is for us the living, rather, to be dedicated here to the unfinished work which they who fought here have thus far so nobly advanced—"

He was back on the scaffold planking now, and he was opening a bundle of shingles.

"It is rather for us to be here dedicated to the great task remaining before us—that from these honored dead we take increased devotion to that cause for which they gave the last full measure of devotion—that we here highly resolve that these dead shall not have died in vain—"

He slid a shingle into place.

"That this nation, under God, shall have a new birth of freedom— and that government of the *people*—"

He hammered home a nail.

"By the *people*."

Another nail.

"For the *people*."

And a third.

"Shall not perish from the earth."

He hammered in one more nail, and then he looked down. "It *was* the Gettysburg Address that you said you liked to recite, wasn't it? Or was it 'Casey at the Bat'?"

"You're quite an entertaining man, Mr. Bass." She was seething.

"Speaking of 'Casey at the Bat,'" he said then. "You should keep your right elbow up."

"What?"

"When you were in the batting cage during the World Series, you kept popping the ball up because your right elbow was too low. Put a big hitch in your swing."

"Right," she said, looking at him, wondering if at this point her best move would be to depart the field. "I thought you said you never watched television."

"I didn't say never. Of course I watch the Series."

He went back to work. From her vantage point on the ground she couldn't say that he was actually smiling, but he sure as hell wasn't frowning, either. She still held the soda in her hand; it wasn't diet and she had no intention of drinking it.

"So you've basically spent the last ten minutes making a fool of me," she said, looking up at him.

"Oh—I wouldn't say you needed any help in that department," he said. He took a shingle knife from his apron and cut open another bundle. "You know you could've just shown up here, told me your name and what you wanted."

"And you would have advised me to take a hike."

"I did that anyway," he said. "I see you're still here."

He took a shingle from the bundle, aligned it into position, and nailed it. Then he reached for another. She held herself in check; she knew that if she were to fly off the handle she would only succeed in pissing him off and she was pretty certain that Dock Bass pissed off would be even less cooperative than he was now. For the time being, he seemed merely amused by her. Of course, that realization only made her angrier.

"Listen," she suggested, her tone as conciliatory as she could manage. "Why don't we start over? I'm Amy Morris, and I'm here for TransWorld Communications. I'd like to ask you a few questions."

The son of a bitch smiled again. Mouth full of nails, smiling, laying his shingles, not even bothering to look down. "So that's your method?" he said around the nails. "Start out lying—if that doesn't work, try the truth?"

"I didn't lie, Mr. Bass. I told you I worked for TransWorld."

"You lied by omission."

She told herself to count to ten. She got to five and then said slowly and deliberately, "Okay—I apologize for misrepresenting myself earlier, and I promise that the next time I come I'll provide you with a full résumé upon my arrival."

"Whoa, Nelly. The next time you come? What makes you think there's gonna be a next time?"

"The fact that you're not telling me anything this time."

He slid another shingle into place as he considered this. On the ground, Amy allowed herself an inner smile; she felt as if she'd actually landed a punch on the elusive bastard. He drove four nails into the shingle and then turned and sat down on the scaffold plank.

"What do you want to know?" he asked in resignation.

"Well, it would be nice if you could climb down and talk."

"You think I'm gonna give you different answers down there than up here?"

She sighed. "At this point, I'm not expecting much either way," she said. "All right, let's start with this. What are your feelings in general about being the man responsible for these significant discoveries?"

To her surprise, he took a few moments to think it over, then he said, "Privileged, curious, bothered, harassed."

"Could you elaborate on that?"

"Which one didn't you understand?"

"Oy," she said under her breath. "I'm just trying to discern whether or not you have a sense of the historical import of what you have here. You seem to be a genuine, down-to-earth, normal guy. And I'm wondering if that makes you more appreciative, say, than somebody who looks only at the dollar value of things."

"Somebody like you?"

"I didn't say that," she snapped. "And you have no right to because you don't know anything about me."

"I know you're a liar and you can't hit a seventy-mile-an-hour, batting-practice fastball."

Being called a liar didn't improve her temperament any. She found herself counting again. "You seem to be obsessing on this batting-practice thing, Mr. Bass. Maybe the network should have sent Derek Jeter to talk to you."

"Maybe by now old Derek would have told me why he was here."

"You know why I'm here."

"Bullshit," Dock said. "You want me to believe that you're here to do a story for TransWorld? You show up without a camera crew, claiming to be somebody you're not, driving a car you probably got from Rent-a-Wreck down in Baltimore, asking dumb questions about how I feel to be the guy who found this stuff. I'm supposed to buy that?"

"It's what's called a *pre*-interview," she told him.

"And they got you doing it?" He showed her the goddamn smile again. "I don't think so, lady. They'd send some flunky to talk to me. Not you—you're too big a fish for this little pond. I figured that out all by myself and I'm no Einstein. Or is it Edison? I always get those two mixed up."

"That's very good, Mr. Bass," she said. "You're a cruel man, you know that?"

"And a couple days ago, I was an asshole," he told her. "Seems like I got a lot of people showing up here uninvited, telling me what they think of me. So I'll tell you something—either I'm gonna go back to shingling this roof, or you're gonna tell me what you're doing here. And just so you know—my preference is the roof. The only interest I have in why you're here is that the knowledge might lead to you *not* being here."

She reminded herself that she was a professional—at this point, it appeared to be her last refuge—and summoned composure enough for one final try. "I'm here, quite simply, because the country at large is interested in what you've found and by the nature and the historical significance of your findings I think they have a right to know the particulars of the discovery."

"If a woman like you is representative of the country at large, then God help us all," Dock said.

"You can go fuck yourself." The words were out of her mouth before she could stop them.

"Congratulations," Dock said. He stood up to go back to work and he flashed her a parting smile. "That's the first sincere thing you've said since you got here. There might be hope for you yet, lady."

TEN

"The man is a total asshole," she said into the phone.

"Why do you say that?"

"He called me a liar."

"And did you lie to him?" Sam asked.

She hesitated. "Maybe—technically."

"He sounds like my kind of guy. What's he going to do with the phonautograph?"

"I don't know."

"He wouldn't say?"

"I never really asked him," Amy said. She was in her hotel room, pacing back and forth, smoking a cigarette.

"And why not?"

"Sam, you're not getting a picture of the man. I might as well have driven out there and interviewed his pickup truck. He was a lot more interested in shingling his goddamn roof than talking to me."

"Your vaunted charm didn't work?"

She exhaled and looked at herself in the mirror. "My vaunted charm was not much in evidence."

"Maybe he's gay."

"He's not gay. He's a fucking nut. He recited the Gettysburg Address to me, Sam. The whole thing."

"Why would he do that?"

"I have no idea," she said quickly. "I guess he was showing off."

"Playing Tom Sawyer to your Becky Thatcher? I'd say the man was smitten with you."

"He was a lot of things. Smitten wasn't one of them."

"What's your next move?"

"Aruba?"

"I don't think so, kid. I want that phonautograph."

Thaddeus, dressed in corduroy trousers, leather bomber jacket with a fleece collar, and an Irish tweed cap, took an early afternoon drive down to Washington. He drove a yellow 1960 Mercedes SL roadster, which he had acquired several years earlier from an estate sale he'd been consigned to handle in Johnstown. The convertible never actually went under the auctioneer's hammer, as Thaddeus had managed to convince the owner to sell it to him, in advance, after spotting a pool of oil beneath the car's engine. Thaddeus had cautioned the owner against selling the car to a stranger in auction, someone who might come back at him if the engine proved to be defective. The owner assented and Thaddeus ended up getting the car for fifty cents on the dollar. Stonewall, at that point on his way back to Gettysburg with the empty oil can stashed beneath the seat, got a steak dinner for his part in the transaction.

The day was cool and Thaddeus drove with the top up and the heater on, and he wore his racing gloves and his scarf. On the thruway he kept to the right lane, held the little roadster at an even fifty-five for the drive. It took him two and a half hours to reach Georgetown.

Helen Middlefield lived in a seniors' condominium complex not far from the river. The buildings were maybe twenty years old yet so meticulously maintained they appeared to be brand-new. There were flower beds all around, although the blooms were shriveled with the season, and a man-made stream running through a small park at the confluence of the buildings. In the stream were dozens of fat golden carp the size of footballs.

Thaddeus parked in the lot and announced himself in the intercom at the gate. Helen's voice possessed the cracked tremolo one might expect from a ninety-year-old; she told him to come right up.

"Oh, Mr. Stevens," she said as she let him in. "How nice. I was so happy when you called."

Thaddeus had the vase, wrapped in crepe paper, tucked into his jacket and he produced it with a flourish. Helen gasped when he unwrapped it and handed it to her, holding it at arm's length like it was a bomb about to explode.

"I picked it up in Philadelphia," he told her. "But it originally came from Kent. Circa 1775 if my sources are correct."

The vase was about twelve inches high and the glass was rose-tinted. Cut into the sides were flowers with narrow leaves entwined at the stems. Helen held it to the living room bay window, turned it so the daylight shot through the cut glass like a prism.

"Oh, Mr. Stevens—it's beautiful."

Thaddeus took off his coat and hung it on a hall tree inside the door. Helen carried the vase to a glass-front cabinet across the room, placed it on top, then stood back to look. The cabinet itself was filled with glassware of the same period; a good many of the pieces were gifts from Thaddeus.

"I don't know," Helen said of the vase's perch. "I'll have to think about it."

She had tea ready, and they sat in the living room and chatted. Thaddeus asked about her son, who was retired and golfing twelve months of the year in Florida, and her daughter, who was a pharmacist in Hawaii.

"And how are things in New York, Mr. Stevens? I don't know how you can live in such a busy city."

"Been very steady. But a writer's life is full of ups and downs. The ebb and flow can be maddening at times, but I do love it." He sipped his tea. "On the subject of creative composition—did you get a chance to finish the piece on Mary Chesnut?"

"Oh, I did. Just a minute."

Thaddeus poured more tea as she went into the next room. She returned with a loose-leaf binder.

"Such an interesting woman. Of course, I remembered her from when I worked at the Smithsonian, but I had no idea of how prolific she was until I started the research. Did you know she married at seventeen? Of course, that was not at all unusual for the times. Here it is—it's about three thousand words—I hope it's suitable for our little collection."

Thaddeus gave the piece the quickest of looks. "I'm sure it's fine. Any editing it might require, I can do."

"Any news from your editor on when they might publish?"

"Well, they're still culling the pieces. It's a tricky endeavor, a book like this. Everything has to dovetail just so. They'll know when it's ready. And then—you'll know. I daresay some champagne will be the order of the day. My treat."

He stayed for twenty minutes longer, drinking the tea and talking about dogwoods and vases and Mary Todd Lincoln. Leaving, he stood by the door and looked at the vase across the room. "That's the place," he said. "Absolutely. It seizes the eye upon entering."

"You know, I think you're right."

"I was wondering, Helen. Do you know anything of Nathan Bedford Forrest—his life before the conflict? Might make for an interesting sidebar."

"I know a little. And I can certainly find out the rest."

He puttered back to Gettysburg in the Mercedes. When he arrived home, Carl was gone, as usual. Thaddeus sat by the French doors and read the Chesnut piece. It was, of course, beautifully written and meticulously researched. He would be proud to claim it as his own. He would add a typical flowery fore piece, rearrange a paragraph or two, then attach his name and submit it. He hadn't decided where as yet, but *Atlantic Monthly* was a possibility. Mary Chesnut was a woman of irony and wit—she just might be a perfect fit.

"Irony and wit, a perfect fit," Thaddeus said out loud, giggling a little as he sat down at his desk to personalize the piece. As the computer booted up, he took a moment to reflect upon the lonely existence of the writer in society.

He shingled the rest of the day and was interrupted only twice—once by a pair of elderly brothers from Nebraska who were quite sure that they were descendants of Abraham Lincoln, although they spelled their surname Lincon, and once by a pimply faced kid from Harrisburg who wanted to set up a Dock Bass Web site, which would offer, for a price, a virtual tour of the farmhouse and the artifacts.

"We can split the profits sixty-forty, right down the middle," he'd promised.

Dock was back at it the next morning. It began to rain shortly before noon and he was forced inside. He ate lunch in the old house and read the diary as he did. He was now up to April 1860.

> *Today was the first warm day of spring. Silas Trostle asked of me some time ago to make some plates of him and his family so I loded the cart behind Bess and went over ther after breakfast. Maddy cumb along with me.*

Dock read the last line twice. It appeared that young Maddy's appearance had become much more acceptable since he'd last read about her.

> *The Trostle farm is south of town and it sits below Little Round Top. We had the misfortun of an incounter with Josh Burrel on the way. He still smarts that I woudn't sell him Bess and I know he is sweet on Maddy besides. He tried to make a joke and said he wanted to offer on Bess agin. When I asked after it, he alowed that his offer was a kick in the arse with a frozen boot. I do not tolerat langwage like that, in particlar where a lady is envolved. I socked Josh sqware on the nose and nokked him over a snake rail fence. I then put him in a headlock til he cryed uncle*

*and I informed him if he wished to repeat the ofence that I woud
give him more of the same.*

Outside the rain continued. Dock read for a while longer; then he
put the diary away and spent the next couple of hours nailing in fur-
ring along the top of the exterior walls. He was just finishing up when
he heard a knock. He turned from where he was perched on the ceiling
joists to see Klaus enter through the side door. The professor was wearing his parka and a hat with ear flaps. He was carrying a large print under his arm.

"Doctor!" he shouted, not spotting Dock in his elevated location.

"Klaus!" Dock shouted back.

"There you are. Vy do you shout?"

"I don't know what got into me." Dock shifted around to sit on a
ceiling joist, his legs dangling down.

"Look vut I have for you," Klaus said and he turned the print
around. It was a framed shot of Lincoln, taken from one of the collodion plates. In the shot, the great man's eyes were cast downward, his
brow furrowed.

"That's nice, Klaus," Dock said. "You didn't have to do that."

"Is little housevarming gift." Klaus leaned the print against the
sawhorses and rubbed his hands together. "This house could use some
varming, I think."

Dock was down to his shirtsleeves. "Don't they have winter in
Hungary?"

"Yah, cold vinter. That's why I come here, thinking it is varmer.
Maybe I should have gone to Mexico, study Santa Anna instead of
him." He indicated the print. "But old rail-splitter looks good, no?"

"He looks good. A little worried though."

"Is November '63. He has reason to vorry."

Outside, a car door slammed, then another.

"I swear, this place is like a Wal-Mart," Dock said. "Who is it?"

Klaus walked to the window and looked outside. "Is African-
Americans in baggy clothes," he said.

"What're you talking about?"

"You don't understand English?"

"I'll let you know when I hear some."

Someone pounded on the door. Klaus walked over to open it and two African-Americans in baggy clothes entered. Through the open door, Dock could see a stretch limousine in the drive, the motor running.

"Yah?" Klaus asked.

"Whaddup, dog?" the first man asked.

Klaus turned and looked up at Dock. "They are looking for Doug."

That little misunderstanding was cleared up by the time Dock climbed down. The man doing the explaining was thin and he wore a bandanna on his head and a wispy goatee on his chin. He introduced himself as Five Star, and he was a talker. The other man was large, with a bodybuilder's physique and a gold incisor. He wore a Malcom X ball cap, backward. Five Star shook Dock's hand. The second man, whose name was Steel, did not.

"Lookit this fuckin' crib," Five Star said, looking around. "Y'all got a whole Bob Villa trip happenin' here. This where you find all the Lincoln shit?"

"This is it," Dock said.

"Right on," Five Star said. "You a renovatin' motherfucker, dog. Word up—you know a brother called J'Makir Slim?"

"And the Word," Dock said.

Five Star was impressed. "That's the man. You a hip motherfucker too, you know that?"

"I'm pretty much as cool as it gets," Dock said. He nodded toward Klaus. "Him, too."

Five Star looked at Klaus, eyebrows arched. "I buy that. Listen, dog, we here to represent brother Slim. Lookin' to score, understand?"

"Looking to score what?"

"The motherfucking Lincoln recording, what you think? The phone-*not*-ograph. What kind of cash you gotta have for that thing?"

"Where is brother Slim?"

"He in the limo."

"What's he got—iron-poor blood?"

"Me and Steel takin' care of business, that's the way it work," Five Star said. "Slim don't do the transaction thing, you dig?"

"Me neither," Dock said. "It's not for sale."

"Everything's for sale, bitch," Steel said. He was staring at Dock, his eyes flashing chemical menace.

"Shut your fuckin' mouth," Five Star told him. "Me and the man negotiatin' here."

"You don't tell me to shut up, nigger," Steel said.

"Yikes," Klaus said.

"Listen, Slim want that recording machine," Five Star said then, turning back to Dock. "Y'all got to understand, Abraham Lincoln was the brothers' president. Man set all us motherfuckers free back in 1861, you dig? Anybody should have that machine, should be a brother. And Slim will pay the price, don't you worry on that end. He got the Franklins. Brother moved fifteen million units last year alone."

"But you are wrong," Klaus said.

"What the fuck you say, Grandpa?" Steel asked.

"Vas not 1861. It vas 1863 Mr. Lincoln set you all motherfuckers free," Klaus said. "Emancipation Proclamation, January 1863. Also I think you are mistaken about me being your grandfather. I have no children."

"Motherfucker, you ain't even from this country," Steel said.

"You sure about that whole emancipation gig?" Five Star asked. "Because I been readin' on this shit. Right now I'm into this mother-fucker Shelby Foote—I'm talking Fort Sumter right on through to Per-ryville, man."

"Quite sure," Klaus said. "I am reading on it also. You come to the university, I show you copy."

"I'm gonna take you up on that," Five Star said, then turned back to Dock. "What you say, dog? You know you gonna sell that machine to somebody. Don't tell me you don't wanna sell it to a brother."

"I don't know what I'm gonna do with it," Dock said. "Nothing—for the time being. But I'll tell you what—I decide to sell it, then I'll give brother Slim a shot at it."

"This bitch is lying," Steel said.

Dock walked over to the corner and picked up an iron wrecking bar. He hefted it for a moment, and then he approached the man named Steel.

"I don't think Klaus appreciated you calling him Grandpa," he said, and he glanced at Five Star. "And I can't imagine that this man likes being called nigger. But I can't speak for either of them. I'll tell you what, though—you call me bitch once more, and I'm gonna use this bar to remove that gold tooth, and I suspect a few of its neighbors to boot. Now, is there anything else you'd like to say to me . . . Steel?"

Steel's eyes narrowed to a squint, but in the end he opted for continued dental health. Dock glanced at Klaus—whose eyes, in contrast to Steel's, were as wide as saucers.

"This motherfucker is fly," Five Star said, smiling. He took a felt pen from his pocket. "Tell you what—I'm gonna give you my cell. We staying at the Hampton, suite 403. You wanna deal that fucking machine, you give me a call. Brother Slim will beat anybody's price." He wrote the number on a length of two-by-six on the sawhorses.

"Fair enough," Dock said. He was still watching Steel warily. The man was as big as a building and Dock wasn't at all sure he had enough wrecking bar to handle him.

"All right, we outa here," Five Star said to the big man. He looked at Klaus. "What about you, dog? We goin' to the university? I wanna check out the thing—the proclamation thing."

"Yah," Klaus said. "Ve go—all us dogs."

"Peace out," Five Star said to Dock.

Dock walked outside and watched them leave. Five Star regarded Klaus's Volvo doubtfully, but he climbed in. Steel, casting a final amphetamined eye toward Dock, disappeared into the stretch limo, wherein, Dock assumed, J'Makir Slim was deeply bunkered among his units and his Franklins and his newfound appreciation of American history.

When they were gone, Dock walked back inside and began to pick up his tools and put them away. Before he was finished, the next interloper was standing in the doorway.

This one was young, maybe twenty-five, and he wore a leather coat and chinos. His hair was gelled and frosted at the tips. He had at least as much energy as Five Star, but Dock sensed at once that it was not an energy borne of reading that motherfucker Shelby Foote. It was coming from another place altogether, and it was coming fast.

"Are you Dock Bass?" he asked at once. "Tell me you're Dock Bass."

Dock, coiling an extension cord up, tried closing his eyes, thinking it might cause the man to disappear. The trick didn't work for five-year-olds and it didn't work for Dock either.

"I'm Dock Bass."

"John Paul Thompson," the man said, charging across the room, his hand outstretched, the palm turned down. "Just in from New York."

"What can I do for you?" Dock said, returning the hand to the traditional position as he shook it. The man smelled, improbably, of sagebrush.

"Just turn that around," Thompson exclaimed and with the fore-fingers of both hands he demonstrated a turnaround, presumably for the hearing impaired. "It's what I can do for you. Do you have representation yet? Tell me you don't have representation yet."

"I don't have representation yet," Dock said, wondering what representation he might need.

"Great," Thompson said. "What's the date? We should write this date down. We're both gonna remember it."

"I'll remember it in my head and write it down later," Dock said. "Why are you here?"

"I'm here because I want to be your agent."

"Did the Orioles draft me? Because otherwise, I don't think I need an agent."

"You need an agent. Trust me, my friend. The big boys are gonna come calling. Has Sotheby's contacted you yet? Tell me that Sotheby's has not contacted you yet."

"Sotheby's has not contacted me yet," Dock said. "What kind of agent are you?"

"I'm an all-purpose agent, I'm an uber-agent, I'm all the agent you're ever gonna need." Thompson pulled a business card from his pocket. "I'm half of Levine-Thompson, and we are not just the future, my friend. We're the day after the future. And for what you have here"—he stepped back and held his hands out in an all-encompassing gesture—"let's just say we're ideally suited to handle something of this scope."

"I'm not really looking for anybody to handle my scope."

"Listen! We sat down to dinner last night and talked about this. That's right—we had a Dock Bass dinner—*you* were the entrée, my friend. Now the thing to remember here: this is Abraham Lincoln. Nobody else is gonna generate this kind of interest—not Washington, not Jefferson, not even JFK. This is the guy—I mean, the whole idea of the Civil War is sexy—half the country considers itself an expert on that war. Then you have the Gettysburg Address, the battle, the pictures, the whole package. It's Lincoln, man. He's the greatest president. I suppose you could argue that his little experiment didn't exactly pan out, but what the hell? The point is, it's Honest Abe."

"I don't think I need anybody," Dock said slowly, trying to decide what he had just heard.

"That's where you're wrong," Thompson said. "If you wait till you think you need somebody like me, then it's too late for somebody like me to help you. This business is all about anticipating. Everybody on the planet knows what's hot this week; it's my job to know what's gonna be hot next week."

But Dock was still on the previous statement. "What experiment?"

Thompson threw up his palms, like a man being held at gunpoint. "Hey, we had to do away with slavery; that's a given. It was a black mark on the game, no pun intended. I'm just saying they haven't really held up their end. I mean—you can't say they're the most motivated people you've ever seen. I know—you can argue that some of the athletes are pretty remarkable, and I'm proud to say that I represent a number—but hey, we're way off topic here. First thing you need is a plan. Tell me you don't have a plan."

"I don't have a plan," Dock said. "But I feel one coming on."

"We have a plan for you," Thompson said. "We can take the worry out of your life."

"Tell you what," Dock said. "I'm gonna keep the worry in my life, at least for the time being. But you know, I might have something for you. There's a musician in town who's expressed interest in my . . . collection. Maybe I should get you to talk to him."

"A freaking musician . . . has he got any money?"

"You know I think he does. He's a singer-songwriter, and I take it he's quite successful. His name is Slim."

"What is he—country-and-western? No wonder I never heard of him."

"I believe he is a little bit country. Anyway, he's expressed interest. Why don't you feel him out?"

"Well, you and I will have to get something on paper first."

"No," Dock said. "Let's consider this a test—I want to see how you operate. I need to know if you can think on your feet. Are you up to this? Tell me you're up to this."

"I'm up to it. Just tell me where to find this bumpkin."

"The Hampton. Suite 403."

"And it's Slim? Slim who?"

"I guarantee you he'll be the only Slim there."

"Okay, man. You wanna see my moves? Stand back. You're gonna like this."

"I got a feeling I am," Dock said.

When Thompson was gone, Dock plugged the phone in and dialed Five Star's number. He answered on the third ring.

"Yo."

"It's Dock Bass. Where are you?"

"I'm in the Lair, homes. Five Star in the Lair. Man was right about that whole Emancipation gig. You won't believe the Lincoln shit the Klaus dog got. You been here?"

"I've been there."

"Shit," Five Star said. "Professor Klaus, he a cool motherfucker."

"That's pretty much his reputation," Dock said. "Listen, there's a guy in town named Thompson, pretending to represent me. I don't know what he's on, but I hear he's headed down to the hotel to see your boss. Somebody better warn the Slim dog."

"What's this motherfucker—a scammer?"

"Looks that way. And there's something else: I think he's a bit of a racist."

"What you say?"

"You heard me. The guy's got a problem."

"He got nothing, compared to what he gonna have."

"And he's *not* representing me," Dock said. "You got it?"

"Oh, I got it."

Dock hung up the phone and unplugged it. He went into the trailer and opened a beer and sat back. He was looking forward to some peace and quiet.

Not that he thought for a moment that either was on its way.

They were drinking in the Cashtown Tavern, on a rainy November night, listening to a bad country-and-western band and waiting for Tommy Trotter. They had been there for a couple of hours. They'd had chicken wings and garlic bread and a pitcher of beer, and now they were back into the bourbon as they waited.

Stonewall had spent the last three days with the blond woman. They'd gotten drunk at the hotel bar on Tuesday night, after Thaddeus had called him and invited him to join them. Thaddeus had left them after a couple of chardonnays—the little man's limit—and then Stonewall and Leona had carried on until two in the morning, when he'd dropped her off at the West Street apartment she said was her mother's.

The next day he picked her up, and they bought a six-pack of Miller and then drove out to Shealer Road, to the site where her childhood home once stood. Once there, they got out and took a walk around the property. All that was left of the house were a few crumbling concrete blocks from the foundation and some rusted plumbing pipes. Fifty or sixty feet behind the foundation was a gray and tilting outhouse and a woodshed that was completely collapsed, lying on the ground like a flattened house of cards.

"I remember carrying wood in the winter," Leona told him. "Traipsing back and forth in the snow. Sometimes we'd run out and we'd have to burn the furniture. I don't remember this, but my mama used to tell us how my father chopped up an old piano once and burned it in the woodstove."

"The guy who *might* have been your father," Stonewall said, and he smiled as she gave him a puzzled look.

There was a stone cistern between the woodshed and the house, with a broken pump still clinging to the rotted boards of its lid. Stonewall walked over and lifted the pump off, the screws pulling easily through the decayed wood, gave it a glance of appraisal, and then tossed it aside. He removed the boards from the top and had a look down into the well.

"Who owns the property now?" he asked, his voice echoing down the shaft.

"I got no idea," she said. "Mama sold it, long time ago. The guy that bought it tore the house down and then I think he mighta sold it to somebody else. But I haven't been around here in years, I told you that. Why?"

"I might want to have a look in this well."

"You gonna make a wish?"

He straightened up. She was smiling, taking a drink of beer. "I've found some real interesting things at the bottom of a well. People had a habit of dropping stuff down there—accidentally and on purpose. I found a calvary sword once, turned out it had belonged to one of Jeb Stuart's troop—man had his name etched in the hilt. What do you think I got for it?"

She opened another beer—her third. "A thousand dollars," she said.

"Fuck," he said. "Try twenty-eight thousand. Oilman from Texas, claimed to be some kin to the original owner."

"Wow," she said. "How come I only got two hundred for my gun?"

"Because it had no connection to anybody. You need provenance. If you could prove that Ulysses S. Grant had it in his pocket at Appomattox Courthouse, then you'd be a rich woman."

"Hey, did I mention that Ulysses S. Grant had that gun in his pocket at Appaloosa Courthouse?"

"Nice try."

On the drive back into town they stopped in front of the old Potter place. Stonewall looked at the house trailer, parked behind the pickup.

"Son of a bitch, he's living out here now."

The sound of someone nailing could be heard from the far side of the house.

"We used to play in the old barn there," Leona said. "The mow was full of loose hay and we had tunnels dug everywhere. I got my first kiss in that barn."

"Yeah? What else you get?"

"That was it. I was just a kid."

Stonewall shut the engine off and sat there looking at the house. "Your mother used to come visit the old guy, you say?"

"Every once in a while they'd get drunk together, on dago red wine. Me and my sister would have to fetch Mama at suppertime—I can remember the three of us walking down this road. We'd be holding Mama up; she'd be swaying back and forth, singing Patsy Cline." She began to sing. "*I fall to pieces—*"

"All right, I get it," Stonewall said. With her hangover, it seemed that she was loaded on three beers—a sure sign of a juicer. "Was your father gone by then?"

"Yeah, he was gone. What did my mother used to say? 'He was no good when he was gone, and no damn good when he wasn't.'" She smiled at Stonewall. "God, these are going down smooth today—hand me another one, will you?"

"Shoulda bought a case," Stonewall said, but he was smiling when he said it.

Now they were drinking Jack Daniel's in the Cashtown Tavern and waiting for Trotter to arrive. Leona had been drunk for several hours, but she never seemed to get any drunker, in spite of the bourbon she put away. She was wearing the low-cut tight blue jeans preferred by the kids and a white V-neck sweater revealing her impressive cleavage. Fortunately, she had the body to pull the outfit off.

"My man Trotter is a pretty cautious guy," he said to her now.

"What does that mean?"

"He's a fucking wimp, you wanna know the plain truth. I gotta handle him a little."

"Maybe I'll have to handle him a little." She laughed.

She was pretty when she laughed, and, in fact, she was pretty when she didn't. And she was easy to be with. Even the mornings when she was hung over—and that had been every morning in the brief time he'd known her—Stonewall had never seen her in a foul mood. Of course, the proposition they would put to Trotter would improve anybody's outlook on life.

Stonewall had been trying to get her into bed all week, but she'd turned him down, although gently. She indicated, without saying as much, that she was an old-fashioned girl. He was thinking that tonight might be the night, though, depending on how things went. He'd even showered that morning; as a rule, he only took a shower once, maybe twice a month. He was aware that there was an odor to him, but it was a smell he liked. Plus, he considered it part of his wild and woolly image.

He hadn't enjoyed a lot of success with women in his life. Most of his conquests had been of professional girls and it was hard to consider it much of a victory when the sex was preceded by an exchange of cash. His longest relationship had been with Roseanne; they had lived together for six months in an apartment in Carlisle, back when he worked for the Chrysler dealership there, cleaning trade-ins. He'd come home after work one day to find her stoned on grass and necking with the kid who lived across the hall with his mother. In a rage, Stonewall had broken the kid's nose and Roseanne's cheekbone. The judge had given him a two-hundred-dollar fine for the nose and six months in jail for the cheekbone—just his luck to get a magistrate who held the concept of chivalry above that of the equality of the sexes.

The incarceration turned out to be the best thing that could have happened to him. Inside, he met a guy named Platts, who, when he wasn't selling speed on the outside, was a Civil War reenactor. Platts turned Stonewall, who was still Jim Martin at the time, on to the whole subculture of historical interpretation, and when Jim got out, he adopted his new name and immersed himself for several months in the game. He didn't have the discipline to stick it out, though—the hard-core reenactors lived an existence that would have killed him—but he dabbled in the field long enough to meet Thaddeus St. John at a memorabilia auction. Thaddeus had been taken by Stonewall's appearance and eventually hired him. They had been in business together for almost ten years. The partnership was incredibly successful, even though the two men contradicted each other in every way: appearance, vocabulary, education (Thaddeus's bogus degree from LSU notwithstanding). In truth, the only thing they had in common was that each knew the other to be an absolute phony.

Trotter came through the front door at exactly nine o'clock, looking like a man who was uncomfortable in strange drinking establishments, particularly a shit-kicker joint like this. Stonewall watched the little lawyer for a moment as he stood inside the door, as if waiting for the fucking maître-d'. After a moment Stonewall yelled over to him.

"I didn't see you there," Trotter said when he arrived at their table. He looked at Leona. "Where's Thaddeus?"

"This is Leona Anderson," Stonewall said as Leona smiled lazily around the cigarette she was lighting. "This is the noted Gettysburg attorney, Thomas Trotter."

"What're you noted for, Tom?" she asked.

Trotter gave her a look and then he sat. "I understood I was meeting Thaddeus."

"You think he's under the fucking table?" Stonewall asked. "Thaddeus got called out of town. Talking to some pointy-heads in Washington tonight."

"Nice to meet you, Mr. Trotter," Leona tried again, and this time Trotter nodded to her quickly. The waitress approached and he ordered a light beer.

"You guys all right?" the waitress asked the other two.

"We will be, long as you keep 'em coming," Stonewall said.

Trotter sat silently until he had his beer, and then he said, "So what's going on?"

"Got a couple things I need to talk to you about," Stonewall told him. "Leona here grew up on a farm out on Shealer Road."

"Oh, really?" Trotter said. It was all he could do to feign interest, Stonewall thought.

"Yeah. It's the place just east of the old Potter farm," Stonewall said.

"Okay, I know the farm. The house is gone."

"That's the one," Stonewall said. "Who owns it?"

"Orson and that bunch," Trotter said. "They're hoping to rezone it. They will rezone it, eventually. Why?"

"There's an old stone well on the property," Stonewall said. "I'd like to pump it out and have a look."

Trotter shrugged. "Shouldn't be a problem," he said. "The same arrangement as always: they'll expect a percentage if you find anything worthwhile. I'll call Orson tomorrow."

"Good," Stonewall said. He leaned back in his chair, his bourbon glass in his large fist, his expression suggesting that his business was done. He began to smooth his beard like he was petting a cat.

"That's it?" Trotter asked. "Don't tell me you had me drive out here for that."

Stonewall continued to stroke his whiskers and he looked at Leona and smiled. "There was something else," he said absently. "Now what the hell was it? Oh, I know—did I mention that Leona here is the biological daughter of old Ambrose Potter?"

That got Trotter's attention. It took him a half minute to reply. Stonewall passed the silence imagining the scenarios that were running through the lawyer's large head. Leona lit another cigarette and held on to her dreamy smile.

"I wasn't aware that Potter had a daughter," Trotter said at last.

"There she sits," Stonewall said. "And I thought you should know. After all, you handled the old man's estate."

"There was no mention of a daughter."

"I just mentioned it." Stonewall leaned forward and reached for a fresh bourbon.

"Is there any proof?" Trotter asked. "Is he listed on the birth registration?"

"Of course not," Stonewall said. "She's a bastard—these things were kept on the hush-hush in those days."

"Who you calling a bastard?" she asked.

"You, sweetheart."

Trotter picked up his beer and then set it down again without drinking. "Well, it's obvious where you're going with this."

Stonewall laughed. "It is—isn't it?"

"However," Trotter said, "you can't just jump up out of the blue and claim that the old fellow was this woman's father. Especially in light of what's been discovered on the property. Otherwise, everybody and his brother would be doing it. A claim has got to be based on something."

"Tell him the Christmas story," Stonewall instructed Leona.

"What?" she asked.

"The Christmas story," he repeated.

"Oh yeah," she said. "Well, every Christmas, old man Potter would get me a present, but just me—not my brothers and sisters. There were five of us. And I guess I just figured I was his favorite. But then one year"—she hesitated and glanced at Stonewall—"when I was fourteen, I remember he gave me a Barbie doll, and I was pissed 'cause I was too old for Barbie dolls. I really wanted a stereo. Anyway, it was Christmas night—not Christmas Eve, Christmas night—and Mama got real drunk after dinner. She was always real emotional at Christmastime anyway. And she gave me a couple glasses of wine, first time she ever did that, and then she told me. Old Ambrose was my daddy."

"Did he ever confirm that to you?" Trotter asked.

"He used to call me his little girl," Leona said.

"I wouldn't call that a confirmation."

"Would you call it a denial?" Stonewall asked. "What was in the old man's will?"

"Ambrose Potter never had a will," Trotter said. "That's why the farm went to the sister Winifred—she was next of kin."

"Maybe she was," Stonewall said, and he took a drink. "And maybe she wasn't."

"If Ambrose knew he had a daughter, then why didn't he make arrangements for her?" Trotter asked. "He bought her Christmas presents; why didn't he provide for her?"

"Same reason he didn't leave a will," Stonewall said. "He figured he wasn't worth anything. Old knock-down house and an overgrown orchard. If he'd of known what that dickwad Bass was gonna turn up, I suspect he'd have handled things different."

Stonewall watched as Trotter took a sip of beer. Stonewall knew that the attorney didn't like beer, but when he ordered his preference—white wine—Stonewall would mock him without mercy.

"And what that dickwad—as you call him—has turned up is worth, what? Several hundred thousand dollars?" Trotter asked.

"I'd say that's a very conservative estimate," Stonewall said.

Trotter looked at Leona. "And you would like me to handle your claim?"

"I don't give a shit whether it's you or somebody else," she told him. "I just want my due."

"It's gotta be you, Trots," Stonewall said. "You were the old boy's attorney."

"Yes," Trotter said solemnly. "I guess so."

He found an excuse to leave soon after that, having drunk maybe a quarter of his beer and made arrangements for Leona to see him in his office the following morning. When he was gone, Stonewall signaled the waitress to bring the bill, and then he turned to Leona. She reached for another cigarette. Watching her, his eyes fell to her cleavage, how her breasts rose under the V-neck when she inhaled. She looked over and caught him and when she did, she smiled.

"What?" she asked.

"You're a good-looking woman."

"I know," she said, holding the smile. "Gets me in trouble sometimes."

They headed back to Gettysburg in Stonewall's van. Stonewall was pretty loaded by this point and he stuck to the back roads, poking along at thirty miles an hour, fearful of getting pinched.

"That was a nice touch, the Barbie doll," he said.

"It was true," Leona told him. She was lounging in the passenger seat, one foot on the dash.

"Potter really gave you a doll?"

"Not him. Some geek my mama was sleeping with. Shit, I'm already getting laid steady, and the fucking guy gives me a Barbie. You got any beer in the back?"

"No."

"Is that true what he said? A few hundred thousand?"

"Trotter's as dumb as a post. Could be ten times that—depends what's in that fucking room."

"When're we gonna get a look at that room?"

"Maybe sooner than you think. Let Trotter do his thing first." He laughed. "Wait till those tight-asses at the university get wind of this. Arrogant bastards, I'd love to screw them."

She reached for his hand. "You know, I was just thinking about doing the same to you."

They went back to his place, and she did just that. What put her in the mood—the talk of big money or the umpteen bourbons or merely the fact that he'd relented and taken a shower—didn't really matter to Stonewall. As with everything else, methods didn't concern him; the only thing that mattered were results.

ELEVEN

He worked until dark and by that time he managed to shingle half of the rear roof of the house. The temperature dropped with the setting sun, and there were snowflakes swirling in the air when he finished up. He ducked into the trailer and lit the propane heater and then went into the bathroom and had a shower. When he came out, the trailer was warm. He heated a can of beans on the stove and ate the beans with a couple of slices of bread. Then he opened a beer and sat down on the couch with the diary. He came to an entry dated April 17, 1861.

> *It started this week down in south Carolina but it looks like it will be spred everwhere soon enuf. At the markit today, all the men in town were argewing about the reason for it. Some say it's states' rights and others put the blame sqware on the nigra problem. I dont claim to know enuf about it to say what is what, but it seems to me that war is not the thing to fix it. I reckin all we can do now is hope it ends real quick. My ma likes to say that hope is like a handfull of rain. It ain't much but its beter than no rain at all.*

Immersed in the reading, Dock didn't hear the vehicle arrive outside. There was a sharp rap on the door and then Harris walked in.

Upon hearing the knock, Dock scrambled to push the diary beneath his jacket beside him. Only then did he see who it was.

"It's just you," Dock said.

"Just me?" Harris repeated. "I'll have you know my mother thinks I'm quite a guy."

"A lot of mothers are confused that way. Grab a beer."

Harris went into the minifridge below the kitchen counter and took out a bottle of Yuengling. He opened it and then sat down at the counter that separated the kitchen from the living area. "You were expecting someone else? Perhaps some fetching young lass from the glamorous world of network television?"

"How'd you know about that?"

"She tracked Klaus down earlier, at the school. I think the old boy's losing it. He claims she let the air out of his tire so she could give him a ride and pump him for information. This is the woman who brought down Sarah Jane Wright and that oily congressman from out West. I hardly think she would stoop to that type of guerrilla tactic."

"Think again."

"Really?"

"Really."

Harris, eyebrows arched, took a drink. "So what did she want?"

"Who knows? She was doing a lot of pretending."

"Well, she wanted Klaus to show her the phonautograph."

"Yeah, she seemed more interested in that than the plates," Dock said. "Although she claimed otherwise. By the way, the phonautograph is on its way to Boston."

"It is?"

Dock looked at his watch. "Should be there right about now."

"Is it on a speaking tour?"

"That's pretty good, you know."

"I have my clever moments," Harris insisted over the bottle neck. "Klaus never mentioned anything to me about Boston."

"Just came up this afternoon."

"I'm surprised Klaus would let it out of his sight."

"He didn't," Dock said. "Klaus went with it. I was picturing him on the airplane, with the thing on his lap."

"What's in Boston?"

"Some people at MIT are gonna have a look at it. Apparently, they can break the sound down—identify background noises, what's real, what's contamination, whatever. Klaus says he needs to know more about what he calls the physical qualities of the recording. He was being kind of mysterious when he told me about it, tell you the truth. But he asked if it was okay and I said you're good to go, man."

"When's he due back?"

"Day after tomorrow."

Harris took a drink. "Be very interesting to see what MIT says."

Dock shrugged. "At this point, I don't know that it matters to me."

"Why not?"

"Maybe Willy Burns recorded sound before Edison, and maybe he didn't. Doesn't change who he was."

Harris leaned forward to set the beer bottle down, and when he did he saw the box beneath the jacket; the edges of the yellow-brown pages of the diary were visible. "What's that?"

"That? That's a jacket."

"*Under* the jacket."

Dock hesitated. "I found Willy's diary."

"I beg your pardon—you never told me that."

"I just did."

"Good lord, man. What does he say? Did he actually record something in '63?"

"I'm only up to 1861."

"Say, I have a radical suggestion—jump ahead."

"I don't want to do that. I'm doing this in real time. I want to live it . . . the way he lived it."

Harris gave him a long look. "You've developed quite an affinity for this kid."

"I guess I have."

Harris nodded. "Then let me have what you've already read."

"No," Dock said immediately. Then, "I just want to . . . keep it together. Maybe I don't have a good reason. I just do."

"All right," Harris said slowly. "It's your diary."

"It's his diary. I'm just the guy who got picked to look after it."

"This from the man who insists he doesn't believe in fate."

Dock looked at him a moment. "I need a beer—talking to you makes me thirsty." He got up and went to the fridge.

"So what's with the lovely Miss Morris?" Harris asked. "A bit of a twist, her arriving on the scene. By the way, she *was* lovely, was she not?"

"Have you seen her on TV?"

"I've seen her."

"Then you know the answer to that."

"So why is that?" Harris asked. "Why is it that every female on television is gorgeous these days? Even the women doing sports and weather—they all look like they just stepped out of *Vogue*. Where does an aspiring journalist go if she's . . . I don't know—"

"Ugly as a mud fence?" Dock asked, glancing at the diary.

"Okay," Harris said, after considering the image. "What happens to those women—do they get banished to radio?"

Dock, leaning against the counter, took a drink of beer. "I don't know, Harris. But you sure ask the tough questions."

"Oh, I have theories, my good man. I'm the Marshall McLuhan of Gettysburg. What's she like—is she dense?"

"Dense? Why would you ask that?"

"That's the other half of my dissertation: I have this notion that all these good-looking women are as thick as a brick. They get hired solely on their looks, you follow?"

"I bet this theory makes you pretty popular in certain circles."

"I rarely advance it in mixed company."

"She's not dense."

"Then what is she?"

"I don't know. Not at home in the real world, would be my guess."

"That doesn't explain why she's here. This woman is a star, and I mean that in the most negative sense imaginable. What you found is pretty exciting stuff for historians and collectors and public TV. But for the glossy network news, I'd say it falls a little short of the new Harry Potter book."

"Who's Harry Potter?" Dock asked.

Harris indicated the diary beneath the coat. "Harry Potter is another whiz kid—but of the make-believe variety. I could see Amy Morris being intrigued by him."

"I don't know what intrigues her," Dock said. "Maybe I'll find out the next time she shows."

"You assume she's coming back?"

"Oh, she's coming back. That's the one thing I do know."

She was lying in bed, looking at the ceiling, and smoking her tenth cigarette of the morning. She hadn't gone for her run, she hadn't showered, and she hadn't eaten. She had no energy, no ambition. Throw in a few insecurities and some acne and she could pass as a teenager.

Chain-smoking, she knew, wasn't her best move right now; her thoughts were already bouncing around her head like a pinball machine on speed and nicotine wasn't exactly the thing for slowing the process down. But the alternative was to get up and do something. And since she had no idea what she might do upon arising, she remained in idle recline, lighting up and indulging her scattershot thoughts.

One moment she was plotting revenge against Sam Rockwood for sending her here, the next she was revising her résumé in her head, considering what options might be available at Fox, at CNN, at MSNBC. And all the while planning her next move on Dock Bass, the stubborn cowboy carpenter with the sarcastic mouth and the audacity to question her integrity.

She kept returning to these wild rambles of career-change fancy because she had no idea how to approach the problem that was Bass. On one level, she had a notion to tell Sam just to offer the man a shitload of money and get on with it. Keep upping the ante until he got what he wanted. It was the tried-and-true American way and one that had worked for Sam his entire life. But she had a feeling that Bass wasn't about to rise to any monetary bait, no matter how attractively it might be dangled. And she also had a strange reluctance to risk it happening; it would mean that she had failed to get to him. He had gotten personal; for some reason she was determined to make it personal in return.

And that wasn't helping her at all in deciding what her next move might be. She lit number eleven and returned to a scenario where Fox gave her a weekly news forum. A prime-time show about actual issues: the environment, civil liberties, homeland security. It would be a show that mattered. It would be a show that would steadfastly avoid topics like the collecting of obscure historical artifacts. It would also, she realized, be a show that would get canceled within a month because nobody would watch.

She was butting the cigarette—having just been pink-slipped by Fox—when the phone rang. It was Sam Rockwood.

"I thought you'd be out for lunch," he said.

She looked at the clock on the table and was shocked to see it was noon. "No," she said. "I'm just working on the laptop."

"What are you working on?"

"Um . . . a number of things. What's up?"

"I figured you'd be calling me about this latest, startling development."

She was forced to admit that she wasn't aware of any late developments, startling or otherwise. She was particularly loath to confess such a thing to Sam, but she had no choice; she could only bluff so much in this game. Of course, it was entirely possible that lying in bed until noon wasn't necessarily the best way to keep abreast of things.

"A woman has come forward," Sam said then. "She's claiming to be the daughter of the old boy who owned the farmhouse. What was his name—Ambrose Potter? You haven't heard this? I imagined the town would be abuzz."

"I'm an outsider, Sam. I've haven't exactly been welcomed into any sewing circles yet. When did this happen?"

"The papers were filed this morning."

"Wait a minute. That means that virtually nobody knows about it yet. How the hell did you find out?"

"I own a large news-gathering conglomerate. Have I never mentioned that to you?"

"I have a feeling there's a lot you don't mention to me," she said, but her heart was suddenly light. "Well, this kind of throws a monkey wrench into things, doesn't it? I can see this getting tied up in the courts for what—five or ten years? Sounds like I'll be back in Washington for dinner, Sam."

"Don't start packing yet, kid. First thing you're going to do is find this woman. I want to know if your gut says she's legitimate or not. If she is, then I think we can assume—from the timing of this thing—that she might be of a more avaricious nature than your buddy Dock Bass. You might be able to get her to sign something real quick on the phonautograph."

"And if it turns out she's a fake?"

"We make an offer contingent on ownership," he said simply.

"Tell me again who this 'we' is?"

"You make the hookup and let me worry about the rest. Have you talked to Bass again?"

"No. I've been busy all morning."

"You'll be busy all afternoon, too. The guy you need to talk to is a lawyer named Trotter. He handled Potter's estate."

"He's in town here?"

"Yes. He should be easy to find—how many lawyers can there be in Gettysburg?"

"Probably about twice as many as there should be."

Trotter had an office on Carlisle Street, a block and a half from the town center. There was a thin woman with straight black hair sitting at a desk in the outer office. Just sitting, Amy noticed, not typing or filing or reading *People* magazine.

"I recognize you," the woman said when Amy walked in, although her tone suggested that she knew that Amy was somebody, she just wasn't sure who.

"Hi. I'm Amy Morris. I was looking for Mr. Trotter."

"He's not here," the woman said. "Are you on television?"

"Sometimes. When do you expect him back?"

"He's in court this afternoon. If you're here about Leona Anderson, he's not talking to the media. He doesn't want it to turn into a circus."

"I understand completely." Amy smiled, and then as a stalling tactic she walked to the lone window in the room and looked out. It was beginning to rain, and for some reason she wondered if Dock Bass had finished shingling his roof. She turned back to the woman, who was now typing something into the computer. "Busy place," Amy said.

"Always is."

"You know, I used to be a legal secretary," Amy said then.

"Really?"

"Yep. It was in Kansas City," she decided. "I've always said my background in the law was an enormous help in my work now. I find I have an intrinsic understanding of legal matters that many of my colleagues don't. You must feel the same way."

"Yes, I do," the woman said hesitantly. "By the way, I'm Olive Tonelli."

"Tonelli—you're Italian?"

"Second generation."

"No kidding? I'm a quarter Italian myself," Amy told her.

By the time she left the office, Amy had Leona Anderson's address, her family background, and most of the salient details of her claim. Olive also revealed that the Anderson woman was unemployed and, in her opinion, a bit of a boozer. Rumor was she'd been passing most of her afternoons in McClellan's bar off the lobby of the Gettysburg Hotel. When Amy asked what the woman looked like, she thought for a moment that Olive would provide her with a pencil sketch.

The verbal description proved good enough. Amy ran Leona Anderson to ground at four that afternoon at the hotel bar. The blond woman was sitting by herself, drinking bourbon and Coke, and chatting with the bartender.

Amy sat down on the next stool over. "Do you know how to make a cosmopolitan?" she asked the bartender.

"Gee, that's a tough one," he said. "You have to mix vodka and cranberry juice together."

When he moved off to make the drink, Amy turned to see Leona watching her.

"Sarcastic little prick, isn't he?" the blond woman said and she released a throaty laugh. "You gonna tell him about the Cointreau?"

"I think I'll let it lie," Amy said and she smiled. "Are you Leona Anderson?"

"How'd you know that?"

"I'm a journalist. I'm in town doing a story on the budget cutbacks at the university. My boss at the network is a history nut—he heard about the guy who found the pictures of Lincoln, and he asked me to check it out—you know, the human-interest angle. When I talked to the lawyer from the estate, he told me about you. So you're actually the daughter of this guy—what was his name?"

"Ambrose Potter." Leona shook the cigarette package on the bar and found it was empty.

"Right, Ambrose Potter," Amy said as she reached into her purse for her smokes. "You know, I like that name, Ambrose. It smacks of our romantic past, don't you think? Anyway, my boss was saying that you're the only blood relative? Help yourself." She tossed the pack on the bar.

Leona reached for the cigarettes without hesitation. The bartender arrived and placed the vodka-and-cranberry mix in front of Amy without further caustic comment. Amy indicated Leona's glass to him, nodding.

"Thanks," Leona said, lighting up. "I'm a little tapped out right now. Temporarily, you might say."

"So what's the deal on this other dude, the guy who found the Lincoln pictures?" Amy asked. "He thinks he's the beneficiary?"

Leona laughed again. "Yeah, he's out there fixing the joint up for me. I think my lawyer's gonna put the run on him, though."

"Have you met him?"

"My lawyer? Of course I've met him."

"No—I meant this guy Bass."

"Naw, he's not from around here." Leona took the fresh drink from the bartender before he could set it on the bar.

"Pretty exciting though, finding the pictures of Lincoln."

"Yeah? Maybe you and me would get excited about different things," Leona said, smiling as she drank. "I guess it's pretty cool, but I'm not much into history. I mean, I was born here and I never even looked at the battlegrounds and shit."

"So what would you do with the pictures?"

"Sell 'em."

"And everything else in the house? I heard there were, I don't know, books and tools and different stuff."

"What am I gonna do, open a fucking museum? I been told all that old shit is worth a lot of money. The way I look at it is, it's my inheritance. If I can turn it into cash, that's what I'm gonna do."

"Well, you're not exactly the sentimental type," Amy said, and she smiled to show she meant no offense. "What would you do with the money?"

"Open a club," Leona replied at once. "I've always been a waitress or hostess, you know. Always figured on having my own place. This could be my chance."

"You wouldn't do it here?"

Leona snorted into her glass. "You gotta be kidding. Philly maybe—I know a lot of people there. I'm not talking about a fucking Denny's, you hear? I'm talking about a place with class. I'd even put it in the name, call the place A Class Act. Keep the lowlifes out."

"That ought to do it," Amy said. She took a drink and set her glass on the bar. "Did you always know Potter was your father?"

"Yeah, well, ever since I was thirteen. My mama told me then."

"Who did you think was your father up until then?"

"Guy named Pete Anderson. He lived with my mother off and on for years. They were never married, but us kids were all called Anderson anyway. But he was in jail when I was born."

"He could be in jail when you were born and still be your father."

"No, I mean when I was conceived," she said. "He was in jail when I was conceived."

"Oh," Amy said. "Where was he in jail?"

"Auburn, New York."

"What for?"

"Who knows? He was always in jail." She helped herself to another of Amy's cigarettes, lit it from the butt of the first. She inhaled deeply. "Listen, I know what people are gonna say—that I'm just going after this because of the money. You know what? They're gonna be right. Ambrose Potter knocked my mother up, and far as I know he never gave her a nickel. The law says that whatever he left belongs to me. It's rightfully mine. So I don't care what people say. You telling me you wouldn't do the same?"

Before Amy could answer she felt a presence at her side and she turned and looked up at a large bearded man wearing a greasy buckskin jacket. The man was leaning over her, his fist on the bar. He smelled like—well, he smelled like a large bearded man who wasn't exactly a fanatic about personal hygiene.

"What're you doing?" he demanded.

"Having a cosmopolitan. Sort of."

Stonewall looked at Leona. "What's she been asking you?"

"Nothing."

"Do you know who she is?"

"Yeah, she's a journalist," Leona said. "She's doing a story on the setbacks or something at the university." She laughed her cigarette laugh and looked at Amy. "What was that story you were doin'?"

"She's no fucking journalist," Stonewall said. "She's a talking head from TransWorld, and I got a feeling she's sticking her nose where it doesn't belong."

"Hold on, Wild Bill," Amy said. "I believe you've got me at a disadvantage here."

"Wild Bill," Leona repeated over the rim of her glass. "I like that."

"You bet your ass I've got you at a disadvantage," he told Amy. "And don't think that's gonna change." He looked at Leona. "What'd you tell her?"

"None of your fucking business," Leona said, laughing. "It was girl talk. Wild Bill."

Amy got down from the stool. She opened her purse and put a twenty on the bar, then she smiled at Stonewall. "I'll be going now. You never did tell me your name. Or your connection to Ms. Anderson."

"My name's Stonewall Martin. I'm her *adviser.*" He waggled his fat forefinger back and forth to indicate the suspected exchange between the two women. "I better not see any of this on the news. Or my name neither."

"Kind of full of yourself, aren't you?" Amy asked.

"What?" he snapped.

"You really don't seem all that newsworthy to me," she said and she left.

Attorney Trotter showed up late in the afternoon, wheeling the big Lincoln into the driveway and parking it behind Dock's pickup. Dock, nailing ridge cap on the roof, watched as the little lawyer departed the big car, like a cartoon mouse leaving a steamship. A second later a man got out of the passenger side. He was of regular size and he wore a uniform. Seeing the man, Dock slid down the roof to the ladder leaning against the eave and then he made his way to the ground.

He crossed the yard to approach the two men, who were now standing between the Lincoln and his truck. Trotter had a briefcase clutched tightly in his right hand, the little clenched knuckles showing white against the dark grip. The lawyer looked in need of a good laxative. The officer, for his part, was more at ease. He was hatless, and his uniform was khaki and had epaulets of dark brown. He had what appeared to be an old-fashioned Smith & Wesson .38 revolver on his hip. Most cops carried automatics—Glocks or Brownings—these days.

"Mr. Bass," Trotter said, his voice nearly collapsing under the gravity of the moment, "this is Sheriff Harmer."

"Howdy, Sheriff," Dock said.

The sheriff nodded and looked at the house. "Got her just about closed in."

"Yup," Dock said. "The rest of the ridge cap and that's it."

"Just in time, if you believe the weatherman."

"We have business," Trotter said.

"Somebody stopping you?" the sheriff asked.

"There's been an unexpected development with regards to Ambrose Potter's estate," Trotter said then and he was off and running. "Now, I think I should at first make clear that I have, from the outset, done everything in my power to ensure that every avenue was explored when dealing with this situation. I was put at a disadvantage from the start, there being no will, and only scattered information available vis-à-vis potential beneficiaries. I spent many long hours looking for leads in this regard and, I might add at this point, it was as a result of this diligence that you are even here today, Mr. Bass. Not that it's my intent to toot my own—"

"Whoa," Dock said sharply, and attorney Trotter whoa-ed, but with the familiar marked exasperation on his face. "I don't know what you're trying to tell me, but I got a hundred bucks that says the sheriff here can tell it quicker."

"A woman has filed a claim against the Potter estate," Sheriff Harmer said.

"Well, I would have won the hundred," Dock said, but he wasn't particularly happy saying it. "Who's the woman?"

"Her name's Leona Anderson. She says she's Potter's daughter."

"And is she?"

"That's what we have to find out," the sheriff said. "But for the time being, the county is going to impose a blanket restriction with regards to any disposition of the estate."

"And then what?"

"Then we try to determine whether or not the Anderson woman is actually the daughter."

"How do we do that?" Dock asked. "Dig the old guy up?"

"He was cremated," Trotter said. "The county has a policy—it's been in effect for some years now—concerning bodies unclaimed by relatives. It was initially put into effect as a cost-cutting alternative—"

"All right, all right," Dock said. He turned back to the sheriff. "I swear, if this guy got paid by the word, he'd be Donald Trump. Does this mean I have to leave?"

"Of course you'll have to leave," Trotter said. "Until such time that this matter is settled, it must be assumed that ownership is in a state of limbo. You'll have to vacate immediately."

"I don't know that that's true," the sheriff said slowly. "My understanding is that the assets are frozen. Nothing can be disposed of until this is settled. Have you disposed of anything?"

"Lath and plaster," Dock said. "Some rotten cedar shingles."

The sheriff looked at Trotter. "Has Miss Anderson expressed interest in lath and plaster and rotten cedar shingles?"

"Hardly," Trotter said.

"I didn't think so." The sheriff turned to Dock. "Everything else will be held in trust. Normally, that would mean the house and property. In this case, there are other items of considerable value."

"A lot of it is at the university," Dock told him.

"I think it can stay there," the sheriff said. "It's as safe there as any place. We'll need to inventory it. I'll send a van out later for the rest. We'll hold it at the courthouse."

Dock thought of the diary in his trailer. "Everything's there," he said. "Can I keep working on the house?"

The sheriff raised his eyebrows and looked at Trotter. "To tell you the truth, I don't know the answer to that."

"Why would you work on a house you don't own?" Trotter asked.

"Five minutes ago, I did own it," Dock said. "And I have a feeling I will again. This thing's got an awful smell about it, Trotter. I find out you're running a scam with this woman, I'll track you down and kick your fat ass."

"Did you hear that?" Trotter said excitedly, turning to the sheriff. "I want him arrested and charged with threatening. This has gone too far."

The sheriff glanced at Dock resignedly; then he turned and had a long look at the house with the new roof. He had the appearance of a man who fervently wished to be somewhere else.

"Well?" Trotter persisted.

"Well, what?" Harmer asked.

"You heard this man threaten me."

Harmer reflected a moment longer, and then he turned to Trotter.

"This guy's a tricky bastard, Trotter," he said. "He sort of qualified what he said. He's only gonna kick your fat ass if you're running a scam. Are you running a scam?"

"Of course not," Trotter said.

"Then I guess he didn't threaten you."

When they were gone, Dock went back up the ladder and finished the cap. The weatherman could do whatever he wanted now. The house would be dry.

No matter who owned it.

When he was done nailing, he remained at the peak for a long while, sitting and looking over the small farm and at the town beyond. The cupola at the seminary was plainly visible in the distance, rising above everything else in the old town. Dock could also see Cemetery Hill, and the Round Tops to the south. He wondered if Willy Burns ever had reason to climb onto this roof—if he did, he would have seen much the same landscape as did Dock. He would have been spared the low-rise Wendy's and McDonald's and Wal-Mart on the east end of town, the car dealers, and the souvenir shops, too. Dock had no way of knowing, but he hoped the kid had been spared the Trotters and the Stonewalls of his day as well.

But the landscape itself, from then to now, would be little changed, and when Dock thought of that which hadn't changed he began to think of all that had. He wondered if any of it had changed for the better.

He'd been thinking lately of restoring the barn, trying to decide if it was a practical move or not. Not that practicality had been his strong suit of late, and purposely so. A man could only stand so much practicality.

He knew he was going to have to do something about this latest development. Probably hire a lawyer and then spend countless hours in a courtroom. The first scenario was at least as unpleasant as the second. Too bad they burned the old boy—a quick disinterment would resolve the problem one way or the other. Now they were going to have to go the long way around.

It was almost dark when he finally climbed down. He went into the house and plugged the phone in and called Harris to tell him the news.

"We've been trying to get you for an hour," Harris said before Dock could speak. "The phone works a lot better if you leave it plugged in."

"I kind of like the way it works when I don't."

"Well, whatever, Klaus is back. We need to talk to you. Something extremely interesting has surfaced. I'll pick you up in fifteen minutes."

Dock was changed and waiting outside when Harris arrived. The moon was up already and he could see beyond the barn and across the cornfield—just recently harvested—to the hardwoods stretching along the fencerow to the west. As he watched, a half-dozen whitetail deer wandered out from behind the barn, foraging for the corn the combine had left behind. A scant hundred yards away, they paid Dock no mind, if they saw him at all. When Harris's SUV pulled in the drive, the headlights swept across the small herd; the deer jerked their heads in alarm and bolted across the field, their tails waving like flags of surrender as they fled.

"Where's Klaus?" Dock asked when they set off. They were driving along Shealer Road.

"At the university."

Dock looked at his watch. "Doesn't he ever go home? Does he even have a home?"

"Oh, yes," Harris said. "He's got a beautiful place along a creek outside of Chambersburg. But his wife died two years ago. Cancer. Now he sleeps most nights at the school. She was the love of his life, Dock. As clichéd as that sounds, she was the love of his life."

"So now it's all about the work?"

"It seems that way. That's all he's got now. Without it, there'd be nothing left of the man. I would venture a guess that you and your amazing little root cellar have added ten years to his life."

They found the Hungarian in his Lair, listening to classical music and eating a green apple. The phonautograph was on the counter; beside it was some tape-to-tape recording equipment and a folder of loose papers, the papers peeking out haphazardly here and there.

"Doctor," Klaus said. "Ve have been looking for you."

"Here I am."

Harris walked to the counter. "The boys at MIT gave your antique Wurlitzer a pretty good going-over. And we have a theory now—and it's just a theory—of whose voice might be on the cylinder. You'd like to think it's Willy Burns."

Dock shrugged. "Does it really matter who? It's when that matters."

"Maybe it matters both," Klaus said.

"They broke down the sound," Harris said. "Filtered out background noise, contamination from the cylinder, and so on. They cleaned it up, in their vernacular. They agree that the recording is consistent with other primitive recordings of the era. However, they've decided on something else. They think they've identified the noise that I thought was static at the end of the recording."

"Is not static," Klaus said. "Hoo, boy."

"What is it?" Dock asked.

Harris looked at him. "It's applause." He hit the play button on the tape recorder, and the voice began the address again. This time the sound was clearer, more distinct. Certain words that had been lost before could now be heard. "The world will little note, nor long remember," which before was just distortion, was now recognizable. "Last full measure" could also be heard, although it faded away on "devotion." And at the end, there was a sound that did seem to be clapping.

"So Willy Burns had an audience on hand?" Dock asked when it finished. "That seems kind of unlikely."

"What if it's not Willy?" Harris asked. "In 1863—who would have gathered an audience?"

"Well, there was quite a crowd on hand the first three days of July," Dock said. "But there was no Gettysburg Address to recite in July and if there was it would have been drowned out by cannon fire." He paused for a long moment as it came to him. "So I assume you'd have to move forward to November and if that's the case then I guess I know what you're gonna tell me next."

"Is maybe him," Klaus said. "Is maybe old rail-splitter."

Dock looked at Harris. "You're not saying we've got Abraham Lincoln on that cylinder?"

"I'm saying we might. I'm saying we might be listening to a voice that up until now nobody alive has heard."

"And the guys at MIT?"

"They won't say it is," Harris said. "But they have no intention of saying it isn't. It turns out the technology was there. Leon Scott visited the United States in 1863, and it's been well documented that he paid Lincoln a visit in Washington while he was here. There's been a rumor floating around ever since that he recorded old Abe on a phonautograph and that the cylinder still exists somewhere. One theory has it stashed away somewhere in the White House archives."

"Wouldn't somebody find it if it was?" Dock asked.

"Ha, you could hide good-sized elephant in those archives," Klaus said. "I have been there."

"The recording seems to match up," Harris said. "For instance, there are a lot of written accounts describing Lincoln's voice. It was usually characterized as flat and thin, kind of a prairie twang. And there are descriptions of the Address itself—what was emphasized, what was understated, that type of thing. Obviously, this recording is pretty rough, but what is there coincides."

"What's the theory here?" Dock asked. "That Scott came to Gettysburg with Lincoln?"

"Nah, he vas Frenchman," Klaus said. "He vud get ten miles from Gettysburg and then surrender."

"There's no evidence he was here—certain stereotypes aside," Harris said, glancing at Klaus. "I'd say there's a better chance that Willy Burns rigged this up himself and then took it down to the dedication. We *know* he was there because of the plates." He paused. "I can tell you this: if it turns out to be Honest Abe on the cylinder, talk about upping the ante. Somebody will hand you a blank check and tell you to keep adding zeroes until you get writer's cramp."

"And then vatch the people show up, looking for those zeroes," Klaus said.

Harris nodded. "You can bet that somebody will come after it."

"Somebody already has," Dock said and he told them about Leona Anderson.

TWELVE

She flipped through the rest of the stations with the re-mote. Any information she found was basically a repeat of the first report from Brokaw on NBC, although the anchorman's garbled baritone seemed to give it more weight than the others. Still, everybody seemed to be taking it seriously. After all, it was MIT on the scientific side and award-winning Lincoln scholar Klaus Gabor on the historical. Not exactly an Elvis sighting in Las Vegas. When the news was over, she clicked the set off and dialed his number.

"Hello."

"You sandbagged me, Sam," she said into the phone.

"I beg your pardon?"

"You knew all along it was Lincoln, didn't you?"

"How could I have known it before, when nobody knows it now for sure?" he asked. "We're just sitting down to dinner, Amy."

"Tough shit. You gonna tell me you never suspected it?"

"I just wanted the thing, in case it preceded Edison."

"Don't you bullshit me, Sam. You didn't know about Scott allegedly recording Lincoln's voice in 1863?"

"Sure, I knew that. It's not exactly a secret."

"Just between you and me," she snapped. "The point is, you knew the technology existed."

"What's one thing have to do with the other? Scott was never in Gettysburg, was he? Your objective doesn't change, Amy."

"I'll tell you what one has to do with the other," she said. "I'm down here on some vague possibility that some yokel recorded sound before Edison while you're sitting at home knowing that it could be Abraham fucking Lincoln on that cylinder."

"Ah, the return of the rogue adjective. Or are you under the impression that his middle name was Fucking?"

"Keep this clandestine shit up, and your middle name is gonna be Mud. What the hell am I supposed to do now?"

"I want that phonautograph, Amy."

"You're beginning to sound like a broken record."

"How appropriate."

She hung up on him. She flung herself crossways on the bed, stared down at the stained carpet there. She'd had it with Sam Rockwood. And while she was on the subject, she'd had it with plate-glass negatives and relic recording machines; she'd had it with perfumed antique dealers and smelly mountain men; she'd had it with eccentric professors, contrary carpenters, bad room service, and alcoholic would-be beneficiaries. And she'd had it with Gettysburg, she realized.

She didn't want to be here. There was something too familiar about the place. She'd grown up in an area marked by poverty and overt racism—the backwoods barn where the local chapter of the Klan met actually had *KKK* painted on the front door. (Amy's father used to marvel that they spelled it right.) She hadn't wanted to be there either and had determined in school to remove herself, both physically and philosophically, at the earliest opportunity. As a teenager, she'd held to the admittedly naive belief that there could come a time when she would never again have to be anywhere she didn't want to be. Although it was still a pretty attractive notion, she was more of a realist these days. While she might fool herself into thinking it was her hand at the controls, it wasn't. That hand belonged to somebody else. That somebody had recently seen fit to dump Amy unceremoniously into small-town Pennsylvania and as a bonus had decided to surround her with an all-star cast of eccentrics and undesirables.

Speaking of the latter, she was going to have to approach the carpenter again. She'd made a mistake the last time she'd visited him. She had, quite uncharacteristically, underestimated the man and shown up on his doorstep thinking that her aptitude and instinct would carry the day. She knew better than that. She'd always known better than that.

She rolled off the bed, went to the desk, plugged in her laptop, and went online. She picked up the phone and against her better judgment ordered a grilled chicken salad from room service. She lit a cigarette and gazed out the window, at the pretty little town she looked forward to seeing in her rearview mirror.

The next morning was foggy and wet as she drove out to the house on Shealer Road again. She abandoned all pretense this time—the son of a bitch hadn't fallen for any of her tricks anyway—and took the Cayenne. The vehicle had returned from the shopping trip to Baltimore reeking of marijuana and red wine, and she'd had to take it to a service center in town and pay to get it cleaned. Apparently, the hundred she'd given the desk clerk hadn't been wasted on foolish long-term investments.

She didn't know if she would find him there, given Leona Anderson's claim against the estate. And she wasn't sure that she wanted to find him in any case, given the way she'd been treated on her last visit. She somehow doubted that the events of the past couple of days had improved his mood any. But the damn phonautograph was her ticket out of town, and she resigned herself to the fact that she would have to put up with some attitude to get it. Driving through the drizzling rain, she assured herself that she'd endured more aggravating assignments. In truth, she hadn't.

His truck was in the drive when she pulled in but there was no one in sight. She saw that the roof he'd been working on was now finished. The back door to the house was open. She called out as she approached but got no reply.

She stepped through the doorway, tentatively, and into a large empty room, the walls stripped down to the studding. Across the room was a doorway leading to another room, this one low-ceilinged and resembling a cellar of sorts. Dock Bass was sitting inside, on a bench in the middle of the room. He was wearing jeans and a T-shirt and a base-ball cap. He heard her footsteps and looked over without expression.

When she approached, she saw that the room was, except for the man and the bench and some bare shelving, virtually empty. She stopped in the doorway.

"This is it," she said, realizing. "This is where you found it all."

"What can I do for you?"

"Nothing. I was just . . . touching base."

"What are we, old army buddies?"

"That's good," she said. She looked around a moment longer. "Quite a day out there."

He glanced toward the rain-streaked windows, but he didn't say anything, didn't as much as nod. She hesitated and then, realizing she'd be waiting a long time for any comment from him, plunged forward.

"You know, it was a day much like this in November of '63, when old Abe gave the Address. Cold and rainy. Lincoln was actually under the weather himself. Strangely enough, just as he began to speak, the sun broke through. Of course, you probably knew all that."

"Nope."

She saw now that he had a sheaf of yellowed papers on his lap, and she realized that he must have been reading when she'd arrived.

"Where is everything?" she asked.

"Sheriff came and took it all away."

"Sounds like a Bob Marley song." She smiled, hoping for a like re-sponse and not getting it. "Too bad—I was hoping to get a look at the collodion plates."

"They're not here."

"You said that," she said. "Just—I would've liked to see them."

He looked at her steadily but made no response. She was getting used to his taciturn manner; she even expected it at this point. She be-gan to walk around the room, looking at the empty shelves, the table, the bench.

"You know, the wet-plate process was revolutionary, when you think about it. I mean, compared to daguerreotypes, which were so ex-pensive, not to mention unwieldy. The interesting thing is, Mathew

Brady is the best-known photographer of the Civil War, but it was Alexander Gardner who was actually the more prolific of the two. Of course, Brady's eyesight was going by that time, and that was obviously a factor. Gardner was the man in the field for the most part. Brady stayed in Washington a good deal of the time."

"You don't say."

"I do say," she told him. "Gardner was actually en route to Gettysburg when the battle was being fought. He arrived too late, but he did take pictures of the aftermath. In fact, it's been alleged that he repositioned corpses for some of the shots. For dramatic effect. Some considered it a sacrilege." She paused, running out of steam. "What do you think?"

"I think the local bookstore must have moved a copy of *The Civil War for Dummies* yesterday. I suppose next you're gonna tell me about Jeb Stuart's superstitions, how he always wore red socks into battle."

"Hey, everybody knows that." She paused, noticing his expression. "You son of a bitch. You just made that up."

He smiled, and she thought that maybe, and it was only a maybe, he was smiling with her. She stepped closer, looked at the papers in his lap. "What are you reading?"

"None of your business."

"God, but you're a charming man, Mr. Bass. You just take my breath away."

He began to stack the papers together. "Well, I got a feeling you're pretty much all breath anyway."

"Again with the charm," Amy said. She hesitated, then pressed on. "I talked to her, you know—Leona Anderson."

"Yeah?" His disinterest could have been real, but it seemed unlikely, given what was at risk. He stood and carried the papers across the room and placed them in a box on a shelf. Symbolically—if not physically—out of her reach.

"Would you like to know my take on her?" she asked.

"I don't know anything about you," he said. "Why would I care what you think?"

"Because I'm a nice person, and if you don't listen to my take on

Leona Anderson, I'm going to start spouting a whole lot more obscure Civil War trivia that I downloaded off the Internet last night."

"What's your take on Leona Anderson?"

"She's only in it for the money. She told me that she'll sell everything if she gets her hands on it."

"What you're saying," Dock said, "is that she's no different from you."

"I beg your pardon?"

"Come on. You're here because TransWorld pays you a lot of money to look pretty in front of a camera. TransWorld is in it looking for some scoop that's gonna up their ratings. They up their ratings, and then they can charge their advertisers more money to sell America a whole bunch of shit they don't need." He paused a moment. "Like soap. I went to the grocery store the other day to buy a couple bars of soap. There's about *five hundred* different kinds of soap out there. I'll make you a deal: explain to me why we need five hundred different kinds of soap, and I'll tell you anything you want to know."

When he finished, he regarded her defiantly, as if she might actually be able to provide the answer to the great soap question.

"Wow," she said after a moment. "You ranted. You actually displayed human tendencies. Emotion even." She smiled. "And it was the soap that did it."

"Forget about the goddamn soap," he said. "I'll tell you something else. Leona Anderson—if she is who she says she is—is a hell of a lot more honest than the rest of you. At least she's up-front with it. She's in it for the money. Everybody else pretends to be interested in the *historical significance* of it all. Bullshit—it's all about what it's worth. How much you gonna get for the plates? How much for the phonautograph? Five million? Ten? And if it *is* Lincoln on the cylinder, then what're we talking? Fifty maybe? Nobody will be able to afford it, other than the dot-com geeks and the odd major league shortstop."

"The dot-commers are in the soup lines these days," Amy told him. "But I think the shortstops are still living large."

"Doesn't matter. My point is, it's the Gettysburg Address. It is what it is. It shouldn't matter who owns the goddamn cylinder."

"Believe it or not," she said then, "I recently had this very conversation with someone who is very much convinced that it matters who owns it. And guess what? I was on your side."

Dock's expression was skeptical; after a moment he indicated the pages on the shelf. "That's Willy Burns's diary. That's what I was reading when you came in. This is the kid who took the pictures of Lincoln, and this is the kid who put Lincoln's words on that cylinder, no matter who spoke them. And because of those words, he enlisted and was killed at Cold Harbor. If he'd have lived, he would've been another Edison, maybe more than that. And today all anybody cares about is putting a dollar sign on everything he touched. There's something wrong with that, lady."

"It's the way of the world, Mr. Bass."

"Your world."

"You think you get to exclude yourself just because you've got an attitude? It's not that easy."

"Far as I'm concerned, it is."

"Is that right? Then tell me what you're going to do about the Anderson woman."

Dock glared at her, then sat down on the bench. "I don't know," he said at last. "You think she's genuine?"

"She could be," Amy said. "Girl's a little rough around the edges, but that doesn't make her a liar. She knows her story. I've no doubt the man was her neighbor, but that doesn't mean her mother was doing the nasty with the guy. There's also the possibility that she really doesn't know who her father was. Have you thought about that? Hey, if you're going to pick a dad out of a hat, why not pick the one who left behind a few million dollars' worth of Civil War artifacts?"

"How does she go about proving it?" Dock asked.

"The question is, how do you go about disproving it?" Amy countered. "I've covered a couple of these things. I can tell you this from experience: if she comes to you looking for a buy-out, she's probably a fraud. But if she's in it for the long haul, you could be in trouble, cowboy."

Dock shrugged. "If she's the real deal, then I won't fight her on it. I'll just walk away."

"Really?"

"A house divided against itself cannot stand," Dock quoted in mock seriousness. "It will become all one thing or all the other. That's from Lincoln."

"I'm aware of that. I had me some book learnin', Mr. Bass. It's not all eyeliner and blush, contrary to what you might think." She paused. "But you could do that—you could walk away?"

"I'd have to. Otherwise, I'd just be like all the rest of you."

"All the rest of us," Amy said. She smiled and shook her head. "You're not going to let that go, are you? You're a stubborn man."

"Look who's talking. I seem to recall running you out of here a few days ago. And now you're back."

"Hey, just doing my job. You'll have to trust me when I tell you that this is not exactly my dream assignment. The truth be known—I have pressing matters elsewhere."

"Don't let me keep you."

He smiled again when he said it, so she took a chance. "So—you going to let me have a look at that diary?"

"I said no. You hard of hearing?"

"My hearing is fine. Why can't I see it?"

"Because you don't get it," Dock told her.

"Why don't you explain to me what it is that I don't get?"

"The pictures, the diary, the recording—it's all about the Gettysburg Address, and everybody wants a piece of it. What they don't seem to realize is that everybody already has it. In a hundred and fifty years they haven't figured out what to do with it."

She drove back into town with that, and not much else, to show for her visit. The island of Aruba was not getting any closer. She wasn't at all sure what Sam expected of her at this point. She supposed that the best scenario, for her and for him, would be for the Anderson woman to be declared the true beneficiary. Then it would just be a matter of Sam showing up with his patriotic smile and his deep pockets and buying the phonautograph, and the plates, and anything else in eastern Pennsylvania that might catch his fancy. Maybe he could convince the folks in Philly to sell him the Liberty Bell. He could haul it down to McLean and put it in his front yard, have Nettie ring it every night at cocktail hour.

She knew one thing. It was highly unlikely that anything was going to happen while the ownership of the estate was up in the air. Maybe she could do something to speed that process along. Maybe she could determine that Leona Anderson was in fact the daughter of Ambrose Potter.

And maybe she could find out otherwise. Either way didn't really matter to her.

When she got back to the hotel, she passed by the front desk and said hello to the woman working there. The woman had long brown hair and was probably in her mid-thirties. At the elevator, Amy paused, and then went back to the lobby.

"Hi again," she said. "Are you from here originally?"

The woman nodded suspiciously.

"Where were you born?" Amy asked.

"Here. I just told you that."

"I mean where, though. Is there a hospital?"

There was a hospital, an extending complex of wings and additions, located on Washington Street. There was a large parking lot off the south end. Amy parked and went inside, found a desk that appeared to be reception although it wasn't labeled as such. A slight man with John Lennon glasses and long hair was sitting there. If he recognized Amy, he never let on.

"I'm trying to locate a birth record," she told him.

"Name."

"My name?"

"The person you're looking for." The guy stopped just short of rolling his eyes.

"Leona Anderson."

"These records are private. Are you a relative?"

"I'm a journalist," Amy said and she produced half a dozen pieces of ID, including her press pass from TransWorld.

The Lennon wannabe looked at her credentials for a moment, then apparently came to some decision. He stood and walked into a glass-walled room to the rear, where Amy watched as he entered the name in a computer. She waited a few minutes longer as he chatted with a woman in nurse's scrubs. Then he glanced at the screen and walked back toward Amy.

"September 30, 1971," he told her.

Which sounded about right. "Does it list the parents?"

The young man regarded her with further suspicion, before releasing a sigh and returning to the computer. "Judith Elaine Tompkins and Peter Daniel Anderson," he said when he came back.

Amy was reluctant to send him back. "Could I, um . . . get you to print me a copy of the birth record?"

"I'm not looking at the birth records," he told her. "I'm looking at our computer records. The information is pretty minimal. The actual birth records are stashed somewhere, probably in the basement."

"Could I get a copy of the actual record?"

"You'd need some sort of authorization from the family for that. I've probably given you more than you're allowed already."

Back at the hotel, she called TransWorld and asked for Marla.

"It's Amy."

"Hey, what's up? Where you calling from—Aruba?"

"Is that a shot?"

"No. I booked you a flight for Aruba."

"Try Pennsylvania."

"The Keystone State."

"That's the one," Amy said. "I need you to check something out for me. Apparently there's a prison in Auburn, New York."

"Okay."

"I want you to find out whether a guy named Peter Daniel Anderson did time there—let's see, it would have to be late '70 or early '71. Anything else is good too—parole conditions, home address when they released him, whatever you can find."

"You got it. You got your cell with you?"

"Yeah. Thanks."

Amy hung up and then walked to the window and looked out over the monument to the south. As she watched, a man on a gray horse appeared at the crest of the ridge. He was wearing a wide-brimmed hat and he held the horse to a walk as they crossed over the ridge and then disappeared to the east, horse and rider sinking slowly behind the hill, like the sun going down. After a moment, Amy put on her jacket and then went into town to have a look around. What she was looking for she couldn't say.

But she was hoping she'd recognize it when it came along.

He found Stonewall at ten in the morning, in the back room of the shop, where the bearded man was fitting a pair of wooden grips on a small revolver. The gun was clamped in a vice that had jaws of protective rubber. Stonewall wore a pair of glasses like those worn by a jeweler and he was bent at the waist, turning the small screws that secured the grips.

"What's new, Trots?" he asked without looking up.

Attorney Trotter, in the doorway, would have sworn that Stonewall hadn't looked his way, yet he somehow knew it was him. How he knew, Trotter had no idea, but he wasn't about to ask.

"Thaddeus around?"

"Off to New York."

"Oh," Trotter said. "And what's he doing there?"

"Oh, I don't know. Buying antiques, sucking cock . . . you never know with our boy Thad."

Trotter determined at once to change the subject. "The store's wide-open out front," he said. "Aren't you concerned that someone could rob you when you're back here?"

"There's over two hundred guns out there," Stonewall said. "And I know how to use 'em. Anybody thinks about robbing the place better be quick on their feet. A fifty-eight-caliber musket ball makes a mighty big hole."

"That's one way of approaching it, I guess."

"It's the Stonewall way," the big man said, grinning. Finishing, he took the gun from the vice and showed it to Trotter. "See here—Allen and Wheelock twenty-two pocket revolver. Just picked up the original rosewood grips off the Web. What do you figure this gun is worth?"

"I have no idea. A few hundred dollars."

"Wrong again. This little gun might be worth a few million, maybe quite a few million."

"How can that be?"

"It was because of this pop gun that we met Leona Anderson. She came in to sell it. And then later—through a combination of my lethal charm and some fine Tennessee sippin' whiskey—she told me about Potter being her daddy. If it wasn't for this gun, we never would've met. Destiny, my son. She could have walked into dum-dum's shop across the street, but she didn't."

He picked up a cloth and then began to wipe the gun clean, walking as he did into the front part of the store. Trotter followed along; he stood and watched as Stonewall unlocked the gun cabinet that held thirty or forty handguns and gently laid the little revolver on the green felt inside. Then he took a price tag from his shirt pocket and placed it beneath the gun. Trotter stepped in to look at the tag.

"Twelve hundred dollars?" he asked.

"That's for the tourists," Stonewall said. "It'll fetch six or seven, unless we get a live one off the street. So what's your story, Trots? You didn't come here to look at guns—a cap pistol would have you pissing your pants."

"I was looking for Leona Anderson," Trotter said, ignoring the insult. "There's never an answer at the number she gave me."

"Oh," Stonewall said vaguely. "I don't think she's staying there any-more. I might be able to find her. What's it about?"

"I have a lead on Winifred Potter," he said.

"Who?"

"Ambrose Potter's sister—we talked about this."

"Right. The DNA thing. Wasn't she cremated?"

"No. That's what we were afraid of. But it seems she was buried in a cemetery near Binghamton, New York."

Stonewall went behind the counter and opened the cash register, then took a wad of bills from his pocket and began to feed them into the till. He seemed decidedly unenthused about the news of Winifred Potter.

"Did they confiscate the stuff?" Stonewall asked, closing the drawer.

"Everything's down at the courthouse under lock and key."

"Everything?"

"Well, the collodion plates and the old phonograph are still at the university. Sheriff Harmer was of the opinion that they could stay there until this thing is sorted out."

"That's bullshit. That stuff is part of the estate. Why do they have access to it and she doesn't? Because that dipshit Harmer is busy kiss-ing Klaus Gabor's ass, that's why. That fucking Hungarian—someday I'm gonna take him down a peg."

"I didn't challenge it because I had no reason to."

"You wouldn't challenge a snake to an arm-wrestle."

"Very funny, Stonewall. What would be my argument? That Leona Anderson wants visitation rights?"

"No. Your argument is that you need to know what's at stake here. And to find out, Leona Anderson wants to retain Thaddeus St. John as an expert adviser on this."

"Oh?"

"As the foremost authority on Civil War memorabilia in the state, I think he's qualified. She wants you to write something up for her to sign. And make it ironclad—we don't want her running off on us down the road."

"I can draw a contract between the two of them," Trotter said unhappily. He wasn't at all comfortable with the inclusive pronouns Stonewall was using. He was beginning to wonder who he was representing. He watched as the bearded man took a feather duster and then walked over to the racks of rifles and muskets along the wall of the shop and began to dust the weapons off. It was a strange sight, the terminally uncouth and unkempt Stonewall engaged in such a fastidious act.

"You don't have much to say about Winifred Potter," Trotter said then.

"What do you want me to say?"

"This is significant. If we can disinter the woman, we can use DNA to prove unequivocally that Leona Anderson is who she claims to be."

"Isn't that gonna be expensive?"

"I would say it will be very expensive," Trotter said. "I've never been involved in such a thing before, but there is the actual disinterment, and then there's the cost of the DNA testing—I would say there'll be considerable expense."

"Who's gonna pay for it?"

"It would be up to Ms. Anderson."

"Fuck 'em. Let them pay for it. Let Bass pay for it—he figures he's the prodigal." Stonewall walked behind the counter and slid the duster underneath. He produced a jelly doughnut from somewhere down below and sat back on a stool and took a large bite. Apparently he was now ready for business.

"I don't understand your attitude," Trotter said. "This is very good news, finding Winifred Potter. This will prove her claim."

"You're absolutely right," Stonewall said after a moment. "Matter of fact, I think you'd better tell Bass that you found her, and that you're gonna dig the old girl up. Let's put some pressure on him."

The front door opened then, and a middle-aged couple walked in. Tourists. They stood in the doorway a moment, looking around, while Stonewall watched them without interest. Finally, the man said hello.

"Hey," Stonewall said.

"We were looking for something small for our grandson," the man said then. "He's quite the little history buff. Do you have minié balls?"

"Not according to my girlfriend," Stonewall told him.

The couple glanced quickly at each other. They were about to leave when Stonewall came out from behind the counter.

"Over here," he said, walking to a glass display case beneath the gun racks. "These were found up near the Devil's Den." He opened the case and removed a misshapen slug and showed it to the couple.

"I see," the man said. "How much are they?"

"Twelve bucks apiece," Stonewall said, on impulse tripling the actual price.

Twenty-four dollars later the couple were out the door. Stonewall put the money in the till and then looked at attorney Trotter. "Draw that contract up between Thaddeus and the woman. We'll meet you at the hotel bar at five o'clock. Once she signs, tell the other side that we want access to everything Bass found at the house. I don't trust that fucker."

"It's hard to know who to trust these days," Trotter said.

"You're right, you know," Stonewall told him. He shoved the last of the doughnut into his mouth. "I couldn't agree with you more."

Dock sat around for the next couple of days and while he wasn't exactly moping, he came, from time to time, dangerously close. It rained the first day and he passed the morning in the trailer, reading the diary. He was up to May of 1863. The news was from Chancellorsville:

> We walked to the town sqware and it was all the news of how Hooker took a thrashing over to Chancelorsville. People are geting right discorage now about the war and there seems to be more opinyun on it than ever. One feller from York, behaveing in a most belicose and pugnacious manner, opined that it was time to end it and let the secesion states go. There was much hollering to that and then another feller said that the war was ment to keep the country togther and that the only way to keep the country together was to at first keep the country together. Sometimes they ain't nothing for it but a stout piece of logic.

The rain stopped midafternoon and Dock went out and took a stroll around the small farm. He often walked the property at dusk, when the autumn sun was falling behind the bush lot to the west and the light took on a timeless, nostalgic tint. As a rule he stopped at the broken rail fence that was the property boundary. From there an over-grown lane led into the hardwood lot. The lane and the small forest, he was certain, had once been part of the original Burns farm. There was a copse of trees in the cornfield, standing out a hundred yards or so from the bush lot, and today he decided to walk over to see if he could determine why it had been spared the axe.

Arriving, he came across an old family cemetery. Clearing away the matted grass beneath the hardwoods, he found a number of head-stones lying flat on the ground. Although bleached white, their inscrip-tions faded and chipped, he found he could make out most of what was written on the stones. A good many belonged to various members of the Burns family, along with the odd Potter or Leach. Outside of Thomas and Eva Burns, none of the names were recognizable to him. Some were dated as early as the late 1700s. Dock sat in the grass by the stones and thought about the lives they must have lived, the mechanics of day-to-day living, the effort that must have been required just to keep food on the table and heat in the house. He wondered if people like that were given much to moping. He decided that it was unlikely. They'd have been too damn busy.

He didn't spot Willy's grave until he was leaving. It was set apart from the others; the small stone was still upright in the long grass along the fencerow and the inscription was legible. It told Dock that Willy had been born in 1843 and died in 1864, the two things he'd already known. There was nothing else to note his time on the earth.

Walking back to the house through the muddy field, he decided he would go back to work. If it turned out that he was restoring the place for somebody else, then that would have to be all right. Better than having someone come in and tear it down. If he could get it past the point where that was a consideration—and he was pretty close already—then that would be something at least.

The studding in the back portion of the house was in worse shape than he'd originally thought. The two-by-fours were shot through with dry rot, and the bottom plate was punky from worms or moisture or both. He decided to remove it all and start fresh. He tore out the old framing in a morning and added the pieces to the burn pile in the orchard, then drove into town and picked up a hundred precut two-by-fours and a keg of nails.

He laid out the first wall—the south wall—on the floor and nailed it together, then knocked together the lintels for the windows and the door. Nailing the lintels in, he smashed the forefinger on his left hand with the hammer, mashing the nail and causing the blood underneath to gather in a black clot. He wrapped it with electrical tape and kept on. By midafternoon, the wall was ready to lift into place; however, it was too long and unwieldy for one man to handle. Dock was considering what to do when he heard a car door slam and seconds later Klaus walked in. He was wearing his parka and carrying a bottle of brandy.

"Just in time," Dock said.

"Vut?"

"I'm gonna put you to work."

"But I have brought brandy."

"Grab ahold of the end of that wall," Dock said. "We'll work up a thirst."

"I am thirsty already."

With the Hungarian's inexpert help, they lifted the wall to a standing position. Dock had already chalked lines along the ceiling joists and on the floor where the wall was to rest. He had Klaus hold the wall in place as he went along and spiked the top and bottom plates. When the wall was secured, Klaus made a show of mopping his brow like a man who'd just spent ten hours in a cotton field.

Dock went into the trailer and came back with two plastic cups, and then he laid a length of two-by-ten across the sawhorses to make a bench for them to sit on. Klaus poured the brandy and indicated the wall they'd just erected.

"So you are undeterred, Doctor," he said.

"Idle hands are the devil's workshop—didn't anybody ever tell you that?" Dock asked him.

"You Americans are full of platitudes."

"Only when they work to our advantage."

Klaus produced a jackknife and a wedge of cheese from somewhere in the large coat. The cheese was wrapped in the waxy bronze paper once used by butchers. He opened it on the plank and then cut it into thick slices. "I buy this from a farmer on the pike. Is good cheese, not like the stuff in the store, full of chemicals."

Dock took a bite of the cheese; it was a sharp aged cheddar and tasted vaguely of grapes. "So what are you doing in this neck of the woods, Professor?"

Klaus shrugged. "I come to see if you are thirsty."

"You worried I might get dehydrated?"

"Maybe I vorry you get discouraged," Klaus said.

"Not easily, I don't," Dock told him. He had a drink of the brandy, felt it warm and welcome in his throat. The afternoon sun had dropped to shine through the window, where the muntin bars on the glass caused the beam to crisscross the two men sitting on the plank. Klaus closed his eyes against the bright light as he chewed on the cheese and had a drink of brandy.

"So vere do you come from, Doctor?" he asked when he opened them again. "For years it is very quiet in the town—except for ven maybe Hollyvud shows up. The only thing vorse than a fake accent is a fake beard." He took a sip of brandy. "But then all of a sudden you are here, and next thing ve have pictures of Mr. Lincoln, and recordings, and all kinds of nincompoops coming out of the vudvork."

"I was born in upstate New York," Dock said. "Little town called Coopers Falls."

"And you are carpenter there?"

Dock nodded. "Up until a few years ago. My dad was a carpenter. Well, not licensed but he could do anything—carpentry, plumbing, electrical. We built houses together for ten years or so. Everything, from the foundation to the cupboards." He paused, then shrugged. "But I got out of it, went into real estate."

"And vy do you do this?"

"Good question." Dock took a drink and wondered how he could possibly explain to the old man what he hadn't been able to explain to himself. "You ever meet a woman you figure is way better than you?" he asked after a moment. "I mean, unattainable? And then it turns out that she's not quite who you thought she was?"

"No. I meet a voman who I think is vay better than me," Klaus said. "And you know vut? I am right."

"Well, you're a lucky man, Professor."

"I *vas* lucky man. No more." Klaus picked up the knife and cut more cheese. "So go on—you meet this voman and she makes you crazy."

"I don't know if she made me crazy as much as she made me different," Dock said. "It's the old story. She loved everything about me and then proceeded to do her goddamnedest to change everything about me. But it was my call in the end—I broke up the partnership with my dad and got my real estate license. Starting making money hand over fist. But it was too much for me and never enough for her. The old man and I had a falling out over my leaving and before I could make it right he had a heart attack and died."

"Too bad, that. Is something you don't get back."

"That's right, you don't get it back. So it ended up I lost a father and gained a wife and if I could've swapped them one for the other, I'd have done it in a heartbeat."

"So vut happen next?"

"I don't know," Dock said. He reached for the bottle and poured for both of them as he thought back. It had only been a few weeks, but it seemed a lot longer than that. "I guess one day I just stood back and had a look at myself and I didn't much like what I saw."

"This is a hard thing to admit."

"Admitting it to you is easy," Dock said. "Admitting it to myself was the tough part. Maybe that's why it took so long. Anyway, I said to hell with the whole mess and just skedaddled."

"Yah, that's vut I thought. You skedaddle to here. I am glad you did, Doctor." Klaus indicated the workshop. "Vithout you—ve don't find this."

"Somebody would've found it, sooner or later."

"Yah, but maybe the wrong somebody. Is good job it is you." Klaus took another large drink of the liquor. It occurred to Dock that the old man was tipsy already.

"Your turn, Klaus. What brought you here?"

Klaus went into his pocket and brought out a handful of change. He selected a penny and then held it up for Dock to see.

"For the money?" Dock asked. "Somehow I doubt that."

"Not the coin. The man on the coin."

"Oh, that guy."

"I come here to study about him, almost thirty years now," Klaus said. "Every year I think I leave, but I stay. Is great man, Mr. Lincoln. Not just great American, but great man. This is vy vut you find here is of such interest. This is the man who made great speeches; but also he write these speeches, I think he believe these speeches." He sipped the brandy, then sighed. "Today, somebody else writes the speeches."

"And nobody believes them," Dock said.

"Yah," Klaus said. "The first inaugural, Mr. Lincoln speaks of the better angels of our nature. Think of that a minute, Doctor. To speak of these angels, first you have to know of them. Today, I am afraid these angels have become strangers. Makes me sad that they are gone."

They sat in the failing sunlight and finished most of the cheese and all of the brandy. From time to time Klaus would bring forth another of Abe's quotations, some familiar to Dock, others obscure. By the time the bottle was empty he had moved on, to Frederick Douglass, to Grant, to Marse Robert E. Lee. But he kept returning to Lincoln.

"What would he say if he was here today?" Dock asked when the bottle was gone.

"You mean here in this house?"

"No. Just . . . here."

"Vell . . . he vud travel the country," Klaus said and he got to his feet, eagerly but unsteadily, and he began to pantomime Lincoln traipsing across the nation, arms clasped behind his back. The liquor had given the old Hungarian a decidedly theatrical air. Dock half expected him to don a fake beard. "And ven he had been across the country from east to west, and from north to south, he vud say—vy in the fuck did ve fight that var anyway?"

"Vy in the fuck did ve fight that var anyway?" Dock repeated. "That's what Lincoln would say?"

"Yah, that's vut I think."

Dock laughed and while he was laughing the door opened and Stonewall Martin walked in, followed by a blond woman wearing jeans and a suede jacket and patent leather mules. Dock wasn't sure at first glance about Stonewall, but the woman looked every bit as drunk as Klaus.

"Trespassers," Stonewall said, smiling and glancing back to the woman. He dismissed the two with a disdainful eye and then moved to the center of the room, where he stood spread-legged, apparently taking command. He wore heavy-heeled engineer boots, which made him look even larger than usual, and there was a damp red stain on the front of the dirty buckskin jacket. The man's presence was such that, in another time and place, the stain would very likely have been blood. As it was, Dock was pretty sure it was tomato sauce.

The woman approached Dock; she had a cigarette in one hand and a bottle of Budweiser in the other. She was a little wobbly on the high heels and she was smiling a wasted smile.

"I'm Leona," she said. "You must be the guy fixing up my house."

"Nothing for you to steal here, Mr. Martin," Klaus said loudly. He spoke without turning to look at the big man.

"If I want any shit out of you, Gabor, I'll squeeze your head," Stonewall said. He walked to the workshop and had a look at the empty room, then stepped back and studied the doorway cut in the stone. "So this is it. Right under my nose all these years."

"What do you want?" Dock asked. He was on his feet now.

"The hired hand has a question, Leona," Stonewall said.

"Now don't be like that," she told him lightly. "There's no need to be nasty."

"You and your boyfriend having a little picnic, Gabor?" the big man asked then. "You sure got your fat Hungarian nose in here quick."

"I asked what you wanted," Dock said.

Stonewall looked at Leona. "Tell him."

Returning the look, Leona pulled lazily on the smoke, as if to tell Stonewall that she'd do what she wanted in her own time. She exhaled and made a move to butt her cigarette on the floor, then thought better of it and went to toss it out the open door. When she turned back, she offered Dock the same wan smile.

"We were wondering if we could look at the pictures and, um . . . the other thing," she said.

"You weren't wondering," Stonewall told her. "And you're not asking. You're demanding."

"They are at the university, these things," Klaus said.

"I thought I told you to shut up," Stonewall said. "We know they're at the university. That's the problem. They shouldn't be at the university. The university has no fucking claim on any of it."

"But still, that's vere they are," Klaus said, smiling. "Too bad for you."

Stonewall stepped quickly to the bench and roughly grabbed the old man by the fringe of hair at the back of his head. He forced Klaus's head down, mashing his nose against the rough plank where he sat. "Too bad for me?" he asked, smiling. "Is that what you said, you old fuck? Too bad for *me*?"

"Hey," Dock said, and when Stonewall looked up Dock hit him flush across the face with a short length of two-by-four he'd picked up from the floor. Stonewall went over backward and all 310 pounds hit the floor with a thud. He managed to roll onto his side before losing consciousness.

Dock turned toward Leona, who was watching with her mouth open. "What have you done to Wild Bill?" she asked.

She seemed surprised rather than angry; she soon recovered

enough to take a long drink of beer. Dock smiled at her in wonder and then he turned to the old man, who was still sitting on the bench, rubbing his nose where Stonewall had pushed it against the plank. It took him a moment to notice the inert giant on the floor.

"Vut in the Dickens?" he asked.

"Sometimes," Dock quoted solemnly, "they ain't nothing for it but a stout piece of wood."

Klaus was confused. "That is Lincoln said that?"

"Nope. I believe it might have been Babe Ruth."

THIRTEEN

By the time Stonewall regained consciousness, went to the hospital for stitches across the width of his forehead, and then made his way to the police station, it was nine o'clock. Sheriff Harmer decided to wait until the next morning to arrest Dock Bass.

Which he did, arriving at the house shortly past nine. Dock asked if he could take the time to lock his tools up and Harmer told him that he could. The sheriff let Dock sit up front for the drive to the station, and he didn't bother with the cuffs.

The charge was aggravated assault with a weapon. Harmer did not seize the weapon in question, as Dock had that morning integrated it into the framing of the back wall of the house.

There was a deputy working at the station and it was he who finger-printed Dock and took the mug shots and checked him for outstanding warrants. When these technical details were attended to, Harmer returned and he and the deputy took Dock into an interrogation room of sorts and sat him down. The deputy was businesslike and humorless to the point of being surly. When he printed the middle finger of Dock's left hand twice and the ring finger not at all, Dock felt obliged to point out the error and the man took affront to the correction.

In the little room, the three of them sat at a large oak table. Harmer was drinking coffee from a cup inscribed "World's #1 Dad." The surly deputy sat directly across from Dock, pencil in hand, a thick yellow notepad on the table in front of him.

"On a charge like this," Harmer said, "you'll have to appear before a judge and make bail."

"Okay," Dock said.

"It won't be a lot of money," Harmer continued. "The problem is—it's Saturday morning. You won't see a judge before Monday. This isn't the big city."

"It means you're going to spend the weekend in jail," the surly deputy said. Evidently, he was still smarting over the missed fingerprint.

"I figured that's what it meant," Dock said.

"You can make a statement if you want," Harmer told Dock. "Or you can call a lawyer. You don't have to do either if you don't want to."

Dock shrugged. "You can ask me whatever you want."

"Okay," Harmer said. "What happened between you and Stonewall Martin out there?"

Dock looked at the ceiling for a moment. "I guess you could say that he was behaving . . . in a most bellicose and pugnacious manner," he said finally.

"All right," Harmer said slowly.

"So I whacked him with a two-by-four."

The deputy took him to the county lockup on Carlisle Road, where he had to give up his personal effects, as well as his belt and shoelaces. After slow consideration by the deputy, he was allowed to keep his watch. Presumably, there was little chance he would endeavor to kill himself with a twenty-two-dollar Timex.

There was a large common cell, with a half-dozen cots and a card table, and a few straight-back chairs. He was alone in the cell all day long. Sheriff Harmer stopped by in the afternoon and gave him some magazines, *Sports Illustrated* and *Field and Stream* and a *National Geographic* with a grizzly bear on the cover. Most of the time he slept, out of boredom and not fatigue. He wished he'd had the diary to read, but it was an impractical wish. At least he was showing some consistency in that regard.

The bail hearing was set for nine Monday morning, but for a reason unknown to Dock it was at the last minute pushed back to ten o'clock. Coming into the courtroom, he saw Harris standing at the back of the room, his arms crossed and his face tight. The judge was a plump brunette in dangling gypsy earrings who seemed little interested in Dock's problems with Stonewall Martin. She set bail at two hundred dollars and added a condition prohibiting Dock from being within a thousand feet of the complainant. The acting DA then requested that the condition be expanded to include Thaddeus St. John as well, as St. John had apparently been retained by Leona Anderson in connection with the lien on the estate. The judge promptly agreed; by her expression she'd already heard more about the matter than she cared to know.

"Is that understood?" she asked Dock from the bench, speaking in a tone one usually reserved for mischievous toddlers. "You are restricted from being within a thousand feet of these two men."

"Can we make it a thousand miles?" Dock asked.

When Dock had put up the money, he collected his belongings and then walked outside, where Harris was waiting, his face still grim.

"What's going on?" Dock asked.

"Thaddeus St. John pulled a fast one this morning," Harris said. "He spent all weekend talking to the press, claiming he's been hired by Trotter and the Anderson woman as an independent expert to authenticate the effects of the estate. When he sent his trusted assistant—Stonehead to you—to the house to inform you of this, you went nuts and attacked him with a club."

Dock smiled.

"What're you grinning about?"

"That's pretty much how it happened."

"Well, there's more," Harris said. "This morning St. John and Trotter convinced Deputy Barney Fife in there to issue a warrant for the seizure of the plates and the phonautograph. Said they have to be included with the rest."

"What'd Harmer have to say about that?" Dock asked.

"Harmer is conveniently out of town for the day," Harris said.

That goddamn fingerprint. "So this means they'll be headed to the university," Dock said.

"They're there and back already," Harris said, and he nodded toward the courthouse. "They seized everything this morning—it's stowed in there with the rest. That's why they delayed the bail hearing. While they were at it, they arranged for Thaddeus—again as an independent expert—to be given access to everything you found. Wouldn't surprise me if he's in there right now, with his manicured fingers all over the plates, the recorder, everything."

Dock turned and looked back at the courthouse. Harris watched him for a moment, waiting for some kind of response.

"You might have to sit down with this woman, Dock," he said.

"Maybe," Dock said without conviction. He watched the courthouse a moment longer; then he turned back to Harris. "Did you know that a grizzly bear can run a hundred yards in less than five seconds?"

The network sent a crew down from Philadelphia and Amy spent a good part of the weekend pretending to do a story she didn't want and chasing people she couldn't catch. Klaus Gabor, Tommy Trotter, Leona Anderson. She knew where Dock Bass was, but she wasn't allowed access to him in the lockup. Not that the words *access* and *Dock Bass* had anything in common where she was involved anyway. So she did the standard pieces: remote shots at the house on Shealer Road, outside the university, at the battlefield. She talked about the plates, the recording, the battle, the looming custody fight. At one point she found herself discussing the weather with her cameraman as he rolled tape. When Thaddeus St. John went public with his involvement, she set up an interview with him in his store on York Street. When she'd contacted him by phone, the little man had assured her that he had nothing to say on the matter but then quickly agreed to be interviewed on camera to say it. Amy suspected that Thaddeus St. John was not one to turn down an opportunity to appear on network television.

As such, he had ample warning that she was coming with a crew, which probably explained the fact that he was wearing more makeup than Amy when they arrived. And he wore it well, she had to admit. A little liner, a little blush, just a hint of color on the lips. He had chosen, for the camera, a tweed blazer over a cream turtleneck and crisply pressed wool slacks. Amy fully expected him at any moment to produce a lit briar from his jacket pocket and plop it in his mouth to complete the pose.

It seemed as if they'd caught him in the process of taking inventory. As they set up, he made a point of ignoring them, moving about the store, clipboard in hand, counting merchandise and making entries as he did. It was an activity that conveniently and—quite purposefully to Amy's eyes—discouraged small talk, but she paid it no mind and approached him anyway.

"What's your background, Mr. St. John?" she asked, removing her coat and placing it on a period slat-back chair.

"Thaddeus," he said absently, his eyes on the paperwork in his hand. "I have an advanced degree in American history from Louisiana State."

"Then you know Charles Lafontaine," Amy said at once.

"Yes, of course," Thaddeus said. He hesitated for the briefest of moments, then looked up from the clipboard. "I wouldn't say we were friends, but we are acquaintances."

Amy nodded. Charlie Lafontaine was a snot-nosed kid she'd gone to junior high with back in Mississippi—he'd dropped out in the ninth grade to become a rock star. The last she'd heard he was still in the music business, working at the HMV in Yazoo City. She was guessing that the closest he'd ever been to Louisiana was when he sorted the Cajun CDs at the store.

They taped Thaddeus in front of the musket display—his suggestion. Apparently, he was going for as masculine an image as he could muster. It wasn't much of an interview. Thaddeus held fast to his pose as a high-end dealer in Civil War memorabilia and a scholar of the conflict itself; he described his role in the custody battle as being merely an expert witness, who could authenticate any of the items in the Potter estate that might have historical—and therefore financial—significance. Other than that, he had no interest in the dispute and, in fact, hinted transparently that it was an inconvenience for him to be involved at all.

"I assume you're being compensated, though," Amy said.

"Yes, I am," Thaddeus replied. "Just as I would assume that TransWorld will be giving you a little something for conducting this interview?"

"You bet," Amy told him.

He smiled at her in triumph and then, perhaps sensing an upper hand, he went on. "What puzzles me is this Bass fellow's reaction to all this," he said. "Are we not civilized men? To attack Mr. Martin for making a simple—and quite legitimate, I might add—request. It's incomprehensible."

"You don't think Mr. Martin could have provoked the attack?" Amy asked.

"Absolutely not. If you knew the man—he reminds me of nothing more than a giant teddy bear, my dear."

"I've met him," Amy said, and she watched Thaddeus's eyes change. "You're not acting as an adviser—or in any other capacity—for Leona Anderson? In other words, you don't have an abiding financial interest in the outcome of the suit?"

"I am being paid by Miss Anderson's legal counsel to examine these found artifacts. I work on an hourly basis and that's that. The outcome of the suit will affect me not one whit." Thaddeus smiled. "I assure you that I'm not in the habit of shilling myself out to whatever sad story comes along. I possess neither the time nor the inclination to do so. I leave that to the network news."

While they were packing to leave, Thaddeus approached. "I really must apologize for that last remark," he said. "Sometimes my passion to defend the integrity of my field of endeavor causes me to speak out of turn. Can you edit that out?"

"What—and dash our hopes for an Emmy nomination?" Amy asked.

He smiled, his eyes narrow, as he took Amy's jacket from the chair and held it for her. "Would this be Italian calfskin?" he asked.

"You've got a good eye, buddy," Amy said. She watched as he fondled the material for a moment. "Tell me, you think the Anderson woman is telling the truth?"

"I haven't the slightest, my dear. I have met her—she's a darling girl who has been dealt some harsh blows in her life. If she is the rightful heir, then I say bully for her. It's her opportunity to raise herself up from the depths. Surely you can relate to that."

"I beg your pardon?"

Thaddeus indicated the jacket. "I just meant—look where you are. You must be very proud."

Amy took her jacket from him and put it on. The cameraman was ready to go.

"Thanks for your time," she told Thaddeus St. John.

"Not at all. I don't know what your plans are, but perhaps we could get together later for a bite. I confess to having a weakness for good old-fashioned Washington gossip and I suspect that a woman of your professional standing in that town must be a font of such salacious tales. I have a favorite café on the hill."

"Sounds utterly charming," Amy said. "But I'll pass. I believe I've been elevated enough for one day."

Marla called at eleven the next morning. Amy had gone for a run and was just walking into her room while the phone was ringing. When it had become clear that she was not going to escape Gettysburg in the immediate future, she'd decided to commit to a daily run. She chose the Baltimore Pike for her route, because it was close by the hotel and because the road offered an incline that got her heart rate going. She ran for half an hour. Returning to town, she grabbed a coffee and the newspapers and went back to her room. She tossed the papers on the bed and grabbed the phone.

"Hello," she said.

"It's me," Marla said. "Breathing kind of heavy there, Amy. Am I interrupting something carnal?"

"You think I'd have answered the phone if you were?" Amy asked.

"It's called multitasking."

"Right. What have you got?"

"Anderson was in stir, like she said. October 18, 1970, to February 28, '71. When was she born?"

"September '71."

"He ain't the daddy."

"It would appear not," Amy said. She was looking at herself in the mirror above the bureau. She threw her Orioles cap on the bed and ran her hand through her hair. She was in need of a trim and high-lights. And she was a long way from her stylist in D.C. As she looked at herself she had a thought. "What about conjugal visits?"

"I'm way ahead of you," Marla said. "Didn't have such a thing. Not there, not then." She paused. "Maybe she's telling the truth."

"Maybe she is," Amy said. "I hate it when honesty rears its ugly head."

"Look at the bright side. It doesn't happen all that often."

"Right again."

"So what're you going to do?" Marla asked.

"Shit—I have no idea."

"Well, this thing is shaping up as one long legal battle. You might be there for a while, Amy. Have you thought about going house hunting?"

"Bite your tongue, girl."

"Might be a good thing if you can convince certain people up there that this chick is legit."

"It might at that."

"Then why do you sound as if you don't want to do that? I thought you had major fish to fry in the Caribbean."

"I do."

"Then what's going on? The Amy I know would do everything in her power to expedite the matter."

She glanced in the mirror again, curious to see if she looked like a woman who was doing just that. "Send me what you've got," she said then. "You're right—I have to make something happen."

★   ★   ★

Dock finished reframing the back portion of the house in two days, then decided to wire the place himself. On top of everything else, he was running short of money now. He wouldn't go back into the Coopers Falls account; in all likelihood Terri would've grabbed it by now anyway. At some point he was going to have to legalize their split. He didn't need complications on his financial situation from that quarter; if Terri was to catch wind of the situation here in Gettysburg, she might decide that she loved Dock just the way he was after all.

Thursday morning he went into town and bought a couple of rolls of fourteen wire and a case of electrical boxes, along with connectors and staples. He set the boxes for the plugs and switches first and was drilling the studs and the joists for the feeds when Amy Morris came calling. The door was propped open; she knocked lightly on the jamb and walked in. Dock turned at the sound; this latest version was wearing jeans and hiking boots and a down vest over a ribbed sweater. She was carrying a large manila envelope. Looking terrific, Dock admitted, but only to himself. Of course, looking terrific was her stock-in-trade.

"Where's your crew?" he asked.

"I'm solo," she replied and added, "I don't have a crew."

"You had one the other day," Dock said. "I saw you on the news."

"I thought you didn't watch TV."

"Sometimes I do—just to remind myself why I don't."

"That's very good—only took you—what?—half a minute to insult me this time. And what did you see on television, Mr. Bass?"

"You—going on about collodion plates and phonautographs and Leon Scott and a whole bunch of other shit that you don't give a damn about. But I'll give you this: you're a good pretender. If I didn't know that you didn't care, I might actually think that you cared."

"Damn, but I've missed you."

"I figured as much, way you keep showing up." He ran the drill bit through a ceiling joist, then looked back to her. "I saw you talking to Thaddeus St. John, too."

"I tried to get a comment from Stonewall Martin as well," she said. "But apparently he's recovering from an assault. On his person, as the local constabulary phrased it. Of course, you wouldn't know anything about that, would you?"

"I might."

"I guess I should count my lucky stars that you didn't give me a whack."

"I don't recall you pushing any of my friends around."

"Oh," she said and she hesitated. "Is that what happened?"

"Yup."

"Then why haven't you told anybody?"

"How do you know I haven't?"

"There's been nothing about it on the news. Just Stonewall's version."

Dock laughed at her. "Everybody doesn't live their life on the television, lady. Like you. Anyone who needs to know, knows."

Amy sighed in resignation. "All right. I swear, you could give a clinic in obstinance." She watched him a moment. "Why are you still renovating? What if Leona Anderson is the real deal?"

Dock was moving the ladder to continue drilling. He paused when he heard the question but then began to climb.

"What if she is?" Amy asked again.

"Then she'll inherit a house with brand-new wiring," Dock said.

"Like she'll care," Amy said. "She'll sell it off, first thing."

"Maybe I'll buy it then."

"I doubt it. She'll sell it to some enterprising huckster. He'll turn it into the Willy Burns museum and hawk photocopies of the Lincoln pics for ten bucks a pop."

"You know it can get real depressing, talking to you," Dock said.

He had the end of the insulated wire hooked onto the top rung of the ladder. He pulled it now to feed it through the holes he'd bored in the ceiling joists. After he'd pulled a few feet, the roll of wire on the floor flipped over and snagged on the leg of a sawhorse. Amy walked over and righted it. Dock kept pulling without comment.

"You always work alone?" she asked.

"I prefer to."

"That's surprising. You being so darn sociable and all."

Dock climbed down and moved the ladder a few feet toward the main portion of the house; then he went back up and continued to pull the cable.

"You know I used to work as an electrician's helper when I was in college," she told him.

Dock laughed. "I'll just bet you did."

"I did," she said. "I could give you a hand."

"Oh, I'm sure you could. Hey, I ever tell you how I used to read the evening news for Walter Cronkite on his day off?"

She walked over to the ladder. "You running a three-way to that light?" she asked.

"Yup. Most people know what a three-way switch is, lady."

"Okay," she said. "This is what you do. You run a two-wire feed to that switch box. You run a three-wire from one switch to the other. Then you run another two-wire to the light. Your white is the common, and the red and the black are your hots. Any of that sound right to you?"

Dock looked down at her for a moment and then he went back to feeding the wire. He moved the ladder once more and was at the wall, where he pulled the cable down and ran it to the switch box.

"Could have been a lucky guess," he said at last.

"Right."

"You know how to rough in a plug?"

"Well—duh," she replied.

"There's a pair of lineman's pliers in that toolbox," he said. "You can take that roll of fourteen-two and feed the plugs in this room, if you're looking for something to do. Start over in that corner—that's where the panel's going. You'll need two circuits, half the room on each."

Amy set the envelope she was carrying on the sawhorse. She went to the toolbox and found what she needed and went to work. Dock, still on the ladder, kept her in his peripheral vision for a few minutes, still not convinced that she was on the level. The woman had a habit of misrepresenting herself.

But not this time. When she'd finished the first box, she stapled the wire to the studding and then stood up and gave him a glance before moving on to the next.

"One of these days you'll have to tell me more about you and old Walter Cronkite," she said.

With the two of them working, they had the room completely wired by noon. They didn't talk much other than Dock telling her from time to time where to put a switch or a plug. He noticed that she wore a look of contentment as she worked that she didn't seem to possess otherwise. Once he caught her singing softly to herself; it sounded like John Prine's "Hello in There." She didn't appear to be someone who would know Prine.

Dock finished up by stapling the wires neatly in a row beside the future breaker panel. He slid his hammer into his belt and turned to where she stood in the center of the room, worrying a splinter from the ball of her hand.

"We're ready for insulation," he said.

"I think you mean *you're* ready for insulation. I'm not getting that itchy shit on me."

"You got an awful attitude for an apprentice electrician."

She managed to remove the sliver. "This from a man who's about as approachable as a cactus."

Dock looked at his watch. "You want a sandwich?"

"Sure."

"We'll eat in the trailer," he said and he started for the door. "I'm thinking at some point you're gonna tell me what's in that envelope."

Amy sat at the table while Dock made sandwiches on the kitchen counter. There were books scattered about the place, most of them opened, lying spine up. Books on the war, on Lincoln, on Gettysburg, some on Lincoln at Gettysburg. She noted with relief that he did not appear to be obsessed with the conflict; there was also a biography of Mickey Mantle and another of Hank Williams. Although each, to Amy's recollection, had battled his demons, neither was known for his connection to the War Between the States. Then she noticed a plate-glass negative beside one of the books.

"Is that from the house?" she asked.

He hesitated. "Yeah. One that they don't know about."

She went over and picked it up, held it to the light. The image was of a young boy standing beside a stocky pony, which he held by a makeshift rope hackamore.

"This is Willy Burns, isn't it?" she said. "That's why you kept it."

"No," Dock told her. "Willy would've taken the picture. I figure it might be a brother, or a buddy. I just kept it because I like it, the look on the kid's face—you can see how proud he is of the pony." He gave her a look. "Must be the same today when little Johnny gets his first laptop."

"Now, now," she admonished.

He looked at the plate in her hand. "You know after the war thousands of these plates were used to build greenhouses. And over the years the sun would bleach them out, and the images would gradually disappear. I think about that—the images of the war and the memories of the war both fading slowly away to nothing."

"What do you think about it?" she asked.

"That there's something about it that's sad and proper at the same time."

She took the plate back to the table and sat down again, looked at it in the light from the window. After a moment she became aware that he was watching her intently.

"What now?" she asked.

"Do you think you'd be where you are if you weren't beautiful?"

Her heart, quite unexpectedly, skipped. "Are you flirting with me?"

"Nope."

"Then what are you asking me?"

"Whether your looks got you where you are. If you tell me you don't understand the question, then that pretty much answers the question."

"I understand the question, smart guy. Why do I get the feeling that you're always talking down to me because of what I do? What have you done that's so bloody noble?"

"Nothing," he said. "I just don't feel the need to be on TV while I'm doing it."

"The viewing public, I'm sure, is inconsolable over that fact."

He smiled as he cut the sandwiches in half and retrieved a jar of pickles from the fridge. "First time in Gettysburg?"

"Yes."

"What have you seen so far?"

"If you're talking about things of a historical nature—not much. I've been busy representing the fifth estate. Talking to phony-baloney antique dealers, contrary carpenters, that kind of thing."

He seemed to come to a snap decision then, and he plopped the sandwiches on a paper plate and grabbed a couple of cans of juice from the fridge. "Come on—we're going for a drive."

He started for the door. She stood but held back. "Hold on—where are we going?"

"You'll see. Call it a picnic if you want."

"Every moment with you has been a picnic," she said, but she followed him outside, envelope in hand. Carrying the sandwiches, he looked like a waiter as he walked toward his pickup.

"We can take my car," she said, trailing and regarding the old truck unhappily.

He dismissed the Cayenne with a glance. "We could. But we won't."

He didn't open the door for her or wear his seat belt; she would have been surprised if he had done either. They drove into Gettysburg, semicircled the town center, and then drove directly out again, heading south. They took the same route she had run a few hours earlier, but a short distance out he turned off on one of the narrow paved roads that intersected the battleground. Soon they began to climb, through brush and rocks. The lane was bordered by split-rail fences.

He had finished his sandwich by this time and was now eyeing hers. "You gonna eat that sandwich or not?" he asked.

"I'm considering it," she said. "I'm also considering the foolhardiness of what I'm doing here. Riding into the wilderness in a pickup truck with a guy whom I—just a few days ago—described as mentally unstable."

Instead of taking offense, he actually whooped with delight. "You think I'm nuts? Hell, I'm the sanest guy around. You might not like it—in fact, in your line of work, it would probably make a great story if I was crazy as a bedbug—but I'm sane, lady. It's the sad truth."

He didn't appear all that sad saying it. After a moment she picked up the sandwich and began to eat. They were ascending through forest now and it was apparent that they were in the middle of the battleground itself. Everywhere she looked there were commemorative plaques, statues, cannons. They met other sightseers, poking along in their cars, or standing alongside the lane, examining the tributes, taking pictures. He drove past them all, steering the truck in and out of the cars parked along the meandering trail, and then finally stopped on a high point of ground, where the lane encircled a huge observation tower and then rejoined itself in the woods.

The tower was made of heavy tubular steel and it featured a series of stairs and landings that intersected at right angles and led to the top, where a railed platform provided a high vantage point over the countryside. The tower, painted in bright blue enamel, was as imposing as it was out of place above the battleground.

It was also closed to the public. The first set of steps had been pulled up to block the second; a padlocked chain denied access to the first landing.

"Come on," Dock said again. He got out of the truck and began to climb the steel trestlework to the first landing, actually using as a foothold a sign advising that the tower was off-limits for the season. Amy got out of the truck and watched.

"What are you doing?" she asked.

"For someone who claims to be an investigative reporter, you don't have a very good grasp of the obvious. You coming or not?"

She sighed, then took her gloves from her vest pocket and put them on. She began to climb. She gained the first landing, had to scramble over the obstructing staircase to reach the steps to the second, where Dock was waiting.

From the second landing on there were no more obstacles and Dock fairly bounded up the remaining stairs to the top. In an effort to keep up, Amy had no choice but to bound as well. In half a minute they were on the platform. Amy walked to the railing and looked out over the town in the distance, the panoramic landscape of the fields in between, and beyond, the forested rise to the west.

"Tell me that doesn't knock your hat in the creek," Dock said.

"It does," she told him. "And I don't even know what that means."

She turned to her left, toward the ridge in the distance.

"How many pairs of shoes do you own?" he asked suddenly.

The question was so incongruous that she looked down to see what she was wearing at the moment; it turned out to be an average-looking pair of hiking boots that she'd paid an above-average two hundred pounds for in London. "Did you just ask me how many pairs of shoes I own?"

"I'll give you a break. Within a dozen."

She regarded him warily. "I own an appropriate number of shoes for a woman . . . on the go."

"I bet you do," he said. "You might appreciate this. The Battle of Gettysburg started over shoes. The Confederates came into town looking for a supply of shoes that was rumored to be here. They didn't even know that the Union army was in the area."

"Ah—at last the Civil War makes sense to me," she said. "Is that what I'm supposed to say?"

He smiled at her. He seemed to be having a hell of a time. Maybe trespassing was his thing.

"That's Culp's Hill," he said then, pointing south. "Where Ewell and Slocum got it on. If Ewell had turned Meade's flank, it could have been a whole new ball game, and not just for the battle. Over there is the Wheat Field. There's the Peach Orchard, where Sickles got his ass kicked. New York nincompoop, Klaus calls him. Below us here is Little Round Top, and over there is the Devil's Den—some of the most fierce fighting in the entire war, they claim. And just over there, in the trees—well, you can't see it from here—is where Chamberlain and the Twentieth Maine saved Little Round Top by routing the Alabamans—although you'll get a different version on that from anybody from Mobile."

As he talked, Amy walked along the south and then the west railing of the platform, following his commentary. And while she had a passing reference to what he was describing, she was more interested in his demeanor than what he was saying. For the first time since she'd met him his guard was actually down, and for the moment, anyway, he wasn't defending anything. All he was doing was telling her how it was.

"That is Seminary Ridge," he said, pointing to the western horizon. "And down here—Cemetery Hill. And in between the two—it probably looks the same today as it did back then—that's the field. Fifteen thousand men trotted across there. They might have called it Pickett's Charge, but it was Pettigrew, too—and Trimble and Armistead and the rest. Fifteen thousand men—and they knew they had no chance."

Amy regarded the armaments along Cemetery Hill, the caissons lined there, the cannon, and the bridgework. Then she looked across the expanse to the ridge. "For every southern boy fourteen years old," she quoted, taxing her memory, "there is a moment when it is still not two o'clock on that July afternoon in 1863 . . . the guns are ready in the woods . . . the flags are furled—" She glanced at Dock. "I can't remember the rest."

"What's that from?"

"William Faulkner—*Intruder in the Dust*," she said. "Wait—I know something you don't? Damn, what I wouldn't give for a megaphone right now." She smiled at the look on his face. "I happen to be from Mississippi. Faulkner was required reading at my high school. The problem is, Mr. Bass, I also happen to be black. And the fact of the matter is, those fifteen thousand brave boys crossing that cornfield were fighting to preserve slavery. So even if I manage to distance myself from that enough to appreciate their courage, I have to say that I'm real happy that they lost. You can understand that, can't you?"

He didn't hesitate. "That's where it always gets tricky for me. Because those boys out there were so poor they didn't own a second pair of socks. Socks—hell, they came here looking for shoes because some of them were barefoot. They sure as hell didn't own any slaves. I think they were fighting for something else. But you're right—the people pushing them owned slaves. That's one thing that hasn't changed; the people that make the war never end up in the cornfield. Be a lot fewer wars if they did."

She looked out over the battlefield again.

"But yeah, I understand completely," she heard him say.

"Not completely, you don't," she told him. She couldn't decide whether she was angry that he would presume that he did, or appreciative of the fact that he would try. There was something contentious about him, even in these—his most conciliatory—moments.

Now he pointed back toward the town. "You look over there— you can see the monument in the cemetery. That's where he gave the Address."

"Whoa—you're not gonna recite it again?"

"No," he said emphatically.

When he didn't elaborate, she wondered if by his tone he was implying that she didn't deserve to hear it again. And it made her wish— for at least a fleeting moment—that she could.

When they got back to the truck, he picked up the manila envelope from the seat where she'd left it and handed it to her. "Well?"

She took it from him. "It's nothing."

"Really? You've been carrying around an empty envelope all day? And you're telling people I'm nuts?"

She opened the envelope. She was no longer in the mood to do this, but she realized she might not get another chance. She suspected that he was as approachable at this moment as he was ever going to be, at least to her. She handed him a photocopied sheet from inside. "Leona Anderson's birth records," Amy said. "She was actually born here in Gettysburg."

"Yeah?"

"A man named Peter Anderson is on record as her father. Problem is, he was in jail in New York State at the time of her conception. I'm thinking that her mother's theme song wasn't 'Stand by Your Man.'"

She found the prison record, faxed to her by Marla, and handed it to Dock, who took a few seconds to look it over. Half of Amy's sandwich was still on the paper plate; she picked it up and had a bite.

"It doesn't mean that Ambrose Potter was the guy," he said then.

"It just means that Peter Anderson wasn't. It's another piece of the puzzle. But it's a piece in her favor. This thing could take a long time to straighten out. I mean, if they start digging people up, it could be years before it's resolved."

"I'm aware of that."

"And you're okay with it?" Amy asked.

Dock put both hands on the steering wheel and sat looking at the tower. "My old man liked to look at things in poker terms. Used to drive my mother up the wall. For instance, he'd call two eggs and three slices of bacon a full house. My mother would say, 'It's just breakfast, for Chrissakes.'"

"Okay," Amy said.

"Right now they've got a four-card flush. They got the Anderson woman, Stonehead Martin, Thaddeus St. Whatsit, and little Tommy Trotter. So it all comes down to their hole card."

"And the hole card is Leona Anderson's father."

"Yup."

"And if it's Ambrose Potter?"

"Then they've got their flush. They win."

He looked over at her as he said it. After a moment, she nodded. She took another bite. "This is good, you know. Is this Virginia ham?"

"I wouldn't know. I bought it at the supermarket. Just down from the soap aisle."

"Ah yes, the soap." Amy smiled. "The thing is—"

"You want juice?"

"What?"

"I brought juice. I forgot."

"No, it's fine," Amy said. "The thing is, like I said before, Leona Anderson admits that she's all about the money. History to her is yesterday's hangover. She only cares about the cash."

"Which doesn't exactly make her an endangered species."

"No, it doesn't. But I don't think the woman wants to cool her heels in this burg indefinitely. I have a feeling she can't wait to get out of here."

"The two of you have a lot in common."

"You think I'm in a hurry to get out of here?"

"You might as well be wearing a sign," Dock said. "Of course, I haven't really figured out what you're doing here in the first place."

"I roam from town to town, doing electrical rough-in," she told him.

A blue minivan came up the road, a couple inside. Their disappointment was obvious as they regarded the off-limits tower a moment then followed the trail back down the hill.

"Law-abides," Amy said.

"You were about to suggest something," Dock said then.

"What's the most valuable item you've found?" Amy asked and then she quickly added, "And I mean in the real world—not the idealistic Dock Bass world. I'm talking dollars and cents here."

"The phonautograph," Dock said.

"Do you care who owns it?"

"No. I told you that before. It doesn't matter who owns it."

"Then give it to her."

Dock opened the bottle of juice and took a drink. Amy watched as he nodded his head slowly. "Tell her it's hers if she just goes away," he said.

Amy shrugged. "It'll make her rich, and that's all she cares about. She told me that to my face. You'd end up with everything else, including the house and farm—which I have a feeling are beginning to grow on you."

"You think so, do you?"

"You might as well be wearing a sign," she said.

Dock leaned back against the door of the truck for a moment. "You think she'd agree to that?"

"I said before, it's possible she doesn't know who her father is. It's possible she's just hoping it's Potter," Amy said. "I can feel her out. You know, buy her a couple of bourbons."

"Why?"

"Because she's a boozer."

"No," Dock said. "Why would you do that?"

Amy nodded toward his hand on the juice bottle. "What'd you do to your finger?" she asked, indicating the blackened nail.

"Hit it with a hammer."

"Doing what?"

"What do you mean? I was working on the house."

"That's why I would do it," she told him. "Because you—in spite of your alarmingly regressive social skills—appreciate all of it. And I mean *all* of it. And she doesn't. You're not going to break it up and sell it off piecemeal to the highest bidder. And if you can save the rest by giving up the recording, then maybe that's what you should do."

He looked out the window. "Be nice to be out from under it."

After a moment he started the truck. She fastened her seat belt. "Don't forget—you could run the risk of losing it all," she told him. "Will you think about it?"

He nodded as he pulled the truck into gear. As they drove back through the battleground, she attempted to cross-reference the sites she was looking at now with those she'd seen from above. It was difficult to do. Up close, things were never quite the same.

Then they were back on the pike, headed for town. She watched him as he drove, his elbow out the truck window.

"You're the first Dock I've ever met," she said. "I've been trying to guess where it came from. Were you conceived on a pier somewhere?"

He smiled. "There was a famous Appalachian folksinger named Dock Boggs. My old man was a big fan. He had all these records when I was a kid. Seventy-eights." They were passing the visitor's center now. "I don't know if my mother was a fan of the music, but I know she didn't care much for the name. I guess they went round and round about it when I was born. The old man won."

"Sounds to me that the contrary gene doesn't skip a generation," Amy said.

He smiled again. "Which means that your old man's got a stubborn side too?"

FOURTEEN

When she got back to the hotel she ran a tub, added some bath oil, and then climbed in with her cell phone and the new issue of *Harper's*. After settling into the warm water, she dialed the number in McLean. Nettie answered.

"Hey, old lady," she said.

"Hello, Amelia."

"The man around?"

"He's out walking the dogs in the rain—I don't know who's dumber, him or the animals. Oh, here he comes now. He's just by the barn."

"What are you up to today?" Amy asked as she waited. "Baking? Embroidery? Making bathtub gin?"

"I generally make bathtub gin on Tuesdays. Here he is, dear."

She heard Nettie tell Sam who it was and then he came on the phone. She could picture him, standing in the kitchen, the two retrievers on leashes circling his legs, no doubt muddying the floor, to Nettie's dismay.

"What's up?" he asked.

"He made me lunch," Amy said.

"He did?" he said, and she could sense rather than hear his chortle. "The reports of the demise of your appeal are greatly exaggerated."

"And we did a little renovating together."

"Is that a euphemism?"

"Hardly," she said. "Sometimes a girl has got to show a man how to wire a switch box to get his attention."

"I have no idea what you're talking about," Sam said. "And even if I did, I doubt it would interest me. So why don't you tell me something that will?"

"How about this? I suggested to him that he make an effort to come to some sort of agreement with the Anderson woman. Maybe offer her something to settle things without involving the courts. Something of significant material worth."

"Like a Leon Scott phonautograph?"

"I may have floated that suggestion."

"What did he say?"

"Well, he didn't hit me with a two-by-four."

"What?"

"He had a problem with some guy last week. A local thug who works for a dealer of some renown—a fop by the name of Thaddeus St. John. You've probably heard of him."

"Nope."

"Well, there was a confrontation out at the farmhouse and Bass hit this guy over the head with a piece of lumber and ended up spending the weekend behind bars."

"He sounds like a prince of a fellow. What'd he say to your proposal?"

"He was kind of hard to read," Amy said. "I'd hate to play poker with the son of a bitch. But I could tell he was intrigued by the possibility of settling the thing without a lot of time and legal nonsense." The tub was getting cool already. As she talked, Amy reached with her left foot and turned the hot faucet on, adjusting the flow so the warm water came out in a trickle. "And there's something else," she said then.

"What's that noise?" Sam asked.

"I'm in the tub. Been working construction all morning, man."

"Jesus Christ," he said impatiently. "You said there was something else."

"Yeah—and it's to your advantage. He really doesn't seem to care that much who owns the phonautograph. I think he cares about the words."

"We all care about the words, Amy."

"Do we now?" she asked and she shut the water off.

"I do," he said, and she could tell he was perturbed. "What do you think—that I collect things just for their monetary worth? If that was true, why wouldn't I eliminate the middle man and just collect money? You're the one with no appreciation of history. Your sense of history goes back to last spring's Paris fashions. And that's okay, but don't suggest that I don't appreciate the spiritual nature of these things. Because I do."

"Tell me again why you keep me around? I mean, I'm so incredibly shallow."

"I didn't say you were shallow."

"You pretty much did."

He laughed. "Not at all. You're not shallow; you just lack . . . depth."

"You're a riot, boss."

"Come on now. It works for you. It prevents you from becoming too emotionally involved. It makes you a better reporter."

"I wouldn't know about that—it's been a while since I've done any actual reporting."

"You'll be back."

"When?"

"When I get the phonautograph."

Dock spent the afternoon insulating and thinking about what Amy Morris had proposed. He wasn't exactly keen on the idea of handing anything, let alone the phonautograph, over to Leona Anderson. Especially when it wasn't even remotely clear that she was who she claimed to be. In his mind, it was potentially akin to aiding and abetting a felon. And, whether she was legitimate or not, he knew that the woman was in cahoots with Gettysburg's unholy trinity of Thaddeus, Stonewall, and Trotter and that they would benefit in some way from the concession.

On the other hand, if he could get himself free of her that easily, he knew it was the practical thing to do. That word again. And after all, he was the one who said it didn't matter who owned it anyway. Time to walk it like he talked it.

That night, reading in the trailer, he came upon Willy's diary entry for the twelfth of November, 1863. He'd been getting close and in doing so he'd slowed his reading to a crawl. "You can only do something for the first time once," his father used to say. Dock was already aware of how much he would miss the diary when he was finished.

He had recently read the accounts of the battles in early July and the sad state of the town from then throughout the fall, of the mass burials, the destroyed crops, the hundreds of dead horses, the flies and the buzzards, and the stench for weeks afterward. The survivors in the two armies, for all the horrors they'd faced for three days, were able to march away when the fighting was done. The civilian population was left with the carnage.

Dock was glad he'd resisted the urge to jump forward in the journal. He encountered Mr. Lincoln on that gray November day as had Willy:

Mr. Everet spoke for a right long time and Mr. Lincoln for a right short time. That seemed to be a surprize for some. I set up my box on the slope and took foreteen plates. The mix was dry on some so they may not be up to snuff. I had the machine with me and I snuck near the platform and set it to running but I ain't any idea if it caught anything or not. The people who saw me thought it was another picture box and I alowed them to think it so. There was plenty noize all around. Some drunks were yelling acting the jackass as always. Mr. Lincoln's words went to my heart. I wish I had them writ down. Maybe the Sentinel will cary them this week.

That ended the entry. Dock went into a cupboard above the sink and took down a bottle of rye and mixed himself a drink with water and ice. He stood leaning against the counter, looking at the pages of the diary where they lay scattered on the Formica tabletop.

"Well, there it is," he said aloud.

He stood there until he finished his drink and then he poured another and carried it back to the table. He read the page again and then placed it carefully with the rest. At the top of the following page Willy had inscribed the Gettysburg Address in full. Afterward he wrote:

> *It snowed last night for the first time this year. We hav more than eght inshes on the ground and the driffs hard on the back of the house are most three feet or better. I and Tom shuveled for near two hours and then went into Aunt Mabel's and shuveled some more.*
>
> *I hav been thinking on how Mr. Lincoln said that the men who died in the summer here should not of done it in vane. I expec he was talking of both sides and not just the Union. Because he talked about the people. Like we all are one people. And if that is so, then I cain't think that it's fine for sum to fight and others not to.*

Dock turned the page and came upon the final entry again.

> *I reckon now that I cain't keep away from it any longer. It was fine to sit back and treat it all like it didn't cuncern me but Mr. Lincoln has showed me that it cuncerns everybody. The people, as he said. And if fighting is the only way to stop people from fighting, then I guess I have to do my part. And when it's over then I hope nevver have to fight any body agin.*

After a while Dock stacked the pages together and then placed them in the cedar box where he'd found them. He sat there thinking about Willy Burns and then suddenly he was thinking about his father again, how the old man would approach a problem, the pinched cigarette always between his lips, the brow furrowed. His father had never once given him any advice on how to behave. Not in his personal life and not in his professional. He had just lived his life a certain way and if he noticed what anybody else was doing, he kept it to himself. Dock tried to recall the moment he decided to turn away from that, toward the pretty and ridiculous woman who was determined to turn him into somebody he couldn't be. He tried to recall the logic behind that. It seemed to him that none existed, certainly not now and probably— since he couldn't remember it—not then. Then why had he made that choice?

He was never going to know the answer to that. And even if he did, it wasn't going to change anything now. What's done was done. But it seemed to Dock that his father had never taken an uncertain step in his life.

He heard a noise against the window and he looked out to see that it was snowing. He got up and walked to the door and turned on the outside light. It was coming down in huge wet flakes, already accumulating on the lawn. If it kept up, there might be eight inches on the ground by dawn.

The next morning he got into his truck and drove to the university. The snow had stopped during the night and the custodial staff from the school was out clearing walkways as he approached. He parked in the area marked for students; there were a lot of students driving Saabs and Lexuses these days. Dock slid the pickup truck in among them and then walked across the lot to the school.

Klaus was teaching a class when he arrived at the Lair. Dock waited outside the classroom for a few minutes while he finished up. The door was open and Dock could clearly hear the old Hungarian as he systematically tore George McClellan into little shreds and then proceeded to dump him into history's wastebasket. That done, he bid the class good day.

Dock waited until the students had departed; then he walked in. Klaus was standing on the far side of the room, gazing sadly out the window overlooking the large snow-covered lawn. He turned only when he heard Dock's footsteps come close.

"Doctor," he said. "Valking softly, like Mr. Roosevelt. And I have seen vut you do vith big stick."

"Hello, Klaus."

"You are fresh from the hoosegow."

"I'm fresh from the hoosegow. Nobody knows the troubles I've seen."

The Hungarian smiled. "I make us tea. And your troubles vill disappear."

"You believe that?"

Klaus shrugged. "Vut the hell—ve can use the caffeine."

He walked to a cupboard in the corner of the room and plugged in a kettle, then produced tea bags and cups as he waited for the water to boil. The old man's hand shook slightly as he dropped the bags into the cups.

"Vy are you here, Doctor?" he asked. "Come to enroll?"

"I don't think so," Dock said. "I'm a little out of my league here."

"Hah, you are twice so smart as these kids," Klaus told him. "You could be teacher. No, I think you are too smart for that too. Sit," he said and he indicated his own chair by the desk. "Is great honor, to sit in my chair. I am joking."

Dock did what he was told. Among the textbooks and papers scattered across the desk was a photocopy of a period drawing of a Leon Scott phonautograph, virtually identical to the one he'd found. Dock was looking at it as the old man delivered his tea and then sat himself in a chair opposite Dock.

"So you are just here to visit?" Klaus asked. "That is nice. But not so."

Dock showed him the paper in his hand. "I'm here about this."

"Vut about it?"

"I'm thinking I might offer it to Leona Anderson, to settle her claim."

"Oh?"

"I'm thinking about it. It doesn't really change anything, Klaus. She'll sell it right off, I expect. To some museum or university, whatever. Eventually that's what'll happen anyway, no matter who owns it."

Klaus nodded into his cup. "She is villing to do this?"

"I got no idea. Amy Morris seems to think so. She's the one who suggested it."

"And you are villing?"

"I'm not sure about that either. If she's Ambrose's daughter, then I'm gonna lose everything. I'd like to keep the house and the property. I know he's not my blood, but for some reason, I feel close to Willy Burns. This might sound strange, but I feel an obligation to the kid. He's not a collectible."

"You are right, Doctor. That might sound strange." And the old man smiled. "But not to me."

Dock took a drink from his cup. The water hadn't quite come to a boil before Klaus had poured it, and the tea was only warm.

"This plan—you say Amy Morris, the TV lady, comes up vith it?" Klaus asked then.

"Yeah."

"This makes sense now," Klaus said. "All the time I vonder vy she is here. Big shot like she is. I should have seen this before. Her boss is Sam Rockvud—you know who this is?"

"I know the name. He owns the Redskins, or he did. You're telling me he owns TransWorld?"

"Yah. And he is big collector, of all American history. I meet him vun time in Vashington. They are giving me award for book I vrite about Mr. Lincoln. In this country, if you can write five sentences, they give you award. Anyvay, I meet Sam Rockvud, and all night he is breaking my ear about Gettysburg. But you see vut I am saying?"

Dock fell silent for a moment. He tossed the paper on the desk. "Yeah, I see what you're saying."

"But vut do you care who she sells it to?" Klaus asked. "If you are resigned to let it go, then you let it go. If it is vut you vant. Maybe Sam Rockvud has already made offer to the Anderson lady. If this is true, she maybe decide to go vith her bird in her hand."

"If he wanted to make an offer, why not make it to me?"

"Because this TV lady—Amy Morris—ven she meets you, she sees you are stubborn man. You don't care so much about your pocketbook. You are not to know vut she is up to. And she is afraid to offend you because her job is to charm you off your pants. She is smart cookie, this TV lady. I tell her the first time I meet her."

Dock got to his feet. "Yeah, she's a smart cookie. Thanks for the tea, Klaus."

He drove back to the house. The day was warming quickly and the snow from the night before was melting in the sun. When he got back to the trailer, he made a sandwich and sat down at the table to eat. The envelope that Amy Morris had left was still on the table. He opened it and had a look at the documents inside.

After a while he packed a bag and locked up the house and trailer and drove into town. He stopped at a gas station and told the attendant—a redheaded teenager with a nose ring and a dragon tattoo on his neck—to fill it up. Dock checked the oil and found he was down a quart.

"I'll need a quart of 10W30, too," he told the kid.

"You got it, dude."

"Better make it two," Dock said after a moment. "I might be gone awhile."

For the first couple of days, Trotter went with Thaddeus St. John to the courthouse to catalog the artifacts from the Potter estate. They would meet at Trotter's office after lunch and then walk over together. Thaddeus opted for a black fedora and a lime green trench coat for these forays through the town. As well, he wore leather boots with zippers up the side and, Trotter suspected, lifts in the soles. Either that or Thaddeus had experienced a rather late-in-life growth spurt.

The walk itself took far longer than it should have. Thaddeus knew virtually everyone in town—save the tourists—and, as he considered himself an expert in most things under the sun, there was much to discuss with the people he and Trotter encountered. Meteorology, politics, sociology, and, of course, fashion were the standard topics for these little sidewalk seminars. The one thing Thaddeus rarely talked about, Trotter noticed, was history, his real arena of expertise. Perhaps that was understandable; no one, for instance, stopped Trotter on the street to discuss the finer points of law. In truth, people rarely stopped him at all.

Thaddeus carried a briefcase and a large leather satchel that resembled an oversized doctor's bag. Inside were his textbooks, a Polaroid camera, notebooks, and a variety of reference materials. The first time they visited the evidence room, Thaddeus was obliged to show the county clerk who admitted them the contents of the bag. After that, he was allowed to come and go as he pleased.

Trotter was little interested in history and as such it was a boring time for him. Thaddeus set up a template for viewing the collodion plates, a simple easel with a lighted background, and he photographed each one and then indexed the shot with his own painstaking description of the particular image—whether it was a local street scene that he could identify, or perhaps citizens, most of whom he could not. The Lincoln plates were, of course, of greater interest, and he took several Polaroids of each and then yet again took pains to describe just what was seen.

"Is it not redundant to be describing a picture in such detail?" Trotter asked on the first day. "After all, the photo is right there."

"You're standing in my light, Thomas," Thaddeus told him.

He cataloged the rest of the items in the notebooks he brought. He wrote down all the information provided in the books, explaining to Trotter that he would check them out further—using the Internet and his own source materials—when he got home.

He was unable to actually play the recording on the phonautograph. He required Klaus's expertise for that, and—after a lengthy discussion—he convinced Trotter to ask the old Hungarian for his assistance.

"Yah," Klaus said into the phone when Trotter called.

"Fuck you," Klaus replied when Trotter made the request.

Thaddeus and Trotter briefly considered attempting to rig it themselves. They were contemplating just how to go about this when Stonewall walked in and saw the two of them staring at the machine.

"Like a couple of monkeys looking at the inside of a watch," Stonewall observed.

They decided to leave it alone. There would be time enough for these technical details once ownership was determined. Thaddeus claimed to know a man in New York City who was an expert in such matters; he was certain he could get it working. If that happened, Klaus Gabor would have to take his own advice.

Thaddeus worked at a pace that snails and turtles would mock. Trotter would watch him for a while, then retreat to one of the chairs along the wall, where he would fall asleep under the sunlight that streamed through the large casement windows above. Thaddeus would shake him awake when he was through for the day.

After the second day, at Thaddeus's suggestion, they stopped off for a drink at McClellan's on the way home. The lounge was half full. Leona Anderson was sitting at the bar.

"Imagine that," Trotter said when he saw her.

Leona was playing video poker on a little handheld machine and drinking bourbon. She joined them at the table.

"How's the catalogers?"

"Ready for a Dubonnet," Thaddeus said. "Can I get you another, dear?"

"You got a silver tongue, Thad."

The waiter came and Thaddeus ordered for himself and Leona. Trotter asked for a Coke.

"You know you haven't responded to my messages," Trotter said to Leona.

"What messages?"

"I need you to sign some papers if we're going to go ahead with the disinterment of Winifred Potter."

"Oh yeah. My friend keeps erasing my messages. I'm gonna have to get a new system."

"Maybe that's something you should think about," Trotter advised. He hesitated, then pushed forward. "I must say I really don't understand your cavalier attitude with regards to this. I would think this would be of great concern to you. Unless you prefer to drag this out for years. I really don't think you understand the machinations of such an undertaking. There are matters of procedure—"

"What's *cavalier* mean?"

"Lawyer talk, my dear," Thaddeus said. "These fellows and their thirty-dollar words."

"Look who's talking," Leona said.

"At least I have the capacity for relaxation at day's end," Thaddeus said. "Our Mr. Trotter is much too tense for the hour. Loosen up, man—it's cocktail time."

"It seems I am required to be tense enough for the three of us," Trotter said.

"You seem to be up to the task," Thaddeus said with a giggle.

Leona tipped her glass. "And we appreciate it, boss."

Trotter watched as she shifted the indolent smile to Thaddeus, who was watching her over the rim of his glass. He had the familiar feeling of being left out. Trotter took a sip of his soda. "Just how necessary is it for me to be with you every day at the courthouse?" he asked Thaddeus then. "I really find it tedious—just watching you basically—"

"Watching me with his eyes closed a good deal of the time," Thaddeus stage-whispered to Leona.

"My point is, I'm falling behind in other areas," Trotter said. "I do have a law practice."

"Why don't you set it up with the good deputy for me to go it alone?" Thaddeus asked. "I was under the impression you wanted to be there."

"Not at all," Trotter said. "They all know you at the courthouse. Heck, everybody in Pennsylvania knows you. I'm sure it will be all right."

Thaddeus nodded and then looked thoughtfully at Leona a moment. "I was thinking that perhaps you should talk to this ruffian Bass as well," he said, looking at her but talking to Trotter.

"About what?" Trotter asked.

Thaddeus shrugged. "See what he thinks about this unfortunate business of digging the old girl up. You might remind him that he stands to lose everything when that happens. Better yet, tell him that he *will* lose everything when that happens. See what the coarse fellow says to that."

"I think we can guess what his reaction would be," Trotter said.

"He won't be turning fucking cartwheels, I can tell you that," Leona said.

"Engage him anyway," Thaddeus said. "He might be in a mood for compromise. Has he retained counsel yet?"

"Not that I've heard," Trotter said.

"A curious thing, that," Thaddeus said. "Anybody with a brain would have taken that step. I suspect this fellow is the dimmest of bulbs. Violent types usually are. And I'll tell you what else I think. He's in love with that decrepit house and that sorry patch of ground. And he's so frightened that he might lose it that he's basically in denial. Why do you think he attacked Stonewall? Yes, this fellow is off the bubble. You go to him, Thomas, and you tell him he can keep the house and acreage if Leona gets the contents."

"Come on, he's never going to consider that," Trotter said. "The contents are where the money lies."

"You don't know what the simpleton might consider," Thaddeus said. "If nothing else, it's a jumping-off point. It might put him in a compromising frame of mind. Perhaps he would be willing to go—say—sixty-forty on the contents. To our advantage, of course."

"You mean to Ms. Anderson's advantage," Trotter pointed out.

"Indeed," Thaddeus said at once. "To Ms. Anderson's advantage."

Trotter looked at Leona. "And you would agree to that?"

"In a New York minute," she told him.

"But if you're the legitimate heir, you'd be cheating yourself," Trotter said.

"She has a life to get back to," Thaddeus said. "This young woman has irons in the fire in Philadelphia which you and I, Thomas, know nothing about. She realizes that she might have to make some concessions, but she's a reasonable woman. She will listen to a reasonable offer."

"Why do I get the impression that the two of you have discussed this at length?" Trotter said.

"Oh, we've become fast friends," Thaddeus said. "Am I not allowed to offer advice to a friend? Are we in breach of some mandate?"

"I don't know about this," Trotter said after a moment.

"Fortunately for everyone, it's not up to you to know," Thaddeus said. "Correct me if I'm wrong, Thomas, but you're basically operating as an employee on this matter. Leona here is a sweet girl—I'm sure she would be loath to seek representation elsewhere."

"You mean fire his ass?" Leona asked, nodding to Trotter. "Yeah, I'd hate like hell to do that." She clinked the ice in her glass to emphasize the fact that it was empty. "Where's that fucking waiter? I'd fire *him* in a minute, if I could find the little bastard."

Thaddeus took another sip of Dubonnet and then wiped his lips carefully with a napkin from the table. He looked at Trotter, who was unhappily rotating his Coke glass on his knee.

"We're going to have to start the proceedings on the disinterment," Trotter insisted.

"But do seek him out first," Thaddeus said emphatically. "You can use the other as leverage if you want, but by all means find out what this fellow is thinking."

Trotter turned to Leona. "Are you instructing me to do so?"

"Go get him, tiger," she said.

"But protect yourself, Thomas," Thaddeus advised. "Have you seen my poor boy Stonewall? I swear—his face looks like a crazy woman's quilt."

FIFTEEN

Amy began to run through the battleground, taking a different route each morning. After a while, she found herself doing less running and more reading of the inscriptions on the plaques and statues along the way. Her twenty minutes stretched into an hour, then two. On Friday she passed most of the morning in the Devil's Den and on Little Round Top, educating herself on McLaws's Georgians and the Texans of John Bell Hood, and on the heroics of an engineer named Warren and two doomed young colonels, Strong Vincent and Patrick O'Rorke.

Back at the hotel she showered and dressed and then ate lunch in the restaurant across the street. Returning to her room, she read the papers and answered a few e-mails and looked at herself in the mirror. Then on impulse she drove out to see if Dock Bass was thinking about offering Leona Anderson a deal. Turning onto Shealer Road, she considered sharing with him what she'd learned on her non-run that morning. But he would assume that she was faking it again, as she'd done on her earlier visit, after cramming all night on the Web. He'd be surprised to learn that this time her interest was genuine. She was a little surprised herself.

The point was soon rendered moot. There was no one at the farm; the house and trailer were locked, the red pickup gone.

Driving back into town, she realized that she could ask Leona Anderson if the matter of a compromise had been broached. Unfortunately, she knew of only one place to look for the woman. And Leona was not at the bar in the Gettysburg Hotel. After learning from the bartender that she hadn't been in that day, Amy walked back out onto the sidewalk and, lacking any fresh offensive strategy, decided to take a stroll through town. She put her collar up—the day was gray under a stiff breeze—and started around the town center. The shopwindows were filled with everything from authentic Civil War muskets to Lee and Meade salt and pepper shakers. There were T-shirts and hats and flags and books and candles and beer mugs, all commemorating the great battle. One diner offered the Jubal Early Bird Special.

Across the town center from the Gettysburg Hotel was a statue of Abraham Lincoln. It was unusual in that it had no pedestal; as a result Abe appeared to be standing on the sidewalk. A plaque indicated that the building alongside was where Abe had spent the night prior to giving his best-known speech. The statue Abe was gesturing with his hand toward some unknown point. Amy walked up for a closer look. She assumed the monument to be life-sized—the old emancipator loomed nearly a full foot above her. She looked at the face for a time. She had no idea if it was a good likeness; of the images she'd seen of the man, no two had ever seemed alike. Still, there was a sadness to the eyes; whether it was a result of the carver's skill or just her subconscious reacting to what she knew of the man and his circumstance, she couldn't know.

"I guess this isn't exactly what you had in mind," she found herself telling him.

As soon as she said it, she realized that there was a couple standing not six feet away, camera-ready tourists, watching her with interest.

"I gotta go," she told Abe, and she started down York Street.

A couple of blocks along, she passed Thaddeus St. John's store. Inside, she saw the little man, standing in the middle of the floor, his hands fluttering in the air as he described something to a man in a navy blue suit. As she walked on it occurred to her that Thaddeus might know of Leona's whereabouts. When she got to the point on the east end of town where the stores gave way to clapboard residences, she turned around and went back. Thaddeus was alone when she walked in. "Hello," she said.

He looked up from where he was sitting behind the counter, an open magazine or catalog before him, and he nodded to her. If he was surprised to see her, he never let it show.

"I was looking for Leona Anderson."

"She's not here."

"Obviously not. Do you know where she is?"

"I might. I'm not at liberty to say."

"I see."

It seemed that Thaddeus was cooler than on her last visit, when she'd rebuffed his invitation to dinner. He immediately went back to his reading. Amy stepped farther into the room, stopped to look at a display case. Inside was a surgeon's kit from the 1860s, complete with bone saw and pliers and laudanum bottles, along with a number of other frighteningly medieval-looking instruments that she couldn't name.

"I'm going to Louisiana next month," she said, her focus still on the kit. "I'll probably hook up with some friends from the university. Who did you say you studied with?"

When she turned, his eyes were still focused on the magazine, but he didn't seem to be reading any longer. When he looked at her, he smiled. He really did need to see an orthodontist.

"What business do you have with Leona Anderson?" he asked.

Amy shrugged. "Just following up. The claim against the Potter estate is a news story and I'm a journalist. I didn't mention that the day I interviewed you?"

"Well, there are reporters and there are TV *personalities*," Thaddeus said. "I'm not convinced under which category you fall, but I suspect that Miss Anderson is not anxious to speak with either species. None of my affair, of course; but it would seem to me that the media would only muddy the waters on a claim such as this. The truth might fall prey to sensationalism, if I may speak frankly."

Amy smiled slightly as he went back to his magazine. He was wearing a mauve cashmere sweater with a scarf that appeared to be silk.

She found herself wondering just how satisfying it would feel to reach out and drag the snotty little prick over the counter and slap him around the room for a minute or two.

She entertained the notion for a moment longer, then let it go. She wondered what was happening to her. A few minutes ago she'd been conversing with a statue. Now she was thinking about bitch-slapping an antique dealer. The heartland, it seemed, was turning her into a lunatic.

If she wouldn't slap him, she would at least try to bluff him. "I heard a rumor that Leona and this man Bass might be considering some sort of compromise."

"Where would you hear a thing like that?"

"I'm not at liberty to say."

"That's very good," Thaddeus said and he smiled again. She wished he would stop. "Is that why you're still in town? Because otherwise, there really doesn't seem to me to be much of a story here. Especially for a woman of your profile. Shining light that you are."

"Maybe it'll turn into a story."

"I suspect not. In fact, I suspect Sam's got you bird-dogging for something other than a story. Furthermore, I suspect I could make a pretty fair guess as to what it might be."

She hesitated. "You know Sam Rockwood?"

"I've known Sam for twenty years. Last spring I sold him a Brown Bess musket which once belonged to Abner Doubleday."

"I wasn't aware that you guys knew each other," Amy said after a moment.

"He's a major collector, I'm a major dealer—of course we know each other."

"Of course."

"Anyway, I was just closing for the day."

"I won't keep you."

"Are you quite certain you don't want to tell me where you heard that rumor?"

"Can't divulge sources," she said, and he smiled as if he was passing a stone.

The sun came out and the wind diminished as she walked back up the hill to the hotel. The street, which had been virtually empty earlier, was now filled with people, drawn outside, she assumed, by the improved weather. There were students on Rollerblades, young mothers pushing retro prams, businessmen and -women strolling to the town center, heading for that first after-work drink. Amy, walking uphill against the traffic, felt the sun on her face as it dropped toward Seminary Ridge.

There were reasons why Sam might have said that he'd never heard of Thaddeus St. John. Maybe he hadn't heard the name correctly, or maybe it hadn't registered—although it wasn't a name that would qualify as pedestrian. Maybe his mind was on the phonautograph. Maybe it was just Sam showing his years—it would happen eventually.

And maybe he'd been lying.

When she got to the hotel she kept on walking and soon she was at the visitor's center. She went inside and passed the better part of an hour there, looking at the maps and the clothing and the weapons and the literature. She eventually bought several books on the battle and one on Lincoln's visit.

She was examining a painstakingly detailed re-creation of a period military bivouac when she noticed an older woman watching her. The woman, who looked like Katharine Hepburn's kid sister, carried a large folder.

"I recognize you from television," the woman said then. "Are you doing research?"

"Just playing the tourist," Amy told her. "Had some time to kill. Do you work here?"

"I'm with the Historical Society. I saw the piece you did on the news, about the collodion plates and the rest."

"I happened to be in the area," Amy said, wondering at her need to shade the truth, even in this. "The network wanted a human-interest piece on the guy who found the stuff."

"But Mr. Bass wasn't in the story."

"Mr. Bass is not an on-air kind of guy. He's a very private man."

"I didn't find him so. In fact, we went for drinks at the hotel."

For some implausible reason, Amy felt a sudden pang of jealousy. The feeling was high school and ridiculous and it passed as quickly as it arrived. When it did, she smiled at the older woman and then turned to go.

"I think he's the right man to have found what he found," the woman said then.

Amy turned back. "And what if it turns out that it doesn't belong to him?"

"That's why he's the right man," the woman said. "He's known all along that it doesn't belong to him."

On the way to work the next morning Trotter stopped by the courthouse and arranged for Thaddeus to continue his examinations of the items from the Potter estate on his own. That burden lifted, he went to the office, his mood improved greatly at the prospect of a day without the popinjay antiquary. Olive was already at her desk when he arrived and he sat with her for a while, drinking coffee and listening to the country music station out of Harrisburg.

"Leona Anderson wants me to approach Dock Bass," he said after a while. "To see if he's open to some sort of settlement."

"Well, I suppose she's anxious to get her hands on some money," Olive said. "It doesn't appear that she has any."

"I guess not."

"I know she hasn't given you any," she said pointedly.

"No."

"Then it's probably worth a try."

Olive called information and was told that Dock Bass had an unlisted number.

"I'll drive out there at noon," Trotter said. "It's only five minutes."

He worked at the office until twelve thirty, then drove out to the Potter farm. There was no red pickup truck in the drive, no one on the premises. The trailer was locked, as was the old house itself. Trotter took a walk around the yard, muddying his shoes in the process, and then he went back to sit behind the wheel of the Lincoln, thinking he would wait until one or so. Perhaps Bass had gone into town for lunch. The sun was shining through the windshield, and he fell asleep under its warmth. When he awoke, it was nearly three o'clock. He drove back to the office in a stupor.

"I was wondering where you got to," Olive said when he walked in.

"I had a meeting in Carlisle," he said.

"Oh." She went into her daybook, wondering if she'd neglected to remind him.

"It was personal," he told her, and he went into his office. He passed the next hour on and off the phone with various municipal types in the city of Binghamton, trying to find one who could grant him the authority to get Winifred Potter out of the ground for an afternoon in the lab.

At four thirty he came out of his office. He was thinking of driving out to the Potter farm again, and while he was thinking it the phone began to ring. He watched Olive as she answered it and then saw her eyes register surprise.

"He's right here—one moment," she said, then offered Trotter the phone.

"Who is it?"

"Dock Bass."

Trotter hesitated a moment before taking the receiver. "Hello," he said then.

Dock Bass said hello back. His voice sounded far away. There were vaguely familiar rumblings and whirrings in the background.

"Where are you?" Trotter asked.

"Out on the turnpike."

"Are you leaving town?"

"Nope—just on my way back. I'd like to sit down with Leona Anderson, counselor. Maybe we can work out some sort of agreement."

"Well," Trotter said, and he stalled again. That Bass was willing to do precisely what he wanted him to do made him suspicious. But he couldn't justify the feeling. "To tell you the truth, Ms. Anderson has suggested something along those lines to me recently. I wasn't sure you'd be open to such a discussion, given your problems with Mr. Martin last week."

"That's got nothing to do with this," Dock said. "But I'll be honest with you, counselor—this wasn't my idea. It was Amy Morris who put the notion to me. I'd like her to be at the meeting if that's possible."

"Land's sakes, man—we don't want the media there."

"She won't be there as media. She came up with the idea—maybe hoping to get herself out of here—I don't know, and frankly I don't care. But without her, I wouldn't be making this call. She seems to know a little about the law. And since our bitter breakup, counselor, I've haven't found anybody yet to take your place."

"Right. I'd forgotten that razor-sharp wit." Trotter imagined, rather than heard, Bass chuckling into the phone.

"Either way, I'd like her to be there."

"Could you hold on a moment?" Trotter said and he cupped his hand over the mouthpiece and turned to Olive. His whisper was louder than his normal voice. "He wants to meet. But he wants the Morris woman from television to be there. She's apparently convinced him she's an expert in this."

"She does have a background in law," Olive said. "And she's very nice."

Trotter regarded her with momentary reproach, then uncovered the phone. "I suppose that would be all right," he said to Dock Bass. "But she is to be on her own. Absolutely no cameras."

"Suits me. I'm not looking to be on TV anyway."

"But it does bring up another point," Trotter said then. "Ms. Anderson might want Thaddeus St. John there. You might say he's taken on the role of her adviser."

"Then you've got a problem," Dock said. "The judge has ordered me not to go within a thousand feet of old Thad. I don't remember your office as being that big, Trotter."

"I see," Trotter said. "As I was not in court that day, I was not aware of that restriction. I wonder if the judge would temporarily stay the condition for the purpose of this meeting. Contingent, of course, upon Thaddeus being agreeable."

"Fuck Thaddeus. He can't have it both ways. Besides—am I talking to the wrong guy here? Can you handle this, Trotter? Tell me you can handle this."

"I can handle it," Trotter told him. "When were you thinking?"

"Tomorrow afternoon," Dock said. "One o'clock."

"Done."

The line went dead before Trotter could say anything else. He handed the receiver to Olive and then with an effort lifted his stumpy body to rest his hip on the edge of her desk. "We're meeting here tomorrow at one."

"And he's not bringing a lawyer?"

Trotter shook his head. "He's bringing the TV star. I'd say the woman has turned his head."

"I could see why. She's a beautiful woman," Olive said.

Trotter turned up his nose. "She's a little too fancy for my taste."

Dock got back to the trailer a little after dark. The snow that had arrived so spectacularly two days earlier had now melted almost completely away, leaving thin rivulets of dirty water running along each side of the drive and a muddy mess around the old house. Dock went into the trailer and turned the heat on and then he walked over to the house and unlocked the door. Inside, he plugged in the phone and called the Holiday Inn. He asked for her room, and a moment later she answered.

"Hello," he said.

"Oh—hi." She sounded every bit as surprised as had attorney Trotter.

"It's Dock Bass."

"I know who it is. How are you?"

"I'm meeting with Leona Anderson and her lawyer tomorrow at one. Do you want to be there?"

"Yes, absolutely." She made a lame attempt to hide her enthusiasm.

"It's at Trotter's office. It's on Carlisle Street. I don't know the number."

"I've been there."

"Right," Dock said. "I guess I should've known that. I keep forgetting you're always one step ahead of everybody else."

"Not always."

"All right. And no cameras."

"Wait," she said then. "Do you want to meet for lunch beforehand?"

"No."

"Why not? We could discuss what you're going to do."

"I know what I'm gonna do."

"Have you decided what you're going to offer her yet?"

Dock was looking at a wire along a switch box that needed stapling. "I bet when you were a kid, you liked to open your presents before Christmas Day, didn't you?"

"As a matter of fact, I did. What's wrong with that?"

"Makes for a pretty boring Christmas. See you tomorrow."

The next morning he got up early and in a couple of hours finished insulating the back room of the farmhouse. By noon he had the heavy plastic vapor barrier on as well. He taped the seams and around the electrical boxes and then he swept up, put the sweepings in a garbage bag, and set it outside. It was garbage day.

He went into the trailer and ate a bowl of cereal for lunch while he read the sports section from the previous day's paper. After he ate, he had a shower and then put on clean clothes. It was a quarter to one. It would take only a few minutes to get to Trotter's office. He took down the cedar box containing the diary and found a passage he'd marked after reading it the first time. It was written in September of 1862.

> *There was a right ferce battle neer a place with the curius name of Antietam last week. Both sides are declareing victory but from the number dead it is hard to see how neether could be right. If the news is to be trusted, Mr. Lincoln is becuming right impatient with McClelan. It becums less clear to me day to day just what it is being fought for. It seems there is plenty of lyes*

from both sides and they just go to make maters worse. For me,
Mr. Lincoln is one who does not deal in lyes. For me, that is the
best way and the only way. Tell the truth all the time and the
truth will win out.

They were all assembled when he arrived: the doughty lawyer
Trotter, the bleary-eyed client Anderson, the plain secretary Olive, and
the television star Amy Morris, looking more fetching than ever in
black jeans and a cream knit sweater beneath a black fleece vest, her
hair pulled back in a ponytail.

Dock walked in, carrying the envelope provided him a couple of
days earlier by Amy. The room fell suddenly silent as he arrived and
he suspected that the conversation he'd interrupted had been about
himself.

"Here we are," Trotter said, assuming a take-charge tone. "Right
on time."

Dock nodded, first toward Amy and then in the direction of Leona
Anderson, who was wearing a short skirt and cowboy boots and a jean
jacket over a black T-shirt. He smiled at Olive, causing her to blush and
busy herself with a urgent rearrangement of her desktop. Removing
his coat, he hung it on a hall tree in the corner. When he turned
around, Trotter was reaching across the desk to take up several sheets
of paper.

"I've taken the liberty," he said as he did, "of drawing up an
agenda, which basically identifies—in alphabetical order—all parties
present, as well as describing their individual roles in this discussion.
You'll see that I've also made notes with regard to—"

Dock took the papers from Trotter and gave them a quick glance,
then looked at the assembly. "Is there anybody here who doesn't know
they're here?" he asked. When no one replied, he said to Trotter, "I
think we can dispose of these," and dropped the papers in the
wastepaper basket beside the desk.

"For the love of God," Trotter protested.

"I'd rather we keep him out of it, too," Dock said and he opened the envelope. "First thing I want to talk about is your birth record, Miss Anderson." He hesitated. "Why don't we all get comfortable?"

When he turned toward Amy, she was wearing a bemused look, but she moved to sit on the leather couch beneath the window. Leona Anderson followed. Trotter was determined, it seemed, to remain on his feet as long as Dock did, although he did move to lean against Olive's desk. When everyone was settled, Dock produced the hospital record from the envelope.

"I'd just like to go through the paternity stuff before making any kind of an offer," he said. "This document was given to me by Amy Morris and it states that Leona Anderson was born September 30, 1971. Is that right?"

"That's right, cowboy," Leona said. She was lounging, her legs crossed, against the worn arm of the couch, lighting a cigarette and smiling at him. Olive scrambled to find an ashtray.

"Well, you look hale and hearty today," Dock said to Leona.

"And what is that supposed to mean?" Trotter asked.

"Just what I said," Dock told him. "She had a rough start in life; she only weighed three and a half pounds when she was born."

"How do you know that?" Amy asked. "The hospital didn't give me that."

"That's because the hospital doesn't have it," Dock said. "I had to track down Dr. Isabel Suggins, who delivered Leona Anderson and most of the other babies in Gettysburg back then. She may have even given Trotter here his first slap—and if she did, I can understand why—I've thought about it myself more than once."

"This is ridiculous," Trotter said. "What is the point in this?"

"Just trying to get all the information out in the open," Dock said. "I visited Dr. Suggins—who now lives in Hagerstown and is still slapping babies, if not lawyers. She has records of every baby she ever delivered, and she informs me that Leona Anderson was born two months premature. Which means that she was conceived around the first of March, not the first of January."

"So I was premature," Leona said. "What's your point?"

"Pete Anderson was in jail on the first of January," Dock said. "But on the first of March, he was not."

The assembly was quieted, but just for a moment.

"What does it matter?" Trotter asked. "We have every intention of proving that Ambrose Potter is the father."

Dock grinned and pointed at him. "You're right; it doesn't matter. I just wanted to get that straight. Let's move on. So from Baltimore I drove to upstate New York, to the prison at Auburn. Now, does anyone here believe in serendipity?" Dock looked at each in turn, then smiled again at Olive. "Olive, do you believe in serendipity?"

"Um, I forget what it means."

"Well, in this case, it means that by chance I did a little time at Auburn myself a few years back. So I got in touch with my old parole officer. Now, it turns out that the guy he replaced was Pete Anderson's parole officer. Can you imagine that?" Dock looked at Leona. "You know, the Pete Anderson who's not your father. The old officer's retired now, got a nice little cottage along the shore of Lake Ontario; he was frying up a mess of perch when I got there. But he remembers old Pete real well, even kept in touch with him after his release."

"Does this little travelogue have any relevance?" Trotter asked. "We already knew when Leona was born and we already knew about Anderson's incarceration. What is your point?"

Dock ran his hand across his beard, as if he wasn't quite sure where he was heading with it himself. He glanced at Amy. She wore a slight smile now—a look that suggested she didn't know where he was going, either, but she had a feeling it was going to be good.

"Well," Dock said then. "I just wanted to make sure her story checks out. You know, about Anderson not being her father."

"And how did you intend to do that?" Trotter asked.

"I figured we could draw some blood when he gets here."

Trotter's exasperation was now apoplectic. "When *who* gets here?"

Dock smiled. "Pete Anderson."

On the couch Leona Anderson was rather quickly lighting another smoke, although there was still half a cigarette burning in the ashtray.

"Anderson's dead," Trotter told Dock.

"Then he died in the past twenty-four hours," Dock said. "Because I had lunch with the man yesterday. He's living in a retirement home in Morgantown. He looked as healthy as a draft horse—claims he hasn't had a drink in eighteen years."

Leona was now eyeing him wildly. But when Dock turned toward her, she looked away.

"You're saying you spoke to him?" Amy asked.

"He's coming in on the afternoon bus," Dock said. "Harris is picking him up and bringing him here."

"What the fuck is goin' on here?" Leona said, finally snapping. "I thought there'd be an offer. I don't have time for this shit. I have to . . . I gotta get back to Philadelphia."

Now Trotter turned to Amy. "Yes—what exactly is going on here? What have the two of you concocted? Is Pete Anderson actually alive?"

Amy nodded toward Dock. "You're gonna have to ask Geraldo there that one. Sounds to me like the man's been doing some serious investigating."

"You bet I have," Dock said. "You're lucky I'm not charging you mileage, Trotter."

"I don't have time for this," Leona said again. It seemed that her husky voice had risen an octave.

"I have a feeling that Mr. Bass wants to see your hole card, Mr. Trotter," Amy said from the couch.

"I beg your pardon?" Trotter asked.

"That's it," Dock said. "After all, we all have our motives in this thing. Well, with the exception of Olive here, who's probably just collecting an honest wage. But Miss Anderson, you're interested in the estate because it'll mean money in your pocket. And you've admitted that. Trotter here is representing you because he stands to receive a percentage of whatever you collect. The lovely Miss Morris—well, she's the wild card in all of this because she's not quite as transparent as the rest of us. She'll say she's here as a journalist, but she's really here because her rich boss sent her to Gettysburg to try and score the phonautograph. And, being a smart woman, she knows that she's got a lot better chance of buying it from you, Miss Anderson, than from me.

Which is why she was so generous in supplying me with evidence on your behalf and then suggesting that I offer you the phonautograph. If she had done her job a little better, she might have turned up Pete Anderson herself, but then she's not really an investigating type journalist—she's more of a high-cheekbones, nice-ass kind of a journalist."

The room fell silent for the second time. Everybody tried to look at Amy without appearing to look at Amy—who, to her credit, remained cool.

"Wait a damn minute here," she said slowly, and she stood up, smiling but barely. "As much as I've enjoyed this nifty little Sam Spade routine here, I think I should set everybody straight. I am in Gettysburg as a *working* journalist. I am in no way, shape, or form some kind of agent in pursuit of these oh-so fascinating knickknacks that you people get so fired up about. And frankly, I resent any suggestion otherwise."

Trotter looked at her. "To be honest, I really don't care why you're here. Your presence doesn't change anything either way." He turned back to Dock. "Are you saying that if Pete Anderson is not the father, then you'll agree that Ambrose Potter is?"

Leona was pulling on the cigarette like it was a lifeline.

"Yup," Dock said.

"I got irons to fire in Philadelphia," Leona said. "I got no time to wait around on this."

"Ms. Anderson," Trotter advised. "This could work to your advantage."

Leona gave him a look of dismissal and then she came off the couch and went after Dock. "I was told there'd be a fucking offer. I came here to make a deal. Tell you what—give me the goddamn Lincoln pictures and I'll forget the rest."

"Don't you want to stick around and say hello to your old dad—or stepdad—or whatever he is?" Dock asked her.

"To hell with him," Leona said. "I got things to do. You gonna make me an offer or not? Tell you what—give me a hundred grand right now, and I'll be out of your hair. Trotter will draw up the papers, and I'll sign. Right now."

"You went from the Lincoln plates to a hundred grand in ten seconds?" Dock asked. "Old Thaddeus wouldn't like that."

"Fuck old Thaddeus. Give me the hundred grand and I'm gone."

"I think we ought to wait for Pete," Dock said. He looked at Trotter and then turned back to Leona. "By the way, did your attorney tell you that you could be convicted of fraud if it turns out you're lying?"

Leona's eyes went to Trotter.

"Hold on now," Trotter said.

"Is he gonna make an offer or not?" Leona demanded of Trotter. "I'm not waiting around for that fucking drunk to show up."

Trotter looked resignedly at Dock. "Is Pete Anderson coming here?"

Dock looked at his watch. "I expect him any minute now."

"Are you, um . . . ," Trotter began, and he looked at Leona, who was executing a not so subtle side step toward the door. "I think I see what you're doing. Are you prepared to make an offer before he gets here?"

"Sure," Dock said.

"And what are you offering?"

"How about a kick in the arse with a frozen boot," Dock suggested.

Leona told Trotter that she would be in Philadelphia and then she was out the door. They could hear her clopping briskly down the stairs. Trotter watched the door, then turned reluctantly to Dock, who was taking his jacket from the hall tree. Amy had walked over to the office windows, and she was looking down to the street below, where, Dock guessed, she was witnessing the rapid retreat of Leona Anderson.

"I don't think we have a number for Ms. Anderson in Philadelphia," Olive said.

"Ms. Anderson won't be back," Trotter said. He was still watching Dock, who now had his jacket on.

"Well, I guess I'll head off Pete Anderson at the bus station," Dock said. "I assume I can send him on home?"

Trotter, his hand now on his forehead, as if stricken with a sudden headache, nodded behind the hand.

"I'll be wanting to collect my stuff from the courthouse, too,"

Dock said. "You arranged to have it seized; I guess you can arrange to have it unseized."

Trotter nodded again, and then he dropped the hand and drew the deep breath of a man about to take on an unsavory task. "I should apologize for this, Mr. Bass," he said slowly and then his voice picked up. "In my defense, I think it should be known that I was approached, unbeknownst to me, by this individual—"

"Don't," Dock said and he held up his hand. "You're just gonna ruin the moment."

He walked out. Going down the stairs, he heard footsteps behind him, but he didn't turn toward the sound, didn't need to.

She caught up with him in the parking lot. He was going through his pockets for his truck keys and then realized that they were in the ignition. He could see them through the driver's window.

"Hey," she said.

"What?" He opened the truck door.

"That was quite a performance."

"Yeah, it was. By everybody."

"Everybody?"

"Yeah. You get a bunch of liars in a room and I guess it's bound to get entertaining, if nothing else."

She put her hand on the truck door. "I could take offense at what you said about me."

"You could," he said. "You should."

"You don't fool around when you've got an ax to grind, do you?" she said. She waited for a response and when none came she showed him a smile of forgiveness. "So why were you in jail in New York State?"

"I've never been in jail in my life," Dock told her. "Wait—that's another lie. I was in jail last weekend, for thumping old Stonehead across the noggin."

"You didn't do time in Auburn?" she asked and she regarded him suspiciously until it came to her. "Shit—you never found Pete Anderson."

"He's dead."

Amy turned and glanced toward Trotter's office a moment. "It was all bullshit, wasn't it?"

"The part about the doctor was true, and Leona being premature. The rest of it was pure horseshit." He waited until she turned back to him and then he said, "That ironic enough for you? This whole thing revolves around a guy who was known as Honest Abe. And for some reason it attracted the biggest bunch of goddamn liars and weasels I've ever seen. Someday I'd like for somebody to explain that to me."

"Why don't we go for a beer and I'll try."

"I doubt you're qualified," Dock said. "Is this your boss's fallback position? If Leona Anderson craps out on her claim, then buy me a beer and see what transpires?"

"You're pretty determined to insult me today, aren't you?" she said. "Up there, I thought it was just part of the act."

"You're the one to know about that," Dock told her. "All you are is an act. And when it comes to liars, you're the biggest frog in the puddle. Tell me something—how far has Sam Rockwood instructed you to go to get the phonautograph? If I'm not interested in money, what're you gonna suggest next?"

"I'll suggest it right now," she snapped. "You can go fuck yourself."

"That's the second time you've told me that," Dock said and he got into the truck. "You better watch it—your boss finds out about that tongue of yours and he might fire your ass. I gotta believe there's a lot of pretty girls out there willing to tell lies for a living. See ya."

She walked back to the hotel and called Sam Rockwood from her room. When she told him the bad news about Leona Anderson's pretension to the Potter estate, Sam accepted it with uncharacteristic resignation and humor even.

"So he bluffed them," Sam said and he laughed. "And it turns out they were running a scam all along."

"That's it. They were four flushing."

"Beg your pardon?"

"Oh, nothing."

"Well, don't worry about it, kid. It was always a long shot."

"That's nice to know now. Next time you want to chase a long shot, send an intern."

"I'll let you know when it's time for you to make those kinds of decisions, Amy," Sam said. "You're a little on the sassy side today."

"You're the second one who's told me that," Amy said. "The first wasn't nearly so polite about it. What do I do now, Sam?"

"Get the crew, do a quick wrap-up on the custody battle—give it a feel-good spin, the truth winning out, that sort of thing. Paint Bass red, white, and blue if you want. Then come on home."

"Yeah?"

"You're going to Aruba."

She left town the next morning. She took one last run to the Round Tops at dawn. This time she climbed the bigger of the two hills, had a final look over the town. It was a gray, misty morning and she could see little, though. The cupola was like a ghost in the distance.

She had breakfast in the hotel restaurant and then went to her room and packed. She couldn't remember ever being so anxious to vacate a hotel room. Still, loading her luggage into the Porsche, she had to fight an urge to drive out to the Potter farm one last time. She wished that her parting statement to him had been something of a more profound nature than simply advising him to fuck himself. Thinking about it, though, she knew that another meeting would in all likelihood end up the same. Like Lee fifteen decades earlier, she decided to cut her losses and head south.

She stopped in town, on Chambersburg Street, for gas. While the kid was filling the tank, she got out and went into the service center and bought a *USA Today,* the only paper available.

When she walked out, she saw Sam Rockwood across the street, strolling down the sidewalk, wearing a khaki jacket and tweed cap. She stopped short, thinking at first that it couldn't be him. But it was. She called over to him. He turned and stopped, then made his way across the street.

"Hey, kid."

"What the hell?" she asked. "What're you doing here?"

"Looking for you, of course."

"I'm on my way home. You knew that."

"Yeah, I did. But Marie and I are heading for St. Kitts for a month tomorrow and I didn't think I'd see you. I've been feeling guilty about this whole thing and I figured I'd drive up here and buy you a cup of coffee."

"You drove two hours to buy me coffee?"

"Well . . . all this commotion has got me going through my Civil War books again. It's been years since I've been to Gettysburg—thought I'd spend the afternoon wandering around the visitor's center and the museums."

"Really?"

"All right," he said after a moment. "I'm going to drive over to the school, see if I can't persuade Klaus Gabor into letting me have a look at the plates, once they're released. I've met the old boy a couple times; maybe he'll do me a favor. I could end up on the inside track if they happen to come up for sale."

This time Amy nodded. The kid had finished pumping the gas. Amy handed him a credit card. "What about the phonautograph?" she asked.

"I think you'll see the university end up with it," Sam said. "Now that the Anderson woman has flown. To quote Mr. Lincoln: 'She was our last, best hope.'"

"You history buffs are always quoting dead people," Amy said. "I'm looking forward to getting back to a world where Donna Karan's opinion counts for something."

They went to a café in the town center and had lattes and croissants. The place was empty except for two young women who sat in a booth at the rear, drinking tea and reading from textbooks, ignoring each other. Students, Amy guessed.

"You might as well take the weekend off," Sam said. "Head for the Caribbean on Monday. Get yourself ready."

"I'm ready now."

"I thought you might need some downtime before heading out."

"This whole assignment has been downtime, Sam," she said.

He smiled and drank from his cup. "Be careful what you ask for, kid. There might come a day when you'll miss this quiet little town."

Amy looked out the window. A man was washing the windows on the ground floor of the Gettysburg Hotel. "Why do you say that?"

"Just that it's a nice little place. I spent a lot of time here in my younger days, weekends with Marie. Norman Rockwell's America continues to exist, Amelia. You just have to look for it a little harder these days."

"This town is full of pretenders and opportunists."

"I'm not willing to believe that," Sam said. "It could be those are the people you happened to encounter here."

"We had a saying when I was a kid," Amy told him. "Takes one to know one."

"You talking about me?"

"I'm talking about both of us."

SIXTEEN

Dock had dinner that night at the Jamesons'. He and Klaus and Harris sat at the counter separating the kitchen from the dining area, while Lynn prepared the meal. Harris and Dock drank Yuengling Lager; Klaus and Lynn had wine. The kitchen smelled of rosemary and garlic, of baked goods and the pungent whiff of yeast.

"So vut you do now, Doctor?" Klaus asked. "You have routed the enemy."

"Yeah, I've routed them."

"Like General Meade, though, you vill not pursue."

"I'm not in a pursuing mood, Klaus," Dock said. "If I press charges, it'll drag on and for what? You can bet that Thaddeus and old Stonehead have covered their tracks on this. They'll lay it all on Leona Anderson. It's not gonna give me any satisfaction to see her take the hit. I'd rather let it go."

"Tell me something," Lynn said. "How were you so sure that she didn't know whether or not her father was alive?"

"I wasn't," Dock said. "I had to see her face when I said it."

"And if she'd been telling the truth?"

"I guess you guys would be having dinner with her tonight," Dock said.

"Don't be too hard on Leona Anderson," Harris said. "This thing had Thaddeus St. John's elegant fingerprints all over it from the outset. And why not? Worst-case scenario, he gets nothing. That's what he was going to get anyway. And Trotter—the man should be disbarred."

"I don't think Trotter was in on it," Dock said.

"Come on."

"I'm telling you," Dock said. "There was the whole bunch of us in that office and the only one telling the truth was the goddamn lawyer. Talk about a world turned upside down."

"Shocking," Harris said and he stood up.

"So now vut?" Klaus asked Dock. "Go see the African-Americans in baggy clothes?"

"I guess I could go and see the Africans-Americans in baggy clothes," Dock said. "For sure, I gotta do something. Because it looks like I don't own this stuff. It owns me."

Harris, returning from the fridge, put a full beer in front of Dock and then sat down.

"Whether you like it or not," Lynn said, "you're about to become rich."

"I think you should know that I'm all in favor of me becoming rich," Dock told her. "I'm not nearly as noble as these guys may have led you to believe. It's just that I'm not thrilled with dealing with guys like Thaddeus St. John and his smelly sidekick. It can't all be ulterior motives; there's gotta be a high road somewhere."

"You'll need Lewis and Clark to find it," Harris said. "In the meantime, what're you going to do with the collection?"

"I don't know," Dock said. "I came here hoping the three of you could tell me."

"I come here looking for roast beef," Klaus said. He sniffed the air. "I think maybe I get it, too."

"There's your ulterior motives," Lynn said.

"First thing—you must qvit to vorry," Klaus said then. "Tomorrow, ve go to the courthouse and gather everything. Then ve sit and figure it out—is not space shuttle. You are too busy in your head, Doctor. That is your problem."

Dock took a drink of beer. "I am too busy in my head. That is my problem."

He and Klaus found Sheriff Harmer at the police station the next morning at nine. Harmer was behind a desk in an office to the rear of the big room, drinking coffee and wearing a ball cap with a leaping brook trout on the front. The surly deputy was lounging against a side wall, talking to a young woman in a state police uniform. When he saw Dock, he straightened up and squared his skinny shoulders. Dock looked him in the eye and then he winked at the woman as he walked past and went into Harmer's office, Klaus in his oversized parka on his heels.

"Mr. Bass," Harmer said.

"Hello, Sheriff. This is Klaus Gabor."

"I know Mr. Gabor," Harmer said. "He owes me about eight hundred dollars in parking tickets."

"Oops," Klaus said.

"You've come for the plates and the rest," Harmer said to Dock.

"Yup."

Harmer got to his feet. "Trotter was here yesterday afternoon, babbling like a running brook. Apparently, the heiress Anderson has skipped town."

"She had business in Philadelphia," Dock said.

"Yah, monkey business," Klaus added.

Harmer raised his eyebrows. "You figure on paying those fines today?"

Klaus immediately made a production of slapping his pockets. "I forget my pocketbook," he said then. "I come by another time."

"Right," Harmer said. "I'm just heading to Cashtown to pick up an idler. My deputy can take you over to the courthouse. Everything's been authorized for release. I want to apologize for this. Under the circumstances, maybe I can get Stonewall Martin to drop the assault charges. You could make a pretty good argument that he had no business being there, especially in light of what happened with the claim. Technically, you could charge him with trespassing."

"Then I'd be no better than him," Dock said.

The surly deputy led them across the yard to the courthouse. Dock had backed his truck up to the edge of the lawn, just twenty feet or so from the building. They could carry everything out the side door and load it in the pickup.

Inside, the deputy used a key from the ring on his belt to open the evidence room. Back in the station he had made them wait while he regaled the woman officer with a story of pursuit and capture, one in which he was the chief pursuer and, ultimately, the hero. Now he went in first and turned on the overhead light. All the items from Willy Burns's workshop were scattered across two large oak library tables. Dock walked to the table with the collodion plates and held several in turn up to the light. Then he began to count them.

"You boys all right in here then?" the deputy asked, his tone every bit as snotty as his look. "Or do you need babysitting?"

"If we did, I doubt we'd hire a baby to do it," Dock said.

"Keep it up, Bass," the deputy said and he started for the door.

"Hold up your horses," Klaus said. He was standing at the farthermost table, where the phonautograph was positioned amid the books and tools and the Bacon revolver. "Vut is this?" he asked, picking the machine up.

The deputy turned and looked. "It's that damned tape recorder you all been fighting over. What do you mean—what is it?"

Dock walked over to Klaus and looked at the phonautograph. "Shit," he said when he saw.

"What's your problem, Bass?" the deputy asked. "You gonna claim it's been tampered with?"

"I wouldn't say tampered."

"Then what?"

Dock looked at him. "Switched."

The surly deputy decided to walk over and have a look at the phonautograph. "What the hell are you talking about? I helped lug all this crap in here. Looks like the same gizmo to me."

"You wouldn't know a Great Dane from a calico cat," Dock told him. "But you do know who's had access to this room."

"Is that what this is about?" the deputy asked. "You're gonna try and tar Thaddeus St. John?"

"Why would we do that?" Dock asked.

"Hoping he'll get Stonewall to drop the assault charges," the deputy suggested after a moment's consideration. "You guys wouldn't try to pull a fast one, would you?"

"I think to fool you it vud not have to be so fast," Klaus said. "You come to university; I show you picture of the real phonautograph. Cylinder here is bigger, for one thing. And horn is different too."

"Thaddeus," Dock said, thinking about it. "He must have switched it yesterday, after Leona bolted." He looked at the deputy. "Was he here yesterday?"

"Who?"

"St. John," Dock said. "Try to keep up."

"He's been here every day," the deputy said.

"This vas—vut you call—contingency," Klaus said. "But he vas prepared. Vy else he has other phonautograph on hand?"

"Is it a Leon Scott?"

"Yah. Just different model, I think. Close, but not close enough, like horse grenades. But now vut?"

Dock went over the surly deputy's head without as much as a sideways glance. "We could ask Harmer to get a search warrant on St. John's place," he said. "But it won't be there. I don't know where it'll be, but it won't be there."

"If by chance this thing really has been switched—" the deputy began.

"He just told you it was," Dock said, indicating Klaus.

"I'm just saying, it probably wasn't Thaddeus St. John," the deputy said. His tone was actually civil. He may have been smarting at being excluded from the loop.

"Why not?"

"For one thing, he's a very respected guy in the business," the deputy said. "You think he's gonna involve himself in some petty theft?" He hesitated. "But there's something else. Yesterday morning, that window was unlocked."

He indicated one of the huge barred casement windows running along one wall of the room. The windows were secured with deadbolts, top and bottom.

"We don't know how it happened, but it was unlocked. Didn't appear like nothing was missing, so we just locked it back up."

"Who discovered it?" Dock asked.

"Well," the deputy said and he paused again. "It was actually Thaddeus St. John who pointed it out. He noticed it when he came to examine the stuff."

Dock looked at Klaus and laughed. "You think this dumb motherfucker here knows what a red herring is?"

Klaus looked at the surly deputy. "Somehow, I am doubting it."

They loaded everything, including the bogus phonautograph, into the back of Dock's truck. There were a few reporters on hand, still sniffing after the Anderson story, and a couple of photographers. Neither Dock nor Klaus mentioned the missing phonautograph. It wasn't much of a story—watching two men load antiques into a truck—and by the time they finished, the press was gone and Sheriff Harmer was pulling a cruiser into the parking lot. He was alone in the car; his idler must have given him the slip. He walked across the lawn to where they stood and when he got there Dock told him about the switch.

"What's my deputy think?" he asked when he'd heard.

"Good one," Dock said.

"Okay," Harmer said. "Do you want me to search St. John's shop and house?"

"You think there's any sense?" Dock asked.

"No. And he'd probably sue the town for defamation of character if we tried."

"So what can you do?" Dock asked.

Harmer thought about it a moment, then he said, "To hell with him. I'm gonna search his shop and house. But you're right; I won't find it."

Dock said. "Maybe it'll turn up on eBay—under used nineteenth-century presidential recordings."

"At least you've got a sense of humor about it," Harmer said.

"I'm only laughing on the outside," Dock told him.

Harris was waiting for them when they got back to the university. He was sitting at Klaus's desk, with his feet up, a newspaper across his lap. He was drinking a cup of tea.

"Get your clide-hoppers off my desk, Harrison James," Klaus said and then he told him the story.

Harris shook his head as he listened, but by the time Klaus had finished, he was nodding and smiling a knowing smile as he slapped the newspaper onto the desktop. "Well, that explains today's paper," he said.

"What's in today's paper?" Dock asked.

"There's a small—very small—news item about Leona Anderson and her failed beneficiary claim," Harris said. "Several long-winded quotes from Attorney Tommy Trotter, exonerating Attorney Tommy Trotter. But then there's an interesting sidebar to the story, in which noted local Civil War expert and Gettysburg gadabout Thaddeus St. John discusses the historical import of the Potter estate. And in general, the man is quite impressed with the collection, refers to the collodion plates, for instance, as a discovery of enormous significance. However—are you ready for this? He suggests that the phonautograph is a fake."

"Son of bitch," Klaus said.

"Smart son of bitch," Harris said. "Think about what they've done here. One day, he tells the world that the recording is as phony as a three-dollar bill. Knowing full well that the next day you guys will announce that the machine has suddenly gone missing. You two emerge looking like a couple of used car salesmen."

"What about the opinion from MIT?" Dock asked.

Harris pushed the paper toward Dock. "Read the sidebar. He sort of vaguely suggests that somebody—he doesn't specifically mention any eccentric old Hungarians by name, of course—pulled a fast one on the eggheads over in Massachusetts. Those people are so screwed up about the Red Sox they'll believe anything anyway."

Dock picked up the paper and sat down in the classroom to read it. Klaus, muttering dark threats, moved to plug in the kettle for tea. The water was still warm from Harris's own tea and in a minute it was boiling. Klaus made a cup for Dock and carried it to him as Dock was finishing the article.

"Pretty slick, our boy Thaddeus," Dock said as he read.

"Yah?" Klaus asked.

"He steals a recording of Abraham Lincoln and then turns around and says that the thing was a fake in the first place. How can you accuse a man of stealing something that never existed?"

"You cannot accuse him, of course," Klaus agreed. "He has covered his traps too good. But vut about this? He only vants it to sell. How can he do that?"

"A very good question," Harris said.

"Maybe it was already sold," Dock said.

"To who?"

"I don't know," Dock said. "If I did, I'd go get it back."

Harmer, with the cooperation of the county force, obtained warrants and performed a futile search of Thaddeus St. John's shop and home. Thaddeus, of course, went directly to the media and spent a couple of days—and eight or nine costume changes—disparaging Harmer, Klaus Gabor, Dock Bass, all the while bemoaning the emergence of a "police state" in Gettysburg.

The meeting at the university was scheduled for eleven Friday morning. Harris went into town first to pick up the papers and a few things from the drugstore. It had started snowing after midnight and continued ever since. There was a wet covering of maybe three inches on the ground. Harris had been obliged to lock in his four-wheel drive for the trip. At the checkout counter in the drugstore, he glanced out the window to see Dock Bass parking his red pickup across the street. Dock got out and put on his ball cap and then starting walking up York

Street. It took Harris a moment to realize that Dock was heading toward Thaddeus St. John's shop.

Harris had to run to catch up with him on the sidewalk. Dock turned at the sound of his footsteps.

"Let me get my breath," Harris said. "I'm a teacher, remember?"

"Buck up, buddy," Dock said and he kept walking.

Harris fell in. "Where might you be headed?"

"See a man about a phonautograph."

The man in question was standing in front of a Confederate flag when they walked in, talking to Stonewall Martin, who was sitting at the counter, a take-out coffee in his beefy hands. Stonewall had matched up his buckskin coat with a pair of faded sweatpants, a cross-century fashion statement that wasn't quite working. Thaddeus, on the other hand, was dapper as ever in a chocolate brown sports coat over a pink silk shirt. The two men stopped conversation when Dock and Harris entered. Stonewall assumed a scowl that seemed to occupy his entire massive head, while Thaddeus, his nose in the air like a hunting dog, just smiled.

"Well, what an unexpected bit of unpleasantness," he said.

"I have some advice for you," Dock said.

"It must be rather pressing advice. I do believe you're in breach of your bail conditions," Thaddeus said. He turned to Harris. "And what is your role in this, sir—are you the peacemaker?"

"No," Harris said. "I missed it the last time Dock knocked Stonewall on his ass and I could've just kicked myself. I was kind of hoping for an encore performance."

"Fuck you," Stonewall said.

"My friend, the minimalist," Thaddeus announced. "But his point is valid. You must be careful, Mr. Jameson; when the gods wish to punish you, they answer your prayers." He looked at Dock. "Now I believe I'll make a call to the authorities, see if they can't get their heads out of their posteriors long enough to take this abrasive fellow back into custody."

Harris stepped toward Thaddeus, who was reaching for the phone. "What did you do with the phonautograph?"

"Oh, that—it's in my warehouse out back," Thaddeus said, stopping. "I'm thinking of using it in a window display. I'll call it 'great hoaxes from the Civil War.' How's that sound?" He narrowed his eyes for effect; in truth, he looked like a man squinting at an eye chart. "I don't have your phony recording machine. I deal in Civil War memorabilia. Why would I be interested in a fake?"

"Because you know it's not a fake, for one thing," Dock said. "But that's not why I'm here. I want you to stop telling people that the recording is a scam."

"I have a reputation in this field, and as such, I have a responsibility to tell what I know. Although I think the matter is becoming increasingly moot. My information is that you are claiming that the item in question has mysteriously vanished." He winked at Stonewall. "I've also heard a rumor that you've somehow misplaced Bigfoot and the Loch Ness Monster."

"You're missing the point, sunshine," Dock told him. "You're telling the world that Klaus Gabor is a fraud. Now, I don't know what you did with the phonautograph, and I might never know. But I do know this: that old man is a friend of mine and the next time you call his integrity into question I'm gonna introduce you and Spanky over there to a brand-new Battle of Gettysburg."

Thaddeus smiled at this. Stonewall's hand disappeared beneath the counter. "You want me to take care of this asshole?"

Thaddeus raised a palm of admonition to Stonewall but kept his eyes on Dock. "You're looking to add threatening to your assault charge?"

"I don't know what you've got under there," Dock told Stonewall. "But I do know what you don't have—balls enough to use it." He looked at Thaddeus. "We're not going to have this conversation again. Lay off Klaus Gabor."

Dock turned around and left. Harris looked at Stonewall and then at Thaddeus. After a moment Stonewall brought his hand above the counter.

"I will have him back in jail," Thaddeus said.

"And piss him off even more?" Harris asked. "Sound thinking, Thad."

Harris left and headed for the university. The meeting was in the dean's office. Harris walked in at eleven and out at five past, slamming the door so hard that he was actually surprised that the glass didn't break. He drove home through the melting snow; he was so angry that his hands shook on the wheel.

Lynn was in the kitchen when he walked in. Her eyes widened when she saw him.

"My God. What is it?"

"They're going to ask Klaus to step down."

"What?"

"There's a reporter from the *New York Times* in town. Doing a story on the missing phonautograph and the question of its validity. The guy's been talking to St. John and he was at the university yesterday, quizzing the dean. Like it or not, the phonautograph has an association with the university and everybody's on tenterhooks about the thing. The thinking is, if Klaus's reputation is at stake, then so is the school's. They want him to step down, temporarily, until the thing is resolved."

"Temporarily?" Lynn asked. "Come on. He's seventy-two years old. He leaves and they'll never let him back."

Harris nodded. "I just got finished telling them that. Rather emphatically."

"It will kill him, Harris."

He looked at her a moment and he nodded. "That's what it will do."

When they were gone, Thaddeus walked to the front of the shop and looked out the window. He could see Dock Bass getting into his truck and driving away and Harris Jameson walking back into the town center. The snow continued to fall.

"Why don't you run that armoire over to Harrisburg?" he said to Stonewall without turning. He continued to watch the snowflakes until he heard the back door open and close. Then he went to the counter and picked up the phone to call the sheriff. With the receiver to his ear, he changed his mind, though, and went through the clutter beside the phone and found the hotel phone number. The reporter answered.

"Thaddeus St. John here," Thaddeus said. "You put it to bed yet?"

"No. What have you got?"

"The ruffian Bass just left my shop. He threatened me and my assistant with violence if I continued to tell the world about the scheme he and Klaus Gabor cooked up."

"He did? Do you have a witness?"

"I most certainly do. Does that sound like the act of an innocent man?"

"It seems a little on the desperate side. Bass won't talk to me."

"Indeed not. If I were a faker, I imagine I too would be reluctant to speak to the *New York Times*. Gabor is behind it all, I'm certain. Trying for some damage control, but it's too late for that."

"Did you report this to the police?"

"The last time we had this individual arrested, he was out walking around two days later. I thought perhaps a phone call to you would serve better. This thing—even aside from the criminal intent—is becoming a distraction to me. My life's work is the preservation of a time and place in history. Every now and then people like this come along and give everybody else a bad name. They're scam artists, nothing more."

"Can I use that?"

"Scam artists?" Thaddeus asked and he considered it. "Why don't we call them snake oil salesmen instead? More befitting of the century in question, don't you think?"

The Saturday *New York Times* had quite a piece about the recent events at Gettysburg. It was a lively recounting, with file photos of Thaddeus St. John and Klaus Gabor and Abraham Lincoln. There was even a recent shot of Stonewall Martin, the line of sutures crossing his forehead resembling a railroad marking on a map, and a mug shot of Dock Bass, the architect of the line, in police custody after the fact.

The article quoted Thaddeus St. John at length; a distillation of his flowery statements seemed to suggest that Gabor's reputation was in tatters as a result of the missing and apparently phony phonautograph. In the context of the story, Gabor's insistence that the machines had been switched did indeed seem the last refuge of a desperate man.

Amy read the paper at Dulles, mired in the two-hour wait for her departure to Aruba. It was the first she'd learned of the switched phonautographs. She read the piece quickly, standing along a glass partition, and then she found a row of hard plastic seats by an escalator, where she sat down and read it again.

After a while she wandered into a coffee shop and ordered a latte. She'd last had a latte a few days earlier in a Gettysburg café, with Sam Rockwood. That day, she recalled that she'd sipped the coffee and silently wondered why Sam had suddenly and mysteriously surfaced in Pennsylvania.

She wasn't wondering anymore.

When she walked out of the shop, she looked at the screen and saw that she had thirty minutes before boarding. She stood there for a long time, glancing every now and then through the plate glass, where outside planes were rolling across the tarmac.

While she deliberated, a middle-aged woman wearing a red fedora and a long leather coat got off the escalator. When she saw Amy, she walked over.

"You're Amy Morris," she said.

Amy smiled and looked past her to the planes again.

"Could I have your autograph for my daughter?" the woman asked. She began to fumble in her purse for a pen. "She's in her first year at Columbia and she wants to be just like you."

"She's studying journalism?"

"Well—she wants to be on TV."

Amy signed the woman's ticket folder.

"Where are you off to?" the woman asked.

Amy looked up at the departure screen once more. "I might have to get back to you on that one."

She walked away from the woman and went into her purse for her

PalmPilot and found Klaus Gabor's number at the university. She
called and got no answer. It was Saturday, she remembered. She wondered at the chances that a man like Gabor would have his home number listed. And if he did, what the odds were that he would answer his
phone on a day when he'd been branded a fraud in the *New York
Times*. She tried Gettysburg information with no luck. Then she remembered that he'd told her he lived near Chambersburg. She tried
information again.

A minute later the old Hungarian was in her ear. She immediately
thought of the first time she'd called him, from her hotel room in Gettysburg. A lot had changed since then.

"Yah?"

"Professor Gabor, it's Amy Morris."

There was a long—and for her, expected—silence. "I don't think I
need to talk to you."

"Answer me one question and I'll never ask you another."

A second pause. "Vut?"

"You guys are claiming they switched the phonautographs. The
one you have now—does it have a dent in the horn about the size of a
golf ball?"

She could hear him breathing. "How do you know this?" he asked
after a moment.

"I just do," she said. "Thanks."

Her luggage was already on the plane and it was no easy chore getting it off. An airline employee recognized her and for some reason decided that there was a problem with the service. The man spent an
inordinate amount of time apologizing for the nonexistent slight.

"If you could just explain what the problem is," he said at one point.

"I don't have a problem," Amy told him. "I've changed my plans. I
need my luggage. If I'm not going to Aruba then neither are my
clothes."

She drove back to Old Town and carried her luggage into the
house and threw it on the floor. There was one carry bag that would suit
her purpose. She dumped its contents on her bed and then carried the

empty bag out to the Cayenne and headed for McLean. It was snowing again, thick wet flakes that melted upon hitting her windshield.

Nettie was at the house, sitting in the kitchen and watching a soap opera on the little TV on the counter. Amy walked in the back door without knocking. The smell of coffee was in the room but also something else, something baking. It was a familiar odor but one that Amy couldn't name.

"Sister," Nettie said when she saw her.

"What's that I smell, old lady?"

"Sweet potato pie. Least, that's what I call it today. If the folks were here, I'd be obliged to call it yam pastry somethin' or other."

"I had an aunt who used to make it with nutmeg."

"So do I, child. That ain't hardly the biggest secret in the world. They all off to the Caribbean, didn't you know?"

"I know."

"What's in that bag you're carryin'?"

"I'm planning a little surprise for Sam," Amy told her. "I have to get into the den."

"You know where it is. Not my job to be no tour guide."

Amy walked through the big house. She was counting on Sam's arrogance now. Anyone else would have it stowed away under lock and key, fearful of discovery. With Sam she was hoping it would be different. He would have to have it on display, even if he couldn't advertise it for what it was. There would be time enough for that—although how he'd imagined to pull it off, she had no idea. He would probably wait a year or two, then announce that he'd rescued the thing from the hands of some unappreciative thugs.

It was there in the den, on a shelf—quite fittingly—above a glass-encased copy of the Emancipation Proclamation. She wondered if the hypocrisy of placing it there had given him as much as a moment's pause.

She took it down, surprised at its heft, and maneuvered it into the carry bag and zipped it shut. She took a furtive look about the room before she left, feeling very much like a burglar in a 1930s movie. When she got back to the kitchen Nettie was taking the pie from the oven.

"Sit and have some coffee," Nettie said, setting the pastry on a plate on the table. "I'll cut you some of this when it cools. I don't expect you eat nothin' but restaurant food most of the time. No wonder you got no meat on you."

Amy started to decline, but then she was taken by a sudden calm. The sense of urgency that had gripped her at the airport was passed. Sometimes the deciding was the hardest part. She set the bag containing the phonautograph on the table and sat down. Nettie brought her coffee.

"So what you planning for the old man?" Nettie said, sitting across from her.

"I'm gonna knock his hat in the creek, Nettie. But it has to be a surprise; you can't tell him I was here."

"I won't even see 'em all till Christmas, don't you worry 'bout me. Way my memory's goin', I'll forget you even here by suppertime." Nettie pushed the bag out of the way and began to cut the pie.

Amy drank the coffee and ate the sweet potato pie and chatted with the old woman about yams and okra and the Redskins' secondary and the possibility that Hillary Clinton would become president. Before she left, she hugged Nettie for the first time ever—and quite probably the last—and then she put the bag in the back of the Porsche and headed for Gettysburg.

The snow turned to rain. It was after two in the afternoon when she got there. She parked on York Street, across from his shop. Through the window, she could see a couple inside, talking to Thaddeus St. John while examining some fading infantry flags in a window display. Thaddeus wore what appeared to be a safari suit. She waited until they left—no sale—and then she got out and retrieved the carry bag from the back.

Walking across the street, she pulled her cell phone from her coat pocket. She made sure it was turned off; she didn't want it to ring while she was pretending to talk into it. She had it to her ear when she walked in the door.

"Are you there?" she asked and then, "Are you there?" She feigned exasperation. "Shit," she said as she hit a button and returned the phone to her pocket.

Thaddeus was watching her narrowly from across the room.

"Have you talked to him?" she asked. Her tone was impatient, bordering on petulant.

"Have I talked to whom?"

"Sam. He said he was gonna call you. He's in St. Kitts—they've had a bloody hurricane, and even the cell phones can't get through. He said he'd call you."

"I'm sure I have no idea what you're on about."

"All I know is I'm supposed to deliver this," Amy said. She unzipped the bag and brought the phonautograph out and plunked it carelessly on the counter. "I thought these things were supposed to be rare. All of a sudden they're a dime a dozen."

"That's—" Thaddeus said, but he caught himself.

"The one from the Potter place," Amy said. "That's what Sam said you would say. It's a dead ringer, according to him anyway. I wouldn't know one from the other and really don't give a shit. Running fucking errands is not exactly in my job description."

"What am I supposed to do with it?"

"I got no idea," Amy said. "Sam knew I was going to this banquet in Baltimore tonight, and he asked me to drop this off first. Apparently, you guys don't believe in FedEx? I don't know what the two of you got going on, but I have the feeling the less I know the better. And I don't care what you do with it. You can cut it up and make fucking jewelry out of it if you want."

Thaddeus hesitated, then reached for the phone beneath the counter. He punched in a number; Amy could hear the faint automated voice mail prompt. Thaddeus hung up, tried another number with the same result. Hanging up again, he looked at her for a long moment; then he picked up the phonautograph and carried it into the back room. A moment later, he was back.

"I'll be expecting his call," he told her and his voice held the tone of a threat.

"You can expect it all by yourself," she said. "I'm going to Baltimore."

SEVENTEEN

Dock drove into town Saturday morning and went to the lumberyard, where he bought twenty-two sheets of drywall and a couple of boxes of compound. There was a teenager working in the yard and he helped Dock load the drywall, which was stored in a building to the rear of the property. It began to snow as they finished—fat flakes floating and swooping like miniature paratroopers as they fell to the ground.

"You want some plastic to cover that board?" the kid asked.

Dock looked out at the sky. "It won't amount to much. And I'm not going far."

He pulled in at the One-Stop on the way out of town to buy a newspaper and some canned soup for his lunch. As he was paying at the counter, he noticed that the woman working there was watching him with interest.

"You don't wanna buy the New York paper too?" she asked at last.

"I hadn't planned to," Dock said. "Why?"

"You're in it."

He sat in his truck in the parking lot and read the article in the *New York Times* as the heavy snow hit his windshield and melted, the water running down the glass. When he had finished reading, he put the paper back together and folded it and placed it on the seat beside him. After a few minutes, he drove over to Washington Street and bought a case of Yuengling Lager. He put the beer on top of the drywall and then drove out to the house.

He set up a pair of sawhorses in the center of the big room and carried the drywall inside and stacked it on the horses. He brought in the case of beer and the *New York Times* and put them on top of the drywall. He opened a bottle of beer and sat there while he drank it. When the first bottle was empty, he opened a second and then went to work putting up the board. The drywall was in ten-foot lengths, and it was a chore to put it up alone. He had boarded the ceiling earlier in the week and had enlisted Harris to help him. Harris had complained from the moment they'd started—his back ached, his legs hurt, his arms were sore—and if he was complaining to ensure he wouldn't be asked back, it had worked.

Dock struggled with the heavy drywall, opened another beer every half hour or so, and wondered what to do about Thaddeus St. John. Truth of the matter was, he knew exactly what he should do about Thaddeus St. John. He just couldn't figure out a way to do it and stay out of jail.

Which, in the end, was what was wrong with the whole goddamn deal. In the past two weeks Thaddeus had stolen, lied, slandered, and conspired to defraud. And yet, in the face of all that unchecked felony, Dock was the one who was worried about going to jail. Even in the simplest of terms, there was something desperately wrong with that. But there was no easy way to make it right.

And why should there be? There'd been something gnawing at Dock ever since he'd opened up the doorway to Willy's shop. He realized he'd been subconsciously comparing his world to that of Willy's, and wondering why it was that 1863 kept coming out on top. And finally it came to him. Everything today had to be *easy*. And if you had to screw over your neighbor or your brother or your friend to make it easy, then get to it. Easy was the way to go in the modern world. Easy was the new God.

But old Abe never had it easy, and, in the end, neither had Willy Burns. It occurred to Dock that if he took easy out of the equation, he would know what to do. With that in mind, he picked up his twelve-pound sledgehammer and set it by the door. He would need it when he went back into town.

Midafternoon, he was attempting to lift a full sheet of drywall into place, hold it there with one hand, and screw it fast with the other. The sheet began to slide, and just as he was about to lose it, he suddenly felt someone lifting the far end into place. Dock had his cheek against the board and for the moment he couldn't see his savior. He popped in a couple of screws and then turned to find Amy Morris holding up her end.

Which was something he never expected of her.

He didn't say anything, just went along the sheet with the cordless drill, screwing it fast to the wall. When it was secure, she stepped away. He looked at her and she was smiling.

"What're you doing here?" he asked.

"Saving your bacon, cowboy."

"I can put up drywall by myself."

"Who said anything about drywall?"

She walked over to the sawhorses, picked up the copy of the *New York Times,* raised her eyebrows at Dock, then tossed the paper aside and sat down. She reached into the case and helped herself to a bottle of beer.

"I asked," he said again, "why you were here."

She pointed her chin toward the newspaper. "What do you intend to do about that?"

"I'll take care of it. Got nothing to do with you."

She took a drink of beer and shook her head. She glanced about the room and saw the sledge by the door. "Would that big old hammer be part of your plan?"

"It might."

"You're gonna get yourself in shit, Mr. Bass."

"Well, I guess I can do that without your help, too."

She smiled again. "That might be the first time we've ever agreed on anything." She got lightly to her feet. "Tell you what—let's put the drywall up on that last wall and maybe the two of us can come up with a plan."

"I've got a plan."

"What would that be—scuttle his shop?"

"I figure I can do a couple hundred thousand dollars' damage before the cops get there."

"And tote you off to jail," she said. "His insurance would cover the damage. So what would it prove?"

"I'm looking at it more as a symbolic gesture."

She smiled at him once more. "You are a piece of work," she said. "I don't believe I've ever met anybody like you."

"You flirting with me?"

"Nope."

There was definitely something different about her. She was loose and at ease. She had something up her sleeve, and whatever that something was, it was pretty evident that she had faith in it.

"I thought you had important matters to tend to."

"I did," she said. "Matter of fact, I was at the airport when I realized I had to come back up here and save you."

"You said that before. What is it you figure on saving me from?"

"Yourself."

It didn't take very long for the two of them to board the end wall. Dock did the cutting, and Amy helped with the measuring and holding the drywall in place. She tried her hand with the cordless drill, but she was too aggressive and had a habit of pushing the screws all the way through the board.

Dock had a pair of electric heaters in the room, and soon the work warmed Amy to the point that she removed her jacket. She was wearing a brown silk blouse and black muslin pants, and both were soon covered with a light sprinkling of drywall dust. Whenever Dock stumbled into eye contact with her, she seemed to be smiling.

When they were fitting the last piece into place, she waited until it was fastened and then turned and walked back to the sawhorses and opened another beer. Dock screwed the sheet into place and stepped back to look at the finished wall.

"When do you plan to carry out this symbolic attack?" she asked.

"After they close the shop."

"Right," she said, realizing. "Because if Thaddeus or Stonewall was there, you just might end up on the wrong end of a murder charge."

"I wasn't aware that there was a right end of a murder charge," he said. "But I've considered the possibility."

"Well, it's good to know that you haven't completely lost your capacity for rational thought."

Dock watched as she produced yet another mysterious smile and then he turned and walked over to the doorway leading into Willy Burns's shop. He put his hands on the lintel above the doorway and he looked inside, even though there was nothing there to see, just the empty shelves and the rough-cut stone of the walls.

"A few weeks ago I took a hammer and chisel and I knocked this doorway open," he said. "And when I did, I found this . . . pocket from 1863. This might be a little too corny for a woman like you, but there was something very pure about it. It was . . . pristine in a way."

"Hey, I can relate to corny," she told him. "Pristine is cool too, for that matter."

He regarded her doubtfully, but he went on. "Ever since then, this room has become a magnet for a bunch of . . . well, Willy Burns would call them ne'er-do-wells. I might not be so polite about it."

"You? Come on."

"My point is, I contaminated this room by exposing it to the world." He stopped, then asked, "Did you meet Klaus Gabor? Yeah, you met him."

"Yes."

"Here's a guy, he was fifteen when the Second World War ended, and he was an orphan. He fought in the revolution in '56, and when it failed, he came to the States. Well, if you recall, we won our revolution. Maybe because of that, he started studying history, and he fell in love with this country. But you know, I think he fell in love with the way this country used to be."

He looked back at the empty room for a moment, although she knew for him it wasn't empty. He turned back to her. "You know what I'm saying?" he asked.

"That Thaddeus St. John is the way this country is now."

Dock nodded. "That crazy Hungarian is more American than that sneaky son of a bitch will ever be. And he's being called a fraud. His life's work is being called into question by this perfumed little creep. Do you have any idea how much that hurts that old man?"

"You're saying Thaddeus St. John is a thief?"

"Yup."

"Then call the cops."

"Yeah, I'll get right on that." He walked over to reach into the case for a beer.

"I mean it, Dock. Call the cops."

He was taking a drink and he stopped. There was something in her tone. "What the hell is going on?"

"You gotta give me a break here, man," she said. "You asked me what I was doing here. I'd kinda like to know what it's like to have you trust me. Even for a minute. On a certain level, you're an absolute shit-head, Bass. From the first time I met you, you made me feel inferior. Like I'm shallow and you're sincere; I'm nothing but a flashbulb, and you're this idealistic stand-up guy. You just asked me if I had any idea how Klaus Gabor feels, being called a phony. Well, guess what?"

"You did show up here under false pretenses," he reminded her.

"Yes, I did," she admitted. "By the way, I could mention that in the few days that I've known you, you clubbed a man unconscious and went to jail for it, brought a dead man back to life to screw a woman out of an inheritance, and are now preparing to take that giant ham-mer into town to demolish an antique shop."

"Hey, I never said I was perfect," Dock said.

"Perfect? You're a damn hoodlum."

He shrugged. "Maybe I did get a little carried away. But I was pro-tecting the kid. Willy Burns deserves better than that bunch."

"You were protecting the kid, and now you're protecting Klaus Gabor," she said. "You ever think about buying a white horse to ride around on?"

"I'd have to fix the barn first," he said. "You ever gonna tell me why you're here?"

"I guess I'm here to protect *you*. Because, believe it or not, I think you—stubborn son of a bitch that you are—deserve better than that bunch, too."

She walked across the room and picked up the receiver and held it toward him. "But I can only save you if you're willing to be saved. So call the goddamn cops."

At that point he was curious enough that he called them.

Harmer had a warrant in thirty minutes. The three of them arrived at Thaddeus's shop just as the little man was closing down for the day. Dock watched Thaddeus's plucked eyebrows arch at the unlikely trio coming through the door. Harmer was in the lead and he walked directly to Thaddeus. Amy, wearing Dock's dusty cap from the lumberyard, followed. Dock lagged behind.

"Why, this man is in breach of his bail conditions," Thaddeus said lightly as they approached, indicating Dock. "And in the company of the high sheriff to boot. I demand he be arrested and put in irons."

"You hush, St. John," Harmer told him. "I'll decide who gets arrested around here."

Dock sidled leisurely along the wall. He stopped at a display of reproduction Civil War headgear and put a Union infantry cap on his head, turned to check his image in a display mirror.

"What in the devil is going on now, Harmer?" Thaddeus asked. "I have an important engagement on the hill."

"You've got an important engagement right here," Harmer told him and he showed him the paper. "I've got a warrant to search the premises."

Thaddeus shook his head and made a sound like tut-tut. "Again? I really thought I was doing the town an enormous favor by not suing the police department last time. But I am afraid there is a limit to my charity. This time I will sue, and I will collect. I suspect that one of the items I'll collect will be your badge, Sheriff."

"Hell, I'll give you my badge, if you want it," Harmer said. He read from the warrant. "I'm looking for—what's that damn thing called?— oh, a Leon Scott phonautograph."

Thaddeus maintained his thin smile while he considered his predicament. "I have an old phonautograph here. But I guarantee you it has nothing to do with this . . . situation." He pointed his delicate chin at Dock, who was still admiring himself in the mirror.

"Where is it?" Harmer asked.

"There are a number of Scott phonautographs in existence," Thaddeus told him.

"We're just interested in the one," the sheriff said. "Get it."

Thaddeus looked pointedly at Amy and then he went into the back room and a moment later came out with the phonautograph. He put it on the countertop. Dock stepped forward, pushing the cap back on his head.

"Is it yours?" Harmer asked.

To Dock's eye it was, but he couldn't be sure. He picked it up and turned it around in his hands. He wished that Klaus Gabor was there. Then he glanced at Amy. She was watching him with the steady eye of a savior.

"Yeah," he said, still looking at her. She smiled.

"This is a joke," Thaddeus said to Harmer. He pointed at Amy. "That woman delivered this thing to me not three hours ago."

Harmer turned and looked askance at Amy.

"Hey, I've been out at Dock's since nine this morning, putting up drywall," she said. "Lordy, look at my fingernails."

So Harmer turned to Dock.

"She's been out at my place since nine this morning, putting up drywall," Dock said. "Look at her fingernails."

"You, sir, will end up a laughingstock, Harmer," Thaddeus said. "These two are playing you for a damn fool. This phonautograph is here on consignment, from a client in D.C. It has no connection to the Potter estate."

"Are you sure it's yours?" Harmer asked Dock.

"Yup."

"Can you prove it?"

"Nope," Dock said. "But Klaus Gabor can."

Thaddeus smiled again, but his voice was now betraying him. "You'd better move slowly, Sheriff. A thing like this could put you into early retirement."

Harmer shrugged and looked at Dock. "Where do we find Gabor?"

"Probably at the university," Dock said. He took the cap off and held it toward Thaddeus. "What's a thing like this go for anyway?"

Klaus was indeed in the Lair. The decision on his suspension had yet to come down, but he was putting things in order in the event that it did. The old Hungarian's face lit up like a quasar when they walked in with the phonautograph. To authenticate it, he produced a couple dozen photos of the machine, taken when it had been in his possession. Then, after giving Harmer a quick tutorial on the transfer of sound from cylinder to tape, he played the recording he'd made earlier. The sheriff stood comparing the photos to the genuine article, and, as the scratchy prairie voice that may have belonged to the sixteenth president of the United States came creaking from the machine, he walked over and put the cuffs on Thaddeus St. John.

Thaddeus wasn't the type of man who would do well in prison—if the company and the food didn't kill him, the wardrobe presumably would—and perhaps for that reason he was reluctant to go there alone. He rolled over on Sam Rockwood and Stonewall Martin before Harmer got him back to the station. Harmer had been hoping to get away for a couple days' trout fishing over the weekend. He could forget about that. He doubted his simple deputy could handle the press that would surely be descending.

At the university, Klaus was sitting in a chair, the phonautograph in his lap, his arms wrapped around it, basking in the light of his rescued reputation. Dock, still wearing the cap, was leaning against the counter. Amy sat in the big chair behind Klaus's desk, her feet up.

"You," Klaus said, pointing at her. "You vere behind this, yah? Ven you call me earlier, I know you have something up your sleeves."

"Not me. I'm a drywaller. I do dabble in electrical rough-in from time to time."

"Bullshit," Klaus said. "It vas her. Right, Doctor?"

"It was her."

"Then you are my hero," Klaus told her. "The doctor's too, I think—but he vill not tell you so much."

Amy looked at Dock. "Yeah, he's the contrary man, white horse and all. But you know, Professor, every now and then he shows a glimmer of potential."

"Maybe so. Maybe ve let him stick around."

"I hope you realize," Dock said, "that the thing you've got your arms around is about to become the star witness in a number of criminal prosecutions."

Klaus stood and walked over to Dock, handed him the phonautograph. "It vill be vat you vant it to be. Enough of the nonsense, enough of the nincompoops. Vut you do now is between you and Villy Burns."

"Okay," Dock said after a moment.

Amy could see that Dock was actually emotional about the exchange. She got to her feet. "Getting back to *me*—I have to say that being a hero is hungry work. What do you say I buy you boys dinner?"

"Oh, no," Klaus said. "I buy the dinner."

Amy went into her purse. "I have an American Express platinum card here in the name of TransWorld Communications. And I'm quite certain I'll have access to this card for a very limited time. So I'll buy dinner."

"I vill buy the dinner," Klaus said emphatically. "Of this, there vill be no argument."

Harris and Lynn joined them. They ate in the dining room of the Gettysburg Hotel, established 1797. They had drinks and hors d'oeuvres, steak and sea bass and lobster. They drank four bottles of expensive wine and several glasses of very old cognac. The waiter gave the bill to Klaus. When he looked at it, his eyes popped like a man in a cartoon; then he slid it across the table to Amy.

She put it on the card.

There was a mist rising from the fields at dawn. Dock found a shovel in the old barn and walked through the wet grass, the canvas bag over his shoulder. The sun was not yet showing as he reached the graveyard. In the faint light, it took him several moments to find Willy's grave again. He laid the bag on the grass, and he began to dig.

He would not go as deep as the coffin, if the coffin indeed still existed. He dug down about three feet, squared off the opening with the shovel, and then he took the phonautograph from the bag and placed it in the hole. He looked at it for a long moment. He picked up the shovel and began to push the dirt into the hole. When he was done, he laid the sod back over the cavity and tamped it flat.

As he walked back to the house, the sun cleared the tree line to the east, filtering through the mist like the memories of a long-ago day.

ACKNOWLEDGMENTS

The author would like to commend the town of Gettysburg, Pennsylvania, for remaining the town that it is. Thank you to Glenn Sage and Allen Koenigsberg for technical guidance. A special thanks to Mike Robinson, who taught me how to tell a collodion plate from a calico cat. My enduring gratitude to Jennifer Barth, a crackerjack editor despite being a Mets fan.

Thanks also to Barbara Berson, the indispensable Lesley Horlick, and the multi-talented sales and publicity teams at Penguin Group (Canada).

Finally, a tip of the saber to that dynamic transatlantic duo—the wandering Jen Barclay and the wondrous Ann Rittenberg.

ABOUT THE AUTHOR

Brad Smith lives near Dunnville, Ontario. His novel *One-Eyed Jacks* was nominated for the Dashiell Hammett Prize. His most recent novel, *All Hat,* is available in paperback from Picador in the United States and from Penguin in Canada.